D1462345

SNAKEBITE
SONNET

SNAKEBITE
SONNET

MAX
PHILLIPS

LITTLE, BROWN AND COMPANY

BOSTON NEW YORK TORONTO LONDON

FIRST EDITION

The characters and events in this book are fictitious. Any similarity to real persons, living or dead, is coincidental and not intended by the author.

Library of Congress Cataloging-in-Publication Data
Phillips, Max.
    Snakebite sonnet : a novel / Max Phillips.
        p.   cm.
    ISBN 0-316-70620-5   (hc)
        1. Man-woman relationships—New York (N. Y.)—Fiction.
    2. Obsession (Psychology)—Fiction.   I. Title.
    PS3566.H487S63   1996
    813'.54—dc20   95-43249

            10 9 8 7 6 5 4 3 2 1

                    MV-NY

Published simultaneously in Canada by Little, Brown & Company (Canada) Limited

Printed in the United States of America

Acknowledgments

Far too many people to list
have made valuable suggestions about this book,
but I especially want to thank
Charles Ardai, John Hansen, Bruce Holbert, Beth Kobliner Shaw,
Maddog McCracken, Fritz Mc Donald, Charles McIntyre,
Noah Millman, Cat Shugrue, John Whalen, and Michael Wolf,
who uncomplainingly read many hundreds of pages of manuscript
and whose responses were a model of large-spirited discernment.
I owe a particular debt to Jordan Pavlin, editor and philosopher-queen,
who knows what to do with a Gordian knot when she sees one.
Stanley Debel, Yossi Friedman, Dr. A. Lawrence Ossias,
Dr. Carolyn Schiff, Molly Schwartz and Cowboy, and Marguerite White
all provided research assistance and other kindnesses,
as did my parents, Constance and Irving Phillips.
Steve Snider and Caroline Hagen were supernally gracious
about my kibitzing during the design and production of this book.
Thanks also to Kevin Silva and Bill Stewart at Superior Copy
for their many good offices over the years.
I'm deeply grateful to the National Endowment for the Arts
for a Creative Writers' Fellowship
and to James Michener for a Paul Engle Fellowship;
both provided crucial support during the writing of this book.
And I am indebted beyond all hope of repayment
to Henry Dunow, agent nonpareil,
who battled stalwartly on my work's behalf for years
after most sensible people would have quit.

JANUARY 1996

Childhood love is boundless,
it demands exclusive possession,
it is not content with less than all.
But it has a second characteristic:
it has, in point of fact,
no aim and is incapable
of obtaining complete satisfaction;
and principally for this reason
it is doomed to end in disappointment.

SIGMUND FREUD

SNAKEBITE

SONNET

A Lash of Brightness Catches You Off Guard

The first time I saw Julia, I wanted to lie down with her, though I was ten years old and had no idea why I wanted to lie down with her, or what I might do about it once I had. Julia, on the other hand, was well versed in the matter of what you did with people once you'd lain down with them. She was nineteen, home from Bennington for the summer, and liked to say, *I'm pursuing my destiny as a poet and a slut.* She was still young enough to find glamour in those appellations.

"She's neat," I told my best friend Adam Frankel.

"She has hair in her pits," Adam said. "Hairy pits."

We fought and he won. Won the fight, that is; I considered the neatness of Julia beyond argument.

Not everyone did. Mom and Dad went odd in the face when I brought her up. Her escort for the summer was an unknown man of thirty-eight, and she was rumored to run around. Her parents had money. (I didn't know what this meant. Of course her parents had money.) *So young, and all alone in that big house,* my mother said sadly. At the time, it sounded like heaven.

According to gossip, Julia was supposed to have summered with her folks in Crete, but had shown up with her new beau and, after a trying week, flown home with him on her own credit card. Back in Silver Crest, New Jersey, she parked him by her parents' pool and took long rides on her Campagnolo dressed in cutoffs and a peasant blouse, or a gingham skirt tucked up around her legs and a man's sleeveless undershirt. Her imperfectly clean hair would flutter in the wind. Her dirty feet would be bare or in sandals. Beneath her arms, as Adam noted, were two lush tangles of auburn fur. I wasn't sure if these were bad or good, but they made me want to hunker on all fours and snarl.

"Father-fixated," my mother called her, and my father nodded sagely.

The Turrells had moved to Silver Crest the previous fall. There wasn't much in town for Julia to do. She was too young to drink at Arno's Tavern or Pete's Golden Memories, and her standards were too exacting for Villa Mulino, Empress Garden, Bagels'n'Everything, or R&J Pizza. (Foraging through the fridge, Julia would eat all manner of crap, but when she went out she was an appallingly learned snob.) Our one good restaurant, Popinjay's, would never admit people dressed like Julia, and she wasn't likely to patronize Lena's Hairliners & Nails Too, NAPA Auto Parts, Silver Crest Volvo, or ValueRite Lumber. What was left? The bank, where she went once a month to get money. Our little public library, from which she departed with her backpack full of Balzac and Djuna Barnes. The Foodtown, where I crept along behind her and her companion as they bought just what my friends and I would have, if someone trusted us with the shopping: Doritos, frozen pizzas, gallons of orange juice and soda, barbecue sauce, candy bars, hamburger buns, and peanut butter with the jelly already mixed in. And Melody's Ice Cream Parlor; Julia had an unconquerable sweet tooth. When she put on a few pounds in her early forties, she told me, "By rights, I should've been fat *aeons* ago."

Julia usually hit Melody's around one. If her friend was with her, they'd take a corner booth. She'd order a mammoth sundae and finish it; he'd order tea and let it go cold. But more often, she'd go alone and perch tailor-fashion on one of the stools along the counter, pivoting back and forth and engaging townspeople in chat. Eventually she would hear about your job and your family; eventually you would hear about the intolerance at Bennington, the glories of Baudelaire, the cloud shapes that preceded that morning's sunrise, and her latest work in progress. You'd conclude the conversation out on the sidewalk. By now, you'd be doing most of the talking, and Julia would wrestle her hair back behind her head, grip it with both hands, and stand with hips cocked, armpits flourished, brown eyes intent on yours. Afterward, you'd say, *But, you know, she's really friendly!* And your auditor would smirk and say, *I'll bet.*

When I saw her first, she was headed for Melody's on her bike. I recall that she began dismounting half a block away, balancing with one bare foot on the pedal and raising her other leg straight out in back like a dancer. She coasted that way for twenty yards, head lifted proudly. Then she swooped to the curb, landed with a little skip, sank at once to one knee, and locked her bike to a vending machine selling the *Bergen County Record* for Monday, May 25, 1970. In a moment, she'd swept into the ice cream parlor, eyes front. She hadn't been showing off for me, particularly.

I now find it easy to see Julia in two ways: the way she seemed that summer – a striding, tall, mysterious, gem-eyed beauty – and the way she almost certainly was. By 1970 Julia had reached her full adult height of five feet two and one-half inches. She was pretty but not very pretty. She was slim and strong but still lightly coated with puppy fat, and her features were puppyish. She had a snub nose, a snub chin, snub lips, and small snub breasts. Like many of the children of the rich, she had flawless skin. Her eyes were a warm but not remarkable brown, and her posture was iffy. Her plentiful, glossy, rust-brown hair spiraled crazily from a white central part to nearly the width of her indolent brown shoulders. Her feet were quite large. If I met this Julia now, I'd think, *Who is this badly behaved child?*

3

I still might want to lie down with her, but only on one of my evil days.

Back then, I had no reservations. But what could I do about my love? My friend Adam would clearly be no help, and none of the other kids knew. After a week of indecision, I took up a position outside Melody's, holding my baseball glove so as to appear rugged. It also made me seem purposeful – *Yes, officer, just waiting for some of the guys. Going to play a little ball* – and helped mask the trembling of my hands. The street smelled of tar, sunned bricks, and clipped grass from the plot in front of the fire station. It was barely June, and not really hot, but when cars passed by, I felt the heat of their engines.

Julia and her friend walked right by the first time. His back was dismayingly broad. But on the second day she was alone, and I caught her eye. She nodded pleasantly. I just looked at her. I had a disconcerting gaze, and even at that age I damn well knew it. She stopped, puzzled. "Well, sir. Hello."

"Hi."

"What's that you've got there?"

"A third baseman's mitt."

"Are you good at softball?"

"Mediocre," I said.

She regarded me. "Well, sir. So was I, once. Now I'm worse. How old are you?"

For a wild moment, I considered *fifteen*. I'd be small for my age due to a fascinating illness. She'd fall in love with my bravery.

"Ten," I said.

"What's your name?"

"Nicholas," I told her. "Nicholas Joseph Wertheim."

"Nicholas Joseph, I'm pleased to make your acquaintance. My name is Julia May Turrell."

"Do you have a boyfriend?"

"Several. Do you want to be my boyfriend?"

"Yes."

"Well, maybe later," she said, smiling. "Ten years old, huh? What a threat you're going to be."

:   :

I was an average-looking child, medium-sized, with dark brown hair. A bit thin. My only distinguishing features were a hooked nose and narrow, squarish shoulders that seemed fixed in a perpetual shrug. At third base I was competent, provided a fly ball didn't give me too much time to worry about dropping it. My wheelies, when we rode bikes, were brief and haphazard. I was a master of the less sophisticated manly art of tree-climbing, and could hook my toes over a branch and dive headfirst toward the earth, landing in an inverted paratrooper's roll and springing to my feet unhurt. I rode in the middle of the school bus, though I had modest credentials as a fighter and could have hung out in the back with the tough kids. I sat in the middle of every classroom unless alphabetical order intervened, and managed, by an unremitting effort of will, to make everyone forget I was one of Silver Crest Elementary's better students. (My twin sister Del's habitual A-pluses helped.) I was fairly well liked, and took part in group doings with the other ten-year-olds – designing go-carts, exploring the gravel pit, murdering frogs – but these were dutiful pleasures. They made me happy mainly as elements of a successful imposture. When I met Julia, I'd spent my entire life impersonating a normal boy from a normal family.

In fact, my family was peculiar. To begin with, there was our house. Silver Crest was well barbered and well-to-do, but the Wertheims lived in a three-room brick bungalette, a converted carriage house tucked in the woods at the end of a dirt drive. Our kitchen and bathroom were small and makeshift. The single bedroom had been divided into two cubicles for me and Del, and could barely accommodate our beds, footlockers for our clothes, and a few rock star posters. Most of the house was taken up by a large room furnished with a couch made of two old mattresses lashed together with rope and covered with tie-dyed cloth, an Eames chair and ottoman, brilliant injection-molded chairs around a plywood table, our parents' water bed, a dust-mauled paper Noguchi lamp, and a Navajo rug in turquoise and umber. From floor to ceiling, the house was dark with books, from *Reading Capital* to *The Upanishads,* from *Querelle* to *Tales of the Hasidim: Later Masters.* (I paid this no special mind. My sister and I had never so much as set foot in a synagogue.) Their bindings were rough, dim, sneezily sweetish with age, and stamped with tiny torches, towers, fish, prancing dogs. My parents would drop whatever they were doing to fetch from a high shelf whichever one I asked to see; I recall Suzanne rising on tiptoe while steadying herself with a joking palm on my head, or my father scrambling up on a chair. All this suited me right down to the ground, but that just made things worse. I knew from my friends what a house should be like. This was the wrong sort of place to love.

My father was an adjunct instructor at Montclair State College and my mother clerked part-time at a Nyack crafts gallery. We were supposed to call them Saul and Suzanne. She had a master's in social work, he had a Ph.D. in American history, and both fooled with scrips and scraps of unfinished advanced degrees. They'd been in their thirties when they became beatniks, and middle-aged when they became flower children, and God knew what they'd become by 1970, except forty-six in her case and fifty-one in his. Anyway, we all swam nude together on camping trips. When my twin sister and I were five, they tried to teach us the facts of life, including the proper use of a condom and the fact that some people liked the opposite sex, while others, who were just as nice, preferred their own. Del and I didn't see what this had to do with anything, and forgot the whole annoying business at once. My folks were atheists, too, though careful to explain that when we were older we would decide these matters for ourselves. This struck me as a lot of dumb bother if they already knew the answer.

Saul was a potty little man, bald, with an untidy fringe of brown hair. He had sly, happy cocker-spaniel eyes and a mustache that hid his mouth. If it twitched, he was smiling. For years he'd reworked his monograph on Eugene Debs. Crouched at the typewriter, he struck me as magnificent, an Atlas upholding the world of wisdom, though he could also resemble a spaniel frantically burying a bone. Then he'd loll with an elbow over the chair back and want his ears scratched and his belly petted, and Suzanne was always happy to oblige.

My mother was tall and curvy, with a silver-sprinkled mane, the hook nose she'd dealt to my sister and me, and pale – almost white – green eyes. When you spoke, she seemed to gaze not at you, but at the blinding light of your spirit. She seldom got Saul's jokes. She'd laugh, all right – a breathy, melodic laugh that began well before his punch lines. But she was clearly responding to his tone of voice, as a pet responds to compliments. One of her old self-portraits on canvasboard adorned the big room: a forward-drifting figure with improbably luxurious breasts and an improbably long neck – both of which she admittedly possessed in real life – clad only in a diaphanous shift, which she'd applied using a dry brush touched with chartreuse. She'd studied dance, and was given to doing vertical splits against door frames, one blue-veined foot indicating the zenith and her dreamily parted lips against her thigh. Like Julia, my mother declined to shave beneath her arms. She had delicate swirls there, like steam rising from a coffee cup in an ad for Maxwell House.

We didn't have grandparents. Saul's folks were dead, and Suzanne was so completely estranged from her family in Michigan that they didn't know we'd been born. It was Saul's second marriage. His first broke up because he slept around all the time, most often with Suzanne. We knew this because they told us.

"I was making a lot of poor choices, a lot of dishonorable choices, too," Saul said genially. "I had a thing for the word *abundance.* I wanted to act *abundantly*. And this most often expressed itself in sex. Of course." He laughed. "At first I was open about this with Rachel, and then not. Because she didn't, you see, appreciate it. So I became diplomatic – that is to say, a goddamn liar. I told myself I was *seducing* her into a more abundant existence, gradually opening up her cramped paradigm of personal dealings. When all the poor woman wanted was for me to honor my compact with her, which after all had been for a monogamous relationship."

"Oh, puke," Del said. I think we were about eight.

"She got pretty pissed, right, Dad?" I said, trying to hang in there.

"Saul," my mother said, "I won't have you taking all this on yourself. Because the frame of reference you're describing – and I admit it was flawed, and I admit we hurt a lot of people unnecessarily – was something we came up with between us, as the result of dialogue, and I think the responsibility should be shared. *I* was the one going on about Reich all the time."

"Fixing the blame, fixing the blame," my father sang. "Whatever. The point is, kids, you can't fuck around on your agreements and expect to be loved for it."

Del said, "*Saul! Su-zanne!* Why are you *telling* us these things?"

I called our folks Mom and Dad, against their wishes, because I loved them and wanted them to act like parents. Del called them Saul and Suzanne because she hated them and had given up.

Another problem was that you weren't supposed to like your siblings. Ruth Adele and I knew this, and were always careful to ignore each other on the school bus. But we were very close. We were fraternal twins who might almost have been identical. (Poor girl.) We shared a nickname at school – Nose – and many of our clothes, and even a bed, until we rebelled at nine and convinced Saul to divide our room in two. Through the wall from then on, we listened to each other fumfering around before sleep. Through the wall, we conducted long, confiding talks. The plasterboard turned her words dull as drumbeats, disembodied as something I'd thought myself.

Del was an ideal companion. We were delighted when our parents left us to ourselves. We'd escort them to the door on a Friday evening – me tranced by Suzanne's Vol de Nuit, Del scowling at Saul's dashiki – and then the lock would click, and the little house would be ours. We taught each other to change the bag on the vacuum cleaner and to somersault off the back of the couch. We taught each other to cook. We could both produce serviceable, if eccentric, soups, stews, and casseroles before we were tall enough to reach the stove. We'd drag a bench over and stand on it side by side, each with an arm about the other for stability. I recall my sister's nervous hip bumping mine as the heat of the burners bloomed in our faces. "Did you *see* what she had on?" Del said. "What was that *thing* she had on her big butt?"

"A scarf." I chortled. "Around her waist," I added loyally. It had been shiny and I'd wanted to touch it.

"A scarf goes on your *head*," Del brayed, waving her spatula. "Doesn't she know the *difference* between her fat head and her fat *butt*? She's gonna get fat. They're both getting fat fatty fatter."

"Fat butts, fat nuts," I cried, giddy with treachery. We broke up. I lifted the pan, and Del eased from it a perfect four-egg omelette made with mung sprouts, Velveeta, black cherries, and cinnamon, which we put in everything.

I had to go through Del's room to leave the house, and Del had to go through my room to use the john. We evolved intricate codes of privacy. On camping trips Del would sprawl happily nude in the sun well into her teens, but at home, she'd insist no one enter the bathroom while she was in the tub. Afterward she'd walk through my room wearing only a towel around her head, and stop to chat affably if addressed. If our parents were around, she'd cover up. If she went into the bathroom to urinate while we were talking, she might leave the door open a bit so we could continue our conversation. If she went there to defecate, she'd lock it and refuse to speak. As for me, my only concern was that I be allowed to read in solitude; I was like an animal that hates to be watched while it eats. Other rules concerned our parents. They would have liked to go naked in the house, but we insisted they wear *something*, so they'd lounge around in big T-shirts or in bikinis; lurid, skimpy, and perhaps satirical in intent. However, their bed was out in the common room, and at night and early in the morning, we couldn't boss them around. We had a name for the muffled noises that came through the wall: *undressed*. "You think they're still undressed?" we'd say. "You think we can go out yet? No," we'd say a minute later, "they're undressed again."

In general, we all touched each other too much. Saul kissed me when he was pensive and drummed "Wipe-Out" on my ribs when he was glad. Suzanne wrapped me in long limbs and nibbled my ears. She bared uneven teeth to make frightening ape faces, scissored me between her thighs and made me fight free, pursued me with gleeful pinches that caused an odd, lovely knotting-up inside. Del watched with rage. My sister usually recoiled from my parents' hands, but after an upsetting day, she'd want to neck with me. She'd wake me by worming herself half under my stomach, apply small, stern lips to my face, lick my breastbone, wedge her head into my armpit. Then she'd want a backrub. Massages were a big deal in our family; we'd been taught to give them at the same time we'd been taught to brush our teeth. I'd always finish up with her favorite: gently thumping her kidneys with my fist. *"Ruth-a-dell,"* I'd croon, *"oh, Ruth-a-dell."* When she was quite calm, she'd get up to urinate, then come back and go straight to sleep.

I didn't know what the routine was in other families, but I figured it wasn't like this.

Still, none of this was really a problem until Julia showed up. It was easy enough to keep kids away from our house by saying that we were *poor* and our parents were *weird*. Since Del and I were presentable, fair at games, and not conceited about our good grades, this wasn't held against us. I did not lack for affection or companionship.

I was happy with my double life. It was Julia who ruined everything – I mean, Julia in the larger sense: love.

At ten, I was just beginning to be aware of sexual desire. I recall a
TV commercial for a blockbuster sale on all '69 Dodge cars. It featured a perky blonde woman in a racing jumpsuit. The sale assumed
the form of an explosion that left her dazed and smudgy-faced,
jumpsuit shredded, still trying to smile. This sent me into such a
frenzy of yearning that I'd race around the house. I could find no
precedent for it. Maybe the nervous, voluptuous, vicious-tender feeling of harassing my sister's gerbils, putting them in a shoe box and
dumping them from corner to corner so that their tiny paws skittered and their glossy eyes darted. I wanted to make large declara-
tions and be beautiful and roll the Dodge girl around in a box. I
wanted to fling back the swaddling quilts of family affection and
stride about in the chill. I'd creep after Julia in the supermarket, finding the postures of concealment distressingly natural, and dream of
presenting myself to her whole, the dashing son of the correct sort of
folk. It was the first true discontent I'd ever known.

I had two chief sources of consolation. One was drawing. I'd been
given a set of Giant Golden Books on subjects like Oceanography
and Atomic Power, which glistened and smelled of cellophane and
were lush with pictures. In the books, one was always bobbling
amongst platelets or amongst galaxies, in deep, velvety-red inner
reaches or deep, velvety-blue outer reaches, in the distant past or the
far future. Here was the Moon, neatly labeled: the Sea of Storms, the
Sea of Rains, the Seas of (clockwise) Cold, Crises, Serenity, Mists,
Tranquillity, Fecundity, Nectar, and Clouds. Here was the Sun,
equipped with a magnifying porthole so one could view the hurry-
ing atoms inside. Here was the Earth with a wedge sliced away,
revealing tidy layers and a nestled plum-pit of molten iron. I loved
accounts of evolution and life cycles – unformed young creatures
completing themselves – and artists' conceptions of the future.

Beneath soap-bubble domes rose towers of milk glass or red wax, barbarous and gorgeous as Aztec temples (those stories weren't half bad, either). Transport was by jet-suit and monorail; chores were handled by robots which had a special arm for every task. Certain words in the captions made it all seem possible: *titanium, bathyscaphe, era, neutron, annihilate.*

I'd browse for hours, then uncap colored Magic Markers and dream, filling sheet after sheet of my father's onionskin typing paper: I stepped from my titanium bathyscaphe onto the shores of the Sea of Mists. Daringly, I snuck toward the domed temple. They were ready to drop a girl into the planet's molten core, shackled in silver and turquoise, her clothes shredded, her belly button bare. Sometimes I rescued her, sometimes I didn't. It was horribly exciting either way. Suzanne was enthusiastic about what I called my "diagrams," and sewed the best ones into "textbooks" with gay fabric bindings.

My other consolation was friendship. Adam was stumpy and muscular, uncoordinated but fearless, with large white teeth. Like me, he read incessantly. He was popular, and it was the foundation of my happiness that he liked me best. We'd hold endless symposia on physics, espionage, zoology, warfare, and sex. "The cells of the body renew themselves once a year," he told me that summer. He was squinting into the sun and curling his upper lip to touch his nose.

"Explain, please," I said.

"They get different. The old ones die, and you pee them away—or shit them, I'm not sure—and new ones get born. And after a year, none of your cells are the same ones. So it's no good you being so hot for Megan Lampert, because she's not even the same girl you got so hot for last summer."

"I don't believe it," I said. "You'd fall down."

"Explain, please," he said.

"Well, the cells of your skeleton couldn't change, because they're what's holding you up."

"They do it gradually. It's like a house, and you just pull out one nail at a time and put in another."

"Cells wouldn't be nails. They'd be boards."

"Same thing," he said doubtfully. "If they were really tiny boards, and you changed them one at a time…"

I wanted to get back to Megan Lampert. "You think she's a fox?"

"She's got a bongo butt. Her bonger sticks way out."

"That's supposed to be good," I explained.

"For what?"

This silenced us. We were down by the lake in the gravel pit, on a little mud island we got to by balancing on the culvert wall and then hopping from stone to stone. One false move and in you went, so our lazing around there was proof of our competence as men. The water shone, creamy and rank. What I really wanted to talk about was Julia, but since the hairy pits fight, I wouldn't discuss her. Adam knew this. It saddened us. I plunked a pebble in and said, "It keeps the ovum warm."

"And?"

"That makes her more fertile. Large buttocks means a girl's more fertile."

"The ovaries aren't down there," Adam said.

"They're nearby."

"Doubtful."

"In special cases."

"Such as?"

"If she's a virgin," I said in triumph.

We figured a virgin meant a girl who was really pretty and maybe kind of snotty. Megan Lampert was definitely a virgin. Maybe Julia was, too.

I knew we both had erections now—well, I didn't know what they were called, but I knew the same thing was now wrong with both of us. The conversation had run out of steam. We had reached the male impasse.

I clasped our virgin's limbs in turquoise and silver and handed her over to the cruel-eyed priests.

:   :

One afternoon I found Julia and her boyfriend snoozing on the grass in Menzies Park. This was a runty triangle of lawn at the end of Birch Terrace, which boasted one bench and a flagpole with no flag. The boyfriend didn't look thirty-eight until you crept up close. Then you saw that his long, streaky blonde hair was thinning, that his gut was growing heavy, that his deep tan softened deep lines beneath his eyes. But if you got that close, he'd reach out – he hadn't been asleep at all – clamp his hand around your ankle, and announce, "We got him, Juju. We got our spy."

I suppose I'd wanted to get caught. On some level, I knew my attentions were adorable. Julia lifted a drowsy face from his back and smiled. He said, "You been taking good care of us this summer, spy. Been keeping a good watch on our shopping trips. I just know you were hired to stop me eating so much garbage." I tried to pull back, snickering helplessly. He had lazy, weighty muscles. "Have a seat," he said, and turned his fist so that I tumbled into the grass.

They sat up, and Julia arranged herself cross-legged. "Nicholas Joseph Wertheim," she said, "may I present Craig Scott Harrison. Mr. Harrison, Mr. Wertheim. We'd offer you a sandwich, Nicky, but we've squaffled them all."

"You should've come earlier, spy. You should've pried them out of my greedy fist. I understand you been courting my old lady here."

"Asked me out the first time he saw me. He's dangerous. I doubt, Craig, that you displayed such initiative at ten."

"I didn't display diddly at ten," Craig agreed. "All I did was pull it and bug my folks to buy me binoculars. For Jap planes," he explained to me.

They laughed. Her laugh was nervous. His was sad.

Craig was a formidable rival. I began interrogating him at once, searching for weak spots and helpful hints. Most summers, he life-guarded in Florida, taught swimming and scuba diving, and period-ically went back home to California for surfing competitions. "I lose. My edge is gone." Winters, he rambled. If money ran low before June, he'd paint houses, wheel concrete, do light carpentry. "Seek out rich women," Julia added. Craig seemed not to hear. It was odd that he'd wound up in Bennington, but he'd been in odder places for a surfer: British Columbia, Thailand. Meanwhile, he was thinking a novel through. Conceptualizing it.

"I'm fond of books myself," I said.

"Yeah? You writing one too?" Craig smiled, quite without conde-scension.

I saw myself showing my textbooks, in their beautiful covers, to an admiring Julia. She walked along the bookshelves, brushing the bindings with one hand. It was my house now.

"All writers together," Julia said, giggling.

For a moment, I was on Craig's side, against her.

"Young Nicholas," he said. He'd lost his soft, matter-of-fact tone. "Maybe you can tell us. What's there to do in this town? When you're done making your rounds as a high-powered grocery spy, what do you do to stave off the pangs of boredom? Heavy boredom here, Nicholas. Steps must be taken."

"I could show you the woods. I know all the best places down there."

"That's very kind…," Julia began.

"Good deal," Craig said firmly. "Nothing like having a man along who knows the terrain."

Julia hesitated, then said, "Yes." She smiled and rapped my sneak-ered toes with her knuckles. "Much better this way. No more sneak-ing around."

I nodded. "Much better."

We provisioned ourselves with canned fruit juice and snack cakes from the grocery, and soon Craig was leading us through the trees,

Julia following, me bringing up the rear in spite of how I was supposed to show them the best places. I kept hustling up beside them
so I could see their faces. They didn't look very happy, and we were
walking a bit on the fast side.

"His path is set with many trials," Craig told me. I'd pestered him
into describing his novel. "Trials of the flesh, trials of fear. But just as
he's reaching the point of being totally wasted with all this – the adu-
lation of the fans, the rewards of being at the peak of his sport, the
world of *maya* – he meets, in a little teahouse on the seedy side of
town, an old man who offers to purify him through the disciplines
of Tae Kwon Do. They retreat to the canyons north of L.A., where
Troy, casting his old life aside, devotes himself to the martial arts. He
couldn't have begun before – he was *apakva*, unripe – but now, working out eight hours a day, half-naked in the broiling sun, his surfer's
nerve and reflexes stand him in good stead, and he soon becomes a
fifth Dan black belt, ready to rejoin the world with new self-respect."

I was dying of envy at this terrific stuff, and trotted up to see how
Julia was taking it. She wore a face I didn't recognize, though I'd
know it today. The face of a hostess presented with a difficult guest.

"But things haven't stayed the same in his absence," Craig continued. "Monique has been kidnapped by a gang of drug-running *vatos
locos* linked to an international cartel. They want to neutralize him
while they move into Venice Beach, or better yet, turn him to their
purposes. Troy goes back to his dojo and his master introduces him
to Brad Grant, a novice martial artist and master spy on sabbatical
from the CIA. A private jet flies them to an underground command
center deep below the Mojave Desert."

"Sort of *Siddhartha* meets *Hawaii Five-O*," Julia said.

Craig began to nod, then hesitated. Julia was examining the trees
and sky. He plucked up a long blade of grass, flicked the root off with
a thumbnail and stuck it in the corner of his mouth. "The rest of the
story gets pretty tangled, young Nicholas. And Julia's heard it too
many times. Like I said, I'm working it out."

Julia was barefoot, in cutoffs and a backless yellow halter closed with a knotted string. From behind, if you squinted, it looked like she wasn't wearing anything on top. My hands felt sensitive, as they did after I'd been climbing trees, when my empty palms would still feel full of the harsh, good bark. I was tired of tagging along behind. Without breaking stride, I grabbed a likely-looking tree and began to climb. Craig heard the rustling and stopped. Julia almost ran into him. When they walked back, I was twelve feet up or so, hanging by my hooked insteps.

"Pretty good," Craig said.

"Come on down," Julia said. "That looks risky."

"Only if you slip," I told her, and let go.

Julia squeaked, and her face, as it zoomed by me, was all eyes, while Craig – time stretched voluptuously when you did stunts like these – seemed interested and amused. I hit the ground perfectly and rolled to my feet, letting myself bounce into the air when the balls of my feet struck dirt, hands at my sides like a gymnast, grinning. There was a tiny line of spit on my chin, but I doubted they could see.

Craig was happy. "Nice. Evil nice. Let me see that again."

"*No*," Julia said. "Wipe your mouth."

But I was halfway up the tree. "I've been doing this for years," I assured her, rubbing my chin as I climbed. "I'm proficient."

She squeaked the same way the second time. It left her angrily giggly.

Craig nodded. "I got it now. You cast your hips this way as you release. Then it's, both palms, left shoulder, left hip – I got it." He caressed my neck heavily. "Nice." He stepped forward and nudged the tree to test it against his greater weight.

Julia said, "For God's sake."

"Easy, Juju. Can't get in the way of fun." He moved up the trunk, slower than I but more fluid, a leopard instead of a chimpanzee. After nudging my branch, he hung by his hands from it, swung his thick legs up, hooked his toes and dangled. "Feels good," he reported.

Julia said, "Don't kill yourself, Craig. I get little enough action as it is."

"Let's have some space here, people," he said.

When he dropped, he wasn't twisty enough. He whomped his shoulder as he hit rolling, then popped to his feet. "You see?" He smiled at Julia. "Fun was had." He took hold of his hurt shoulder. "I'm a fat old man," he said, surprised.

"That's really good for a first time," I told him. "You should have seen the way I creamed myself."

She kissed his shoulder. "You dire asshole," she muttered into it. "I didn't come out here to be a playground monitor."

He draped his hurt arm around her. "Nicholas, old buddy, I hope she treats you better than she's treated me." She was about to speak, but he set a forefinger against her lips. "No more bitchery," he whispered. "Lovely day. Wonderful woman. Your nice friend. No more bitchery. Food now, and nap. Can we just do food and nap?"

All of Julia was now something that radiated out from his tan fingertip. She kissed it.

"Food sure sounds good to *me*," I said.

We made ourselves comfortable and ate and drank. Julia rested one dirty bare foot on Craig's calf and one on mine. Afterward he said, "Nap. No one else for nap? You fuckers're young."

"I can show you some of the sights," I told Julia.

"Good deal," Craig said. He lay back, going *oof*. "Nick? Don't steal my woman, now. That happens too often."

"What did we say about bitchery?" Julia asked.

"Right. Sorry. You kids have fun. If you see the bone wagon, just send it my way."

Off we went, Julia and I, into the woods. They didn't yet have that cooked-out odor they got in late summer. Rain had freshened them. I felt I was smelling – leaves, roots, rocks – the underside of everything: we were alone at last. I watched an angry squareness leave her shoulders and fanny, watched her hips begin to roll again. Finally she said, "So, nature guide. You haven't shown me any nature."

She smiled. She was wearing that look again, the one that shut Craig up. "What do you want to know?" I said.

"Well... what kind of tree is that?" she said.

"That's a birch. Come on, you knew that."

"Okay. *That* tree."

"That's a, let's see, that's a Turquoise Elm."

"Yeah? It doesn't look like an elm."

"A *Turquoise* Elm. They're pretty common around here." This was easy. "Oh, now, this is rather interesting," I said. I scooped up a dingy, ovoid something. Pulling out my pocketknife, which was razor sharp, if slightly ragged, from being whetted on the chunks of concrete at the mouth of our driveway, I split the whatsit in a scholarly manner. It was full of half-rotted goop. "This is the pupa stage of the Dowager Fire-Ant."

She grunted softly.

Shit. Ants didn't have a pupa stage, did they? "The Dowager Fire-Ant—it's more properly known as a moth, but it loses its wings about a week after it hatches out—is a pretty infrequent visitor to these parts. It doesn't sting like a true fire-ant, of course. But its wings..."

We waited.

"Its wings. If they brush against you. Leave a reddish trace that resembles fire. The wings themselves are the color of titanium, with turquoise spots. It builds a domed hive when in its usual haunts, which might come up to your knee." I indicated her brown knee with my knife. "This bit is the *pusa*," I said, pointing at some of the gick with the tip of the blade, "and this is the *gerbilium*, and the *echinodorl*, which here is very imperfectly developed." I dropped the glob, wiped my knife on my shorts, and pocketed it. "It's kind of amazing to see one this far north," I concluded.

She'd been listening open-mouthed, and now began to laugh open-mouthed. "You little shitter. I'm beginning to almost think you're not making this up. I'm beginning to think you actually know this stuff."

I explained that you had to have your facts straight in the woods, that proper identification of a species of leaf might mean the difference between life and death.

We were having a good time now, so as we ambled, I pointed out a Lampert's Tanager on the wing, a cluster of Dodge Lady's Slipper and, because it happened to be around, an actual chunk of mica schist. This brought us to the edge of the gravel pit. "There's kind of a nice island out there," I said. "Would you care to visit it?"

"What's the *island* called?"

"Julia's Island," I said.

Her mocking smile vanished. "That sounds lovely, Nick."

"Maybe it's not such a good idea. You have to balance on junk to get there."

"Now don't talk down to me, Nicky, just because I admitted I was mediocre at softball. I'd love to balance on junk with you. Where do you start?"

She did just fine cat-footing along the lip of the culvert. Even so, I kept twirling to check up on her until she made a swatting gesture in my direction and said, "*Quit*," almost falling then and there. But halfway across the wobbly stones that led to the island – she took them one by one, with little squeals – she overbalanced. I started to grab, but so much of her was bare! Julia splashed down and sat, legs spraddled, mouth wide and soundless. The green water lapped her chest. She held dry hands above it. I'll admit I hesitated (I'd never fallen from the stones, and you hate to screw up a perfect record) before jumping into the knee-high water to rescue her.

She began to laugh. "You *goof!* What are you doing in the *muck?* What am I doing on my *ass?*" She flung herself gleefully backward and submerged.

I crouched, drenching my shorts – it wasn't gentlemanly to stay dry – and tried to bring her to the surface. She whipped her sparkling curls from side to side, spraying my face. "*Oops.*" Cackling, she staggered to her feet. Her shorts were soaked black. I took her arm, which was warm in its film of cool water and shook with her giggles, and led her to shore. "Oh God, that's good," she said, panting. "Oh Jesus, you can only be tense for so long, and then you just, *bwaaah!* Nicky, what are you doing?" My T-shirt was the only half-dry piece of clothing we had. I'd taken it off and was spreading it in the grass for her to sit on.

"Such gallantry," she said in a small, hoarse voice. "I'll weep."

She smothered a laugh instead, and set her gritty haunches next to, but not on, my shirt. Perhaps I looked disappointed: quickly, she lay back across it.

I stood there, not quite looking down at her. Then I sat beside her. Then, casually, I lay back myself. "A smooth operator. Another," she whispered merrily.

"What?"

She shook her head and smiled. "This is nice," she said, thoughtful.

The grass on Julia's Island grew high and cushiony, and I tucked my hands behind my head and eased my limbs. The sky seemed to pulse with my heart, though my heart itself seemed to rest in the earth below me, beating up at my shoulder blades. My vision was grainy from exaltation, and I wanted to blow up buildings or run at top speed, Julia running beside me, though I would be faster. "Nicky," she said to herself. "Nicky," she said to me, "have I been… are you having a good time today?"

"Sure."

"I am, too," she said. "That's the strange part."

"Well, good."

"Yes, good. It's good, all right. You are, as they say, showing me a good time."

"Um, good. What's so funny?"

Smiling, she shook her head. Our faces were very near. I wanted to eat her breath. "Listen," she said. "Can you keep a secret?"

Then her mouth writhed, and she began to laugh.

"Oh, your face," she said, and couldn't continue. "I can't," she snorted. "If you could just. Your *face*," she explained. She rolled help-lessly onto her back, hands in a loose, fending-off position, and kicked her legs up in the air, her damp belly surging with laughter. Then she let her legs thump down in the dense long grass, and screamed.

Finger-thick, blackish, with vermilion spots and belly, the snake attached to her inner thigh looked unspeakably vicious. I gripped it, jamming my thumb in behind its head. It tried to twist and bite me as I whipped it away. I seemed to be holding a rock, so I brought it down with a little cry – *iiigh!* – again and again until the head was pink-gray mash, then dropped the jerking thing with a sob. Two red spots jeweled her leg. "Nick," she said, with the perfect diction of panic, "was it poisonous?"

"Might be a variant breed. I can't be sure," I said desperately.

Still, I *had* read about this. I seemed to recall that you began with an X-shaped incision between the punctures. I wiped my knife again to make sure all the bug juice was off. Then I hesitated with the blade poised above her gleaming leg.

She grabbed my fist and yanked the knife into her thigh. A short, jagged gouge. My second cut was neater. Up welled a bright cross, which I covered with my mouth. If Julia had to die for me to suck her leg, then it was worth it. I'd die too, of course; fair's fair. She gripped the hair at the back of my head and pressed my face tighter, hissing, "Give me your belt. Your *belt*. We need to make a tourni-quet." I fumbled it off and gave it to her. I couldn't bear to spit Julia's blood on the ground, so I swallowed, thinking, *Better not*.

Craig didn't seem to be moving fast when I peered over the hori-zon of her knee, but one moment he was a blur in the woods and the next he was loping across the stepping-stones onto the island. "I think I got all the poison," I said. Julia's gore ran down my chin.

He snatched up the snake and examined it. Then us. To this day I can't imagine what he was thinking, seeing this muddy, bloody mess comprised of the child he was fucking and the infant who wanted to fuck her. Craig said, "You didn't get diddly, Marlin Perkins. This is a baby mud snake. See the red belly? No poison. All you got was a mouthful of girl blood."

He pulled my belt from Julia's thigh and handed it to me. He tucked the small corpse in his back pocket. Then he picked Julia up the way you'd pick up a kitten and, padding back over the rocks and along the culvert's edge, headed for town. I followed. My ambition was to neither cry nor fall in, and here I succeeded.

Salty and metallic, her blood tasted like gold. I remembered how the cells of the body renew themselves once a year. But I also remembered that if you dumped a glass of water into the ocean and mixed it around, and came back a year later, and scooped up some more, a few molecules from the first glassful would wind up in the second one. So maybe everything wouldn't be lost. I had a little of Julia's blood in me now, and with luck that bit of Julia would stay with me forever.

Of course, Julia didn't have any of my blood in her.

But maybe she had a little of my spit.

In Childhood · It Completes You · You Change Size

Melissa Perlman was the first girl in our class to develop. She was hulking and sweet-faced and, without quite being fat, larger than most of the boys. We had nothing against her personally. But we recognized her big new tits for what they were: the end of the world. They refuted everything. They made us retreat the few painful steps we'd taken from our animal selves. We had the truculence of boys trying to swagger off a punishment. We told each other what we'd do if we ever got hold of them, but this was just the kind of big talk that moths like to swap about porch lights. We knew that to get next to them meant blinding, universal immolation.

We wanted facts. Would they float in water? In *salt* water? What did they weigh? Were the nipples like ours? Did they point up or down? Could she make them move, no hands? Did they get blotchy red the way Melissa's face did when we taunted her? We squeezed our own bony chests and tried to think things through. Her breasts were a hammer blow on a fault line running crookedly through us. They divided us: some wanted to dangle frogs in her face, and some wanted to fuck her doggy-style. And some wanted both.

The girls weren't much easier on her, and poor Melissa grew quite prim and standoffish. Still, she was always fond of me. Perhaps because I hung back when the others were full-throatedly torment-ing her. I was a private child, and my explorations were private.

Most boys outgrow drawing after a few years, but I liked it and stuck with it, and by 1973 was the preeminent draftsman at Senator Edgar M. Currie Junior High School. I was the guy who did covers for the yearbook and posters for the school plays. I signed my work with the initials NJW; the J had a long, sporty tail, and the N and W were cunningly intertwined. I also accepted commissions from the guys in my study hall to draw comic book superheroes of their own design. This began when I sketched a character called RePulsor, whom Adam had invented. RePulsor had a chainsaw in place of his left forearm. Then a kid named Gerald Meade asked me to do one he'd dubbed Dr. Light, who shot rays from his eyes that turned peo-ple inside out, and soon each boy wanted his own. They'd crowd around my desk, arguing over features and poses. Generally they requested huge muscles, hands poised to grapple or clenched in fists (which were easier to draw), and trapezoidal mouths baring both rows of teeth. A deft and breezy destruction was the order of the day. My new friends included some of Currie's elite (big Gerald, for instance, was the star of our school's offensive line), so I'd never have shamed myself by admitting it, but this stuff bored me. I secretly liked things shiny and well thought out and nice. In the backgrounds of my drawings I placed glistening towers and monorails straight out of my old Giant Golden Books, and it was over these I'd labor, seeking perfection, as boy after boy drifted away from my desk until only Adam remained.

Hunched at the edge of my bed after school, I'd assemble whole cities. I'd set them among fuchsia parks full of intelligent plants, and shelter them under spotless domes. I lit their home world with three pastel suns. I named it Omega Seven. I spent hours making things glitter with a few four-pointed stars, or shading them smooth, like the airbrushed album jackets I admired. Tacked to the wall above my bed was the sleeve from David Bowie's *Aladdin Sane* – the red-and-blue lightning bolt adorning his white face could have leapt from a radio tower in my volume on Electromagnetism. Bowie was scrawny like me, but seemed to hail from some glamorous and sensible future in which you didn't have to prove yourself as a boy, or even as a girl. I peopled Omega with bony, silver-clad youths, all the consorts of a beautiful round queen with a bosom of matchless splendor.

My preferred medium was blue ballpoint pen. I'd evolved particular techniques for its use. Once the buildings and boys were in place, I'd start sketching with the pen capped, marking the paper with luminous, almost invisible grooves until a figure glimmered in the main plaza of my city. There she'd be, plump-shouldered and dainty-footed in chromed boots and wristlets, a spiked tiara on her head. If I was alone in the house, she'd wear nothing else, and stand unashamed, fists on hips. About some things I was confident, like the clean, cheery little pouches in which her dark blue eyes sat. But how did you show the *distinctness* of her knees without spoiling the smooth flow of her legs? And how did those splendid big things fasten on? I scored the paper with conjecture after conjecture, sometimes retiring to the background to shade everything I was sure of with endless feathering strokes until the fusty, curdling sweetishness of the ink rose from the paper. I hoped a number of different versions of the same optimistic line, made one over the other, would average out to truth. But as I fussed at those white grooves, I'd begin to feel bungling, and furtive, and as if I'd let her down, and these drawings I tore from my sketchbook and shredded, reviewing each bit for unrecognizability before burying it in the trash. My best efforts, though, I stashed in a battered Canada Dry carton under my bed. The box seemed good luck, stenciled as it was with a region chill, fabled, northern, empty, and vast, like inspiration itself.

That was the year Saul lost patience with his book on Debs. He roared in the kitchen that he was fifty-four years old and had *nothing.* He brandished a hunk of goat cheese and a short knife as if they were the nothing that he, at fifty-four, had, then retreated to his office at Montclair to write undisturbed. Del took this more or less in stride: of course he didn't have anything. He was old. But it was cruel to Suzanne. She seemed to test the floor with her feet as she padded about the house. As I worked in my sketchbook, she might ease in and stretch out on the bed behind me, asking, when she was comfortable, "Am I bothering you?" Then she'd tell me stories. Of course, she was half nude, her body disgracefully youthful in a wee bathing suit or frayed T-shirt. My mother didn't believe in deodorants, and I remember her scent – rich and sharp, like spiced bread – and that spongily undermined feeling you get when you're sitting at the edge of an old bed and someone bigger lies down behind you.

"I lived at home until I was twenty-four," she told me. "It was common back then. And my family wasn't like Saul's. They needed my paycheck." Her parents were from a small village in Lithuania, and Detroit filled them with awed misgivings. It grieved them to buy meat from a man whose family they didn't know, and for a few days prior to each Pesach, a big carp cruised around the family's bathtub, waiting to be made into gefilte fish, a steamy procedure that took Suzanne's mother from morning till night. Suzanne and her parents fought constantly. One battle concerned a dress she'd made for a heavy date. They wouldn't let her out of the house in anything so immodest. At last she hurled the dress into a corner, pulled on a prim frock in Eleanor blue, and thundered downstairs, pausing at the sewing basket to grab pinking shears, chalk, needle, and thread. Then she plumped down on the front steps and, working by eye, recut the dress on her body with a deep scoop neck and a hemline above the knee, as her parents watched in rage through the curtains. They wouldn't come out on the porch for fear of making a public scene worse. Then she flung the shears into the little lawn so that they stuck ("Like a dagger!" she said delightedly), and stamped off to meet her boyfriend. Charmed with the story and the dress, he drove them at once to a tourist cabin, which is the part of the story I'd rather not have heard.

"*Such* an ugly dress," she said.

When I took a break, Suzanne would bounce up and sit beside me, kneading my neck with one hand and resting her chin on my shoulder to see what I'd done. One breast lay silken and heavy against my arm. I couldn't point without stirring it. Gesturing cautiously, I explained that cars were a thing of the past. People got around on rocket-powered roller skates. Suzanne nodded. If she saw anything odd in my jabbing at blank paper with a capped pen, she didn't say. She studied the white trenches I'd dug and, once, shyly offered to pose for me. As a young art student in New York, she'd supported herself by figure modeling. I suppose I could have regarded it as just another camping trip, but I declined.

I always waited until I was alone to uncap my pen. With delicate strokes I'd darken the pale grooves, stopping often to wipe the point on scrap paper so I wouldn't get blots. It was a caressing touch, and like a caress it made things realer. Wondrous things would appear. At first I'd be excited, and feel I'd established the facts we'd all needed for so long. Then, one by one, I'd notice all my guesses and bluffs and lose heart. And then I'd see: *it was all good enough for the time being.* Here I'd stroll musingly to the bathroom and lock the door. Within, as I labored among the cool smells of worn porcelain and water, my queen squatted and became the blue world, my domed city dimmed into a bloodlit cavern through which I clambered endlessly until, with a dying effort, I rose through the cavern roof into a blazing field where perfect animals galloped.

Then I'd wash my hands and shred the drawing.

I did not consciously include Julia in these investigations. Shortly after that afternoon at the gravel pit, the mail had brought me a note, on creamy, cardboard-heavy paper engraved with her full name in letters of ravishing elegance and certitude.

Dear Nicholas Joseph –

I had a lovely time at the picnic last week. Sorry to leave so abruptly. Chiefly, I want to thank you for rescuing me; that snake <u>could</u> have been poisonous, after all. Craig and I are going to New York in a few days, so I may not see you again for quite a while. I tried looking up the Dowager Fire Ant, you little shitter. You are a <u>threat</u>. I'll write when I have my next address. Yours with a sore leg,

   –J

I reread this hundreds of times. Still, the second letter never came, and eventually I tucked the note away. I stopped mooning over her, stopped expecting to meet her again. In fact, I seldom thought of Julia, as you seldom look up at the lamp that lights the room.

:   :

As I said, Melissa Perlman liked me. And I have to give her credit for suavity and guts, because she got me to go with her on a couple of walks and a date. That couldn't have been easy. In fact, we were thirteen before she backed me against a locker and asked what I was doing after school. Her chestnut hair shone, her smile was puckery, and I had no way of identifying the gleam in her eyes as fright.

"Studying," I improvised.

"Isn't that terrific of you," Melissa said. "And tomorrow afternoon, I guess you're studying too? Then I guess you can't walk me home until Thursday, Nose," she said. "You know, walk? Walk walk?"

"What do you need me there for?"

"That's a dopey question, dope."

"If I'm such a dope, and you're asking me on a walk, what does that make you?"

"*You* asked *me*. Girls don't ask boys," she said, and stepped gently on my foot with her small white sneaker.

Melissa found me burrowing in my locker right after eighth

29

period. All day she'd given me secret half smiles. Though she usually dressed as if about to give a piano recital, that day she wore rakish new hip-huggers and a sweater that revealed the pale excellence of her tummy. We walked to the main doors through a gauntlet of growling boys and avid girls. Outside, yellow buses trembled and lunged, filled with dim, peering faces. I felt the ghost lines in my drawings had been inked in crude blue swathes and that everybody could see what I was up to.

We turned into the side yard, descended a gentle slope, and were alone in the birch grove behind the school. "Is this the way to your house?" I asked.

"You're just full of dopey questions, Nose. What's your big important hurry? Am I so terrible to walk with?"

"You'll do." My hands seemed unwholesome. I kept them in my pockets.

"Do. Oh, that's nice. Maybe I should turn around right now."

"No, don't. Sorry. Ironic understatement."

"Whatever it is, cut it out." We passed behind the chain-link backstop of the baseball field, plunged into a rain-dug gully, and were in the woods. "I hope you're not starting in on me, too. I'm not big on purpose, you know. But everybody uses it as an excuse. Well, I mean, you never do, Nicky. Except for a few times," she said sleekly. "What if people never stopped talking about your nose?"

"Huh. Seems like you've called me Nose quite a lot lately."

"Well, it's not the same," she said, and gave her sweater a victorious downward tug. "Anyway, I'll stop."

"I don't mind. It's nice when you've got a nickname. It's like, people are thinking about you."

"Well, I don't want people thinking about me. That way. All the time. How would you like to be called Melly Melons? I'm sorry, but that's not a compliment."

"Well, maybe they subconsciously mean it as a compliment, and they're just being jerks about how they tell you."

"Subconsciously. I don't know what that means," she said severely.

"It's when you think about something without noticing you're thinking about it."

"Oh. That makes sense. I do that all the time."

"Yeah? What do you think about? Subconsciously."

After a pause, she said, "Sometimes I subconsciously think, when I'm walking to school, that I'm walking someplace different. Like, beyond that tree it'll all be different. And then, okay, you know, beyond *that* tree."

We laughed. I said, "Different how?"

"Oh, I don't know. Nicer. Like, the school will be nicer. Maybe there'll be flowers in front or something. And the people will be that way, too. In how they talk to you. This is probably sounding really dumb."

"No, I think I know what you mean."

"People are always acting like, every time you walk into the room, you mean some big *thing* by it. You're doing it on *purpose*. And so therefore they get to make remarks."

"I know exactly what you mean. Like when I first got here and everyone treated me and my sister like some kind of Brainiac."

"I don't think of you that way," she said, and went blotchy.

"Well, good." Then I couldn't think of anything to say, and just looked at her.

She shifted her books to one hip and draped an arm over my shoulders.

I became as still as I could without stopping walking. Her thigh grazed my knuckles with each step, and I was implicated in her scent: girl-soap and girl-hair, which smelled like a heated steam iron on linen. I couldn't get us synchronized and our hips bumped. The weight of her breast was salient against my upper arm. "Friends can touch and it doesn't have to mean some huge thing," she said. "Most guys wouldn't understand. Some guys can be real handsome, but they're jerks."

31

If I crossed my arms, my elbow wasn't mashed into her bosom like that. It might even make me seem tough or thoughtful. She let me go.

"But you're different," she said apprehensively.

Soon we emerged on the banks of the gravel pit. "What a smell." She wrinkled her nose. "I sort of like it," she decided. She set her notebook in the grass and sat on it. I sat beside her. "I didn't know there was an island out here. Does it have a name?"

"Nah, it's just an island," I said.

"We could go swimming, if we'd brought suits. And had someplace to change. I don't mind if the water's a little icky."

"Maybe we could bring some. Next time." I had retreated to the future. I picked up a twig and began noodling in the dirt.

"Mm-hmm," she said. "Nicky, which would you rather have, true understanding, or that somebody be really good-looking?"

"True understanding," I said. I nodded.

"I'm glad we agree. What are you drawing there? A crown?"

"It's, ah… made of chrome."

She leaned closer to see, and her cheek hovered near mine. Again her breast reposed, warm and ponderous, along my arm. I understood that there was some protocol one followed to kiss a girl, which everyone knew except me. But whatever it was, I couldn't see how I could get started without moving that arm. I sat thoughtfully stubbing the twig against the dirt. Then I reached the limits of stubbing, and just sat. I could feel Melissa's heart working determinedly under her ribs.

At last, she got up and sadly brushed off her clothes, saying, "Well, I guess we can't sit here all day."

Being sexually backward gives you all sorts of advantages you never get to take advantage of.

:   :

I stepped off the school bus the next morning after an immoderate night of self-abuse, my groin raw and buzzing, my head still lit-tered with Melissa. It was one of the first cold mornings of autumn, and the moans of the buses traveled with new clarity through the chill. The concrete apron in front of the school was dark with kids waiting to be let in. What I wanted then, as badly as I wanted my next breath, was to take my accustomed place among them and vanish. But I was the first boy to manage a date with Melissa, and even Adam's face wore a look of lewd glee. They clustered around and big Gerald Meade said, "Did you get them out?"

It occurred to me then for the first time: that's what I was supposed to have attempted to do.

I tried an unsettling gaze on Gerald, but he was not a boy who'd mind, or even notice, an unsettling gaze. He repeated his question, and the other boys joined in: How far had I gotten? Did she french? Was she hot for it? Did she say stuff? *Good* stuff? Did she really put up a fight? Gerald asked once more, "Did you get them out? Were they whoppers?" and I saw that something was very wrong with me.

I struck out to drive this thought away, and my fist landed in Gerald's stomach.

A sensation. Gerald went down making a big wug-face, and the monitor seized my neck and hauled me into the school, opening the locked doors with her own special key. I was headed for the principal's office, a place I'd never been. Inside, it was quiet. You could hear the humming fluorescent lamps and the clack of our feet. The floor shone and smelled of wax. It was the smell of consequences.

Melissa cornered me the next day in the audio-visual depot. I was a member of the third-period AV squad. It was a great way to get class credit for loafing and snickering and running dirty drawings through the thermofax so they'd come out as colored acetates for the overhead projectors. We always wanted to sneak one into a teacher's presentation. The question was, how could you do it and not get caught? I was lounging at one of the tables in the front room, scheming, when Melissa stepped before me and said, "Hi."

"How's it going?" I said with a start.

"Can I sit down?"

She'd heard I'd punched out the biggest kid in school for speaking disrespectfully of her person. Now here she was, cheeks glowing, tricked out in a new denim skirt and a pink blouse of jaw-dropping snugness. A phrase flicked through my mind: *on a silver platter.* "Actually," I said, "I was just going in to get some projectors ready. Well. Why don't you come in back and we can talk there? It'll be okay if you're with me."

I hated to withdraw my loins from the shelter of the table.

We walked behind the row of gray steel shelves that marked off the back room. I rolled out one of the powder-blue Bell & Howells, cracked a film can at random, and peered at the opening frames with a judicious frown. "Don't mind me," I said, popping the reel on the spindle. "I'm listening."

"Oh." She hesitated. "I just thought I'd stop by and say hi. How you are. I mean, I had a nice time the other day."

"Good. Like to keep our customers happy." I began threading the machine.

"Nicky, will you stop with that? Isn't there anything you'd like to say?"

"Oh, yeah." I smacked my forehead. "Will you marry me?"

"Stop it."

"Kidding. Kidding kidding kidding. So sorry."

"Why must you be nasty?" she whispered.

"Oh, come on. Look," I said, and looked at her. Her clear eyes were wet. I was stunned. I'd thought all this was exclusively my problem. "Look, why don't, can we see a movie? Friday or something. Look, I'm really sorry, Melissa. It was just a dumb joke. Melissa, I would never make fun of you."

"You could, a little." She attempted a smile. "If I knew you meant it all right. You could say things to me, Nicky, if I knew it wasn't in a bad way."

I didn't know what to say, so I smiled back. We stood and smiled at each other. Then she stopped smiling. She murmured, "*I'm being a dope.*"

She stepped forward, took my shoulders, and kissed me.

My mouth vanished inside hers. I tried to think of something to do with my lips. Her tongue bumped up against them and retreated. She kept kissing and was soon so far ahead, I'd never catch up. Melissa's lips were soft, the softness rich with choices. Which was the correct one? and how could I concentrate with her *distracting* me? She pulled away at last, and shook her head fractionally: *No?*

We went to the movie anyway. (*The Poseidon Adventure.* She felt sorry for poor Shelley Winters.) There were also two more nature walks, on which she again talked bravely about true understanding.

Then she cut her losses. Soon afterward, I saw her chatting in the hall with Ronnie Leckner. Ronnie was a year older and wore his fair hair long. He was thin but wide-shouldered, kept his shirts half unbuttoned, and actually looked a bit like David Bowie, if David Bowie had had tiny gray eyes and the desire, though not the ability, to grow a mustache. Melissa clasped her hands behind her as they spoke, which brought her bust and hips into extra prominence. At the end of their conversation, she stepped gently on his foot.

They were right in front of my Spanish classroom. I plodded over and Melissa met me with a serene smile and tense jaw. "Nick? Ronnie? I think you guys know each other."

"What do you say," Ronnie said.

"What do you say," I replied.

Nodding pleasantly, I walked into Spanish class and flung my books on my desk. *Nuestros Vecinos Dos* skidded off and smacked the floor, and everyone turned to watch me pick it up.

:   :

They sat together at assemblies and walked together in the halls. She hooked her thumb into the back loop of his jeans. He slung an arm around her plush shoulders with dazzling ease and authority. *He'd* gotten them out at once, that's what I'd heard. He'd made her bend over and jump around like that. He'd frenched her – boy, she loved french – and gotten her pants off and done intricate, authentic-sounding things. It never occurred to me that Ronnie's love life was of a piece with the natural history of the Dowager Fire-Ant. I believed he was a fitting consort for Melissa. I believed she'd been right to dump me. I lay on my bed with my sketchbooks all day, my legs weak and vague, doodling cities without queens, watching kite-shapes of sunlight lengthen and dim across the wall.

It drove my sister nuts. Lately, Del had blossomed into a difficult proposition. She squirmed on the rug with a copy of *Seventeen*, legs twined impatiently around a leg of the dining table. She returned from clothes shopping with a bright, wobbly look about the eyes. When she swept from the shower, the tuft at her groin seemed a badge of femaleness and betrayal. Then she bought an aqua bath-robe with magenta piping and began to wear it. She hopped on my bed and tried to jog my pen, she peppered me with questions, she ignored me. The more I sulked, the more she tried out new phrases and ways of crossing a room, the more she slammed her brushes and combs around her dresser and glared. Plainly, we were due for a ruckus. One afternoon when our folks were out, she stationed her-self in my door. She nudged the jamb with a thumbnail, and said, "Show me what you do with Melissa."

I'd been lying with my cheek on my closed sketchbook and my nose in the sheets. I hadn't moved for an hour, and I didn't move then. The sheets had begun to smell like my breath, which was gross but comforting. We listened to the gerbils' wheel squeak.

Del climbed over me and sat against the wall, her legs across my back. She thumped the backs of her knees down on my ribs. "Used to do," she amended. "I mean, you know. Some of it.

"Oh, *cut* it," she said. "You just like feeling sorry for yourself. If she can stand to even let that creep near her… Anyway, she's not pro-portional."

"What do you want to for?" I asked.

"Forget it. Forget I even said anything."

"I believe they call that incest, Nose."

"Kissing isn't incest. Not very. Besides, we deserve to get some advantages out of this mess."

"God!" I agreed, and sat up, knocking her legs aside. Now we faced each other.

"They're so nuts!"

"They like it that way."

"They won't let you live! He's such a *prick!* And her!" she said viciously. "Sticking her big *body* into everything."

"Flumps down in my lap and asks, 'Am I bothering you?' *Am I both-er-ing you?*"

"Don't you think she's beginning to get a little fat? I just meant as *practice*," Del cried. "So I don't come off like some weenie with Shawn."

"Shawn Connolly? You want to go with that dweeb?"

"Shut up. You haven't said yes or no."

"I haven't, have I?"

Sorrowfully, she said, "You wouldn't've let her go if you really cared." She hitched over to the edge of the bed. I wanted to establish that this was all her idea, but I didn't actually want her to go. I managed to catch hold of her long hair. It tightened diagonally across her cheek as she turned. Her face seemed stripped of expression.

Slapping my fingers away, she said: "That's what I figured. Wait here."

She pattered into the bathroom and came out with a fresh towel. "On your feet," she said. She folded the towel and tucked it between us, a thick pad separating our loins. She draped her arms around my neck. I placed tentative hands on her back. She gave me a bossy shove with her hips and I held her for real, one hand low on her back and the other in the tender region between her shoulder blades. She twiddled the hair at my nape and looked dreamy.

I touched her cheek with my lips and murmured, "Nothing personal, Nose. You're just too ugly." I could smell the iron-scented local water on her skin.

She formed herself lightly against me as if we'd been made to fit together. I hadn't known that was possible. I was glad for the folded towel. Her voice hummed: "Look, are we going to or not?"

Eyes closed, I moved my mouth out and slightly slantways.

Her lips were cool and thin. She moved them one way, and I moved mine the other, nibbling as if drawing in a strand of spaghetti. I broke away.

"That wasn't so rotten," she said. "Try again."

She gripped the back of my head and levered it forward. This time our lips engaged firmly. It seemed like brother and sister roughhousing, where the idea was to win. She said, "Easy."

Our mouths bumbled for a while, then began to get the idea. They seemed to fatten as we kissed, and soon we could form a seal, engendering suction I'd feel down in my belly and the backs of my knees. She laid a hand on my butt, then tucked it quickly into my back pocket. I put a hand on her breast. She removed it. "Practice," I said.

Her chest looked sharp, as if she'd been swimming in cold water. "That doesn't prove anything," she said, and hid it against mine.

It was okay, we discovered, to bite a little. You could also just barely brush lips, or try and get right down each other's throats. Some kisses were like an argument, and some were furious but coordinated, like a three-legged race, and some were very sleepy: a state you inhabited. You could grip each other by the shoulders, you could bear-hug, you could lean forward and touch only at the mouth. You could try to climb up each other; the towel kept dropping, and once or twice we'd pretend not to notice – I'd expected her groin to be an absence against mine, but it was a hard, padded crest, and she released a whistling whimper from deep in her throat, like a mournful collie. We found tender places: the hollow of the temple, the hollow beneath the ear, the tense spot between the eyebrows, the cusp of the collarbones. The kiss I liked best was very light and simple, no tricks, with me steadying Del's jaw with my fingertips.

Meanwhile, our hips moved in long, warm waves. Abruptly I found myself rising through the dark cavern until I'd reached the blazing meadow. All the bright creatures were there. Then I fell, opening my eyes in fright.

Del's nose was murderous and her mouth was frightened. "You didn't."

My face was sweaty.

"You didn't. You *didn't*," she wailed, and ran from the room.

I sat on the bed. I stretched out again. After a while, I opened my sketchbook. Wielding my eraser until the paper took on a furry thinness, I stripped away the crystal domes of Omega Seven, rooted up the brainy flowers, yanked down the pastel suns. In their place I set bitter drifts of frozen nitrogen. Now my hero was probing strange ruins beneath the bluish wastes of the Ice Planet. There was a woman in his past about whom he never spoke. Soon a storm imperiled his buddies, and he plunged out to rescue them through gouts of snow that drew sobs from his tortured lungs. He stumbled deeper into that hell of blue ice until death brought peace to his heart.

:   :

On the school bus the next day, I peeked uneasily at my schoolmates. Part of me was sure no one had ever smooched his sister before, and part of me was certain everybody had and that the liars just wouldn't let on. Del and I ignored each other as usual. When we got home, she went right on ignoring me. She didn't act as if I were horrible, or as though the whole thing hadn't been her idea. She acted as if she had no brother. I was afraid to argue the point. I was afraid to *think* — anything I thought of seemed to split open and ooze. I'd ruined everything that could ever happen to Del or to me, and I'd somehow ruined everything that had already happened to us, and our entire family. *Destruction*, I thought, *destruction*, and

39

this would momentarily empty me of thought and shame. I thought all this would last forever, that these were the new terms of my life.

Then, a week or two later, Del wangled a date with Shawn Connolly, and everything else was forgotten.

On the appointed evening, my mother set up her folding vanity on the kitchen table. There were little hinged boxes filled with umber and putty and dark rose, and caskets of powder fine as gas. The lights around the mirror were lit. In the circle of grimed glass, I could see one of Del's eyes. It regarded me, then went back to regarding itself. She sat on a kitchen chair and Suzanne stood behind her, wielding something like a pair of nail scissors, which ended in a sort of tiny guillotine. She applied this to Del's lids, and when my sister opened her eyes again, they were larger. Around Del's wrists Suzanne clasped silver bangles, her own face lined and pale, and I recalled my old stories of virgins and Aztec priests. Finally she turned Del to face me. I was there as a sort of sample boy. My sister's face was haughty and smooth. She asked me unsteadily what I thought. I said she looked great, and resolved to be careful for the rest of my life.

After she left, I made myself dinner and tried to draw. Around eleven, I turned out the light. Del and Shawn would be part of a band of kids who'd see *The Poseidon Adventure*, then have pizza at R&J. I pictured them moving through an illuminated night, comely, touching each other in code; I smacked my forehead. It hurt in a stupid way. Only a creep would lie in bed hitting himself. Some creep who had to make out with his sister. The clock on my dresser was far off, then farther off. Then I slept.

I woke to the snick of the doorknob by my ear. I didn't know what time it was. Del walked through my dark room and into the bathroom and locked the door. I heard water splashing. It went on for a long time. When she emerged in the moonlight, she'd wrapped her new robe tight around her gray body. She stole back into her room and closed the door. Her bed squawked. Then nothing.

"Nicky?" she whispered through the wall. Her voice was dulled and hollow.

"I'm awake," I whispered.

We waited.

"I – He was there. Shawn. He doesn't – There was a girl. With him."

I managed: "He's a jerk."

"So – Don't hate me, Nicky. Please don't hate me."

"What?"

"Ronnie was there. Leckner. Not, not with, Melissa."

I couldn't breathe.

"He started out – He was very nice. At first. I didn't – well, we found a place. And I kept my things on, I didn't really let him – We didn't actually –" Her words twisted into the sad-collie whine. "Oh," she whispered, "it was horrible."

Weeping, she appeared at my door in pajamas which had no color in the dimness. Her mouth seemed primitive. She stole into the bathroom and returned with a folded towel. Setting it across my hips, she climbed on top of me, clasped me with arms and legs, and tucked her scalding face into my neck. "*Shhhhh,*" I murmured, my arms around her. "*Ruth, oh, Ruth-a-dell.*" And I thumped softly on her kidneys.

The next morning we let Del sleep in. It was odd riding the bus without her there to pretend to ignore. The school's doors were open. Ronnie's locker was easy to find. He dropped his books and came out to meet me, tiny gray eyes flat. I wanted to smite him unthinking, as I'd vanquished Gerald, but I'd known what I was going to do all morning, and Ronnie had known the moment he'd seen me. Sidestepping as I swung, he hammered my chin, a marvelous punch, and everything rushed away from me.

It was nice for a moment. And then everything rushed back.

:   :

We fought for weeks. We avoided the school; we didn't want to be interrupted, questioned, kept apart. We also avoided hitting each other's mouths and eyes, so as not to leave telltale marks. (A bitter constraint. I wanted to spoil his Aladdin Sane prettiness.) If either of us was in a crowd, the other would pass by, eyes front, but now and then we'd find each other alone, and go at it without a word. I rejoiced to see how ugly he became when we fought, all elbows and a wrinkled chin.

Fighting changed you. If you fell on gravel, your body became a constellation of hurt points. If you cracked your head, your body grew abstract and spread out from the bruise like a peal spreading from a bell. But if you won, you were perfected, a column of punishing righteousness crowned with a numb fist. I couldn't get enough of that feeling, and I think Ronnie felt the same. As soon as one of us had been knocked down or paralyzed with a blow to the stomach, the victor stalked away, frightened of himself, because a beating was not enough. One of us had to be broken, ruined, destroyed. I remember standing over him, screaming, *"All right? All right?"*

"All right!" he bawled back from the dirt. It was agreed.

He gut-punched me under the stadium and between cars in the ValueRite parking lot, and whipped an elbow across my jaw behind the movie theater. I toppled him with a huge haymaker beside the supermarket dumpsters and, under the bank's revolving digital clock, gave him a clout to the neck that put him in turtleneck sweaters for days.

I thought we would fight forever. Still, the last fight came quite soon. It was November, and everybody was eager for an early snow, and I was lying on my back on the frozen mud while Ronnie's windbreaker retreated into the trees across from the firehouse. A beige windbreaker. The sky was a deep slate color. There was that nice feeling of everything rushing away. Then there was a girl's voice somewhere, and golden flecks. Late afternoon sun striking the fine fair hairs on a young woman's calves. The blood in my mouth tasted like Julia's, so I wasn't really surprised to see her.

Julia had come forward as if to help me up, then stopped. Someone had been teaching her tact.

"Took a tumble," she said.

"So it would appear," I said, getting to my feet.

"Are you all right?"

"I'm dandy."

"If you're dandy, would you please straighten your head?" She put gentle fingers to my temples and righted it.

"Sorry. I thought it was straight."

She laughed. "Oh, Nicky. Come have some ice cream."

"Why ice cream?"

"Because it's good," she said.

Julia wore a gingham skirt and a bulky white cable-knit sweater. She looked very pretty and, I thought, womanly. I was surprised to note that she was shorter than I. She led me down the street into Melody's, settled us at the counter, and ordered for both of us. Then she swung back and forth on her stool, one foot tucked beneath her, the other trailing in a sandal and a crumpled white sock. She mistook the direction of my gaze and amiably twitched up her skirt, presenting the inside of one thigh just beginning to lose its tan. I saw a faint, silvery X: the jagged stroke she'd made crossing my neater one. "Seven stitches for my cut, none for yours. Still, Nicky, you left your mark on me. Now, what was all that about?"

"I'm sorry. I'd rather not say."

"All right. Fair enough. Are you sure you're okay? He was a pretty big guy," she said sympathetically.

"Don't—" I drew a shaky breath.

"Sorry."

"Ronnie Leckner is almost exactly my size. Maybe a little skinnier."

"All right."

"He's faster than me, though. Which is why he often wins. As you saw. I don't mean to snap at you."

"You've been fighting with this guy as a regular thing?"

43

"I guess."

She leaned forward. "All right, then. What's the score? Go on, tell."

I'd won three, and Ronnie had won five.

"I don't keep score," I said.

Our spoons clicked against the dishes.

"Well," I said, "what brings you back to Silver Crest?"

"Fighting with my folks. Why else does one come to Silver Crest?" she said airily.

"Why indeed," I said.

We ate some more ice cream. Its sweetness seemed a reproach: I was a child.

"Well," she said. "What have you been up to? Weren't you writing a book?"

"No. I don't write."

"No?"

"No. Actually, I like to draw."

"Yes? Draw what?"

I'd never told anyone.

"Cities. I like to design cities."

"Who lives in them?" she asked.

I was silent.

"Well, what are they like?"

"I guess they're supposed to be some sort of perfect world."

"Those are nice." Then, "I'm not making fun. Please go on. I want to hear."

"I call the place Omega," I said warily. "You know, as in ultimate. It's all under a plexiglass dome. And all the weather is planned. I mean, they have rain and snow and so on, but there's a guy in charge, and he orchestrates it, like music. It's on a planet with three suns, so there's always daylight, but each sun gives off different-colored light. People tell time by color."

"They *don't!*" she cried, but I understood she was not contradicting me.

Omega, I told her, was a peaceful society. I expatiated on its history, customs, and architecture. I had a kind word for the talking plants, nor did I omit the rocket-powered skates. Enclosed vehicles were considered too isolating and conducive to closed thinking. Perfect human interaction was held to be the highest good. The crystal pylons set throughout the plazas contained recording devices. "They're linked to a huge databank under the city, so whatever you talk about, with your friends or whatever, there's a permanent record and you can always go back and replay it. So no conversation is ever lost."

"But that's so wonderful," she said.

"Is it?"

"I wish I could live there," she said dreamily.

I tried another spoonful of ice cream. The chocolate was delicious. I began to lose that rickety feeling you get after a beating. My bruised jaw felt gallant. "I guess it's just science fiction stuff. Frankly, I have, as yet, no technique. The thing about being thirteen is," I sighed, "you're such a terribly rough sketch."

"*Are* you, now?" she said. "But that's so true. You should've seen me."

"Really? I can't imagine you as a rough sketch."

"Believe it," she said solemnly. "Rough. My poor family. That's why I'm still coming back on these… Well, they're very nice people," she said flatly.

In fact, as she described them, they did sound very nice. Her father had been trained as an engineer. He did not work in an office. He attended conferences, though, and had a number of projects in mind. She recited all this as if by rote, and I didn't listen very attentively. Her lips looked very dry. I wanted to lick them. She'd been talking for quite a while about her family, and was still on the subject of her father. She listed his complaints against her in a singsong voice, and moved her eyes and mouth a lot, as if speaking to a little kid: she was "airy-fairy," she was "blatant," she made "unsound

45

choices," she had "unsound friends." Making an exaggerated about-to-cry face, she said, "He thinks I'm too *vivacious* with the boys. *Me*. Now." She poised the spoon. "When I walk into a room…" She declaimed: "When *I* walk into a room…"

She appeared to have forgotten all about me.

I said, "People assume you're trying to create some sort of an effect."

She lowered the spoon.

"Yes," she said.

"They figure you're doing it, whatever *it* is, on purpose. And therefore they're entitled to make remarks."

"Go on."

"Have you ever thought," I said, groping for words, "that the world would be a little different around the next corner? And then, you know, the one after that?"

She smiled, slowly and hugely. "You little shitter. I forgot what a threat you are." Her eyes seemed pale, her lashes illumined. "Around the next corner. Walk into a room. Who's been teaching you about women? No one, eh? What was that fight about?"

I shook my head.

"Would I like her if I knew her?" she said softly.

At last I said, "I think I ruined everything."

"Oh… I don't know about that. If I were that girl, I'd want another chance. Because you're a real little threat. You are. And you know how to listen. And you have that saving little touch of bullshit, and that's why I can talk to you. I was so low when we ran into each other. So low. Nicky, I've sort of taken a beating today, too. And I'll tell you the truth: you've made me feel good. Nicky, do you remember, on the little island that time, I was about to say something?" She leaned closer. I could smell the chill fall air in her hair and sweater, and the warm girl's body inside them. "I was going to say: I wish I was ten years younger."

I blushed madly.

"Oh, look at *you*," she crooned. She took hold of my nose and gave it a gentle shake. "Look at you," she said.

We sat there together.

Then she said, "My God, is it that late? I have to go. My friend expects me back in New York in…" She laughed. "Well, now, actually."

Her friend.

Desolated again, I lurched off my stool. She settled the bill and we walked down the block to her car, a deep green Triumph two-seater convertible with wire-spoke wheels and rusted rocker panels. It was *wicked*, it was almost enough to distract me from my sorrow. From the corner beyond it, a crowd of kids watched. Ronnie was among them. They'd been spying on us. Well, good. Here I was talking to a beautiful older woman with a wicked car. "Can I drop you somewhere?" she said.

"That's okay."

She wrenched her hair up behind her head, then dropped it. "It was good talking to you, Nicky. Take care." She touched the door handle, and it was then that she noticed the staring boys.

She turned back to me, a small complicit smile in her eyes. Setting her hands on my chest and lifting her face, she brushed her parted lips against mine. For a moment, our mouths clung and stirred together, and I steadied her jaw with my fingertips, like a man of the world, like someone who'd had lots of practice.

Then, waving, she ground off in a burst of blue smoke.

I twirled on my heel and sauntered past the guys. Ronnie's little pale eyes were sick. He was stumbling out into the wastes of the Ice Planet, broken, ruined. Destroyed.

THREE

In Dreams of Smelly Water, Catch Your Eyes

The next time I saw Julia – four years later, in Ithaca, New York – she was undressing near a boulder shaped like a goat's head minus ears and horns. The stone had an unwholesome yellowish tint. Julia wore frayed white fishnet pantyhose and no underpants, and her pubic hair snarled the cotton mesh like crab grass growing though the tines of a discarded rake. After rolling the pantyhose to her ankles, she sat on the goat's head to remove her hiking boots. That's when she looked up, and we recognized each other.

What was I doing there, anyway?

Well, to begin with, Saul had finished his book. My sophomore year in high school, *Bright Chains: Debs, Marx, and the American Century* was published by a midwestern university press. It was carefully reasoned and gracefully written, and enjoyed a respectable sale for a scholarly title, and on the strength of its success, Saul was offered an associate professorship at Cornell's School of Industrial and Labor Relations. The summer before my senior year, we left Silver Crest for upstate New York. I had to start my life over. It was the worst thing that had ever happened to me.

I'd been doing well at Silver Crest High. I even had a girlfriend: Jo Ann Corvino. Jo Ann was agreeably svelte, as she often reminded us with prim, dowdy clothes of an alluring tightness. Her face, though, was quite homely. She'd been born with a harelip, and the cartilage dividing her nostrils had been snipped out and used to repair the gap. This left her with a ragged mouth and a boxer's mashed-in nose, and lent a quacking tone to her voice, so that she kept silent when in groups. Jo Ann was cautious, studious, and fiercely Catholic. I was the first boy she'd seriously kissed, and she meant to remain a virgin until marriage. Still, the combination of a body we all wanted to look at, a face we didn't, silence that could be taken for stupidity, and parents, by the way, who were infamous drunks, was enough to brand her, in the eyes of us would-be men, as a slut. I believed this, too, and was terribly disappointed to learn the truth.

Jo Ann made up a monthly study schedule, and stuck to it. She attended Mass each Sunday, alone. Before donning a halter top, she secured her nipples with crosses of scotch tape. "Otherwise, it doesn't look *neat*." And she did have a powerful libido, one she was determined to conquer. Her great weapon was routine. For a year and a half, our petting schedule seldom varied: two sessions a week, often in her cousin's basement den (her cousin was usually out with her ex-husband), either On Top or Down There. For an On Top session we stripped to the waist and dry-humped to orgasm. For a Down There session we doffed shoes, socks, and pants, and did the same. We never removed our underpants, and to have removed both shirt and pants at the same time was unthinkable, though I thought about it constantly. She liked being caressed In Back, and encouraged me to slip my hands under her panties to do so, but even through the shield of our clothing, we could never touch each other's In Front. There was a distinct boundary between In Front and In Back. At the end of eighteen months, if you'd handed me a grease pencil, I could have marked it with a dotted line.

We didn't, frankly, like each other that much, so when I told Jo Ann I'd be leaving Silver Crest, her reaction stunned me. Her keen dark eyes filled with tears. "I'll never see you again," she whispered.

"I'll come back and visit," I offered.

She sneered. She wasn't dumb.

I said, "We can still go steady. Maybe we can see each other on summer vacation. Maybe you could apply to Cornell and we could both go there."

Her contempt turned to something like fear. Was I insane?

Our last date was a Down There session at her cousin's. Around midnight, after we'd each made two excursions from the dark cave to the lit meadow, Jo Ann took on a look of fierce resolve. She reached under her sodden jersey and, grimacing, pulled away the crosses of tape. These she stuck to the arm of the couch for safekeeping. Then she slipped off the jersey and slumped back, eyeing me over the dark, stiff, fretful-looking tips of her breasts. Her white cotton panties were nubbly with wear and soaked to grayish translucency. Within, a shadowy wedge. She watched me stare. Her black hair was stuck to her mashed-in face. She was beautiful. Unbelieving, I settled a palm upon her pubis as one touches a stove that may be hot. From it rose an odor both smothersome and light. I curled my fingertips into her waistband. She seized my wrist. We remained motionless, the cleft summit simmering in the hollow of my palm. Eyes slitted, she surveyed the front of my jeans. "He still at it?" she asked.

"Yes."

A tremor washed across her body and her knees went lax.

Adoringly she said, "I think it's time for you to go."

Ithaca proved to be a very pretty town, but sixteen-year-old boys don't live for scenery. My one year at Ithaca High was a desolation. These kids had grown up together. Their alliances and hatreds and codes were fully formed. Now, in their last year before college, they were not looking for new friends. I was used to doing well and being liked, and it hadn't occurred to me that I'd one day live among people to whom I simply did not matter. They already had a girl who drew posters, and she was better than me.

Saul had bought us a big house on a tree-dark street. It had a broad staircase of caressable mahogany, big closets with mysterious little cabinets inside, fresh yellow paint in the kitchen, and a sunny rotunda where Saul placed his new electric typewriter. If you put in all the leaves, the dining room table was lozenge-shaped and seated sixteen. Without, it was circular and seated six, and the four of us sat around it each evening like the four points of the compass.

We avoided Saul's eyes. His mustache dragged on his lower lip that year, and he wielded knife and fork with gray fists. This was to have been his time of triumph, the one he felt he'd been born to. Saul liked to say, *My folks were the real Galitzianer royalty, hot shots who came over in time to cash in on the Civil War. See, you could get your uniform from the corner tailor, but it had to have the right buttons. My zaydeh provided the buttons. Gutter genius, but they thought they were Morgans.* Little Saul's parents used to buy his crayon drawings from him for a nickel. He'd crouch in the corner, scribbling in a torment of greed. At Columbia he was famous for the number of prizes and scholarships he applied for, not one of which he ever got, and for the eloquence of his rages afterward. He'd believed the Twentieth Century would one day confide in him, like a princess in a courtier. He saw no reason why presidents should not seek his counsel. But Saul was an indifferent student, *a real thick one*, as he liked to say, and at thirty found himself instead with a lackluster doctorate and a perfectly adequate wife (Rachel, his first). The academic career that followed was a long stumble through a weedy field.

Then *Bright Chains* was published, and Cornell bestowed upon him a fine salary, a fine office, and, more to the point, a graduate assistant, a glossy, twitchy beauty named Carla Hirsch. Carla did not exactly count as infidelity. My parents still had an "open" marriage. But Suzanne was aging and lonely and four hours from her beloved New York, and it was, at the least, poor manners on Saul's part. In her grief, my mother was learning to cook. Each night, shamefaced, she ladled out the slop of her sorrow. Saul sorted through it in a temper, nose bustling with excuses. Slumped and glum, I was probably no bargain myself those days. Only Del was stubbornly cheery. She'd met a curly-bearded Cornell freshman named Robert Martz, and came home only to eat and sleep. We weren't her problem anymore.

I'd recently set aside my ballpoint pen and was trying to teach myself to make linoleum block prints. Still lifes – I was sick of girls and boys and imagination. Over at Cornell's Fine Arts library, I'd discovered Giorgio Morandi, who'd spent his entire life making sober, dull-toned pictures of a few old bottles and jars. Good stuff. I decided to outdo him. I'd pick a single object – pencil sharpener, soup bowl, sneaker, garlic clove – and squint at it for a quarter-hour at a time, willing it to surrender up its essence. I had forbidden myself to sketch in pencil. That made it too easy to erase or fudge things. No more leaving the cap on my pen; I'd draw with the blade or not at all. The blocks came either in a dim custard color or a dim mint, and were clean and pleasant to the touch, and the main thing I remember is that I always hated to spoil them.

When the gouge at last touched down, the block resisted. Gently but firmly, I had to force the issue. Too deep an angle and the point burrowed in, crunching against the wood beneath. Too shallow, and it skittered off, leaving a sere little scratch. But if I was lucky, sometimes I could briefly lose myself in relaxed attentiveness, so that long curls of linoleum rose from the block with a clayey, secret smell, and my line chose its way with buttery ease. I thought of this as "thinking with your arm," and wished there was someone to whom I could use the phrase.

When I finished a block, I proofed it. I recall the dankly hearty odor of the ink, and the tiny sucky crackling as I rolled it out on an old mirror with a rubber brayer. Then, when it was the right consistency, the rumbling, felt in the bone rather than heard, as I rolled it onto the block. I'd waft the paper onto the inky surface and buff it down with the back of a big soup spoon. The bowl of the spoon would grow hot with friction. Then I'd peel back the new print, examine it, and sigh. I filled my Canada Dry box several times over that year, and each time emptied it into the trash. If only some part of the mint rectangle were forbidden! – cordoned off like Jo Ann's In Front – at least I'd know where I was trying to get.

I missed Adam painfully. I missed climbing the cyclone fence behind the drive-in and watching movies from the roof of the snack stand. I missed the galumphing one-on-one basketball. I missed Adam's basement, where we'd read or noodle on his guitar all afternoon among the marshy smells of new wood-grain paneling and old magazines. He'd taught me the introductory vamp from "Stairway to Heaven." It hurt my fingers, but it sounded perfect. I missed the rock fanzine he was going to edit and I was going to design, the film we were going to produce using paper marionettes that I'd construct and he'd animate with the Super 8 camera down in the AV center. I missed the warm tables at R&J Pizza and the long counter at the Hiamack Dunkin' Donuts, the pleasure of cupping hot food or drink in our hands and speaking brashly through the rising steam: once I was done with Cornell and he with NYU, we'd get a loft together in SoHo, wherever that was, and have wild times with wry, uninhibited women who looked like Carly Simon. He thought they should be dancers, or back-up singers in his band, and I thought they should be fellow artists or something. I wrote him often: *I walk, sulk, wank. Buddy, everything in my life is about two notches below pathetic. Del's got a new romance going and is unavailable for comment. I'd weep with happiness if some-body here had some opinion of me, no matter what it was.*

I even wrote Jo Ann: *Three deep gorges divide the town, each fash-ioned of brown-gray granite dabbed with thin afternoon light, and through them I trek each day, killing time. Much loneliness. I think of your warmth, your passion and subtle courage.* I was already writing with an eye to my Collected Letters. She had sense enough not to encourage this with a reply.

I didn't write Julia, though she'd sent me two letters back in Silver Crest. True to her word, she'd mailed the first a week after our parley at Melody's. *Everybody talks in this town, me more than most, but how many listen? Thank you for that. Alan, my friend, sends his best.* To this I'd posted a brief, strangled response. (*Thank you for your thoughtful note.*) But I didn't write back when, two years later, she wrote: *Know who I was thinking about the other day? You. Sorry to be such a lousy correspondent. I've thought of giving poetry a rest and taking a shot at a performance piece. Though Alan reminds me (we try to keep in touch) that it's boresome just to épater le bourgeois, because they never stay épatered, and anyway, why bother? What are you now, fifteen, sixteen? Write. Let me know what's become of you.*

:   :

In May 1977 I turned seventeen and was graduated from high school. The only friend I'd managed to make was Kenny Sobel. He was a tall, bony, plump-faced, anxiously smirking guy who seldom spoke, and when he did, he ducked his head and let the words slip out in a soft, rapid mutter, as if trying to sneak through the sentence before you hit him. Kenny and I had a lot in common. We were both Jewish, with high SAT scores, tense shoulders, and a kind of bashful secret arrogance. But basically, we spent time together because nobody else would have us. It was a grim, expedient friendship that bordered on hatred.

I'd resolved that my time at Cornell would be nothing like my year at Ithaca High. My appetite for inconspicuousness had been glutted for good. To ready myself, I got my ear pierced, grew my hair long, and dressed all in black. Coats struck me as uncool and fussy; in cold weather, I just piled on black shirts until I could barely move my arms. I wanted to be noted, admired, marveled over, resented, ridiculed, hated – to stamp myself on the blank page of Ithaca like an inky capital I. Now, when I stood in the corner, I set my hands on my hips, studied the passing scene with a tiny, lopsided smile of my own invention, and waited for someone to look at me so that I could suck the smile away with a little shake of the head. *Don't mind me. I guess I've always seen things differently from other people.*

Central to this new persona was my weirdo family background. I stopped hiding it and began wearing it like a Croix de Guerre. I told Kenny stories – often true – about the poverty I'd never noticed at the time, and retailed some of my parents' more flavorful sayings. I frankly stated that my sister had taught me to kiss, and explained about the skinny-dipping. Naturally, these days, I swam bare-ass at the Lower Reservoir whenever I could. One day, smirking and nodding, Kenny asked to come along. Thank God. I never had the nerve to talk to anybody there, and always felt pitifully lonely.

The Lower Reservoir lay half a mile into the woods above Giles Street. Halfway along the path, we met a group of college kids. We wanted to get an advance look at the girls among them, but the trail forced you to walk single file and we only caught glimpses of them from the back. One smallish gal was ludicrously overdressed: hiking boots, fishnet stockings, a flouncy saffron skirt, a denim jacket hand-painted with a sunset and palm trees, and an old fedora crammed down over kinky brown hair. More promising was a tall, fair girl with a drowsy sway to her walk. Kenny mumbled, "I don't know. This may be too strange."

I instructed him: "You can always keep your trunks on if you feel uptight, Ken. It's not like there's a dress code."

"Undress code," Kenny said. We knew this wasn't funny, but we laughed. We were really getting to hate each other.

After five minutes or so, the trail opened out onto a terraced stone bluff overlooking the reservoir. To the right, the green water slid smoothly over a spillway and thumped into an invisible basin below. Heads bobbed on the dull waves. On the opposite shore, a long rope hung from a tree so that enterprising individuals could climb up, swing out, and jump. The water smelled ancient and lewd. The convoy began to disrobe, and so did I. So, after some skittish reconnoitering, did Kenny. I gossiped with him, stretched, admired the green trees, the blue sky, and everything else but the women disrobing around us. I permitted myself to glance toward the big girl. She held her army fatigue pants in languid hands and gazed at them as if she couldn't imagine what they were for. I removed my sneakers, paying great attention to the laces, and glanced at the short one.

As I said, when we saw each other, Julia had rolled her pantyhose down to her boot tops. She stopped and stood. Rather than shuffle over with bound ankles, she smiled and curtsied. Her brown triangle curtsied as well. It was lush as her armpits, and a faint line of hairs trailed up from it to her navel.

I sort of waved. Then I jerked my eyes aside just as she shucked off her brocade vest. There was nothing beneath it. In that sliver of a second before I forced my attention to the opposite trees, I saw that her smallish body had shed its baby fat everywhere but at the hips and thighs, which were still slightly blurred; that her calves were graceful and her torso almost childlike; that the sun had turned her fat nipples a syrupy brown and that each rested on a minor swell of flesh beneath which her ribs were distinct and orderly; that her stomach was strong (though, childlike, she made no effort to suck it in) and her navel pronounced; that her shoulders and arms were delicately made but capable-looking; that her fingernails were badly chewed. Then I dragged my gaze into the trees. I still remember those fucking trees: there was one little runt who didn't seem to have a chance. But I couldn't control my peripheral vision: Julia in boots and hat. She removed the hat, and her mashed-down hair rose like bread dough.

So did I. By now I'd stripped down to my jeans, which were rapidly getting too small. I bit my tongue and thought *dead babies dead babies dead babies.* I pictured a horrific jet crash I'd seen on the evening news. I pictured myself castrated with poultry shears. Meanwhile I stood, hands on hips, as if lost in the scenic splendor. Kenny watched me, fiddling with the snap of his plaid shorts. I took a breath: *Smell that air!* By this time the poultry shears had reduced me almost to normal, so I yanked my jeans down, said "Uh huh," and dove in.

The lake was icy. My warm head clanged and I saw white stars. I stayed under and took another stroke in the green silence, then another, gliding heavily forward through bitter cold and warmer currents curling up from the bottom. Two more strokes, and my chest hurt. One more stroke. I burst to the surface. I'd hoped the cold would deflate me, but the impact of Julia's body – an On Top and Down There of such quality, and seen all at once, too – was overwhelming.

Julia scanned the water until she spotted me, then smiled, dove in, and closed the distance with a few graceful strokes. "Where are you running? Nicky, I haven't seen you in forever."

I glanced down nervously, but the green surface was opaque. "Wanted to cool off a bit. Kind of hot today."

"No, it isn't." In fact, people were already climbing back out of the frigid water. "Nicky, it's good to *see* you."

"What are you doing here?" I tried to smile.

"I'm coming to school in the fall. Doctorate in French Lit. Rimbaud," she said, giving it the full French pronunciation. There was something loose and scary about the way she spoke. "Anyhow, I hadn't made my mind up, and I wanted to see the place, and I've got a friend who's letting me crash at her place while she's out of town."

"I thought you had to let them know earlier than this."

"Well, I *said* yes, but I thought I might change my mind. But isn't this lake or whatever marvelous? I've just been *living* here. Stop running away," she added. I'd been sculling slowly backward as she sculled forward. I expected to jab her in the belly any minute. "Is it too weird, that we meet after all this time, and we're naked? But you can always put your shorts on if you're uptight about nudity."

"I'm *not*... Skip it."

Back on the bluff, Kenny was talking to the tall girl. He stood before her, arms crossed, hands clutching his own shoulders, the most enormous dick I have ever seen dangling furtively between his thighs. The tall girl gazed into his eyes, nodding, dressed only in a beige brassiere. She reached back to unhook it, seemed to forget why her hands were back there, and scratched her long spine with long fingers.

"Nice, I agree," Julia said, "but you're supposed to admire my beauty before you ogle other women. Who's the guy?"

"Just a guy I know," I said quickly. "Why don't we talk when I've finished swimming? Thought I'd swim a few laps."

"Okay, okay. I'll let you be."

Then she heaved herself up and dunked me.

Just before I went under, I noted on her breath the hard, sweet tang of liquor.

I swam leftward to the farthest shore, then back, a distance of perhaps a third of a mile, breathing as seldom as I could in the hope that anoxia would rectify my condition even if hypothermia couldn't. No luck. I lost all feeling in my fingers and feet, but it still tugged at the base of my belly like a stubborn rudder. On the returning lap, I saw Kenny hurtling from the hanging rope down into the water. Cautiously, I swam closer. The tall girl was trying to clap and tread water at once. "This is great," Kenny told me. "Have you met Sam?"

She extended a willowy hand. I shook it. "Kenny's something," she said, pale eyes full of wonder.

"He is," I said.

"Listen," Kenny said, "were you thinking of swimming much longer? Because Sam's getting kind of cold. Sam and I thought we might go get some tea at the Rosebud. I mean, if you wanted to come?" he added reluctantly.

"No, nope. You kids have your fun. I'll just do another few laps or two before I turn in." I could barely talk.

"It was nice meeting one of Kenny's friends," Sam said.

Julia shouted, "Yo! Nicky! C'mere!" She sat on the edge of the bluff, making a bullhorn of her hands.

"You devil," Kenny said. "Better go see what the lady wants."

I swam over to keep her from shouting again. "If you can talk to your friends over there, you can talk to me."

"Just saying them goodbye. Goodbye to them. Thought I'd swim a couple more."

"That water's ice. You can't be enjoying this. Don't make me come and get you."

"*No.* I am," I said. "It's fine."

"Nicky, I haven't seen you for years."

"One more lap."

"Come up and talk for a little first."

"Be right there. One lap."

"I'm coming to get you."

"Bye."

"This isn't funny, you little shit. Why are you avoiding me?"

"Jesus Christ, Julia," I hissed, "why do you think?"

She smiled radiantly.

"A stiffy?" she said. "A boneroo? Oh, let's see."

"Shit," I said, and paddled away.

She began to laugh. "Oh, be a sport. I promise I won't look, Nicky. Well, I won't *stare.* Where are you going? I've got your clothes right *he*-ere."

Kenny boosted Sam shrieking up the slope to the rope-tree with a hand on her rump. I coughed water from my nose and set out again.

When I returned, I could scarcely move my arms, but my temperament was still flourishing. The dim sky was darker. Everyone was gone but Julia, still naked on the bluff's edge, reading a book. "All done?" she called. "Come on up and I'll *towel you off.*" She cackled and nearly dropped the book in the lake.

"Please go away."

"Look, I've still got your scar! If you know me well enough to carve up my leg, you know me well enough to show me your prong. I am putting on my *skir*-irt, Nicky," she sang. "And now I am putting on my *vest.* And now I am all clothed and no threat to anybody."

"Julia, goddamnit, will you please just fuck *off?*"

59

"Ooh, that does it," she said. "Here I come."

I took a huge breath and, with the last of my strength, swam straight down toward the bottom of the lake. The cold squeezed my temples and ears. Kicking vigorously to stay under, I took a firm grip and jerked myself off with three brusque strokes.

By the time I rose gagging to the surface, I was close to dead. I crept up the bluff trembling and raw-throated. The goat's-head boulder was a dour gray. "You look tired," Julia said sadly.

When I was back in my uniform, she said, "Well, you can't go far wrong with basic black. I can lend you a string of pearls, if you like."

We didn't talk much on the way back through the woods. My responses to her questions were brief and delivered through a rigidly friendly face. At Giles Street, I declined her offer of a ride. Ducking her head like Kenny, she murmured, "I suppose I can be obnoxious sometimes."

"Not at all."

"I'll be in town another week or so, Nicky. Look, here's my phone number at my friend's place. Maybe I'll see you?"

"I'm sure," I said. "Bye now."

I strolled away. Soon I began to swear. I swore harder when it began to rain.

By the time I flung myself, soaked, on my bed, it was time for the poultry shears again.

: :

How often could I call Adam in Silver Crest? Once a month? Once a week? Once a *day*? I'd settled on once every nine to eleven days; I didn't want Adam to notice I was calling him every ten days exactly and realize I was rationing my calls to keep from wearing out his friendship.

The next afternoon made eight days, but I called anyhow.

He said, "Hey, sugar." Adam's nasal voice started deep in the chest, and even a long-distance connection couldn't weaken it. I was lying on my back on the rug in the upstairs hall. I propped my feet on the wall and crossed them at the ankle. "Hey, hoss," I said. "How's every little thing in Silver Crest?"

"Pretty good," he said apologetically.

There had been a wealth of stirring doings back home. First and foremost, Naomi Singer. She was a burnished brunette who kept one eyebrow perpetually cocked and had built a reputation as a wit by repeating the phrases "Isn't that *curious*," and "Oh, I'm *sure*." Early one morning she'd succumbed to Adam's stumpy charms on the sliding pond behind Silver Crest Elementary School. Now he was struggling with premature ejaculation. It seemed an achingly adult and glamorous problem to have. Then there was the midnight party down in the half-empty municipal pool. Megan Lampert had arrived in a red party dress. She was soon crawling through the black rainwater on all fours, refusing to stand for fear of high winds. When her date left in disgust, Ronnie Leckner tried his luck, and she vomited in his lap. For his part, Adam had been careful driving home, but the next morning found he'd painstakingly parked the car on the wrong side of the whitewashed stones lining his parents' driveway: on the lawn. It had been great.

"All fours?" I sighed. "Listen, when are you coming up?"

"Oh pal, I'm busted. And with the lawn thing, it's not like I can exactly go ask my folks for money. Maybe sometime this summer."

A small glum pause.

"Anyhow," I said. "Listen, guess who I saw out skinny-dipping the other day." My pulse began walloping my throat. "Julia. I gather she's become a sort of a fixture at the Lower Reservoir."

I met his bus down at the State Street Greyhound Station that weekend. We hugged, and he said, "Where is she?"

Though short, Adam was fearfully dense through the torso and arms. A band of flab softened his waist. His dark hair was curly, his broad brows emphatic. Beneath them, his eyes were balls, barely marked with pale-gray irises and nestled into ball-shaped cheekbones. His soft lips were ornately curved and always parted over square white teeth. His cheeks were round and his chin deeply cleft. Adam had a handsome, baroque ferocity, like a bronze Chinese Fu dog. An electric guitar suited him better than the acoustic guitar he'd brought; what would have suited him best was a scimitar.

I assumed things would be wonderful now he was here, and so they were. We hiked through Cascadilla Gorge, padding along the rapids down slippery greenish stairs carved from the rock. We waded one of the slowly spinning pools and I pointed out the gazebo of a frat house balanced far above us and told Adam the old story of the guy who toppled backward off the wooden rail one night and landed in the stream unhurt, too drunk to break a bone. We stood under the steel-grate Stewart Avenue bridge, blurred our eyes, and watched the cars seem to soar over us on a band of green haze. They made a great groaning *AAA-aaaooooohhmmm*, like a vast harp slapped by a vast hand. We tossed a frisbee on the Arts Quad and smoked a joint in the old cemetery on a stone balcony overlooking the town. The gray of the roofs deepened to black and the lake at the center of the valley was an ingot of gunmetal edged with new copper. All the tiny lit windows looked warm and clean. Finally, Adam and I had a big midnight breakfast down at the State Street Diner, where the fubsy home fries sweltered in lascivious grease, and the extra coffee they slopped into your saucer seemed a promise of life abundant.

The irritating thing was, Adam was supposed to pity me for living in such a hell on earth.

On Sunday we went, with Kenny and Sam, out to the Rongovian Embassy in Trumansburg. The Zobo Funn Band was playing, and their fans were as usual drifting in clusters like seaweed on the ocean floor, or zipping at top speed through the crowd, sometimes knocking one another down. One gawky man in a body stocking wore elbow and knee pads in order to rebound off the floor with greater ease. We were soon soaked with sweat. Sam blew down into the collar of her wobbling T-shirt, noticed me watching, and panted to remark the heat, tongue lolling.

When the band took a break, Adam and I smoked another joint by the creek in back. I felt the familiar wheezy exaltation. I was reclining on the bank with my elbows on the ground and my forearms and hands up in the air. They felt good that way. "Nurse?" I called softly. "Oh, nurse!" We cackled.

"My friend, you are fucked up," Adam said.

"I'm a hot tamale. I'm a seventh son. I can foretell the past and regret the future."

"You are fucked *up*. Listen, what's the story with this Sobel?" His eyes widened. "And that *girl!*"

"I know," I said, and we lay there for a moment in pain. "Listen, when a woman pants like a dog at you, isn't that considered a good sign?"

"Exactly. She should be with you."

"Well, she's with Kenny."

"Tonight."

I thought it over. But when I opened my mouth, he said, "You're not going to start in about the goddamn lake again, are you?"

"I've been talking about it, huh?"

"You have. I don't know why you're so wound up in the first place."

"I told you. She deliberately humiliated me."

"What you told me was, she wouldn't go away until you got out, and kept saying, 'Let's see it, let's see it.'"

"Well, words to that effect."

"Sugar, why," he said softly, "do you imagine she was behaving in this singular fashion?"

"To harass me," I said unsteadily.

"Nothing else? She loiters naked on shore, demanding you show her your hard dick... It didn't occur to you that you two might have found a soft spot on the bank and made rather a good thing of your bowungus?"

"She's crazy. But not that crazy."

"It's lucky you're beautiful, sugar, because you don't have half the brains God gave a chicken. Give her a call. *Now.* She'll be *embarrassed* about it. You'll have the *whip* hand."

Silence.

"You are doing this deliberately to destroy me. You get one fabulous opportunity after another. Melissa, Jo Ann, Julia. And you do nothing. And blithely tell me all about it, and watch me shrivel. Look. Here is a shiny new dime."

"All right. Let's just say you can't understand my feelings and leave it at that."

"Don't shit me, sugar. You're not not calling because you're hurt. You're not calling because you're scared."

"I'm not a child," I said quietly. "I don't respond to dares."

"Nicholas Joseph!" she cried when I finally got through. I cupped my other ear against the music, hunched closer to the pay phone, and nodded. She sounded happy to hear from me—what about that whip hand I was supposed to have? "I've been meaning to call you," she said.

"Well. I've called you."

"Oh, I know. I'm sorry about the lake, I was utterly obnoxious. It was just a joke. I was, I don't know what I was."

"Drunk," I suggested.

"Well, yeah."

"Why are you drinking at ten in the morning, Julia?" I said clinically. "Anything up?"

"I guess that's a good question. I guess you have a right to ask."

"I don't want to pry if it makes you uncomfortable."

"No, it's fine. Well, stuff with my writing. Stuff with men. You know, the usual."

"Actually, I don't know the usual."

"Look," she said angrily. "Are you beating me up about this? I said I was sorry, Nicky, and I never apologize twice for anything I do. Just like I never expect anyone else to apologize twice to me, and believe it or not, I've been fucked over myself a time or two. People fuck up, Nicky, and you can't keep forcing them back into some mode of constant contrition for things that are *over*. And I *am* sorry. And that makes twice."

My face grew hot. "It does. I'm sorry myself. I didn't call you up to lecture you."

"No?"

"Well, yes," I said. She laughed briefly. "But I was also thinking... I don't know if you already have plans... it's kind of late. We're, I'm, down at the Rongo. I don't know if you know where that is? And, ah... are you free?"

"Thank you, Nicky. I don't think I'm in the mood now. But I'm glad you called. I don't want you to be sorry you asked me."

We said goodbye and I went back to our table. Kenny, asprawl in his chair, said, "Pull up a pew, Wertheim. I've delegated Miss Sammy for a dance or two. That gal wears me out."

Jesus, I hated him.

Sam danced with Adam until he was staggering, then towed him back to the table by the hem of his T-shirt. "*Next*," she said gaily, and pulled me to my feet. She danced like a buxom rag doll being violently shaken. Everyone got whipped with her damp hair. She scowled comically until I realized I was scowling, turned her back to me and performed a complex ratcheting maneuver. She glanced over her shoulder to see if I approved. When a slow number began, she drew me close, and I was enmeshed in her sweat and patchouli. I searched for neutral places for my hands. Then I noted Kenny's complacent moon face and let them drop to her hot, soft flanks. They rolled. I was wondering if I might conceivably separate her from Kenny, and how, and how soon, when Julia said, "Hi. I came anyhow. Anger's boring."

I spun in Sam's arms. Julia wore harem pants crammed into white vinyl go-go boots, a yellow bowling shirt identifying her as Ed of the Big 50 League, and sunglasses. She kissed my cheek. "I'm flying back day after tomorrow, and I didn't want to spend tonight sulking. I wanted to spend it with my friends."

"We were just dancing," Sam said. "My lover's over there."

Julia said, "Nice to know where they are, isn't it? Don't let me barge in."

She walked off toward our table.

When the song ended, I suggested we sit the next one out, but Sam said, "You go," and I left her dancing with herself, wet hair swinging half a beat behind the music. Adam met me halfway to the table. "A word with you, my friend. You got that look in your eye," he said, "of someone who's about to fuck things up. Okay. She's here. Start talking about relationships. Then: dinner." He furrowed his brow. "Rhythm guitar's lagging. Look, just ask her to dance."

"I can't."

"Why not?"

"She saw me dancing with Sam. She'll think we – She'll think I just – I can't."

"Be my brave little soldier. Try. *It's what you're both fucking here for.* Sugar, it's the next step on the golden path to dinner. C'mon, say it with me. *Dinner.*"

Julia came up and said, "Secrets?"

"My friend here was wondering…," Adam said.

I was silent.

He said, "My friend here was wondering if you'd care to dance with me."

They walked out onto the floor, and I went back to the table. I drank my Coke. I thought about having another. When the song was over, Julia danced with Kenny. *Kenny.* He looked no dumber out there than I. She shimmied with vigor, her face smooth and happy, eyes lidded, lips parted – I stood up. Sam spotted me. "*Next!*" I was hauled out and flogged with her hair again as the others sat down to rest.

By closing time, Julia had knotted her bowling shirt across her ribs, so that her stomach and gleaming breastbone were bare. She carried her boots in one hand. Kenny said something and she laughed and dropped one. I still hadn't danced with her. She kissed Adam, Kenny, and Sam goodbye, then turned to me. I was trying to pluck one of Sam's hairs from my mouth. I quickly wiped that hand on my jeans.

She shook it. "Well, thank you for inviting me, Nicky," she said. "Maybe I'll see you in the fall."

We watched her toddle off.

"She's leaving," I said.

"You know," Adam said, "you could be right."

I sprinted out into the street. Julia had just gotten into her car. I leaned on her door and said, "Anger's boring. Somebody once told me that."

She smiled. It was a wonderful smile. An invisible chin strap seemed to tighten about her face, dividing her snub chin from the rest of her smooth jaw. "What a silly-ass thing for her to say. Actually, I think anger's fascinating."

I said, "You'll find me a fascinating fellow."

: :

Julia was staying a mile north of town in the upper half of a shabby two-story tract house across from a field of alfalfa. She'd offered to make me a chili dinner, and I'd insisted on bringing the fixings. When I pulled into her drive the next evening, she was seated barefoot on her front stoop in an antique prom gown and at least ten bracelets. She kissed the corner of my mouth – whiskey again – and surveyed me. "A six-pack in one hand and a pound of beef in the other. Nicky, I've been waiting for a man like you all my life."

"Every woman has," I assured her.

She led me around back to an outdoor staircase. It mewed insinuatingly as I climbed after her.

The mottled, mustard-yellow kitchen had once been off-white; rectangles of that color were revealed where tacked-up charcoal landscapes sagged away from the walls. The vinyl chairs were patched with gummy duct tape. The old stove was adorned with flecks of egg and soy sauce and one crinkly rust-brown hair. The place looked frowsy, half-clothed. Amidst the surrounding heated fug, a clean sharp smell drifted from Julia's low bodice. The frayed sateen dress contained that small, smooth, bare, well-remembered, somehow unfinished body, now balanced on the balls of her feet, as if she were about to swoop in and kiss me or, only slightly less bizarrely, bolt from the house. Nervously? she wrenched back her hair in the old gesture, and the scented fur of her armpits rose into view.

The poultry shears were no longer equal to the job.

I tugged down the hem of my T-shirt. This may have lent me a disapproving air. She said, "I cleaned. It was worse."

"How?"

"You little shit. You don't drink enough, that's your problem."

Julia pulled two bottles from the six-pack and handed me one. "Let me rinse you out a glass." She had to fit the glass between dirty dishes to get it under the tap. "Well, forget about giving you the tour, then. If this bugs you, the bedroom would probably kill you." Beans already simmered on the stove, and now she broke open the package of meat, her hands moving quickly among a jumble of groceries. "I don't know what I'm doing yet. Sit. What has it been, three years?"

"Three and a half."

"Well, tell me everything." She nibbled a smidgen of raw meat. "This is so bad for you. But delicious. And here you are at Cornell. Studying art? Next year? Somehow I pictured you more the Columbia type. Brooding in Broadway coffeehouses with darling little chain-smoking beatnikesses. I'm closing up the Mercer Street loft. The place is *infested* with Alan. When you've lived with someone you'll know. I mean, it's three years, and I'm still finding his junk. Then, Lisbon, because it's a stupid time for a vacation and I'm stubborn. There's this *farmácia* that sells saints' tears in these green plastic vials – I'm fresh out of saints' tears – and the Azulejo. A last fling before the adult world. If you want to call grad school the adult world."

Was it my turn to talk? "What are you working on?"

"*God*. No – good for you. Someone needs to keep me on the stick. I'm working on everything I was working on last time I saw you, basically. I mean, Creeley says a poem is a dance, you just dance the dance, you don't revise it. But if you can't make anything but a… *blob* that way, you have to push stuff around endlessly. Like it was your life. Which is another kind of honesty, the honesty of saying, *This is the best I can do.* I have no intrinsic problem with the poem as product. Especially considering this one's, ah, subject matter. 'Love.' " She snorted. "Which is always supposed to be a moment, too, but winds up being something you kill yourself adjusting, and never get qui-i-ite right. Come taste this."

"I trust you." I didn't want to stand.

"Come *on*." She cupped a hand below my chin and brought me a forkful.

"It's great," I said, mouth full. "Can I see it?"

"It isn't ready yet," she said, and banged down the ladle. She padded to the screen door and leaned her forehead and hands against it in the attitude of a pet that wants to be let out. "Warm," she explained, gazing quizzically at the alfalfa. "I want *you* to chop the onions. I cry enough as it is."

Rising cautiously, I went to work. "Oh, your hands," Julia said. "Something about the way you move. Maybe I just like tall men."

"Julia, I'm barely five ten."

"That's pretty tall, isn't it?"

"No. And I'm not a man, I'm a boy. Seventeen, to be exact." I smeared tears from my cheek with a wrist.

"Oh, let's be inexact, Nicky, you pompous little fart. It's more fun." She began mashing garlic with a little press. "Exact. No wonder I take a belt before you arrive. Should've seen your face. No wonder I talk a lot of tripe about art. Nicky, I don't like being judged. And by all *means*, don't forget to remind me that you're half my age and I'm pushing thirty."

"Pushing twenty-seven."

She stamped her foot. "To be exact. That's what I *mean*. You just sit there with your big face and take it all down in some inner notebook. I despise levelheaded men." Anger made her cheeks heavy and babyish.

"Well, at least I'm tall," I said.

She glared a moment more. Then her mouth crinkled and she leveled the garlic press at me. "Why do Jews have big noses?"

"Because air is free. Come on, Julia, you can do better than that."

"I *can't.* That's the only Jew joke I know. Alan would never teach me."

I took another onion and began slicing.

"That's enough. I shouldn't have made you chop so many." She rose on tiptoe and blotted my tears with a handful of her hair. We stood like that, with our faces near. My hands were covered with bits of onion.

She thumped down on her heels. "Cumin. Have you seen the cumin?" She scrabbled through the cupboards. "I remember, we don't have any. I'll run down and borrow some. It's important. I'll just be a minute." She smoothed her dress. "Keep stirring the chili." The screen door flapped, and she pattered down the stairs.

She pattered back up. She slammed bourbon and a glass down in front of me. "Now, I don't want to catch you *swigging* this stuff. You're too *young.*"

She bumped me with her hip and scurried chortling out again. A rap at the downstairs door, and then their screen door flapped open and shut. Then silence.

I washed my hands and sniffed them. They smelled funky. I washed them again. I adjusted my pants. I stirred the chili, then poured a little bourbon and forced it down. Jesus, was it awful, but it made my legs warm and courageous. So, the bedroom would kill me, eh? I eased over and pushed the door open.

My blood knocked at my middle, leaving my extremities weightless. I deployed my numb feet stealthily. Beneath them, I heard Julia's laughter, another woman's voice, two chairs scraping. The room's disorder was terrific, a nest of flung clothes. A tear dropped from my nose to the bed. I covered the spot with a blanket. There, through an open door, was a toilet that had recently supported Julia's bare buttocks. I bent toward the bowl in all sincerity, but kissed the seat feeling theatrical. Then I slid open a drawer and sniffed a lacy camisole, but smelled nothing but bourbon fumes streaming up from my mouth. I bit it, and noticed a large, sturdy underwire bra beneath. This was her friend's apartment. I was biting the wrong woman's underwear.

By her bed I spied a small portfolio in oxblood leather, badly scuffed. It was full of sheets of lined yellow paper, some frayed, some new, some typed, some touched with a light, jostling script. I riffled through, wanting to hoard each page in a perfected memory. Then a phrase caught my eye: *a lash of brightness.*

I read more slowly. *Lash of brightness... as sun and moon wear hot grooves through the clouds... bewildered body, puzzled sucking mouth...* The two principals seemed to be a wounded woman and a boy with his mouth pressed to her leg.

The downstairs door clapped shut.

When Julia came in I was stirring the chili, throat pounding, a bar of glowing iron in my jeans. I displayed the spoon to show her that everything was under control. She displayed the cumin. "Been a busy little cook?" She sniffed my glass. "Good."

"Julia, could you calm down? Could one of us calm down?"

"Aren't you calm, lover?" She poured me another slug.

"Stop pouring that stuff." I took a sip.

"Something about you standing by my stove. You look so, I don't know. Domestic. No. Capable. No. Do you have any girlfriends? Any cute little hippie chicks?"

"Not at present."

"Then may I ask you a question? A really, *really* rude question?"

"Yes?"

She took me by the shoulders, smiling faintly into my eyes, and with the light, lingering, and determined touch of a bored cat romancing one's ankles, brushed her loins against mine.

"Uh huh," she said. "There's my answer."

Stepping back, she wrenched her dress over her head.

There it all was, the fine shoulders and dirty feet, the dainty calves and chubby nipples, now tightened to brown rosettes, the carelessly outcurved belly and the large, snarled, soil-hued, blazingly central shield of her cunt.

"Perhaps if you got undressed as well?"

I hunted for the buttons on my shirt.

"You're wearing a T-shirt. Here." She tugged it over my head as I undid my jeans. Then I was naked, my cock twitching between us. Julia cradled it in both hands. "Well. I finally got him."

"What?" I sang.

"The snake that bit me," she said with a roguish roll of the brows, and bent to give it a neighborly peck.

Julia moved quickly and surely, but I didn't give her time to straighten. I nailed her in the collarbone, a silvery streak leading toward her breast. When she sprang upright, I got her again in the hip, and again directly in the navel. The final shot looped down and nicked her knee, clinging to the golden hairs on her calf.

I stood there. My mind was calm and lucid. I'd have to leave the country and start a new life under another name.

She drew two fingers across her belly and licked them. Her smile grew fond and reminiscent.

I picked up my jeans with trembling hands.

She smacked them to the floor and said, "Don't be a *jerk*."

:   :

The bedside lamp stood on the rug, her dress draped over its shade. The room was gilded with the muted light and with its own dirt, every color touched with yellow. Julia was sometimes gold and sometimes tallow. The wrinkles of the sheet beneath us zigzagged out into a continued chaos of clothes and books. The windows were black. I knelt over Julia as she licked at my perineum and drew the length of my cock efficiently into her throat with languorous, muffled groans. Her tongue was hot, her lips cool. I heard the faint huff of air through her nostrils.

My penis looked very odd pumping in and out of this lovely woman's face, with its blissful eyelids and newly hollow cheeks. She drew it reluctantly from her mouth – it emerged with a pop – and nibbled the underseam, then rubbed it over her cheeks and snub nose. "I don't often get to play with a prick when it's soft," she murmured, and soft is what it was: heavy, drowsy, half- or three-quarters erect, but never, that entire night, for quite long enough to serve. Freed to follow my inclination, I'd become a cloud of pleasure with no crux or plan. We seemed to have left behind the world of cute girls and boners, remarks and schemes. We attempted no squashy intromission. It would have lowered the tone of the proceedings. Instead, I wonderingly passed my hand over Julia's belly and hot forehead, tugged Julia's earlobe, lightly gripped Julia's beating neck. I explored Julia's anus, that pale brown star, as Julia's cunt slithered against my wrist. Her breastbone was smooth as a new linoleum block beneath my palm. I had the same sense of being indefinitely poised before infinite possibility.

Washing my fingers with spit, I parted her sex. Inside were tender crannies and swollen little cushions, delicate ribs and hollows. I scooted down and fit my face into the groove of her vulva. Her thighs mashed my ears shut so that I could hear my pulse, or hers. I tried to contain her hectic little bottom in my hands. Her ruff blurred past my lips and tongue-tip, chafed them sensitive. Julia's cunt smelled like almonds, cinnamon, my fingers, gerbil fur, a gym locker, honey, hot tar, lox, pond mud, raw beef, seawater, and a field of heated weeds, and tasted like apple cider, cinnamon, Julia's blood, my lips, olives, seawater, and wild mint. You had to suck that tiny bud out of its sheath and release it; flatten your tongue against the bony shelf of her mons and let it drop off into the soft hollow beneath; nip at the tense cords of her spread inner thighs; nose her wrinkled labia, then drive your tongue as far in as you could. Lying there, a weary ache growing in my throat, I felt like a sick child sipping ginger ale in bed: feverish, pampered, endlessly idle. She choked off a series of little cries, all the while trying to escape across the bed – I wouldn't let her – then jerked in a breath and let out a long, heartbroken wail. Finally she lay as if dead, cheekbones dark and swollen, a tear trickling into her smiling mouth.

We spent the night voyaging between complex caresses and sleep, watching over or being watched, or waking together as if at a signal. Lying beside me, her arms around my head, her lips bumbling against mine, she said, "When did you first want me? I wanted you when you were in the water and couldn't come out. Why *wouldn't* you?" The words puffed into my throat. "Then at the club you were so awful. I hadn't done anything that bad. I wanted you to come dance with me."

"I wanted you to come dance with *me*. How could you dance with Kenny?"

"I'm glad you suffered. You were such an I-don't-know-what. Dear God, are you really just seventeen? Don't let me think about it."

"Everything outside this bed seems so long ago."

"You really haven't done *anything* with other girls? No one else has had… Oh, where are you touching me, are you touching me there? Oh, if I'd never met you. If we'd never had this."

When we were exhausted, I saw what a gift Julia had for torpor. She reclined as wholly as a cat, her little limbs models of indolence. How did her flat chest seem so pillowy? My cheek drowsed on it. "So good," she whispered. "Uhn, so good."

"What do you want?" I slurred. "Let me do something."

"Oh, no. Just your head. Your head right there. Can you hear my heart?"

"It's beating." This struck me as funny, and I laughed.

"Oh, yes. Oh, it's beating."

:　　:

At seven we woke for good. The chili on the stove was a cold, clotted ruin. Julia wore a dressing gown traversed by dragons, which I obliged her to pull shut again and again. "I'm kicking you out. I've got to clean this place and be at the airport by twelve-thirty."

"Let me help."

"No. I don't want you scrubbing my gick."

She shooed me out the rusted screen door and closed it. Then she drew open her robe and pressed her hips against it, and I knelt and kissed the occluded triangle through the mesh. She said, "Oh, I feel so small and wonderful. Should I cancel this trip and just love you?"

"No, you've been looking forward to it." I rested my cheek against her hips. The sun warmed my shoulders, and the fields behind me seemed very vast.

"Don't you dare let somebody else teach you. I'll be back in August or so, and after we've done everything nine hundred times you can have other women, just so you can see I'm better. Actually, I'm the best new girlfriend there is. By New Year's you'll want to murder me for my moods, but first you'll think the world's being made again, fresh. You know, I rather like you on your knees like this."

"I kind of like it myself."

"Well, that's not a good sign," she said, laughing. "You'd better get up."

"All right, I'll get up."

I kissed her again through the screen. Then I stood and went down the stairs, still feeling the rusty wire against my face.

FOUR

Impersonating Something Bright and Hard

Two weeks later, I moved into a group house on Buffalo Street. It was
time. For one thing, I couldn't exactly see myself, on Julia's return,
inviting her up to my bedroom at home to listen to records and
make out. I took a job at Gnomon Copy to cover my rent, and
secured an airy attic room with a dormer, big enough for two, if
that's how things worked out. I set my Canada Dry box beside the
desk. I bought a new paisley bedspread in burgundy and teal. After
work, I'd stretch out beneath the window and let the breeze trace my
eyelids and bare chest.

Yellow House Cooperative had once been a splendid home for
one well-to-do family and their servants. Now fourteen college students sailed luminous frisbees down its halls. In its ample, sagging
kitchen we garnished heaps of eggplant parmesan with corpse-pale
mung sprouts; to its beautiful wainscoting we stapled Escher prints
and United Farm Workers posters; on its broad porch we sprawled
in socks and shorts. We were local kids, and mostly faculty brats. Our
friends had voyaged to faraway schools. Left behind, we were hungry
for distinction. I wasn't the only one destined to be an artist, or
blessed and cursed with a complex inner life. We'd sit by twos on the
floor in front of the sofa late at night and have long, serious talks.

These seemed more serious because we were sitting on the floor, while the others slept all around us. Even our voices grew lower, down there on the indoor-outdoor carpeting some pragmatist had installed throughout the house. I remember the smell of that carpet – it was dank and harsh, and seemed honest – and the tang of Dr. Bronner's peppermint soap on a young woman's neck as she leaned into my shoulder, hugging both her knees and one of mine, confiding some new sorrow. My female housemates liked to tell me their troubles. I was embarked upon a tempestuous affair with a mysterious, jet-setting older woman; I must know things. Their confessions could be quite detailed, but I didn't mind being teased. I knew their bodies well from trips to the Reservoir and long massages. That we hadn't slept together was a detail. I considered them a harem. That summer, I looked upon each passing girl as if I'd just screwed her senseless on a whim and was now trying to let her down easy. When we spoke, my housemates liked to hold my hand, perhaps to keep it out of action.

I was proud of my new place, and glad when Del and her boyfriend came to visit. Robert was a hippie biology student, a tall, bearded boy with red lips and a deep voice. Del would pencil her name and his on the Real Food Co-op work roster taped to the fridge, then sit with me on the porch steps – even they were carpeted – while he played flag football with my friends on the lawn and dusk climbed Buffalo Street. Del had always had a trick of setting one hand on her hip and shading her eyes with the other. Even when she was three, in the middle of suburban New Jersey, she'd pose on our back stoop like a farm wife scanning the fields for her menfolk. Now, as Robert fell back for a long bomb, she guarded her eyes against the slanting glare; the gesture was no longer comical. There was a new clarity in the line of her jaw. Her mouth was wry and comradely, her narrow body narrowly in bloom. "What a bunch of beauties," she murmured, eyeing my housemates. "I don't know. You getting any off of any of 'em?" We were solicitous with each other, like wistful ex-spouses. "Wasn't Julia supposed to be back by now?"

"We didn't say just when," I said comfortably.

"Well, it's better than home. Ready for the latest? The girlfriend got pregnant."

"Oh boy. Well, we saw that coming."

"And Dad paid to fix it, so guess who had to know? I mean, with the house and everything, it's not like she wouldn't notice three hundred dollars gone from the checking account."

"What did she say?"

"She went with Carla to get it done."

"Oh Jesus. I wish you were out of there."

"If Saul went, goodbye tenure, so this is her solution. I think it's like four hours for the whole thing, and there's Mom next to this poor birdbrain, making with the moral support. Why the heck don't they both just *end* it? It would be such a relief."

"I guess I better go see for myself," I sighed.

"What did we always say about martyrs?" Saul shouted at the big dinner table. "You piled up the logs, and you lit the kindling, and you tied yourself to the stake. You wouldn't be half so angry, we wouldn't be in half so much trouble, if it wasn't for your grand fucking gesture." He forked up some stir fry and gave it a punishing bite.

"No woman should have to be alone through that," Suzanne said calmly.

"At least *my* mistakes are not made from self-righteousness and drama. I make my mistakes with my *heart*." He thumped the wrong side of his chest.

"Put your heart away. We're trying to eat."

"Okay," I said. "What I'm hearing is that there's a disagreement about parameters, and it's understandable Mom would be unhappy." This is how we talked at Yellow House. We were putting these matters on a rational footing over there.

"There are other people involved," Suzanne said.

"Leave us out of this," Del said from between her teeth. "Just keep pretending we have no feelings."

"That's pure self-indulgence," Saul said.

"You should know," Del said. She overturned her plate and walked quickly from the room.

"She's upset," I explained.

They glowered.

I was glad to get back to my harem and wait for my new life to begin.

During the first week of classes, I got a telegram:

LOVELY NICHOLAS DETAINED EXPLAIN LATER MUCH MUCH LOVE
BELIEVE ME J

Two days later I got another:

LOVELY NICHOLAS DETAINED EXPLAIN LATER MUCH MUCH LOVE
BELIEVE ME IN SPITE OF EVERYTHING J

Early in October I got an airmail letter with a smeary red post-mark like the bite of a small animal.

Dear Nick –

What a fall it's been! No time to write properly, but I did want to drop a line before we head back. Well, Paris is beautiful, and my favorite town (What an original choice!) and I'll be sorry to go. No, I haven't abandoned my plans for a degree, just put them off. You are often in my thoughts, and I hope to see you not TOO *far in the future. How are the "cute little hippie chicks" of Ithaca? How's school? I want you to know I'm happy. Forgive my penmanship; I'm writing this on the Metro. Well, not much of a letter, was it? Next time I'll do better.*

– J

There was no return address, and no next time.

She wasn't in the new Student Directory, no matter how often I looked. I tried her Mercer Street loft, but the number had been disconnected. Uris Library had two vast banks of shelves loaded with phone books, but hours of research revealed no plausible Turrells. At length I mustered up my nerve and called the friend at whose house she'd stayed in Ithaca. (And whose underwear I'd chewed.) "Oh. Nick, huh? You, um, you know Julia? Well, she's been traveling around a lot. I'm sure she'll write you."

"She did."

"There you go."

"She wasn't very informative, I'm afraid."

"Well, she's been traveling around a lot."

"You wouldn't happen to have a phone number for her?"

The voice sounded relieved. "No. I don't."

"Or an address."

Tense again: "Um, I really don't think I do."

"It's just that, ah, she didn't – Did she mention her plans to you?"

"Do you go to school here? As an undergraduate? You sound young."

"Yes."

"You do. Well. I'm sure she'll write you. Listen, I really have to go."

Finally, despairingly, I wrote to her Mercer Street address. I went through over a dozen drafts. The final product was six sentences long and said almost nothing except that I wondered how she was doing.

Someone sent it back unopened, enclosed in a fresh envelope, with an unsigned note in a strange woman's hand: *She doesn't* LIVE *here anymore. And for the last time,* I DON'T KNOW WHERE SHE WENT. *I feel sorry for you guys. I really do.*

:   :

Once, if I remember truly, Rimbaud wrote, and I read, with the aid of my Cassell's French dictionary, *my heart was a banquet where all hearts opened and all wines flowed.*

One evening I seated Beauty on my knees – and found her bitter – and cursed her.

I armed myself against justice.

I fled. O Witches, O Misery, O Hate, to you has my treasure been entrusted!

In a Dryden Street thrift shop I found a black overcoat that reached to my ankles, and tall black boots with jingling whatnots. Rigged out in these, I swept along the corridors of Goldwin Smith Hall, my heels clunking and echoing. At night I stumped down Buffalo to the rank, heavy lake, or up Dryden, through the black-gold sleeping farms. I swung my arms, cherished the scent of mud and hay, listened for the one streetlamp among hundreds that trembled and droned. *Easy*, I told myself. *Easy*. Memory was a steel blade sweeping over me. I began working to blunt it. My moment with Julia had arrived too soon (ho ho), and I'd flopped (ho ho), centrally, irretrievably. And hadn't there been something fondly mocking in her manner, hadn't she been amusing herself with a feverish child? Of course, as soon as she'd found a more viable male, she'd moved on. I brought them together again and again in a Paris that was all spiral alleys and amber passageways. I wanted him to be beautiful and I wanted her never to have cared for me. I wanted to perfect my betrayal, as if arguing my case before a celestial grievance board. A council of dark women with merciful eyes. They let me rest awhile, my head against their fragrant hips.

A round-trip bus ticket to New York cost about thirty-five dollars. I went as often as I could afford. Adam was wonderful: he expressed no opinions and asked no questions, and kept me stoned and in constant motion through each night. Each day I left him and wandered through SoHo. The metal sidewalks and bare wood floors were soothing under my boots. There was fresh white paint on the walls, on the tall iron columns and stamped tin ceilings. I noodled in my notebook, drank cappuccino at marble-topped tables, and wandered, an emissary on some enigmatic business. It was the heyday of

Minimalism. The galleries were stocked with arrays of enameled steel boxes, with black-and-white photo "sequences" fixed to the walls by straight pins, with shaped canvases hotly striped like the hoods of racing cars. Single neon tubes glowed in corners. I entered small rooms empty but for a single whispering speaker. I reviewed videos of sunlight on windowsills and "projects" for vast mounds in the wilderness. The general idea seemed to be to sweep out the old crud and begin fresh.

Back in Ithaca, I dismissed my block-printed still lifes as "charming." I chose, as my new exemplars, the Russian Suprematists. It irked me now that no one I knew seemed to have heard of El Lissitzky or Kasimir Malevich. I, too, wanted to refine a few simple shapes to the point of madness. I was taken with the notion of distillation: perhaps the frothing roil inside me could be boiled down to an essence that would command from all a respectful hush. Before making a print, I now did study after study on graph paper which I made myself with a Schaedler rule marked out in sixty-fourths of an inch, a steel straightedge, and a sharp 6H pencil. I used heavy all-rag trace, and tore it off against the straightedge instead of cutting it. The edges looked better that way. I pictured each study mounted in a plain frame of white oak, and my signature, which steady practice had made jagged and handsome, in the corner. I could easily conjure up a monograph with my name stamped in small chaste type on the cover, containing an entire career's worth of works. Inarguable objects, immaculately presented.

Cornell's architecture school was world-renowned. The fine arts department, next door, was not. Most of our instructors were obscure middle-aged artists who spent their days obliging us to replicate their styles. My painting instructor, for instance, specialized in studies of women draped in bright cloths, strongly lit from a single source. He had us do them, too, with an emphasis on hot highlights and cool shadows, which he handled in his own work with great deftness.

My sculpture professor began each semester by inviting the model into his studio. There he measured her: nose to occiput, nipple to nipple, breadth of hips, length of foot. Using a calculator, he scaled these measurements down to fit an eighteen-inch figurine. He distributed them to the class on xeroxed sheets. We squeezed plastilene over an armature to make a flat form like a gingerbread woman and scribed in where her various parts should go, using his diagram as our guide. Next we packed on plastilene in front and back, bent her into position, and put in details like pubic hair and toenails, which he showed us how to make. When the professor was done with his own figures – he got them very smooth – he'd accessorize them with little ballet shoes or sun hats. He had a studio full of these statuettes. They all wound up looking like his wife.

As for the students, I remember as typical a chubby, fluffy little senior who'd spent four years drawing and painting the same personage: towering and mantis-thin, with a triangular polychrome head and huge eyes. Once, seeming hurt that I needed to be told, she explained that these were all self-portraits. There were guys in the department too, I guess, but I mainly recall sleek suburban princesses gone bohemian, gesturing with cigarettes, doing little work and maintaining an air of luscious fatigue.

All this was fine with me. I wanted people around to be better than.

I carried a new scene in my head in those days: a tiny black-clad young man moving diagonally across a field. Choosing his own way. If I were assigned, say, three landscape studies employing chiaroscuro in our choice of charcoal or ink, I'd show up with a dozen sheets of coarse sandpaper meticulously striped with roofing compound, and there'd be an open debate about the validity of my methods while I sipped my coffee, thinking, *Small-town*. I was the only one in my year working non-objectively. (I disagreed on philosophical terms with the word "abstract.") The girls with cigarettes squinted at my new hard-edged block prints: a gray cross on a saffron ellipse, a crimson arc on a black square, all cut with a sharp knife and crisply printed on tissuey Kitataka.

I equipped myself one evening with paint, ruler, masking tape, and scale drawings, and visited the Stump, a truncated elm at the crest of Libe Slope. It was a tradition for students to repaint it periodically with messages like HAPPY 19TH, KRISTI – KAPPA SIG, or RED-MEN RULE THE ICE! I labored until dawn making a "site-specific work" of it, dividing it vertically into halves: charcoal gray and glossy black. If you stood at a certain spot on the pavement, the border between shiny and dull aligned precisely with the edge of the library's clock tower. Was I some sort of threat, or some sort of twit? Anyhow, I was being talked about. My instructors gave me equivocal grades, then took me to lunch to chat about my ideas.

What I wanted to cap all this success, of course, was a girlfriend. Over the phone from NYU Adam spoke of a series of raffish conquests, of other people's toothbrushes, of bare mattresses stained with bongwater. For my part, what I wanted, if I couldn't have Julia, was a lean, anguished beauty to share sullen coffees and nights of scalding, despairing sex. I had several candidates in mind among my louche young classmates. I also worked up a few scenarios in which Carla discovered how much better a man than Saul I was: gentle and sensitive and careful about contraception.

But the tiny striding fellow seemed to do best at a distance. For one thing, I still assumed you had to ask girls out in such a way that they didn't notice you were doing it. I tried to remain reassuringly sardonic. One girl complained, "Every time I talk to you, it's like I'm *interrupting* your train of thought." And I may have grown too devil-may-care when I spoke of my affair with Julia. "I'm not going to be one of your conquests," another said bitterly, thrusting me away after an hour of necking. "You're not the sort of man who'll stay with one woman long." This was thrilling, but not particularly helpful. With my housemates, who knew better, I seemed stuck in the role of confidant. And after all, it was difficult to give up my chaste harem, give up the trust and regard and the flow of shy detail. "Do you need to be held?" I'd ask, then sigh angrily as they moved into my arms. Then, late each night, sinuses caked with cannabis resin, my friends would pair up and straggle off to bed, and I'd gaze at myself in the bathroom mirror, thinking, *Yes. Of course. Now I see.*

"Nicky, why can't my men be more like you?" said the woman who smelled of peppermint soap, bouncing my palm between hers.

"But *I'm* like me," I said, "and you wouldn't fuck me on a *bet*."

She clamped my hand tight while deciding whether to laugh.

I remember those days as a fond, nervous pressure across my knuckles.

One afternoon in the middle of my junior year, I went to resell some old texts in the basement of Triangle Books. "*Une Saison en Enfer*," I said, and tossed Rimbaud onto the pile. "I wonder if you could recommend a better edition?" One with a translation, though I didn't say so. The clerk offered to talk to the manager about my "complaint." She said that it was tough trying to learn a language when the books they gave you weren't good. "I take Spanish," she told me. She kept stroking the counter, I noticed, with her thumb.

Terry Buchalter was an A student and a star gymnast who neither smoked nor drank nor saw the point of a picture that didn't look like something. Her favorite saying was, "And?" *I've got three papers to write this weekend.* "And?" *Face it, Ter, neither Carter nor Reagan offered a true alternative.* "And?" She was a diminutive, muscular woman with an acrobat's bow legs and a dull brown pixie-cut. Compact little tush; compact little bosom: to have grown bigger breasts, said the tilt of her nose, would've been *dumb*. Her face had been roughened by adolescent acne. Her eyes were slotlike; she seemed to peer through a visor. I kept misremembering her little gold *chai* as a cross. Perhaps because at the end of a full year of dating her, at twenty-one years of age, the man who'd never stay with one woman long was still a virgin.

It was appropriate for the tiny trudging figure to be burned out and aloof from women, or to stumble from bed to bed, trying to drug his tormented soul with pleasure. But it was not appropriate for him to be desperately, plaintively, petulantly, unsuccessfully trying to drag the panties from a pint-sized jockette with a 3.91 average and a Cathy Rigby 'do. Was *she* a virgin?

"Don't be rude." Then: "I've done some things."

"Things. Meaning…"

"Don't be rude."

Well, did she want to be a virgin *forever?* "Just let me just slide these over a little."

A brawny little hand clamped my wrist. "I thought I could feel safe with you."

"I should fucking well hope not."

"*Nicky!*"

Eventually I had to be content with a good-natured, competent hand job. At the last minute she'd aim my nozzle back toward my belly, so I wouldn't get stuff on her sheets.

She asked to see my work. "These are very modernistic," she decided, and looked at me hopefully.

When I mentioned my night of splendor at the Stump, she nodded and said, "I think that's okay."

"You think that's okay."

"Yes. Because it's *meant* to have graffiti on it. Because it's the Stump. It's not like it's private property."

She thought my father's behavior was horrible and that Del and I were to be pitied. Nettled, I said, "Oh, I don't know. Maybe it's good Saul's got a lover. My folks are… difficult. Even if you're one of us."

"But where does that leave your *mom?*"

"Saul's made his choices, and Suzanne's free to make hers. As long as everyone's honest –"

"You think she should be the same way."

"Of course."

"But Nicky, when Julia, you know, when she didn't come back… where did that leave *you?*"

I smiled world-wearily. "There are no guarantees against pain. I know it's important to honor your agreements with people, but isn't it just as important to honor your feelings? Besides, what we'd had before that…" I raised my palm. "Anyway, can you really expect two people to be everything to each other? Forever?"

"Why not?"

That, I intimated, wasn't the way I'd lived *my* life.

"Great. So you and your dad have a lot in common. But how do people keep from winding up *divorced* if that's how they act?"

"Maybe my parents would be better off divorced. I'm not sure I believe in marriage, anyway."

"What do you believe in?"

"Passion."

She looked ready to cry, but said no more than, "Well, I wish you and passion a lot of luck."

:   :

In the spring of 1981, Del announced her engagement to Robert. If she'd wanted to stick it to Saul and Suzanne, she couldn't have picked a better way. The prospect of her June wedding, at twenty-one, to a nice Jewish boy, the first and only man she'd ever slept with, was almost more than they could bear. Suzanne's whitish eyes blazed with panic and hurt. "Honey. You're closing down your life before you've begun to *live* it."

"I love him. He is my life."

"Love does not exclude," Saul said. "It includes."

"Your first wife didn't think so."

"All we're suggesting is, live together a few years. Learn to know each other. See other people. Sweetie, it's only reasonable."

"What would either of you know about reasonable? If you hate the idea so much, none of you have to come to the wedding."

"Good," I mumbled.

"Shut up," they shouted.

It was big news, and no one took it bigger than Terry. Overnight, she became Del's closest pal. Suddenly they spent all their time conspiring on our parents' living room floor in a welter of *Modern Bride* magazines, strutting off arm in arm to scout the local shops for bridesmaids' dresses, stalking Saul and me with smirks and measuring tapes, and dreaming, over spiral-bound notebooks, of celestial flights of catering and special theme colors (rose! cream! chartreuse!) designed to embed the event forever in a sugary aspic of memory.

Del took me aside and said, "I'm *happy*." She seemed afraid to be overheard. I told her I was happy for her, and she said, "Okay," then, "I want you to be *happy* for me. Terry's *great*," she said. "You know, she honestly is a lot of fun." She held me by the arms and surveyed me, digging her thumbs into my biceps and giving me a look I knew to be her most seductive, though a stranger might have mistaken it for beady-eyed rage. "You'll be all right," she said at last, and grinned. Then she asked if I wanted to be one of her bridesmaids.

On the big day, a striped canopy covered half my parents' pitted back lawn. Beneath it, *tzimmes* vapor, wine breath, and pot smoke hovered in a disk-shaped cloud. The guests were hippies and aging New York beatniks, and they gawked at the uniformed caterers, silvered warming trays, and chopped-liver swan, at high-rises of Jell-O and endless suburbs of cold cuts. They crept along the tables clutching empty plates, pining for whole wheat carrot cake and cold sesame noodles. And Saul in his tux and Suzanne in a new Laura Ashley dress blinked like old dogs dressed in baby clothes, reckoning up the cost.

Del shot them an occasional look of triumph. She and Terry raced in circles, nipping at the caterers' flanks, as Robert beamed from a folding chair, hands on knees. Who was this doofus and how had he been permitted to ensnare my sister? Then someone led him to meet

Del in the shade of the satin *chupah* – I suppose it was Del; all you could see was an explosion of white tulle – and they exchanged vows; Suzanne gasped as Del promised to honor and obey. Apologetically, Robert smashed the wrapped tumbler beneath his heel, then stuck his head into that burst of white. A dazed cheer went up. I decided to get drunk. As I drained a plastic cup of wine, I heard a car door thump, and swung toward this embarrassingly late arrival, hoping for awkwardness, wanting a scene.

It was Julia.

She wore an antique communion frock with little white gloves. She held herself very erect. Maturity had beveled her snub nose, and she'd tied her disorderly hair back along her fine skull. I could feel the hammering of my heart, but not the ground beneath me. Gamely she paced forward like a Confederate general come to surrender his sword. She halted a yard away and said, "Well, I was hoping there'd be some statute of limitations."

She lifted and dropped her gloved hands. "Nicky, I'm *sorry*.

"I've been back for a month," she continued. "I was afraid to call. I was afraid your parents would answer, I was afraid *you* would answer. I drove by here a few times, but I never did see you 'til now, and then I thought, *It's a wedding, a happy time, they won't want me there.* But what if I could never do it if I didn't do it right then? So I went home and changed, and here I am."

"Here you are."

"You look gorgeous," she offered.

This nearly unmanned me. The thing is, slim in my tux, hair gleaming from one hundred strokes of the brush, I did hope I looked slightly gorgeous.

But I rapped out: "What kept you?"

She began plucking at the seams of her gloves.

"I guess you've figured out there was someone. Oh, Nicky, what do you want to say to me? What do you need to say so we can go on from here?"

"You sound like a, a *therapist*. This is not *my* little problem."

"You're right. I know you're right."

"I would think that, after everything… I would hope the least I could expect…" One more sentence fragment in the subjunctive and I'd cut my throat. "If I hadn't…"

She whispered, "Could we please go someplace where everyone isn't looking at us?"

I said, "All right," and led her in the back door.

Inside, Del, in white gown and oven mitts, was setting a tray of her special lemon cookies on a trivet. Terry stood beside her, pen poised over notebook. The theme color they'd chosen was aqua, and Terry's bridesmaid's dress featured a system of aqua straps crisscrossing the bodice. She looked cheerily at Julia, waiting to be introduced. "Right through here," I announced in tour-guide tones, and shoved Julia past them. Julia shied at the few people in the living room, pelted upstairs, and pulled me into the first bedroom we reached. This was Del's. She sank down on the bed and leaned back on stiffened arms. It is a position in which a wrestler can postpone being pinned almost indefinitely.

"Better?" I barked.

Nodding guiltily, she scooted forward and sat at the edge of the bed. The duvet was plaid, trimmed with lace. I seated myself across from her, in a little French Provincial chair made of ivory formica trimmed with gold. "Well," she said, "I didn't expect I'd see you next at your wedding."

"This is not my wedding. It's my sister's."

"Oh," she said. "But you're seeing someone?"

"Yes."

"I knew you would be. I'm glad. Is she here?"

"In the kitchen as we came through. Aqua dress."

"She's – pretty."

"Thanks."

"You deserve someone good."

"Thanks."

"Does it make anything better to say I'm jealous of her?"

"Are you?"

"Yes. By now you must be the most wonderful lover."

"I wouldn't know."

Then I wanted to pluck my tongue out by the roots.

"You wouldn't..." Her eyes widened. "You're *joking!*"

"Have it your way," I said, blushing furiously. "I'm joking."

"But, Nicky, for God's sake, you were such a *monster*, I thought by this time you'd be the biggest dick artist in the school."

"No. As it happens. I'm not."

"How long have you *been* with this woman? The one in the silly-ass blue?"

"About a year."

"And she hasn't come across *yet?* Is it made of *gold* or something, does she keep it in Fort *Knox?* Oh, this is none of my business, but my *God!* Well, you don't have much luck with women, do you?"

It seemed I had been waiting a long time for someone to notice that I did not have much luck with women.

"Nicky... have I ruined *everything?*" Entreatingly, she held out her hands.

I slid forward and wound up kneeling, bracing my forearms on the bed on either side of her. I bowed my head, and my hair spilled across the lap of her dress. I could recall the glories beneath with great clarity. Gingerly she smoothed her hands down my nape, combing them into my hair as she went. "I missed you," I said dully.

"Oh Nicky! I missed you too. Even when–" She moved her fingers impatiently in my hair. "I kept wondering how things were with you, and it seemed so wrong that I didn't know. I wanted, it was so crazy, I wanted to sit down and talk it over with you, what was happening between me and him. Did you want to talk to me about what was happening with you?"

"Yes."

"Are you glad I came here?"

"Oh God. Yes."

"I was stupid," she said. "I was stupid not to come back."

"I missed you."

I raised my face and she took my cheeks in her gloved hands. "Do you think they could spare you for, say, half an hour?" she said softly.

"Half an hour."

"Does that door lock? We could start bringing matters up to date. We've both lost so much time."

Holding tenderly onto my jaw, she began to lean backward, and her knees began fluidly to part. I leaned out farther and farther over her, as one glides over a landscape in dreams, gazing brainlessly at her parted lips. In a moment I'd overbalance and collapse on her, and she'd be able to do with me anything she wanted. My stomach touched the crest of her groin. A sort of shock shot through me, and I scrambled to my feet.

"Are you *insane?*" I grated.

"I don't know," she said, startled, trying to sit up and close her legs. "Am I?"

"Thanks. I'm not a charity case quite yet."

"But I didn't mean it like that."

My strength, my spite, came roaring back, and I was safe. "You take me to bed, and you talk all kinds of… *talk*. And then you disappear for four years."

"I'm sorry!"

"And then you try to fuck me at my sister's wedding with my girl-friend bustling around outside the door."

"But she's down*stairs!*" Julia cried.

"You're dangerous. You are dangerous. Listen to me, Julia. I'd rather stick my schvantz in a bear trap."

I turned on my heel – wearing a tux encourages you to do things like turn on your heel – and left.

Out on the lawn I found Terry brandishing a camera about the buffet. "Isn't it all so *precious?*" she said. "Who's that girl you were talking to? She's pretty." I noticed she'd bought kitten-shaped aqua earrings.

I said, "We're going."

"You want to go soon? I thought I'd –"

"We're going."

"But they're… we haven't… *what did I do?*" I hustled her out onto the lawn. As usual, the keys were in Saul's car. I drove through a low hedge and was on the road.

We were silent on the way to her apartment. I escorted her upstairs and locked the door behind us. "Nicky, if I've –" she said, and I kissed her savagely, yanking at the straps of her aqua dress. My idea was, her mouth would remain cold and horrified under mine. Then she'd break away for good, so instead of a sexless little buddy she liked having around, I'd be a man she'd rejected, vile and free. She was kissing me back hotly, but never mind. I yanked her panty-hose to mid-thigh, baring a matted auburn brush. This I gripped as a stablehand grips the bit of a rearing stallion. Then I was flying backward. I came to rest against the dresser. It hurt.

"Now you've done it," she said, and disappeared into the bath-room.

I heard the clack of the medicine cabinet, then hollow, metallic rummaging.

I barged in. Terry was squatting nude by the sink, a white tube of something in one hand and the other between her legs.

She was putting in a diaphragm.

I picked her up bodily. She cried, "*Wait*," and tried to wipe her fingers on a towel. Then she grabbed at the towel rack as I slung her leg up in the air and crammed myself into her with one curt thrust.

It was a warm surroundingness, much vaguer than my own hand. Terry's eyes were large. My prick had vanished. Well, one organ at blood heat inserted into another… We were sliding down the wall. I flopped out when we landed, and she hissed, *Sorry*. I reinstalled myself, legs wedged between the tub and the toilet; folded double on the bath mat, she began coasting away. I lurched after her and thumped against the end of her womb. She yelped. I quickly covered her mouth with mine. I could feel the smooth edge of the diaphragm. I could smell the toxic perfume of the contraceptive cream on her fingers; the harsh, swarming odor of the acrylic bath mat; the scent of old grout between cool tiles. Her thighs fluttered against my ribs, her ankles clamped my cheeks. I thumped into her a few more times and grew ticklish. Then I felt a dull report inside, as if a distant someone had slammed a distant door, and collapsed on her wet, jerking stomach.

Awww, she crooned, *awwwww*.

Frisky and proud, Terry tucked me into her bed as the late afternoon sun skidded under the curtains. She laced her fingers across my chest, set her chin on them, and beamed. A stranger with a red face. I asked why she'd made me wait so long. She said, "If you're just going to sit there and wait for the girl to do everything."

"But I thought you didn't want—"

"… talk so much," she murmured, and cuddled under my arm to sleep.

But just as I was drifting off, she gave my scrotum a brutal squeeze. I squeaked.

"See how *you* like it," she said merrily.

As Sun and Moon Wear Hot Grooves in the Sky

Terry doted on me for a week afterward, and our nights were informative. Still, I remained logy with self-dislike. I couldn't stop reviewing that afternoon, from Julia to Terry and back again. My
gracelessness, timidity, spite – these fit no picture of myself I wanted to
recognize. Terry asked why I kept wincing and whipping my head
back and forth. Her face, so like a scrubbed and pert gladiator's hel-
met, shone with gladness. We'd been swept away by passion, which she
knew I was in favor of. I couldn't tell her how I ached to go back and
make it all come out different.

This time, at any rate, the operator had Julia's number.

"I don't know whether I'm calling to apologize or to ask for an
apology," I said. "I'm pretty sure I was… I was pretty bad."

"We were both pretty bad," she said. The spirit had left her voice
when she'd recognized mine. "I was very irresponsible. I could explain
what I thought I was doing, Nicky, but it was just bad behavior. At any
rate, I'm glad we're not leaving things like that. So. What now? If you
don't want to see me again, I *will* understand."

"I just don't see how it could work."

"I understand. I have no claim on you."

"I just think it would be a bad idea."

"I'm sure you're probably right."

A silence.

"Well," she said. "What are you working on these days?"

I don't suppose there's anyone who's really comfortable answering this question. I muttered something self-deprecating about circles and squares.

"Sort of Suprematist? I always did love Malevich," she said yearningly.

We met at a Collegetown saloon called the Palms. Its windows were smeary little portholes, and red-tipped crew oars hung above the bar. One sat at picnic tables deeply carved with initials and names decades old. There was a mural of dogs drinking at a dog bar under an oil painting of a svelte lady poodle. Julia wore knee-length green tights, plastic sandals, a short jacket of mauve lace, and a silvery bustier. These did not go unnoticed at the bar and, I couldn't help noting, did not suggest contrition. "My Slave-Girl-from-the-Pleasure-Planet look. Like it?"

"Very eye-catching."

"Oh, foo. Come on, Nicky, I just, you know, get dressed in the morning."

I had a sip of my drink.

"You drink whiskey now," she observed.

"Yes. And cross the street by myself and everything."

"A regular little man."

"That's the idea. So. Why don't you fill me in on your last four years? You mind?"

"Not at all." She took a drink of her bourbon. She sipped as if expecting the glass to be snatched away. "Well. Let's see."

"Bad beginning," I found myself saying. "Start again?"

"Oh, *yes*," she said. She held out her hand. "Julia Turrell."

"Nick Wertheim," I said, shaking it. It was fine-skinned and warm, the small bones clear in my hand, and I couldn't let go. I kissed it and then couldn't raise my head.

Into her chewed fingers I said: "I've been such an asshole. I hate everything I said at the wedding. Can we agree I didn't really say it?"

"Oh God, Nicky." She ran her other hand into my hair and gripped my skull. "You have such pretty hair. I wanted to touch it. And when you let me – well, never mind. But I didn't think you'd be such a little *shit*. I was so frightened the whole time."

"So was I."

"Like when you feel something so strong that your legs start to go. And all you can think is, *Please don't let my knees shake so he can see.*"

"Yes! Or just fall down."

"Exactly. I wanted to touch your hair so much."

"You hurt me," I said wonderingly. "You have no idea how you hurt me."

"I'm so sorry! I shouldn't be doing this. You've got a lover." She took her hands away.

"Yes," I said gloomily.

She folded her hands before her. "Sorry. I'm a flirt."

"I don't mind."

"I know. That's why *I* have to mind."

She'd brought along a stack of manuscript. To end the ensuing pause, she shoved it across the table. My eye fell on the name typed at the top of the first page. "Julia *Hargreave?*"

"I sort of married him. The guy."

"Sort of."

"Shush. And divorced him."

"What's he like?" I said helplessly.

"Um, let's see. He's British."

"What does he do?"

"He's Cubby Hargreave's boy. He doesn't have to *do* anything. No, sorry, he designs lighting. Lamps. He's actually very good. Lately he does these teetering sort of things like sails, made of silk and flexed nylon rods and teeny little halogen bulbs. Artemide's just asked him to do some prototypes and he says the wops have to be very impressed before they'll commission a non-wop. That's how he talks. He's an ass-hole," she said as if saying, *He's an Aries.*

"Where'd you meet him?"

"The Azulejo. He was working in his sketchbook, and I thought, *A good-looking rich boy amusing himself with art, and isn't it cozy he has a bit of talent.* Well, I found he was funny. I was right about the rest, but I wouldn't have thought that, and it somehow made me helpless. I kept thinking nothing I did with him could really affect you because it was a different world, and I decided you'd be having some little fling back in Ithaca, too. And then we were waiting for our luggage at Orly, and he was arguing with some security person in that French of his, absolutely machine-gun French with almost perfect Parisian syntax, but all in the most piercing upper-class Brit honk, as if he couldn't be bothered to master the accent of this absurd little frog country he hap-pened to live in, and I thought how I'd never put up with it if I wasn't in love with him. Then I thought: *Uh-oh.* It was pretty bad. No, it was as if I'd finally found someone just like me, a male Julia, and seen how little I was worth, so there was nothing left but –" She shrugged. "We'd wake up at two in the afternoon and go out with our hair all stuck down our faces and he'd say, *Dear me, look at all these ugly little shites. How they hate us, just for being us.* I'd have pulled on yesterday's dress and I thought everyone could smell him on me. As if I was some bitch in heat trotting past the other dogs. I *wanted* them to. If I was just rich trash, I could be so wanton. I should shut up. This isn't fair to you."

"You took his name, huh?"

"He wanted me to. *I* wanted to. You think I want to go through life with my fucking *father's* name?"

Feebly: "Oh. What was his first name?"

"Larry. Oh, my husband? Ex-husband? Chris. Forget Chris."

"Except you slip and call him your husband."

She pillowed her cheek on the table and murmured, "Don't pick on me."

"And don't lean close and whisper along my arm," I said. "That's picking on *me*."

She drew herself up angrily. Then she nodded. "Right. We won't pick on each other. And Nicky? I am so horribly sorry I came on to you at the wedding. I thought poaching other women's men was something I outgrew in my teens. Anyway, I want to be a good friend, and someone who can be relied on, not this arty femme fatale who's always, *Oh, that's just Julia*. And I want you to know that I will never do anything, ever, to hurt your relationship with Terry."

Hope died in my breast.

:   :

Terry was not ardent by nature. She soon reverted to her usual bustling affection, and made time to see me only once or twice a week. She didn't like being "dropped in on"; these meetings were punctiliously scheduled in advance. It left me with a lot of free evenings. Warily at first, Julia and I began meeting at the Palms. Soon it was a weekly ritual. I was careful to explain that Julia was just a friend, but all Terry said was:

"Isn't she kind of old to be hanging around a college town?"

"Thirty."

"Is she a graduate student?"

"Not this semester."

"But she's still hanging around town?"

"Yes."

"I always promised myself I'd never do that."

Julia was looking very well. Things had been done to her trove of russet hair; it spiraled with added vivacity. Her lipstick was a defiant shade of red. Still, the distracted way she perched in her seat suggested sorrow and chastened longing. At first she spoke in a cheerless, circling way of Christopher, and I formed the picture of an unlikable little cuss with an unfortunate amount of sex appeal. Then she decided to disallow the subject. "It isn't fair to you."

"Let me worry about what's fair to me."

"No, I think I'll worry about it, thanks just the same."

The safest thing was to talk about our work, and I, for one, had plenty to talk about. By the time of my senior thesis show, I'd attained a measure of prominence within the fine arts program. Even those who considered me a twit considered me a twit of talent. After graduation, I took a job managing the soup kitchen in the local Unitarian church, where my family and I had often volunteered, and set to work on a major project. The city had built a new parking garage downtown, a modernist hulk featuring expanses of rough-cast concrete. It had occurred to me to do something about it. Why should painters and sculptors hog all the architectural commissions? I proposed a mural executed in hard-ground etching.

I'd experimented with mounting heavy Rives paper on stretched canvas with methyl cellulose glue. I varnished it front and back with two coats of clear acrylic medium and found that the result could be left out in the rain and snow without ill effect. The piece would be a diptych, each panel twenty feet long and composed of twenty-four etchings mounted edge to edge like tiles. Together they'd form five simple forms in three colors; two cool, one hot. I taped my miniature studies to the inside of a shoebox and cut a peephole in the opposite side, so that you had to pivot your head to view the whole composition, as you would when the full-sized mural was installed above a narrow street. The box enchanted Julia. She also loved to hear tales of my trundling persistence with the city fathers, of how I'd wangled a bigger studio to construct the stretchers in, how I'd cozened my classmates' help with pizza from the Chariot and baggies of the tuneful Sonoma Valley Green I got from Saul's connection in Mecklenberg. A masterful organizer of small pleasures, my father had a genius for finding good dope.

"You're a pushy little brute when you set your mind to it," she said approvingly, and gave me a speculative look.

She was working on an extended prose poem called *Music*. It was to be comprised of one hundred individually titled paragraphs. Each week she'd bring a few more. One called "Certificate" read, in full: *And then each morning at six the concierge pours water into the enamel bowl as if setting the seal on a certificate.* Another called "Blue" was three pages long and began: *The woman has faith in the color blue. Not that it will save her, but that there is nothing she can do to spoil it.* Once, scribbled in pencil on the back of one of the pages I found:

BITTEN

The woman sees her blood spring up, twin jewels in smelly water, or a dream of changing size without pain. ~~The boy's mouth~~ ~~The boy's hands~~ *The boy's mouth draws a lash of brightness* ~~deep within her~~ *deeper than* ~~knowledge~~ *the spine   spring up bright and hard as false eyes [touching her? telling her?]   turmoil, wet friend, wet*

Beneath this, she'd drawn:

First I saw two stylized faces in profile, nose to nose, one upside down. Then: a jagged stroke crossing a straight stroke between two dots like the marks of fangs.

Below this she'd written *serpent à sonnettes.* I looked it up. It meant rattlesnake.

We'd close down the bar and often stroll to Yellow House, where she'd "come up a moment" to "finish our talk." Then we'd fix tea and slouch side by side in my room till our eyelids sagged. Often I'd have her take my futon for the rest of the night, then go down the hall looking for open doors and sleep in the first vacant bed I found.

At eight, I'd come in to wake her. A sweaty little personage swaddled in my blankets, her fists jammed into her lap. A woman. I was then having sex with a woman for the first time in my life. It seemed an exacting business. Terry insisted I keep kissing her throughout, to demonstrate affection. Oral sex she dismissed as squalid and show-offy; Terry getting on top fell under the heading of Making the Girl Do Everything. She didn't like me to rear back on my palms – she didn't want "to be *mounted*, like a *mare*" – but sometimes I did so anyway, in order to look down at our joined parts and try to convince myself we were, in fact, screwing. "Don't prove things," she'd say if I ground away too long. Then she'd roll onto her belly, and I'd wedge my thumb into her marshy vulva, grip her mons, and begin massaging her, inside and out, until she released a long, aggravated note into the mattress.

Still, it cured me of wanting and made it possible to consider Julia with what I believed to be dispassion. She'd led me to believe she'd return from Lisbon and be mine, she'd led me to believe that sex was a great deal more fun than it apparently was. Lash of brightness, indeed; the woman was a menace. At last I'd shake her gently awake. She'd smile blearily up at me, then kiss my cheek and toddle home.

"Kiss your cheek," Adam said dully, "and toddle home." Though I could not see him, I knew he was clenching the phone with one hand and scrubbing rapidly at his face with the other.

"I have a girlfriend, Adam."

"You have *Terry*. That you are *plodding* around with this little *drone*, when you could be – It's unwholesome. I got your number, you shit-head, you think it's grown-up to be bored with your love life. When you were guzzling Julia's snatch, was that boring? Look, nuts Julia may be, but she wants a chance to treat you well for a change."

"That's not how the smart money bets."

"All right, forget about Julia, because that'd obviously be too good for you to even consider. Kiss your dwarf jock goodbye and come down here. I'll find you a job and I'll find you women. I got a better idea of your type than I wish I did."

"What are you on, Adam?"

"This astonishing brown Peruvian flake," he said. "Come to New York. I'll save some."

As it happened, Julia beat me to it. After some months of this, she left me a note on the back of a blank check voided with a single stroke of the pen:

> *Going NYC few days & see about Things sorry no warning. Have one for me a/t Palms. See you* SOON.
>
> *—J*

LOVELY NICHOLAS, I thought, BELIEVE ME IN SPITE OF EVERYTHING.

Then the murals were finished, and the city sent a crew with a motorized winch to install them on the sides of the garage. I was there to supervise. The workers got a big kick out of me. They kept thumping me on the back and admitting in prideful tones that this modern stuff was beyond them. Afterward, Terry arranged a celebration at the Palms. She wore one of my black shirts like a dress over pink leotards and red gym shoes: her idea, I guessed, of boho couture. "Terry, what's with your *hair?*" She looked like a Breck Girl caught in a wind tunnel.

She checked her reflection in a window. "I used Tenax. That's not how they do it?"

It became a joke between us. She'd applied most of the tube, and all evening she'd twist her hair into barbarous whorls and peaks and then glance at me as if to say, *Hey Nick, is this how they do it? How about this?* The place was packed. She'd invited my coworkers from the soup kitchen and everyone who'd helped fabricate the mural, as well as my old thesis adviser and some models, who had that costumed air the professionally nude seem to assume when clothed. She kept bouncing off across the room to see that people were enjoying themselves, especially the construction workers, who didn't know anyone. They were delighted with her. There might be, they seemed to indicate, something in this modern stuff after all. Meanwhile, my ex-adviser grew increasingly fatherly as the evening wore on. He was a stocky, tweedy man with a patriarchal beard, who was undergoing a punishing divorce and kept patting young women on the wrist. "You're…," he said, and gripped my shoulder in order to focus his thoughts. "We're going to be hearing from you," he said. Terry hugged my arm. A few of my prettiest former classmates came up to do a little ceremonial flirting. They shot Terry looks of mock envy. Jovially she advised them to go on and take me, since I was getting such a swelled head that there'd be no living with me. I'd never been out in public as part of a couple before, and all this had a powerful effect on me. It struck me that it was one thing to be beautiful and bright and exotic, and another to be there when it mattered. What, I found myself thinking, if Terry and I just said the hell with it and got married? If nothing else, it would drive my parents right around the bend.

That weekend, they asked Del and me up to the house and announced they were getting a divorce.

"We decided some months ago," Suzanne said. "But Del had just gotten engaged, and we agreed that that should be your time, and not to spoil it."

I wiped my mouth with my napkin. Then again. Somehow it seemed I must have food all over my face. Perhaps what amazed me most was that my parents had kept mum about something awkward. "But you were getting on again," Del said. "But Saul stopped seeing that girl. You were loving each other again."

"We got on better," Saul said, "because we knew we just had a little time left together. Anyhow, the issue was never Carla. It was my need, real or perceived, for a Carla. Or Carlas."

"You don't even want to *try* any more?"

Suzanne said, "Del. Honey. We've been married nearly twenty years. Saul and I will stay on in the house, for the time being, and I'll start looking for a job in New York. Honey, you said you and Robert were headed for the city. We'll be closer there."

Saul said, "Guys, guys. We know this is painful. But you're adults now, with your own lives. I don't understand the horror I'm seeing in your faces."

"ADULTS?" Del screamed. "WHAT IN FUCK WOULD YOU KNOW ABOUT ADULTS? WHAT IN FUCK WOULD YOU KNOW ABOUT *US?* YOU'VE BEEN DANCING AROUND IN YOUR LIT-TLE PLAY WORLD AND NOW YOU SAY THIS MARRIAGE IS OVER? *WHAT* MARRIAGE? THIS IS SESAME STREET! WE WERE RAISED BY BIG BIRD AND ERNIE! I GREW UP INTO SUCH A BITCH BECAUSE THERE WAS NOBODY TO STOP ME AND IF I HADN'T TAKEN CARE OF NICKY HE'D BE EVEN FUCKEDER-UP THAN HE IS NOW AND JUST LOOK AT HIM! YOU'VE GOT HIM TRAILING AROUND AFTER ANOTHER LITTLE FRIZZLE-HEADED PSYCHO JUST LIKE YOU AND WHAT CHANCE DO YOU THINK HE'S GOT? THE FIRST TIME I MET A GROWN-UP I MARRIED HIM BUT WHAT FUCKING CHANCE DO YOU THINK NICKY'S GOING TO HAVE? AND I WANT YOU TO KNOW I'M *PREGNANT!* AND SHE'LL BE *NOTHING, NOTHING, NOTHING* LIKE ANY OF US!" She ran out the front door.

I looked helplessly at my mother and father.

"We know, Nicky," Suzanne said. "She's upset."

I guessed I'd been waiting, after all these years, for them to shape up and be parents. In any case, the news stunned me. Everything seemed loose, wobbly, up for grabs, everyone seemed perilously *imaginative.* What I needed was Terry. I made a beeline for her place, practicing nonchalance. *Oh, nothing. Just wanted to say hi. Nothing special; do I need an excuse to see you? No big deal, I just –* She opened the door, puzzled. "Well. Hi," she said.

"Oh, nothing," I said.

"What?"

"*Hi.* Can I come in?"

She figured she'd better kiss me.

I walked past her. "Nice place," I said crazily.

"About like always, I guess." She tittered. "Listen, is anything–"

"You doing anything tonight?"

"Well… Nick, we always plan these things out."

"Oh, okay. I just thought if you weren't." I dropped into the sofa. "Listen, come over here a minute. You studying tonight, or…?"

She moved obediently into the crook of my arm and I kissed her, then slid an open hand down her stomach and into her jeans. She surged against my palm, her stubby body a long hot wave, then plucked my hand out and sat up, laughing. "Whoa. I wish you'd give me some warning when you're going to be like this."

"Oh. Sorry."

"No. It's not that at all. It's just that, well, you're not usually like this." She smiled shyly. Her skin was a clear dusty red. "I just mean this is just really bad timing, Nicky, 'cause I have to kick you out really soon."

"Oh." I tipped up her face and began kissing her again. We began to tremble. I pulled my mouth loose and murmured, "Cancel whatever you were going to do. I want to fuck you so badly."

"I can't do that," she said distinctly.

I sat up. "Okay. No problem."

Reluctantly, she sat up as well. "All I meant was, it's usually not like that first time. Almost never, really. I guess I'd been meaning to say it."

"How was it different the first time?" I asked leadenly.

"Well, the way you acted. Like a man."

"*What?*"

"Well, I don't want to sound terrible, but it's true. A girl doesn't want to have a committee about everything she does with a guy. Is it all right. What do I think. You just, you know, do it. Like a man. Ask anyone. No, don't, they'll lie. And now I've made you angry. I know you think I'm an awful lay. But I'm not that bad. Not with everyone."

"With everyone."

"I've wanted to tell you. I've been thinking about all the stuff you've been saying about honesty."

"*And?*" I shouted.

"Well, we haven't been, it hasn't been that long," she said very rapidly. "It's just sort of a thing of passion like you were saying. He's very nice. Well, you've got Julia, and I knew you didn't believe in marriage, and you've got Julia. I know she's been spending the night there. It's okay. I know she's the one you love, it's obvious, so don't make like this is so terrible. You don't even want me. You have to lie there and shove me with your thumb."

"Okay. This is a little – Sorry," I added, because I'd begun to cry. "I'm a little off balance. My folks just decided to split up."

"But isn't that good? You kept talking about how you didn't care! How it would be so great!"

"Yes. I did say that."

"You were *bored* with me!" she cried. "Don't tell me it's like that with Julia. Don't tell me it's like that with your other women."

"My other women."

The realization that I'd never had any other women struck her like an open hand.

In guilt and fright, she shucked off her clothes. "Do what you want," she begged. "Do anything." She dropped to all fours and presented her neat little hams. She crouched and busied her mouth, she gave mine free rein. Her cunt was bitter as smoke, and lunged despairingly back and forth so that I couldn't get properly started. Nothing was possible.

She whispered, "You *lied* to me."

Eight forty-five came – the new guy was due at nine – and I had to go. At the door I gave Terry a jaunty, miniature wave. I couldn't have asked for a more soul-pierced gaze in return. Then I strode away from her apartment in that anesthetized sort of state, that then-I-noticed-a-severed-leg-beside-me-in-the-trench-and-realized-it-must-be-mine sort of state. I walked straight over to Julia's place. I stared at her darkened window. I started walking again.

It took Julia two more days to return, so I know I couldn't actually have spent the entire time walking, but that's how it felt. Through the next afternoon, I plodded up Dryden through the unending farms to the north. At dusk, I climbed the empty stadium and watched a single figure circle the track. I pissed in the black lake at 4 A.M. Every few hours I rattled Julia's doorknob and peered through her curtains. Early the second evening, as I sat numbly on her step, she came toddling down the street with an overnight bag. She didn't look up until she was almost on top of me.

"Oh!" she said, starting as if caught at something naughty.

"Here I am," she offered. "I – did you get my note? I left you a note. I was in New York. I finally decided I had to see him. Chris. I guess it didn't go all that terribly well. I thought, I was pretty sure, but I just had to – Well, I guess it is. Over." She began to cry: long, horrible, groaning sobs. "*Please* ignore me," she said, leading me inside. "I'll be done with this" – she waved at her streaming tears – "in a minute. Sit. I don't know what I'm doing yet. But I had to see him. I knew it would be bad. But he didn't have to – No, he's right. My God, I'm so *hungry*. Can I fix you anything? There's some eggs. There's some mustard. There's some ground beef, can I fix you some chili? You know, we never actually got to –" She took out a package of ground beef and began to wrestle with it, teeth gritted, wrenching her body from side to side. I tried to help. "No, I have it. *I HAVE IT.*"

The cellophane ripped, the meat sprang out onto the filthy floor, and Julia sank down next to it, bawling. I knelt beside her. She pressed my knuckles to her breastbone; it strained like an overwound clock trying to strike. "Did you have," she said, "any plans for the evening?"

My knuckles ached. She would not let go.

:   :

Soon after this, my parents began fixing up the big house, getting ready to sell. Since Saul's back was frail, I went over there often to lend a hand. Suzanne would be on elbows and knees in the front garden. She'd lined the rose beds with wood mulch and jars of sun tea, and weeded them daily. Smiling over one shoulder, she'd wave me on with a dirt-crusted salad fork, saying, "Help your father." Saul and I replaced the upstairs toilet and reenameled the tub, secured a loose rain gutter, pried up the old linoleum and rotted underlayment of the kitchen floor. Meanwhile, bit by bit, he moved from my mother's room to my old bedroom down the hall. Once I found him upstairs, dragging his Selectric along on a blanket. "It's not so bad," he explained. "See? I sort of bounced it across to the bed, and then I put the pillows on the floor and let it slump down, and when I got to my room I was gonna think of something." I scooped up the typewriter and carried it in. "This huge fucking empty house," he said, "and we're both huddled in one room. It was so *A Rose for Miss Emily* I kept waiting for myself to rot."

He sank down on the bed. A frownlike crease divided his belly. He was seeing a forty-eight-year-old anthropology student. "She'd have forgiven a tootsie much quicker than a woman nearly her age."

"Don't tell me Mom threw you out."

"Who threw? I ran." He seated himself before the typewriter, poised his hands as if typing and gazed at the wall before him. He relaxed and struck a key at random. It clicked inertly. The machine wasn't on. "So. Nickel. What's the story with that girl?"

He didn't have to specify which girl. When I saw Terry in town, she smiled and waved from a distance like a beauty queen on a parade float.

Julia and I had spent the night together, fully clothed, hugging like frightened children. In the weeks that followed, she slipped into dazed inanition. Gone from her wardrobe were the child's ruffled vest, the vinyl poodle skirt, the weirdly short denim dress with shoulder straps like overalls, the blouse whose long filmy sleeves were patterned with spectral roses. Now each morning Julia brushed her teeth, dabbed her face with cold-cream, and crept into the world in the plaid shirt and jeans she'd worn all week. Her dwindling haunches moved timidly beneath the frayed denim. A tang of dried sweat wafted from her open shirt. She dropped out of grad school again. She would not speak of Christopher, or say what had happened in New York. I learned never to ask.

She'd scattered legal pads around her apartment and at intervals would pause at one and fall into a brief trance of work, scratching away with the page on a diagonal, gnawing her lip like a young girl practicing to be a sex kitten on the basis of old Kim Novak movies. Then she tucked the sheets in a small portfolio, tied it shut with a gray ribbon, and abandoned it on her dresser top, trusting me never to pry. I undid the ribbon every chance I got. *So this is the starling on the sill,* I read, *about whom everyone has been complaining! / Her particular ruckus balanced / on eight fastidious points. / Her tiny, blistered, brownish heart / beating hundreds of times a minute.* I read: *A string of ponies driven into the water. / The disordered water against their disordered breasts.* I read: *A web of ruin inside her, rich as lace.*

She began to smoke a great deal of my dope. It had a disastrous effect on her. Her speech grew sloppy and expansive. She'd conceived a character called Makey the Face, and when she felt like doing Makey she screwed her face up and yammered nonsense syllables in a piercing quack, and whatever you said, she responded in Makey-talk. She seemed to have no idea how much it cost to get her stoned, and sometimes I felt quite ill-used. But dope plainly eased her as few other things did, and it was better than watching her drink.

It wasn't a nightly event, thank heaven, but Julia seemed determined, several times a month, to get hammered flat as a coat of paint. At first, I admit, I hoped a few belts might be good for her. Later, I tried to keep her out of the Palms. But home was worse – she kept a bottle or two forthrightly out on her bookshelves – and if I had us meet someplace that served no liquor, she'd fortify herself beforehand, then spend the evening chafing to get home. At least at the Palms, where both principal bartenders liked Julia, she'd be handed, in place of her fourth or fifth order of the evening, a free Coke. She took this more meekly from them than she would have from me. She already had a drinker's appreciation of the puissance of barkeeps.

At first she'd try to conceal the degree of her inebriation. Each stimulus was interpreted as a challenge, and a trip across the room required visible forethought. Then she'd give up, and merely hope to be the wittiest and most fascinating drunk you'd ever met. Her face became a sort of pretty puppet theater within which she acted out the emotions of your story as you spoke. Beyond this point, however, she could only choose between the one endless, desperately elaborated sentence, and stooped, yellow-eyed silence. She'd be bitterly humiliated by the collapse of her gaiety.

It was terrible to see her wandering lost like this. Around then, the soup kitchen I managed needed a half-time coordinator. On impulse, I offered the job to Julia.

The impulse proved an inspired one. Though she'd been hired to work twenty hours a week for a fraction of what she received anyway from her trust, Julia was soon devoting forty or fifty, and dumbfounded me by proving painstaking, efficient, and shrewd. She was skilled in parting wholesalers from food and foundations from grants. She hadn't balanced her own checkbook in years, but she kept our check register impeccable, inscribing each entry in a small, regularly looping hand. There were two advantages to this new setup, both debatable. One was that Julia now drank a bit too much, instead of quite a bit too much. The other is that we were together every day.

We'd run errands for the kitchen in Julia's old Fiat, another dashing little two-seat rattletrap with a convertible top. If she drove, I could admire the sureness of her bitten fingers and the gallantry of her wrists. If I drove, she lifted her face into the wind as blissfully as a dog. And unloading supplies with Julia was always a treat. Though fetching and carrying was not, she made clear, her métier, she also made it clear she would not dream of fussing about it, that it was her *job*. We'd haul the boxes down into the church cellar, which was all low fieldstone arches and narrow passages, one of them housing a walk-in fridge. Every available niche had been crammed with steel shelves bearing scrounged dry goods, or clean metal trash cans lined with heavy plastic and filled with pinto beans, chickpeas, powdered milk. Back upstairs, I set the day's menu on the chalkboard for the benefit of the volunteers. Then we tucked our hair up into Moore Paint caps and began the meal. Julia's repertoire did not extend past simple omelettes, spaghetti, and the chili she still hadn't made for me; learning new recipes raised her to a state of panicky hilarity.

"I'll forget. I'll ruin it. I'll put in too much basil or something."

"Not for eight gallons of stew you won't."

"Okay. Don't tell me now, even if I ask."

The refectory in which we served our meals had been tacked onto the red stone church in the sixties. It was a big white box with a hardwood floor and long windows of pebbled safety glass. There were two basketball hoops, usually folded up against the ceiling. I loved to look out the serving hatch at the long clean tables early in the morning. When we finished serving, we took our plates out to eat with the "guests": outpatients, some aging hippies, a family of struggling soy farmers, a seventy-year-old amateur sinologist on Haldol. "Digest your food," he'd shout, mastering his spoon with two drug-palsied hands. "Who loves a worrier?" Julia was angelic with them all, though sometimes her beautiful manners were pierced by vast, nose-wrinkling yawns during which the whole of her pink mouth was revealed, down to two molars with fillings.

It was central to Julia's beauty that she always knew precisely how beautiful she was. Her beauty had, always, an element of generalship. She weighed ninety-seven pounds that year, and subsisted on bourbon and moisturizer, but she was still capable of mustering her decimated troops for a last-ditch assault. She held her wrists high and a bit tensed, so that one was compelled to admire their hard, intelligent lines. Her hair seemed always just to have tumbled undone. She presented herself in a ravishing *déshabille* of the heart, as a great beauty stripped of elegance by sorrow, and I don't think I was wrong to believe that, however equivocally, I was being courted.

I waited a few weeks, until she'd settled into her new job and the first bitterness of her grief seemed to be waning. We were sitting thigh to thigh on her sofa after work, still in that first state of shared surprise and pleasure at how well things were going at the kitchen. I felt it would be advantageous to have her facing me. I set gentle fingers on her jaw and turned her head. "What are we doing?" she asked nervously.

Fighting to keep my voice level, I said, "You're not familiar with the procedure?"

"Yes," she said, eyes downcast. "I am familiar with the procedure."

It was, oddly, her jeans and not her half-open shirt that came off. My fingers flopped and slithered in her sedgy drawers. Arrhythmically she snapped her legs shut, conscientiously she reopened them. Her kisses continued, pouncing and avaricious, but her hips kept shying back. Finally, humbly she asked, "Can we have a little break, and can I have my pants on?" She put her pants on, and we had tea, and her relief and shame were so intense that only a brute could have asked her to take them off again.

It was the beginning of a year of erotic limbo. I spent the night in Julia's bed fairly often, and these nights were not entirely chaste. She kissed me eagerly, she loved to be held tightly, loved to touch me. But she could not bear to be touched ("Not, you know, *specifically*," she admitted) or to have that plaid shirt or those panties slipped from her shoulders or hips. Her nipples would be hard as knuckles and her groin equatorial, but her eyes and lips would whiten. She expected murder. "I'm sorry," she'd say, "I'm not, I guess I'm not quite… I'm sorry, Nick."

Only when I'd given up, when I lay quiet and defeated, could Julia relax and let loose her great store of tenderness. She devoted hours to my back, legs, and arms, kneading, kissing, nibbling, and brushing them with her hair. She kissed my ass. She kissed my toes. I'd once told her how Del and I, when we were little, had played Submarine under the dining table: I lay down and, because the submarine was very small, Del lay down on top of me. One steered with one's feet. Julia loved the story, and if I rolled onto my stomach I found us at once playing Submarine, her legs trailing along mine and her lips against my neck, stroking my forearms almost imperceptibly with her finger-tips. Finally Julia might slip her hands beneath my hips and dispatch me with remorseful palms. She wiped them on her stomach when she was done.

Afterward I'd lie awake and she'd flinch and wiggle in the grip of bad dreams. She ground her teeth, paddled her feet, pleaded and explained in murky syllables pitched to seem reasonable and to conceal her panic from some inquisitor, until I nudged her awake. And sometimes, riven by spite, I did not: I'd gaze across her tumbling hair at a radiator she'd half-painted gold, listening to her grunting and mewling, smelling her rich female scent, gripped by a leaden rage that strained pointlessly at her sacral dimples. And sometimes, half-asleep, she reached back and adjusted it with a nurse's pragmatic touch so that it lay more comfortably along her spine.

Nights like this left her abject. "I almost want to. I *want* to want to."

"All right."

"I hate that you're always so angry. I'm your friend, Nicky. And I'm your girl, I really am. All right, I know I'm not, but I'm your girl as much as I can. I'm afraid you'll just never forgive me for this."

"You've been as clear as possible about what I can and cannot expect, Julia. If I'm still hanging around hoping for more, that's my decision, and if I'm frustrated, that's entirely my responsibility."

"That's what I mean, you'll never *forgive* me! I know you deserve more. Listen, you know that girl I was talking about, down at the Co-op store?"

"You've mentioned her."

"I've been down and had another look. She deserves some thought. I'm serious. She's got such a lovely long nose, and wonderful curves. And that dark, knowing look, that sort of matronly self-possession Jewesses all seem to have by the time they're about eight. As if they're ready to birth their first children while the rest of us are doodling unicorns with big hysterical eyes. I think she'd be good for you. As long as we could still sleep close like this."

I had to smile. "She might not be too keen on the idea."

"Oh, she wouldn't mind. You Yids are all pervs," she said fondly. "Even a prig like Terry was ready to let you have a whole stable of chippies on the side to give you what she couldn't. You know, you seem to get some sick gratification from all these crazy women who say, you can do that, but not this, and you can't ever get enough, and I hate to be one of them. You should steer clear of me. What are you *fucking* laughing at?"

"This sounds like excellent advice, Julia. Would you give it to me if there was any danger of my taking it?"

She grinned, shamefaced. "Oh, all right. But Nicky, isn't it good, any of it? Isn't it good to sleep close and know how I'm so happy and glad you're there? I know it's more than I deserve. But right now I need more than I deserve. And don't I give you any pleasure at all?"

"The nice thing is, when I get tired of my own pleading, I can listen to yours."

She laughed, and then I did. Then she grew serious. "But I can't. You *know* I can't. Not when I'm so awful and rotten inside. Like rotted cobwebs. So filthy inside with unhappiness. It's as though it would make you a part of the filthiness, too, and I couldn't bear that. This is such a horrible tease for you, and maybe you *should* leave me. I'd be all right, you know. Believe me, I'll always find some sort of company. And maybe later, when I'm more myself, we could have everything. But not now, Nicky. It would be so bad."

She spoke matter-of-factly. I was, all at once, very uncomfortable. "Julia, are you going to keep striking tragic poses atop a heap of dirty socks, or are you going to tell me, for God's sake, what Chris *did*? Did he beat you?"

"Boy, do you perk up. No, he didn't *beat* me. Chris was always very careful about that."

"Then what?"

"It wouldn't sound like much even if I told you."

"Maybe I'm not as dull-witted as you think."

Wearily: "You're here, aren't you?"

We fought often. One point of contention was the powdered milk we served. It was, Julia said, spiritually costly to drink such awful stuff. Of course, I'd grown up drinking the awful stuff, and so took great satisfaction in explaining why it was impossible, financially and logistically, for an organization like ours to serve real milk, and this relish was not lost on Julia, and led to many a fine talk about whether I hated hope and cherished disappointments and whether she was an ignorant princess and an oblivious little dabbler. Another time, we nearly came to blows over an offer of four hundred pounds of flour at a meeting with a Catholic relief organization staffed largely by radical nuns in jeans and chambray shirts. We already had a year's supply of flour in our cellar, but Julia was relentless.

"We don't even have a place to *put* it, Julia. I'm sure –"

"Our job is to distribute food, Nick. We are being offered food. We will think of something."

"There are more effective ways to utilize our time…" And so on. Finally I asked the poor nuns to excuse us. Out in the hall, Julia wrestled her hair back in the old gesture, then tightened her fists until the skin of her forehead crept up and her eyes were distorted. Through these inhuman slits she regarded me. It looked painful. I hoped it was. At last she said, "I will be responsible for storing the flour."

"Fine. How?" I wore the calm ugly face I so often used as a bludgeon.

"I will be responsible for storing the flour through means which I have yet to determine."

"Fine."

We returned and thanked the nuns for their flour, and Julia went home and sold it to a Trumansburg bakery for a fraction of the market rate, using the proceeds to finance a month of real milk for our lunches, delivered in woefully uneconomical gallon jugs. "Julia! *You cannot solicit free food and then sell it!* To anyone, for any reason! Julia, these people all *talk* to one another!"

"Calm down. It'll be fine," she said uneasily.

It was fine. No one ever said a word. In a sulk, I mixed a pitcher of powdered milk for myself, and Julia went around asking people whether the real milk wasn't much better, and they assured her that it was.

But more maddening than our fights were the times when Julia compelled me to be happy. For instance, she somehow found out just when my murals had been installed – I couldn't have named the date, myself – and on their first anniversary presented me with a dozen yellow roses and a handmade card on which she'd striven to replicate the murals' design. Her calligraphy was laborious and I could tell she was proud of it. I remember drifting off on her sofa late one afternoon and waking as dusk puddled in the windows. She'd slipped off my shoes and tucked a blanket around me. I could hear a chill rain clicking on the glass and, from the kitchen, the comfy, settling-in noise of water in a kettle approaching a boil. I remember walking with Julia when the weather turned cold. She'd bundle her fists up in her sleeves, angle her arms out like flippers, and squint tormentedly until I put an arm around her. Then she'd hug my waist and jam her temple against my shoulder. I remember going out with her to see the Northern Lights. We went to the lookout above the cemetery and, side by side in a silent crowd, watched titanic drapes shimmering and refurling in the night sky. Afterward we walked wordlessly home as if carrying a brimming bucket between us. From time to time she'd direct at me a look that seemed to say we'd both done so well. I remember Julia dawdling over my art books. She found it most convenient to set the bigger ones on the floor and crouch over them – she could squat endlessly without discomfort, like a Zulu – turning pages between her splayed knees, her mad hair brushing the color plates. I couldn't interest her in the sour sublimity of Duccio's line. She preferred saccharine Raphael, the porcelain eyelids of decorous Madonnas. Her own round head had a touch of Quattrocento sleekness. I did very little work that year, but I did do one drawing I still like: Julia hunkering like a lovely little frog, raking back her hair and inspecting Annunciations. Her shirt was deeply unbuttoned; I traced the line where her shoulder muscle met the plane of her slight pectoral, as clear as a boy's. I loved cooking for her. She seldom ate a full meal, but at least some portion would be so favored, and I'd watch as it vanished between her skilled lips and judicious teeth. And over the next twelve hours I could reflect with satisfaction upon the morsel I'd prepared, now descending her tan throat, now squelching audibly for a time through her concave, deep-naveled, dyspeptic belly, and finally exiting her dear little rectum, which only a few years earlier had so cheerily hugged my dazzled forefinger.

And of course, there was our work at the soup kitchen. As we stocked the cellar with victuals, or scoured pots side by side, I'd dream of a life like this, of abiding affection and good management. I imagined Julia's graceful forearms flecked with paint as we furnished our house. I pictured her graying and my dark hair tangled across one pillow. I dreamed of a body softened by years, entirely mapped by kisses, a warm haven for my face. I grew serious and equipped us with children. There was Noni, the eldest, a poet like her mother, and Ezra, whom many people thought was my spitting image, and Mariah the pragmatic one, and little Josh. I counted them up. Four children! What was I thinking? I eliminated one or two to spare Julia's poor hindquarters. I dreamed of a study for her work and a studio for mine. I designed and furnished them. I considered how we might best get our work done with a houseful of kids. I dreamed of feeding her up, of Julia serene and sleek, sipping two-handed from a mug of hot tea; in my revery it had somehow been arranged that she no longer drank. Sometimes I saw us in the city, and sometimes in a big sunlit house in the woods. I had to admit that with Julia's money we might as well have both. I promised myself I'd always keep a paying job, as a matter of principle.

After these orgies of domesticity, I felt sick and stupid. "Like a pet waiting for table scraps," I'd tell my reflection in the bathroom mirror. "Do better," I begged. The little black eyes peered back with no sign of comprehension.

In good weather, we spent a lot of time at the table out in my back-yard. I remember Julia's face simplified by strong sunlight. After a morning in the sun, the yellow-painted steel beneath our forearms was nearly too hot to touch. There'd come a moment when it stopped burning and began to feel warm, and one's entire body prickled and went dreamy. Here we sat and talked about ourselves, and art, and, of course, Julia's folks.

"Mom was always in her room," Julia told me, "paralyzed with something or other. Migraines, hay fever – she called it 'rose cold' – Agatha Christie. Luminal. She's had no sort of life at all, poor dear. But back then I had no pity for her, I just thought she was a frump who didn't deserve Larry. My brothers were a lot older than me. Big dumb jocks, always on the bustle. I wanted them to be my beaux, like you and Del – I'm *serious*. But they saw me as a nuisance, this fragile thing that needed watching over and had ideas, and used all the little brains they had to find ways to dump me and take off. I considered myself too charming to be disregarded in this manner. My father has every last bit of the brains in our family, and he squanders them on a new brainstorm every other year. When I was twelve, it was these micro-miniaturized looms spinning teensy wet strands of polymer, sort of the way they make pantyhose. But these would make these rigid *structures*."

"What sort of structures?"

"All sorts. It would be very strong and light. It was supposed to replace steel, plastic, concrete. You name it. The invention of the century. He kept doodling it on menus and then demanding to take the menus home. Larry always had a certain demented style. Anyway, he hired a young engineer to set up shop in a spare bedroom and work on this full time. I remember I'd just read *Madame Bovary*. When I first saw it in my father's bookcase, I thought 'bovary' was a word for those rude parts of me I wasn't to fiddle with. And I was upset, because I didn't want my bovary up there where anyone tall enough to reach the book could read about it. But then *I* read it, and wanted to be a fabulous and tragic *amoureuse*. I remember vamping the poor engineer mercilessly, the way I'd read Emma had vamped Léon. My great-aunt gave me pointers. She was the only good one. I guess she was slightly crazy, but she knew how to enjoy herself, and she'd *talk* to me, and teach me things, like how to dress and how to keep myself nice. You shit, why are you smiling? I know I've let myself go a little."

"You smell," I informed her, "like the lion house at the Bronx Zoo."

She laughed. "Not, at any rate, the monkeys? The lions don't sound so bad."

"Oh, I like the lions."

"Well, I've let myself go. I'm having a breakdown. But even now? I do my skin, and I always floss twice a day. Laura told me. Men will forgive anything sooner than bad teeth. A woman with good dentition can expect to retain her attractiveness seven years longer than one without. Seven years, that was the estimate. Look." She spread her lips back with her fingers and complacently displayed two rows of small-ish choppers. They seemed quite ordinary to me.

I praised them.

"Where was all this going on?" I said. "I can never keep straight where you lived before Silver Crest."

"Oh God, neither can I. Everywhere. We moved and moved. I always remember myself weeping in a strange bed, boxes all around and my parents fighting down the hall."

"Nasty. Empty houses have that way of echoing."

"Oh God. I used to hump up the rug against my bed to make a cave. It was an old Persian, and it smelled of old hemp and old dust, sort of fermented. It smelled like incense. I'd huddle up in my cave and each time a door slammed downstairs, I'd tell myself my parents were leaving me, because I'd been so awful. I pictured their big ugly suitcases and their smiles of relief. And so on, until I cried. And then I'd be so kind to myself. I imagined my cave was deep within a mountain, at the end of a maze of tunnels. No one would ever find me. I'd be safe with all my favorite things. My flashlight to read by, and a brass finial from an old lamp that I called the Queen, and a Venetian glass paperweight which was her domain, full of colored bubbles, who were her subjects, and tall spirally blobs."

"Minor royalty."

"Exactly. And my miniature magnetic Parcheesi board, and my Bible."

"The one on your dresser?"

"Yes! It was a great comfort. The thing about the Bible is, everything's numbered, so you always know just where you are. And there was also all this great smutty business in Genesis, like when Shechem raped Dinah, and then decided he wanted to marry her, and she said, 'Not till you and your brothers are circumcised,' and then they killed them all, all the Hivites, while they were too sore from being circumcised to fight back."

"Resourceful."

"Wasn't it? Then there was Tamar, who disguised herself as a temple harlot and got her father-in-law to sleep with her and promise her a kid from his flock, which I figured she wanted as a pet. She got his staff and his signet, too. It seemed the possibilities were endless for a girl with a little imagination. I used to beg to be taken to church the way some kids beg to be taken to the circus. My favorite was St. John the Divine. It was off in the city, and we'd only go there for Christmas Mass. We'd sing in our coats. If you coughed, it echoed, so I loved to cough. There were these mangy kneeling cushions, but I wanted to kneel right on the cold floor and look way up into the roof, very deep-looking and shadowy, and frighten myself with notions of somehow falling *up* there. And the nave seemed its own little *realm* leading up and up and back and back, and finally there was Christ, very stiff and gold and preoccupied with his pain. I wanted to be Christ's girlfriend and tend his wounds. *My* Christ would come home with me and get better."

One day she asked, "Did I ever tell you about my father's convertible?" Her tone made it clear she knew she had not.

"It was a Larry's big idea for 1965," she said. "A red Mustang convertible wasn't, to put it mildly, what you did. We already had a gray Land Rover and a white Saab, and if he absolutely needed a sports car to get him through his midlife crisis, instead of doing something seemly like quietly drilling a friend's daughter, which he was probably also doing, or divorcing Pru, I guess he should've gotten a Jag or an Austin Healey. Something British and pearl gray. But I consider it the most brilliant thing he ever did. It was such a fuck-you, so luscious. There it was, all flaming and squared-off and sort of rumpy, and it started up with this snarling farting growl, and I'd've been, oh, fifteen? and what I wanted most of all, of course, was to drive it by myself, with the top down. *Fast.*

"Well, good luck with that. My family by then had a policy of not letting me do anything at all I might want to do, which I now agree was sensible. Luckily, the keys were never in Dad's pocket – that would spoil the line of his slacks. He'd hang them on a coathook by the front door instead. One night when he was upstairs with a thriller, I stepped up big as you please and grabbed them, and cat-footed down to the driveway. But he popped open the front door right as I put the keys in the ignition. 'Just going out,' I said gaily. 'Can I get you anything?' He walked around behind the car, so I'd have to run him down if I backed out, and closed his hand over mine, and took the keys.

"After that, he kept them close by. So I had to wait for a night when he was soggy drunk. Pru wouldn't let him in, and he'd sleep in the guest bedroom, and there'd be an opportunity. Of course, this was not a long wait. I remember how I just *cuddled* my weight up against the door so the lock wouldn't snick. He was asleep with the lamp on. It had one of these 'hand-blown' glass chimneys that throw little wibbles of shadow all over the room. His mouth was open. He didn't have his bit of stomach held in. The keys were by his wrist. I *smoothed* them up off the endtable and tiptoed downstairs. And then I fired 'er up! and by the time he collected himself, I was down the block, headed for the freeway.

"It was so wonderful. I remember how the wind ran over my face, like ice water. The overpasses went whumping by, it's as if I were passing through gateway after gateway. I was outrunning my father, and all pity, and all shame, and I was young and pretty and in danger, and I think I loved myself most because I knew I'd go home and write – there might be a poem in it – and I saw my head studiously inclined and the lamplight on my face. And then something white jumped up into the headlights, so quick! Oh God. I got the car stopped and walked back to see. It was a rabbit. Half a rabbit. The front half was still all sleek and brown, but then everything just tore off into twitching gray bulbs and strings. And it was trying to crawl. Oh God. I rushed around like a maniac but there was nothing to kill it with, only pebbles. Finally, I backed the car over it, again and again, all crying and my nose running, till there was nothing left.

"My father met me as I turned into the drive. His hands were in his pockets. His shirttail was out. 'What'll she do?' he asked. He was looking at the fender.

" 'I had it up past 130.'

" 'That's good to know,' he said. 'The keys go on the hook by the front door.'

"That was the summer that Larry left my mother for the first time. I believe it was her suggestion, but he'd know she was speaking rhetorically. He very gleefully rented a furnished apartment above someone's garage in the very crappiest part of town, with his own private entrance by the trash cans. The stairs up to his room were steep as a ladder. And from the rabbit night on, I had free use of the Mustang, just me, not my brothers or my mom. And when he went to parties – it was so cozy for the hostesses, they could invite both my parents and know Pru'd never show – he took me along. His date, his chauffeur, and that way he wouldn't have to count his drinks. I had some wonderful dresses that year, and I want you to know it was really something entering a room on that man's arm, and an education too, because everyone considered Pru a persecuted saint, but it was Larry they wanted at their parties. I don't think I'm kidding myself, we were a gorgeous couple. Then I'd go about my business, and he'd go about his, and maybe I'm wrong about him and his friends' daughters, because he always went home alone. This was not what Larry was used to. He'd joke about my being his chaperone and make everyone uncomfortable, but he was striking out, plain and simple. So I'd drive him home by eleven, just *dissolved* in Dewar's, and help him inside. I remember him going up those stairs like they *were* a ladder, using hands and feet. I'd dab his face with a wet washcloth and pull off his shoes and tie. I knew how to do this from Cheever stories in the *New Yorker*.

"One night – we were on the landing outside his door – he said, 'We are not destined to be cherished, you and I.'

"'Everyone cherishes you, Daddy. That's the problem.'

"'I chose my words poorly. Destined to be...' He touched my cheek, and then he took me into his arms. I hugged back, of course. I tried not to notice how excited he seemed, because that was probably a mistake, or my fault, in that little dress. It was all those little bitches' fault for not giving him a thing. 'Goodnight, Daddy,' I said, but he didn't let go, and from then on if I let him keep hugging it was my idea too. Now, I was no virgin. I'd had two or three boys in the past year and acquitted myself pretty well, but now I forgot everything – I thought he was about to rip me apart, leave me all bladders and strings on the road, because he had a tusk or something there, I could feel it, that they used for executing horrible little girls. I thought I was being punished for taking the car by being made to turn my father into a *beast*, something *unrecognizable*. And at the same time! – part of me knew I could lead him into that little dump and know just what to do, and so after all his bullying, I could make him do anything. But if anyone asked, he was just hugging his daughter.

"If he'd held me down and raped me, and trust me, you wouldn't have heard a peep out of Pru or my brothers, he still couldn't have raped me as completely as he did by just standing there and letting it all be up to me. Like a coward. Such a coward. I'll tell you what I did. I had this little trick for when things got bad. Just, you know, generally bad. I'd press my thumb and forefinger together, like this, just quietly down by my side. I'd press and press and think *Here I am, between these two fingertips. Whatever happens doesn't count, because I'm here, way down in the grooves of my fingerprints, only here.* Finally he let me go, and I gave him a little push and he sat down hard on the stairs. I said, 'Goodnight, Daddy,' and went back to the party. And here's the part I really don't recall, whether I took one of his friends out to a parked car, or only made him want to blow his brains out for not going.

"And then, even years afterward, when I was with Chris, sometimes, I'd…" Again she displayed a ring made of thumb and forefinger, the fingertips pressed white. "Not that he ever forced me, Chris never *had* to, but… That's a kind of force, too," she said vaguely.

"It was so bad," she said.

I don't know what she saw in my face then, but abruptly hers filled with remorse. She snatched up my hand and ardently kissed my palm. An onlooker, observing her lovely closed eyes above the bone of my thumb, would have assumed Julia adored me; she seemed martyred by adoration. Then she smoothed my hand back and forth in both of hers as if trying to chafe a small frozen animal back to life. "I'm sorry this is so *difficult* for you. It's difficult for me, too. Nicky, I just can't make any promises."

The only thing worse than living in despair is living in hope.

And You Lurch Toward Conclusion · Here Your Strange

The warm weather had come again, and the long windows were open in the refectory. Outside, a jet passed over with a noise like a vast ball bearing rolling on glass. I damp-mopped the wooden floor in practiced arcs. The folding chairs were stacked in their carts, the guests and volunteers had gone. Julia was in the kitchen finishing up the silverware, for which she had a knack. It was my favorite part of the day. When I reached the far wall and turned to admire my work, I saw a figure in the center of the refectory, motionless in the chalky light. He was dressed in dusty black jeans, cowboy boots, and a dark shirt, and his dark hair fell past broad shoulders. He was no less than six feet four. He was such an obvious heartthrob, in fact, that it should have been funny. It wasn't. "Are you here for lunch?" I said. "You missed it, but there's some leftovers."

"Jewels." He was British.

"Yes?"

"Julia?" he called. "I've come to get you."

"Just a moment," I said.

I went back into the kitchen. Julia stood with dripping hands and a white face. "Oh my God," she whispered. "It's Christopher. My husband."

"Ex-husband," I said weakly.

"I can't, Nicky, I can't see him now. Could you – I *can't*," she explained, and pattered out the back door.

In the refectory, I found Christopher half-crouching, half-craning, trying to peer through the serving hatch into the kitchen.

I said, "I'm sorry. She doesn't want to see you."

She'd called Chris a male Julia, so I'd always assumed he was dainty and auburn. But here was a dark bruiser, very long in the leg, with narrow hips and a wide, flat torso. His hands and deltoids were exaggerated, and he had the faintest beginnings of a gut. Sallow, hairless skin, like mine, but tightly packed with long muscle. Probably in his late thirties. Wide black brows, a columnar nose, and the full, smooth, subtly fashioned mouth of a stone pharaoh. His dusty hair slipped into his eyes, and he shook it away. He smelled like heated tent canvas. "Jules," he said, and started forward.

I stepped in front of him. Dear God, he was big. He eased me aside as if I were a sliding door, then made for the kitchen with a dancer's gait. One shoulder smacked the doorframe as he passed through. He was very, very drunk.

He walked around the worktable, rapped the counter, picked up an egg whisk and, weary of all egg whisks, dropped it on the floor. He stirred the suds in the dish sink with a pinky. He lifted a pot's lid and examined the contents with frank incredulity. "She's not here," he said.

"I'm sorry," I said. "I'll give her a message, if you like."

He nodded, striding past me. "Kind." He bypassed, thank God, the back door and went into the hall. I circled in front of him and stood there, chiefly because I was terrified to do so. He stumbled on my instep on his way past. "You're underfoot," he remarked. He halted before an office door decorated with a rhinestone crucifix and a quotation from Genet. "Hers," he said confidently and tried the knob. It was locked.

"Listen," I suggested.

Frowning, he twisted harder. A metallic ping, and the lock grated open. Christopher went in and flipped through the ledger on her desk. He peered into the kneehole to see if she was hiding there and almost overbalanced.

"Listen, you can't just come in here and start busting things up."

"But I am," he said reasonably. He pushed past me into the hall – use your head, Nick, why try to keep him from *leaving?* – and paused. "Perhaps in the sanctuary, clinging to the cross. A sense of drama, has our Julia. It is *our* Julia, isn't it?" he said, and gave me the same look he'd given the leftovers. Then I followed him into the church proper. "Shit, shit, shit," he said, pacing down the aisle in the fruitcakish light of the stained glass windows. "Not in the vestry." He turned and came toward me. "Out back, perhaps. Preaching to the birds."

I stepped in front of him once more. "Perhaps. But you're not joining the congregation."

Bored, he reached for me. I knocked his hands aside.

At once Christopher's smooth mouth warped and his nostrils flared. He swelled. His huge hands rose. Then he held himself perfectly still. I watched him force the amiable contempt back onto his lips. Finally he smiled – wasn't I a right little bugger? – and patted me on the head.

I punched him.

Or meant to. Second thoughts slowed it to a gesticulation: arm stuck out, hand curled. Still, he accepted this into his face and, nodding, sat down. He brushed his chin as if brushing away a crumb.

From under shapely brows he examined me. "They're getting younger. No offense meant, no offense in the world, but surely she can do better than you?"

"Yes. And apparently she can do worse."

"Clever," he remarked. "That's good. Apparently worse. That's good." He put up tentative fingers and began combing the hair from his face, very slowly. Since he couldn't seem to raise his head, it flopped back. Finally he tugged a black hairband from his pocket and whipped his hair dexterously into a ponytail. He lifted an arm. "Would you…"

I hauled him to his feet. He was heavy.

"Thank you."

"Okay."

"You helped me off my arse."

"You're welcome."

"That's good. Men must help each other off their arse."

I took a deep breath. "Let's go."

Christopher parted his lips in sadness or nausea and glanced around. "Yes, perhaps you're right. Let's go."

I escorted him out the front door of the sanctuary like a security guard walking a suspected shoplifter out of Bergdorf Goodman.

Outside, the sun dazzled us. A vast black motorcycle, a Harley, I thought, rested on its kickstand on the sidewalk in front of the church steps. He wove toward it. I said, "You came on that? You're not getting on that."

"No?" he said, surprised. "I thought I was."

"You'd kill yourself," I said wistfully. "You're drunk."

"Drunk. How right you are. Should have thought of that myself." He tried to brush his hair back again, but it wasn't in his face. "You are not catching me at my best," he confided. "You dismal little Hebrew *shite*. That trollop. Be shagging dogs and cats next." He shook my hand off. "I'll be fine," he assured me. He headed for the Harley again.

"How would you like your ribs kicked in?"

He stopped. "Oh, don't do that," he said. "I'll be sick."

"Come here." I grasped his arm. The muscle was ropy and warm. He let himself be led back into the church, and, when I saw the coast was clear, into the kitchen. Parking him before the rinse sink, I turned on the tap and said, "Here. Get some cold water on your face. I'll make coffee."

He studied the flowing stream.

"Come on."

Resting his elbows on the edge of the sink, he inclined his head slowly toward the water. When his head dipped below the level of his shoulders, something kicked inside him, and he vomited.

"Oh boy," I said.

Still puking, he waved a hand to indicate that I need not concern myself. The something kept kicking; I could see it through his shirt. "Oh," he said. His voice was clearer. He turned off the cold water, turned on the hot until it smoked, and drank calmly from the scalding stream. He spat. "My breath. What a nasty item. Poor Jules."

The door flapped open. "Jesus," Julia said.

I noticed she'd shaken her hair from her Moore Paint cap and tried to fluff it out.

She flung him stumbling away from the sink. "Thank you for not whoopsing directly on the dishes, at least. Nick, I'm so sorry. I had no right to subject you to my dirty business. That was wretched cowardice." She'd fished out a strip of cardboard box from the trash and was scraping his vomit out of the sink. "Christopher. You'll have to go."

"Hallo, Jules," he said. "Your boyfriend helped me off my arse. That was good of him. Men must all help each other off their arse. Arses." Wiping his mouth with the back of his hand, he gazed down at Julia with absolute pleasure. He wore the expression of a small child who'd been promised a trip to the circus if he was good, and who had not been good, and who'd been taken to the circus anyway. "How well you look," he said. "How well you look. I suppose this juvenile's been taking good care of you."

Standing before him, Julia braced herself, as against a gale. Her bare feet were spread and planted and her hands hung half-tensed at her sides, like a fighter's; she set the puke-stained cardboard on the sink's edge, so as to have both hands free. She seemed to stare at Christopher with her parted lips as much as with her eyes. "Chris, you shouldn't have come. We agreed."

"Listen, Jules, I said, we were in the church there and I said, surely you could do better than him? And he said, with a look, and surely not as well. Wasn't that good?"

"Not bad. Chris—"

"He said it better than that, actually. I make such a muck of things."

"Yes."

"He'd every right to hit me, I think. I was being a cunt."

"Yes. Chris, I'm not going to let you get started."

"You are, though. What is all this shit about your not living with me?"

"You're a drunk and a child."

"Bad luck for you. I'm staying."

"No."

"I love you. And you love me."

"That doesn't matter."

"You're my wife."

"*I am not your wife.*"

"You're my wife. Stop dancing *about.*" He gathered her close. She put out both arms hard to stop him, found she couldn't, and looked up at him, bottom teeth bared. "You have to go away, Christopher," she said into his grave and curious face.

"I don't. I have to stay."

She began to cry. "Please. Please. Why don't you just find some girls? Find lots of little girls."

"I've *been,*" he said impatiently. "*Won't* you kiss me?" He hunched to squash his face into her spiraling hair. "Oh God, Jules. Oh God. I've been so miserable. So miserable. Is that child with the nose still there? Send him away."

"You have to go, Christopher. Please. Chris, please."

"Oh God, Jules."

"*Please.*"

"Excuse me," I said, and left.

Out on the front steps, I seated myself, already thinking that I'd better rest, that I was embarked on an ordeal. It was a lovely day, breezy and warm, with the freshness of the air full of little sounds. I hoped this would come in handy if, in a while, I needed something to be good. I thought, *I'm not feeling this yet. I'll start feeling this in a while. This will be very bad.* From the open door behind me, a steady murmuring. His Harley leaned before me, black and dusty. I strolled over and touched a finger to the scarred chrome of the exhaust, which looked bright and cool. It burned me. After a while the voices stopped. I strolled back and peered into the kitchen.

Julia's forearms were still hard against Christopher's chest, her hands and fingers curved rigidly away from him. She was on tiptoe, her mouth joined to his. Their eyes were closed, and their heads barely moved, in tiny jerks. His big right hand cradled her head and his left covered the small of her back, a long, spatulate finger with a gold wedding band resting on her jeans just where, I knew, a small mole adorned the crease between her buttocks. I heard small noises from within her throat.

I went back to the front steps and sat down again.

In a few minutes, I heard a snorting, ripping roar, and saw them take off on the black Harley, Julia's arms tight around Christopher's back, her cheek pressed between his shoulder blades.

Well. That settled that.

In the kitchen, I found the sink still foul with his vomit. I took Julia's bit of cardboard and finished scraping it up. It wasn't bad. Almost pure liquor. Though some time in the not too distant past, he seemed to have been eating Spaghetti-O's. When I'd gotten the few solid bits up, I rinsed the sink with cold water and scrubbed it hard with cleanser, twice. Then I rinsed it with more cold water. Then I drenched it with near-boiling water from the power nozzle for a while. I sniffed and could smell nothing. My burned finger stung. I started on the pots.

I'll start feeling it pretty soon, I thought.

I felt, not for the first time, afraid of my heart and what it could do to me.

:　　:

I did not sleep that night, and in the kitchen the next day I picked things up, and set them down, very carefully. Julia did not return until I was mopping up after lunch. When I turned my face to her, it was like turning a chair to point the other way. She didn't seem to notice. It was just a face to her. She stood in the door, smiling weakly, holding herself gingerly. "Hi," she said. "I'm going home now and get some sleep. But I wanted to see you."

"Hello."

"What time is it. I missed lunch. I meant to call."

"That's all right."

"Did you get someone to cover for me?"

"It was fine."

"I didn't fuck him," she said wonderingly.

"No?"

"No."

"That's good," I said.

She nodded. Then her eyes hunted mine. "What do you mean?"

"Well, did you want to?"

"No."

"Well then, that's good."

"I mean, of course I wanted to. So much. But do you see?"

"I suppose I see."

"I sent him away."

"Uh huh. Why?"

"I had to send him away. Don't you see?"

"I guess I see."

"Be proud of me, Nicky, *please.* This was the hardest thing I've ever done."

"Proud of you," I said. "You don't expect much, do you?"

Her mouth opened in bewilderment.

I said, "I'm sorry. This is the wrong time for... Go home, Julia. Get some sleep. We'll talk some other time."

"You've folded all the chairs," she said. "If I could just sit down a minute."

I unfolded two chairs. We sat facing each other in the middle of the gleaming floor.

She said, "You look terrible."

"Probably."

"You haven't slept, either."

"No."

"You were being jealous of us."

I blew out an exasperated puff of air. "All right!" she cried. "All right!

"Maybe I never made it clear," she went on. "What you've meant to me. All those years – and maybe you don't know that so much of it was ugly – but I still thought of you as my dear friend. And it helped so much."

"Yeah, I was here being your dear friend, and you were off in Paris fucking Christopher."

"We weren't fucking. We were making love," she shouted.

"What's the difference?" I shouted.

"I forget," she said, and snickered.

She rubbed her red eyes and said, "So, what now?"

"I don't know. But I can't go on being your dear friend anymore."

"Then what's left is the other," she said.

"Oh Christ. Let's just –"

"Yes. I haven't been looking at this properly. But now we're being sensible."

"Please go home and get some sleep. This is more of your melodrama."

"No. We're being sensible now. Tonight's Friday night." She smiled with her lips, and then I saw her work the smile over herself as one works one's hand into a tight glove. Her eyes smiled and her small rib cage rose. Then she was a beautiful young woman, eager and alert and only a little fatigued from the excitements of youth and beauty. At the same time, she was smiling with me at the success of this masquerade. "Let's go on a date. I'll wear lipstick. I'll carry a *purse*. It's not too late for this day not to be terrible."

"Julia," I said feebly, "this is grotesque."

"I knew you'd be pleased," she said.

:   :

I'd picked a handful of daisies for her. She'd pinned them to the table with a finger and was now gently worrying at a petal with her thumb. Absently, she began to pluck the petals one by one, then caught herself. She looked up with an apologetic smile. We were at a hippie restaurant in town – my choice – a collective where the wait staff hunkered by your table and told you their names and I could afford to pay our tab. Since the weather was nice, I'd chosen a table out on the sidewalk, and there we sat, Julia and I, in silence. Her hair was still damp from the bath. She wore a dark red velvet dragon-lady sheath, gray sweatsocks, and beaded moccasins. For a purse, she had a Flintstones lunch box. She wore coral lipstick. Beneath the tan, her skin was like paste, but the kind of which false diamonds are made. I was just about ready to call it quits for the evening. Maybe we could try again when we were less tired. Or maybe we could just – She stopped smiling. "Oh my God, Nicky. Oh my dear fucking God," she said, and I turned to see Christopher striding over the railing that divided the restaurant from the sidewalk.

Drawing a chair from a nearby table, he seated himself between us. "No, I'm not eating," he told the waitress. "Just a double Wild Turkey, no ice. I see. Then just tea. Ordinary Darjeeling, please, nothing *herbal*. *Well*." He surveyed us genially. The flesh of his face looked like sun-eroded snow. I doubted he'd slept, either. "*Well*. *What* awkwardness. I said to myself, there can only be a limited number of places in this foul little encampment where Julia might conceivably have taken him. What odds, after all, she'd do dinner herself? Surely you've noticed by now the woman can't cook? Except, of course, for her famous *chili*," he sneered. "Isn't it good?" he asked radiantly.

"Oh, Christopher," Julia wailed. "You're on your ass."

"Do you know, I believe I'm not. Do you know, I believe I've drunk myself sober. Now. What is all this piss about your not living with me?"

"Oh Chris, you promised you'd go."

"An error."

"We discussed this last night. We discussed *everything*."

"Didn't we, though?"

"I cannot do this all over again," she whispered. "I can't."

"Yes, that's what I'm counting on."

I said, "I think—"

"Respect your elders, sonny. How well you look, Jules. How well you look when you're not in those fetid little lumberjack rags. And all for little what's-his-name."

"You have to go, Chris. There has to be an end to this."

"Not everything in the world has a beginning, a middle, and an end, Jules. This isn't one of your tidy little fables of redemption. Has she mentioned those? They're new. Just a page or so. Apparently Christ must come down and attend to her muddle personally. In the absence of His blessing, she'll just keep changing her outfits. And with each new outfit, a different personality. Whatever-your-name-is-*Nick*, do you honestly think you can keep up?"

"I don't know."

"Well, I can. And that's why she's coming with me."

"You make her unhappy."

"I didn't make her unhappy. God did. Or Daddy, she gets them mixed. I am simply proposing to make the best of God's bad bargain. Did you get that, Jules? Isn't that quite high-flown-sounding enough to be going on with? Look, what exactly do you plan to *do* in this bucolic vacuum?"

She began, "As I said—"

"Admirable. Saint Julia of the Saucepans. Let's both write Nick thumping great checks and let him get on with it. What else? Have you been writing? *Will* you write?"

"I've been considering—"

"You haven't a single sensible idea," he complained.

"Look at your idea of a sensible idea. Living with you."

"I don't claim that it's sensible. I merely remark that you're going to do it. Because, in fact, you want to. *I* wasn't the one who came down to New York and threw herself at me. Begging. Because she simply couldn't *bear* it. I fucking well bear what I'm given to bear. I couldn't have lasted four years with you otherwise. And those years are not over. *Are they.* Julia? Well?

"Hel-*lo-o?*" he said.

"Julia," he whispered, *"for God's sake."*

With a great effort, she drew her small head up.

"Christopher," she said, as if struck by a fresh idea. "Would you please go?"

"You want me to go," he said dully. He touched his cheek with his fingertips.

"Yes."

"You're choosing this child over me," he said.

"I am choosing not to be with you. Because you're bad to me. You're bad to me. And I deserve better."

"With *him?* Oh Christ. You get everything so wrong. This child's not like us, Jules. He has an *attention* span. You'll play house with him until something distracts you, and then you'll move on, and he'll heartache over you his whole life, and you'll wonder why he doesn't want to be your little *chum.* Now listen. I have tried living without you. And it is simply not tenable. *It ain't happenin', maaaaan."* His pronunciation was pedantic. "Can't we keep this on a grown-up basis?

You're b-b-bad to me. Can we, at a bare minimum, continue this in private?"

"*No. I can't. I can't*, I cannot *be* with you anymore, *ever*, Christopher, *please*."

Softly, he said, "But I know you, Jules. I know you. There isn't anyone made for you the way I am. It can't be right for us to be apart. I know we haven't been happy. Quite possibly we won't be. But we're meant to be together."

She was crying. *"Please."*

"If I leave now, you'll always be alone. No matter how many men you have. No matter how they love you."

"I *know. Please* go."

" 'Please.' I don't understand this 'please.' You know that I love you. That you're everything to me. And you want to destroy all that, and take everything away from both of us, and leave us solitary forever. 'Please.'"

"Christopher."

"What lovely manners. Please."

"All right," I said, and stood.

"*Pretty* please," he said.

I grabbed him by the throat.

I think I intended to pick him up by the Adam's apple and throw him… It wasn't too well planned out.

The entire street seemed to heave toward me. Gripping my shirt, Christopher hoisted me off my feet, my hand still on his neck. His smooth pharaoh's lips were skinned back over blazing horse teeth. His gums were black. He had no eyes.

A flash of metal distracted us. Julia was on her feet. Her red lips were skinned back over blazing cat's teeth. She gripped like a weapon, not her knife, but her teaspoon. I guess it was closest to hand.

We gazed at her, appalled.

Christopher set me down again. He raised his hands chest high in surrender. He achieved a smile.

"Well played, young Nicholas." He patted my shoulder. "Game, set, and match. Goodbye, Jules."

He stepped over the railing and was gone.

Then the outsized, ripping din of the Harley sprang into being. It receded up Buffalo and bore right on Eddy, heading for State Street, Route 17, New York. You could see it striking Julia, like wind on a pond. Everyone was staring. I said, "Check, please."

She yanked me close and pulled my mouth down against hers. The spoon in her fist scraped my temple. "This is not Chris's evening. It's ours. It's *ours*," she said. "He doesn't get to take things away from me anymore."

: :

Clutching each other's waists, we stumbled up the hill. Inside the Palms, we began to giggle. "So that's the guy," I said. "He's immense."

"Isn't he large?"

"I thought he'd kill me."

"He seldom kills people. Isn't he lovely?"

"Are all your husbands like that?"

"Ex-husbands. And doesn't he drink? Doesn't he drink much more than I do? He had such a hold on me. Oh Nicky, *had!*"

Julia could not stop smoothing my forearm, rubbing my shoulder with her cheek, nudging my thigh with hers. The bartender brought us two more shots. "These are on the house. I never saw you two happy before."

"We're celebrating my divorce!" Julia sang.

"Divorce? Then give me that." She made them doubles.

We walked back to her house in silence again. As soon as we'd closed the door, Julia dragged my hands over her breasts. The velvet was thick and I wasn't sure I'd found them, but I felt desire engage

139

my belly with a jolt and draw me forward, like the chain that draws a car through a car wash. Pulling off my shirt, I said, "Don't you have to...?" "It's in," she told me, and glanced at her watch. "Should be good for another hour." She slipped off her dress, stepped out of her shoes, and stood clad only in lipstick and gray sweatsocks. Five years later, she still wasn't bothering to suck in her belly. Her russet cunt was still a lush blot. Her calves and forearms were brown, her body white, her nipples slack pink discs. She held her arms awkwardly and seemed dazed to find herself all skinny and bare. Then she raised a foot and hooked her finger in a sock. On impulse I said, "Leave them on." She lowered her foot. "Come here," I said. She shuffled over. I lifted her chin and her mouth opened to my tongue as if she were being fed. My prick ached, a monstrous lever prying at the base of my spine. My first thrust would bruise the underside of her heart. *Good.* I was sick of this deal whereby Julia hurt me and Christopher hurt Julia and I never got to hurt anyone. I bit at her neck and squeezed her buttocks. I gripped her between the legs, and she was dry there, cool and fragile. I stopped.

I kissed her docile mouth, then knelt and touched the piano-wire tensity of the tendons behind her knees. Her brush tickled my nose. She placed hands on my head, in benediction or restraint. "I've wanted to kiss your cunt all summer," I murmured. This sounded polite. I was already looking beyond an unhappy first night to the necessary work of love ahead. I applied my mouth to her; she was clean and slightly stale, like water kept too long in a canteen. But eventually her knees began to move indecisively, the flesh of her meager thighs warmed and loosened, and I carried her to the bed and deposited her on her back. She placed sock-clad feet against my chest. When we were joined, everything would be all right. Her nipples were more or less erect. Kneeling with my thighs bracketing her hips, I pressed my shaft against her slickened vulva and slid it back and forth, as one checks the bolt of a rifle. Her face held a desperate serenity. I stopped.

"It's all right," she whispered.

I centered myself against her soft folds.

"Do it."

Half-hidden by the curve of her hip, her thumb and forefinger were pressed together so that the fingertips were white. She saw me noticing and let go.

I got up, walked to the bathroom, turned the cold water on full in the shower, and jumped in.

When I returned, Julia was dressed and sitting on the edge of the bed, fingers knotted between her knees. I sank down next to her, still dripping. "That looks so painful," she said, and tried to take hold of it. "At least let me suck you. I know I can do that."

"And can I watch your hands while you do it?" I bent to pick up my pants and a tide of exhaustion coasted forward, submerging me. I said, "I quit."

"I know!" Julia said, and began to weep.

"I'm going to New York. Just as soon as the reverend can replace me. We'll talk tomorrow about replacing me. Actually, would you like my job?"

"*Please* shut up." She cried in earnest then, thin shoulders quaking. Her nose ran, and she didn't wipe it. "I would have given you everything. You didn't have to mind about me."

It was difficult to fasten my clothes. I finished dressing, and she followed me to the door. She said, "Can't you even kiss me goodbye?"

I put my arms around her. "Goodbye? I'll be seeing you *tomorrow*," I said exhaustedly.

"Can't you –" and she began to kneel. I tightened my embrace, but she made herself dead weight, and at last I let her down with a thump. She lifted her hands to my belt buckle. I took and held them.

"I can't keep losing people!" she cried.

SEVEN

Illumined Limbs Betray You · You Must Change

The first two things I did when I arrived in New York, ten days before my twenty-third birthday, were to grow a scraggly little chin beard – a soul patch – and give myself a tattoo. I sterilized three needles at Suzanne's gas burner and bundled them together with thread to get a nice strong line. My mother was eager to see, then disappointed I hadn't done something pretty. But working the needles along my leg, tongue extended and teeth bared, I'd known what I wanted. Ugliness, definiteness, a scar: physical proof a wound had closed.

I found a fourth-floor walkup on Fourth Street and B. The craters in the walls writhed with BX cable and paint-globbed dust mice, and one wall of the tiny kitchen was covered with orange vinyl tiling, which clacked when you pressed on it. But it was cheap. I dumped my Canada Dry box, my case of tools, two plastic milk crates full of art books, and my duffel bag of worn black clothes in the center of the floor. Then I went down to scout the terrain.

The corner bodega bore a sign: *"We Accept"* WIC/FOOD STAMPs. A chubby Latino in a red tank top had driven a rusted Buick up on the sidewalk and toiled beneath it with a friend. His family sat on their stoop and watched a TV they'd placed by the curb. Here was a roll-down steel grate blazoned with a spray-paint mural: an LSD-lush sky and a large tombstone reading RIP SHARITA • CAMI • JOSO • MIGUEL • NEWCOMERS 4-EVER WE LOVE YOU '82. A carefully rendered Betty Boop shed tears. Nearby, a homeless woman hurled a can of pineapple slices against a cinderblock wall, trying to burst it open. A young black man walked by with three cellophane-wrapped steaks, hawking them to passersby. I noted mysterious storefronts operating behind painted-over windows. Inside one open door: gilt papier-mâché globes, purple sateen bat-wings passing through a sewing machine, a whining circular saw, a young man bent over a light table. A couple paced down Thirteenth Street on opposite sidewalks, arguing over the parked cars. "Asshole, you fucked up for the las' time," she shouted. "No, I didn't fuck up for the last time, 'cause I didn't fuck up for the first time," he said. At the corner, still hollering, she crossed to meet him and they walked shoulder to shoulder down the avenue.

When I'd looped back to the bodega, I nerved myself, strode inside, and made my choices from half-empty shelves bearing unfamiliar brands of goods; I selected a jar of Goya honey. Then, cradling my groceries the way a schoolgirl cradles her books, I waited while the boy at the cash register gossiped with his friends in Spanish. I tried to summon a phrase of easy camaraderie from my labors with *Nuestros Vecinos Dos*, but they were preoccupied with an associate at the pay phone who was pleading with someone named Inez and flicking the change return with a finger.

"*Hola*," I finally muttered to the cashier.

"*Shalom*," he said, stone-faced, and dropped my honey in the bag with a clack.

When I opened it, I found a chunk of actual honeycomb, a clot of wax that filled the jar. I threw it out and next time bought Golden Blossom.

:   :

Work was not hard to find. I hauled furniture for a moving company, proofread for a law firm, and sold Christmas trees off the sidewalk from midnight to 8 A.M. for two Israeli brothers, cramming the trees through a funnel-like gadget and wrapping them, as they emerged, in plastic netting. But the job that suited me best was with a downtown bike messenger company. Dodging through traffic was like diving from trees. You forbade yourself to think, trusted your reflexes and, afterward, knew you still had some usable luck.

I'd rented a place not far from Adam's. His friends had dubbed his apartment the Bunker. It was a basement storefront, its display window covered over in plywood and expanded steel. The front door sported a massive padlock instead of a knob. The floor was half linoleum and half bare concrete, strewn with scavenged throw rugs and sections of carpeting. Adam's mattress lay in the back, walled off by metal bookshelves. Layers of old quilts had been nailed to the ceiling to shield the upstairs neighbors from the noise of his band's rehearsals. Up on cinderblocks in case of burst pipes stood some fifteen thousand dollars' worth of guitars, including the red '64 Fender Jaguar with the Duncan pickups, the scuffed gold-flake Gretsch Duke, the Martin acoustic with the abalone inlay, and the pinstriped black '69 Precision bass. Mattress and floor were buried under a sort of moraine: a steel-toed boot no one had come forward to claim, a xeroxed Kingsmen fake-book, a set of barbells, a ceramic hash pipe shaped like the Starship *Enterprise,* a tattered copy of *JUGGS* magazine, and dubs or originals of every album on which Dick Dale had ever played. I recall Adam kicking his way through the dreck, clasping me about the ribs, then lifting me and thumping my feet on the floor as if trying to loosen ketchup from a recalcitrant bottle. "You came!" he cried. "You poor puppy, you finally actually came! We'll pick your carcass clean in a *week*."

Adam had become what metalheads call a "monster," someone who could play vast numbers of notes quickly and cleanly. He also had a prodigious musical memory. Having once dialed your number on a touch-tone phone, he'd thereafter be able to hum it to you on request. He'd held his band, the Detonators, together for three or four years now. This made them, by East Village standards, an institution. Of course, I was on the guest list whenever they played. Adam's warmup chords would ruffle my shirt. I remember shouting above the ruckus, my lips by a young woman's ear. Now and then the lights caught the chrome scratchplate of Adam's Jag and made a blinding blot, a gap in the known universe through which the outer brightness could be glimpsed. If they got their favorite 1 A.M. spot on the bill, Adam would close the set by announcing, "Ladies and Gentlemen, it's once again time for our Question Mark and the Mysterians Medley!" Then they'd play "96 Tears," repeating the chorus until the regulars who came to every show stormed the stage and unplugged the amps. We'd leave near three, stinking of cigarettes down to our underwear, feeling, out in the sudden silence, as if our ears were crammed with cotton wool. The sidewalk would be startlingly hard beneath our feet. A new world.

The Bunker served as a sort of clubhouse, and you could always find an assortment of musicians and artists scattered through the debris. Oftenest in attendance was Joey Hale, the Detonators' melancholic, faunlike bassist. When not with the band, Joey made cartoonish, extensively captioned autobiographical drawings about growing up queer on an East Texas soy farm. He shaded his figures very carefully; they seemed cast in lead, with tiny skulls and big bottoms. For a living, he tended bar. I also met a photographer/dress-designer/office temp by the name of Essa Travers, and a painter/poet/margarine heir named Walter Mock whose hair, as it happened, was the color of butter. He did abstract acrylics on slowly spinning 45 records. These people became my friends.

I recall two coffeepots on the hot plate outside Dojo, twin plumes of steam swerving in unison with the chill breeze as we sat at a sidewalk table over brown rice and vegetables and discussed our lives with the eager intentness of near-strangers who have discovered themselves to be foolish in similar ways. I recall afternoon light in underfurnished apartments. We took the Detonators' van to East Hampton, bouncing around on the steel floor in back with a case of beer. Once there, we disposed our white limbs over the gray shore. Joey fired his long body into the surf and then, when we were sure he'd drowned, emerged to stretch out on the sand, happily isolate. Walter prowled despondently amongst the daughters of writer/producers, his hair flopping about his peering eyes in two wonderfully-cared-for yellow swoops. "It's no good," he reported back. "Their fathers all work for my father." "Walt, your dad's three thousand miles away." "You don't know him," he said. Phone lines divided the sky into great vacant trapezoids. Weeds scribbled up and down the dunes. I sketched, then lay with my head on Essa's stomach. She and I appeared to have a great, wordless understanding, but once back in town we somehow lost the thread of it.

I was then busy with an artistic crisis. It was 1983 or so. The heyday of Minimalism was past. People had tired of my beloved SoHo, had tired of austere, iconic images showcased by expanses of mold-made paper. There was an influx of young impresarios who stocked their new galleries like junk shops and promoted them like cabarets, and of suburban painter-brats who singly and severally did not give a fuck, and these kids were not tramping across any twilit fields. They were having a party. And this was all going on north of Houston Street, right in my neighborhood: Scharf and his wiggle-tailed, candy-hued 'toons, Schnabel and his sticky crockery, Fischl and his naughty patio scenes, Haring and his radium-dogs. It was still understood that SoHo was "the art world," while the East Village was merely a "scene," but it was also understood – even the editorial writers understood – that the scenesters were winning, and that the old avant-garde, with their spotless khakis and "shocks" of gray hair, with their MoMA-certified work and Gwathmey Siegel-designed beach houses and rather dear notions of purity, were *over*, and would thenceforth have to content themselves with wealth and fame. I studied slides of my rigorously refined murals. They now seemed the sort of thing an enlightened Chamber of Commerce might commission for a third-tier municipal airport. Sighing, I began to teach myself to schmear.

I developed a crush on Jonathan Borofsky. His disintegrating bunny-men were then making quite a splash. When he drew a head in three-quarter view, he'd set the eyes artlessly side by side, leaving the skull halibut-flat. Borofsky shaded his figures as a schoolchild shades a cylinder, and the shadows were ashy, made by adding black. You were *never* supposed to add black. He employed a cacophony of cheap magentas, smudgy sepias, shameless harvest golds and powder blues. Impressed by the exuberant badness of his technique, I returned to figuration (*I am returning*, I told myself, *to figuration*) and began a series of outsized females with bumptious heads and sloppy limbs. In a doubting moment, I copied out an epigram of Matisse's on the necessity of influence. It was a very comforting quote. I have since mislaid it.

Still, it was an uphill path for someone who'd schooled himself for years in the triangular organization of the picture plane. Trying to work this way left me sullen and stupid and yearning for sweets and sleep. My friends were floundering, too. As we sat drinking in my apartment one afternoon, I started aimlessly snipping at one of my newer efforts, and soon we were all solemnly cutting my work into strips.

One night when the bars had closed and bed would have seemed like defeat, we began wandering the Latino badlands between C and D. Our talk was a little too peppy. We were not as comfortable there as we liked to think. At length we coasted to a halt before an abandoned tenement. The front door was painted bright red. I'd reached the state of drunkenness where this seemed an important truth. It was padlocked. An official notice had been pasted across it. The windows had been sealed with sheet steel. Someone pointed out that the metal in one second floor window was loose. I wondered if I could reach the ladder leading to the fire escape... actually, I was *climbing* the fire escape, to cheers and admonitions from below. I squeezed through the window and into blackness and the cellar-smell of earth and cement and damp-softened wood, then clambered and fumbled down to the front hall, where the light of the streetlamps strained through scratches and pinholes in the black-painted fanlight. When I tried to open this, it fell into the street and shattered. The sound was unreal and musical. I popped my head up in the opening and grinned down on the upturned faces.

There'd been some fire damage to the upper floors, we found, but the ground floor front apartment seemed in fine shape, and big enough for performances, readings, a show. And it was, apparently, all ours. The next day Adam dug out his hacksaw and dealt with the padlock. A stage electrician friend of Joey's helped turn on the electricity. Painting, we decided, was easier than cleaning, so we each bought a gallon of our favorite color and made the place quite festive. At the end of each night, we'd sprawl among the drop cloths, drinking and chatting and admiring our fatigue, and Essa and I would do a little mild, comradely canoodling as Walter made unhappy wisecracks and Joey reckoned the work still to be done. It put me pleasantly in mind of high school. Back then I'd always envied the kids in Thespians. As each school play approached, they'd throw private work-parties to finish the sets, and these were always attended by the prettiest and most interesting girls, all sporting ragged T-shirts and paint-freckled noses and having affairs, as I understood it, right and left. Now, reclining like a pasha athwart Essa's powerful, leotard-clad lap, I proposed an anti-exhibition: we'd provide scissors and encourage visitors to snip out pieces of the art to keep. When there was nothing left, we'd close. It was Essa's idea to call it the Take It Away Show.

Walter and I drafted a press release and were astonished to actually get press. There was even a brief article in the *Daily News*: 'PUNK' ARTISTS TAKE IT AWAY. I told the reporter we were the Fourth Street Collaborative – this was a phone interview, and I didn't have to keep a straight face – and so we were duly called. Her description was pretty accurate. One entered the gallery to a tape of aimless riffs on a bass guitar. The lights were red and blue: Essa's friend again. We'd turned the front room into a maze by hanging clear shower curtains, which Essa had silk-screened with floral and military motifs. Walter did some paintings on snippable flexi-discs, which we hung from the ceiling, and Joey daubed one of his anxious cartoon narratives on tarpaper and stapled it to the floor. In one corner was a looming woman guyed upright with fishing line and reinforced inside by bent wire hangers affixed with blobs of tub sealant. I'd constructed her from rolls of heavy paper stenciled with my new "trademark" splotches of random color. Inside her we'd set an egg timer on a tin plate, to magnify the ticking. In the other corner of the labyrinth, a gaunt figure lay completely mummified in masking tape. Me. "It's *got* to be you, Nick," Joey had said. "No one else is passive enough." Two or three times an evening, the gallery would be closed while I hopped and shuffled to the back door to relieve myself, but aside from that, I did find lying there for hours disturbingly easy. The coiled tape buzzed in my nose, rich and rank. It filtered the light gold. Sometimes a visitor shyly snipped a bit of my tape, or prodded me with a curious foot, and I obliged with a wriggle, but mostly I lay in my pungent gold cocoon and dreamt of fame, of my swarthy and brooding face on the cover of *ARTnews*, of a piece in the Whitney Biennial and shows at International With Monument, or Fun, or – disloyally – at eminent SoHo galleries like Mary Boone, Leo Castelli, Nan Parrish. And I dreamt of love.

"I've never met a guy like you for convincing girls they don't want to fuck," Adam said. He suffered from no such difficulty. If you were a single female, south of Fourteenth Street and of forty, the safest thing was to assume you'd eventually sleep with him. He was not particularly comely. His eyes had a staring look, and his cheeks were red, as if freshly slapped. His thick back passed uninterruptedly into thick legs, bear-fashion. He dressed, except in the harshest weather, in one of half a dozen stolen short-sleeved green hospital orderly's shirts and ragged cut-offs; his mighty globular calves seemed impervious to cold. But Adam was also naturally kind, sexually efficient, and a stranger to shame and memory. He'd make himself convenient, a jolly mutt with whom one might toss the stick until bored. He remained on excellent terms with all. "There's a lot of women out there."

"There's also a lot of men. And they got there first."

"Wait. They have no staying power."

He was right. Sometimes in those years I tried to seize women as I'd seized Terry, and sometimes I tried to ease them into bed through such a gradual series of adjustments that they drifted away in puzzlement. Still, I did, for example, spend a few nights with Essa. Beneath mine, her pale body became loaflike and unwieldy. I was using a condom for the first time. When I got going, she'd say, "Calm down, calm down." If I managed to come, she'd say, "There you go." And a few young women were impressed by the *News* article. There was a cheery, chubby NYU student of nineteen who had dyed her hair sarcastically yellow, with decided black roots that seemed to say: *You don't think I'm actually* blonde, *do you?* Also, an elfin video store clerk with translucent ears. She wore at all times a necklace of big wooden beads, which left our chests mottled with bruises. Well, brief and joyless amours were what a young artist ought to have while forgetting a doomed passion, probably. In any case, I was not discontent.

One night we threw a record-release party at the Bunker for a new Detonators cassette. All the regulars brought friends. By midnight, the crowd spilled out the door and up onto the sidewalk. It was hard not to feel affection for such a mob of people, so many of whom knew my work. I noticed Joey cuddling with a beautiful young black woman by the fridge. Unless he'd changed his proclivities, this seemed unfair. Sort of dog-in-the-manger. She was delicate, in floppy checked knickers, a man's blazer whose sleeves hid her knuckles, a bowler hat that almost hid her eyes. She was blue-black. Joey leaned against the refrigerator door and she leaned back, laughing, into his arms. I felt she was putting on some kind of show. When they parted,

I wandered over. She was licking her contact lens with a pointed tongue. Her irises were spiced with crushed terra-cotta, her nose was smooth and minute. Her top lip was a dusty purple and her bottom lip faded to pink, with a faintly shining bluish rim. "Hello," I said, defeated.

"Oh, hi," she said in a clear precise voice, looking queasily about. "I was actually gonna come over, but I was afraid I might step in something. Joey said I should go talk to you." She popped the lens in and blinked experimentally.

"Why?"

"He said I was wasting too much time with faggots and I should go talk to a real man."

"What do you think?"

"That I been wasting too much time with real men. We don't have to keep chit-chatting at this rate, do we?"

"No."

"Good. I'm tired."

"Why?"

"We're chit-chatting again."

"Which one is he?"

"Who?"

"The ex-boyfriend you're all knotted up over. The one you wanted to spite by necking with Joey."

It brought her up short. "You got a fresh fucking mouth on you," she observed. She worked her own gorgeous two-toned mush in a dissatisfied manner. "Listen," she said, "you enjoying this party a lot?"

Out on the street, she said, "My, that was decisive of me. Don't jump to any conclusions," she added.

"You haven't said who."

"The beanstalky one with the Zorro hat."

"You like your men skinny?"

"I ain't liked you yet."

We passed one bar and coffeehouse after another. Finally we crossed the no-man's-land of Houston Street into SoHo. Enemy territory. "Where are we walking?"

"I dunno. These places all stink."

"My name's Nick."

"I'm Charlotte Keane. These places stink. Don't make any assumptions, but would you like to come up?" She indicated a steel door set with a tiny square of safety glass. "We're home."

Inside, the halls were painted a glossy pale gray. Charlotte had a studio apartment, neat and bare and almost taller than it was wide. A miniature TV screen set into her intercom displayed a twitching monochrome image of the vestibule. I noted plastic Parsons tables piled with copies of *Artforum* and *ARTnews.* A drafting board with a T-square. A big old wooden flat file. In a corner, an array of artists' portfolios. Two walls of the room were lined with cardboard cartons – she would have fit easily into the smallest – neatly labeled in magic marker. OLD TOPS 3. FAKE FUR SCRAPS. 70S STYLE MAGS. HATS C. PATTERN SCRAPS (GEOMETRIC, CLOTH). She put on a John Zorn album, turned it up, turned it down, made an espresso for me and steamed milk for herself. Gleaming new, the machine emitted an irate hiss. She grimaced again and set a hand on her waist. "It's not anything," she explained. "Pyloric channel ulcer. Looked it up in my mom's Merck Manual. She's a doctor. My dad's a doctor, too. Isn't that fascinating. You like the place?"

"It's a hovel."

"Chit-chat."

"You just move in?"

"No, I have a lot of boxes."

"You're an artist."

"I'm in printing paper sales. I'll be an artist when I get some more shows."

Sympathetically: "It's tough getting a gallery."

"Oh, I'm with Nan Parrish. I just need to have some shows."

"Ah. Well, I'm a messenger."

"How real."

"Chit-chat," I said, examining the flat file. "What's in here?"

"Don't look," she said, without inflection or emphasis, and I slid a drawer open. Inside I found ranks of palm-sized paintings on wood. She'd taken frayed, scraped bits of magazine photos or fabric and collaged them over muted sketches in oil: hands, flames, bones. They suggested diagrams for unbuildable gadgets, or half-effaced blueprints for structures of obscure purpose and claustral design. They were tartly lovely and – strict in their elisions – called the eye to order. My own pyloric channel twitched.

"He's cruel, in fact," she said, gazing sightlessly down on her work. "How come I always pick the cruel ones? The icky kind of cruel, the kind that's all, *Oh, I'm sorry.* Meant it, too. I'm the one who left him, so how come I feel so bereft? How come that? He had this li'l habit – Oh. Boredom. No."

I went to lay avuncular hands on her shoulders.

They landed on her breasts. These were very pointy, and therefore seemed to be the center of her agitation. Her nipples burrowed against my palms like the noses of gerbils. If I could just quiet them down… She clamped her hands over mine, then released them. "Do you have to do that?"

"Um, I think so."

She squirmed out of my grasp, then turned and held me. "This is complicated," she muttered. "Don't kiss me yet." Then she shoved me away. "Hugging you, my God. You just find a woman you like and grab 'em by the titties? I'm not hugging you. You think I need another man who doesn't know how to act?"

"I'm sorry. I don't know what you need."

"You for damn sure don't."

And I'd planned to be so tender! Charlotte smirked at my confusion. "You're not good at this, are you? Don't apologize. If you were good at it, I for damn sure wouldn't want to speak to you again. Now get lost. I'm tired. You tire me."

But at the door she scritched my soul patch with a thumbnail and said, "First thing we do, we get rid of *that*."

:   :

After the Take It Away Show closed, the Fourth Street Collaborative was stumped for a second act. We'd sent a press release to the police, too, and were rather pleased when they re-padlocked the place. But now we lacked a venue, or even a new project we could agree on. Nearly two hundred people had left their addresses in the "TIAS" guest book. It would have been nice to invite them to something. We played for time with a xeroxed 'zine called *Razzoo*. Like most affairs of its kind, it employed a sort of scrapbook aesthetic, and achieved formal unity largely by means of a staple gun. *Razzoo* featured covers decorated by hand with sparkle-glue, as well as photocopied body parts and a poem on absence by Essa, out of which we sliced a hole in each copy. Thin stuff, and we knew it. I can't speak for the others, but I wasn't giving the matter my full attention.

When I called Charlotte, I had the wit to keep matters on a professional footing. I asked if she knew a good place to get slides done and invited her to an opening. We went to the opening and to dinner and, at the end of the evening, moving with deliberation, I bussed her cheek as she stood stock-still by her armored front door. When four or five evenings had gone by this way, I reached out a palm and smoothed it over the satiny spot I meant to kiss. She inclined her head to accommodate me, so I traced those astonishing lips with a light thumb. Dartingly she kissed my wrist. Then she took hold of it and, as if my arm were a rope, hauled me near, hand over hand.

I was too dazed with triumph to properly enjoy what followed. But the pattern of our courtship had been set.

A number of buildings in SoHo have stairs that run from the street to the top floor in one long, unbroken diagonal. I recall the sense of hope in my calf muscles as we climbed them. They seemed to lead to heaven, but they'd lead to yet another gallery opening: folding tables loaded with plastic cups of wine, the almost fruity smell of fresh whitewash, and intricate shoals of art and acquaintance. I was used to beer and to walls less faultlessly white, but basically we both knew the drill at gatherings like these. Me especially. Printmakers are small fry to a gallery owner; far more than painters, we sell our work through branching chains of friends and relatives, and are always on the prowl for the enthusiastic amateur, the well-heeled architect or dentist who enjoys the scene and may want to play patron. I was aware of being Charlotte's New Boyfriend in the eyes of those I met, and sometimes I suspected she was dating a man of my attainments and looks in much the same way that a rich girl might affect ragged jeans. But the bone of her shoulder was delicious in my palm, and delicious also was the envy of other men. It wasn't so bad reimagining that *ARTnews* cover as his'n'hers. We were a striking couple. Everyone thought so. We thought so ourselves. I'd descend with her toward food and bed each night with a measure of tranquillity, rubbing musingly at the spot where my beard had been.

I briefed Charlotte about Julia. She listened with mounting horror. "I need something like you in my life," she concluded. "I've had everything way too easy. That girl left you a *mess*," she said proudly. Then: "Oh, Mister Face. Don't you know little girls always dream of some handsome wounded man they can nurse back to health?"

"What if he's not handsome?"

"Well, I ain't a little girl anymore, neither," Charlotte said. "Anyhow. Now you're with *me*."

"Yes." And I nodded.

Her fine large eyes misted over with unease. "She musta really been *something*."

My living room looked much cozier once Charlotte moved her cartons into it. They dwarfed my lone Canada Dry box, but I didn't mind. I loved watching her rummage through them, seeking raw materials for her wardrobe or her work. Sometimes Charlotte would dress as a form of doodling, trying one barbaric combination after another. At last she'd announce in triumph, "Now! Now I look like a *ho'!*" She'd pivot in my arms then, smiling coarsely up at me under thickened eyelids, all at once a little B-girl. Her gifts as a mime had made her the darling of Skidmore's art department.

While there she'd learned to make her own sketchbooks, and now she taught me: cutting the boards, smoothing the paste, wrapping the cloth, stitching in the paper. These we filled at a great rate. She sat for me often. Charlotte had a sidling way of entering a room. Her eyes were large and considering, her fingers quick. She'd been an only child and a star student; she was used to being the prettiest, the most gifted, the most industrious. She was used to being the black girl, to being looked at.

Melville devoted a chapter to The Whiteness of the Whale. I, whose horizons are bed-sized rather than ocean-sized, could easily do one on The Blackness of the Girlfriend. Charlotte's knuckles were inky, but her breasts swelled from her ribs with a faint yellow luminousness. Her vaccination scar glinted like a flake of mica. Her pubis, at first, daunted me: peppercorn pubic curls, outer labia black as the lips of a Doberman. The inner ones glared like a dog's pink tongue. *All* of her daunted me; she was perfect and stylized as a hood ornament, and difficult to get right. "A leg doesn't fasten on that way, Nick. Not all in there by the ischia." Then, remorsefully: "That's cool, that's cool. You're not a portraitist." As I drew, I found myself darkening the tricky lines of kneecap or nostril until they vanished, until my litho crayon skidded on a slick swath of pigment and Charlotte was a stream of black zigzagging the page. She frowned over these drawings, then pronounced them as good as anything I'd done, and we framed three of the best and hung them above the bed.

Beneath them, we strove. I felt some stage fright; making love to such a beauty seemed somehow public. She was slightly swaybacked, and it was natural for her to arch her slim body; she seemed still to be posing. Her beauty seemed somehow undeserved. As we worked, Charlotte would skid along on her tiny rear. I'd hitch forward in pursuit. Our heads always wound up crammed against the wall or cantilevered over the edge of the mattress.

Afterward, there were those minute internal adjustments a woman's body makes to a man's weight. She'd press my rib cage to test its sturdiness, gently honk my nose. "Nifty tattoo," she said once, and traced it – it was on my right inner thigh, just above the knee – with a finger:

"Mean anything?" she asked.

I was twenty-five and no longer an utter goddamned fool. I said, "Nah."

:   :

When we were well into our second year together, Charlotte's dealer wangled her a studio visit from a curator at the Whitney. Of course, we knew – everyone we *knew* knew – that the Whitney was then finalizing the roster for its upcoming Biennial exhibition. To be included would be to find oneself, abruptly, with a significant career. Charlotte and I scoured the apartment clean and replaced the cracked toilet seat. We hung her best work on every available piece of wall. We removed mine to make room. I waved off her protests. "I'm jealous," I said, "but the Whitney's the Whitney."

"But we can't take *these* down," she cried. She hovered before those three crayon studies. I had to admit, they looked pretty good.

"Well," I allowed, prickling with ambition, "maybe not those."

The curator was as nattily bony as a greyhound. His hair was the color of tin, his face a shade lighter. He shook hands with mechanical courtesy, declined coffee, and proceeded straight to Charlotte's work. He stood silently before each piece for a measured interval before addressing the one beside it. Behind him, we danced in place. It was agony.

"I depend on Nan not to waste my time," he said at length. He did not turn around.

He added: "And I must say, she seldom does."

Another quarter-hour crept by.

"There are no guarantees," he remarked tonelessly, never removing his eyes from the work. "You do understand, it would be irresponsible to make any sort of promise."

I thought she'd swoon. I could have swooned myself, with envy and pride.

Finally he worked his way around to my three little Charlottes.

"I'm going to be a bit plain-spoken," he said. "The self-portraits are not a fruitful direction. Can I assume they're much earlier work?"

A brief and hideous silence. He still didn't turn around.

"Well," he said. "It would be helpful... if I knew who did what."

Charlotte and I never really discussed what followed: the complete and unequivocal collapse of our sex life. We didn't need to understand this better. In fact, it would have been a mercy to understand it less well. We tried, instead, as best we could, to forget the matter. It was like willing yourself to remain asleep as the room fills with daylight.

Strolling through Dublin with a college buddy, Stephen Dedalus divided art into the beautiful, which moves one to contemplation, and the "pornographical or didactic," which moves one to action. It must be said in Charlotte's defense that she did her best to be pornographical. Writhing beneath, above, around me, she muttered into my ear a catalog of vile delights. She dug through her cartons for piquant bits of lingerie. But Charlotte in high heels and some trifle of worn lace, stunning though she was, seemed more than ever to be in costume. Dressed up like a naked lady. Wrapping the sheet about her, she'd say, "If I only knew in advance each night, so I don't get my hopes up."

"We'll post a schedule."

"*Shit.*"

"Do you know what we're reduced to?" I asked Adam. "Twice a month, *maybe*, we get busy. And I make it work – *maybe* – but it's like trying to fuck through bulletproof *glass*. Then when I'm alone, I'll remember what we did. And whack off! And it's *great!* As a *fantasy*, she's unimprovable. You know, a photo of someone who looked like Charlotte, naked, taking this position and that… but the real thing's unconvincing. It's like a page of philosophy, and you know all the words, but you read it a dozen times and just don't *get* it. This isn't just she's a better artist, this isn't just the Whitney. It *predates* that shit. And the more I think the situation through – All right. One. She's too beautiful. I don't believe she's there. Two, she's too beautiful to be with *me*. Three, she's this little black princess, and it's like spitting in Martin Luther King's face if I touch her disrespectfully – if I want doggy-style, that's got to be bad for black-Jewish relations. Three, she's *waiting*, this shit's earning *interest*. Four, she's *perfect*, so I don't even have the right to have a problem! Five… have I already done five?"

"Boy, are you working hard. If there's no chemistry, there's no chemistry. Leave."

"But guys dream all their lives of a woman like this."

"Then cling to this estimable woman you don't want to fuck. Until *she* leaves *you*."

My relationship with Charlotte's parents had always been strained. They were an imposing couple, spare and immaculate, with the circular eyes and neat beaks of barn owls. Whenever they came in from Westchester, they invited us to join them at the Paradise Grill. It was on upper Lexington, the sort of place that in those days spread the tables with white butcher paper and set out jars of crayons so you could doodle on them, and I always worried I'd doodle the wrong thing, something talentless, low-rent, white. At the end of the meal, the Keanes would pore over the bill, then apologize for not driving us home. They didn't like to take the car into our neighborhood. Charlotte speared her gnocchi with an air of dazzling boredom, and spoke in the accents of a bored blonde teenager from Encino, but these dinners were tough on her, too.

I remember the two of us escaping into the subway after one of them, and the intensity of our relief. When the doors opened on the downtown 6, we dove for the last two seats. Then I saw we'd entered with a young black woman and her daughter and, half-seated, I began to rise again. Charlotte drew me firmly down beside her. The woman wore an Adidas T-shirt hacked off at the fourth rib, and tiger-striped shorts, brutally tight. She gripped the rail over our heads and stared at Charlotte. Her smooth brown navel stared at me. There was an agreeable smell of heated cocoa butter, which I felt I ought not to be smelling. I lurched upright, nearly biffing her in the bosom with my head, and indicated my seat. "Please."

The woman spared me a glance. Then, buttocks lordly, she led her daughter away, parting the passengers like weeds. Stupid with fatigue, I stared after her. Those shorts cut painfully into her loins. At night, it would be a relief to remove them. I pictured her removing them. Within, a wedge of black peppercorn curls, tongue-pink at the core. Her enmity would make things simple. I was exhausted with caring and being cared for; I pictured the warm wedge descending upon my mouth, silencing my nattering thoughts. Here I called myself to order, but Charlotte was gazing at me, eyes opaque. I'd snatched the most lurid crayon in the jar and implicated myself beyond redemption.

We left the train at Astor Place in silence.

A block from our house, Charlotte asked me to stop off at the bodega and pick up coffee and bread. "Comparison shop," she suggested. "Gimme, oh, half an hour."

"Charlus. Are we having a fight?"

"We'll see what we're having. Now git."

I returned with my groceries to find our door chained from the inside.

I knocked, then called, "It's me." No answer. "Charlotte?"

It opened. A sinewy black girl with her hair tufted randomly in pigtails peered up at me through heavy-lidded eyes. She wore running shoes without laces, fuchsia spandex shorts, and a sleeveless white T-shirt reduced to ribbons by innumerable parallel slits. Through this I saw a lumpy grayish brassiere. Around her glossy hips she'd slung two loose black belts and a length of fake gold chain. Her lower lip stuck out like a shelf; she was chewing gum. "What you want," she said.

"Jesus, Charlotte. Have you always had this stuff?"

She smiled lazily. "Mah stuff? You ain' seen mah stuff, white boy. You wouldn' fo'git it." She strutted into our apartment. She'd somehow made her little ass shelflike, too. I closed the door as she flung herself onto the sofa, knees splayed, pelvis forward. "All right, Charlotte. I'll admit I'm impressed."

"Who Charlotte? My name Rayella. Boy, you gonna creepy-crawl round that door all day?" She thumped the sofa and I sat beside her. She flicked her fingers through my hair. "You prutty cute fo' an ofay white devil."

"I don't think I'm equal to this."

"But you sho' am separate. Now, why you sittin' so fah from Rayella?" She straddled my lap and ground her bosom across my face. My nose kept catching in the slits of her T-shirt. She hissed, "Ah jes' know you been starin' at all us li'l nigger bitches on the subway. Starin', and they all twitchin' round and sticking they shit in yo' face and you be thinkin': What they got? Do I know what they got? Little nasty-wet boodle to jam fulla what *I* got?"

"Is this supposed to be some kind of turn-on?" I breathed, as we slid to the rug, knocking the groceries and Charlotte's neat stack of *Artforums* across the floor.

Afterward, we lay spent and soaking. Rayella's hair-ties terminated in large clear plastic beads, which had rattled on the floor and probably bruised Charlotte's scalp. She removed them and lay her sore head on my chest. I kissed it. Her pigtails unraveled slowly in my face. "Tell me I'm your little brown ho," she whispered. "Your hot little bitch without a brain in her pretty head."

"Hardly," I said. "You're my bright, and beautiful, and wonderful girlfriend."

She tried again. "It's your big dick leaves me so brainless. Your big Jewish dick."

"Actually, I believe it's pretty average."

"What," she said, curious, "is *wrong* with you?"

"Sorry. Let's start over. From little, gorgeous, ah, ho'. "

"Gorgeous *brown* ho'. "

"If you insist."

"You hate me to say that, don't you? *Brown.* I see you jump. You just hate me to talk about my blackness. You never mention it. And when you do, it's always a joke, a rude one, so I can see how carefree you are. Like, 'Smile, so I can find your mouth.' You're *allowed* to notice I'm black, Nicky. You're even allowed to have an opinion on the subject."

"Thanks. I don't."

"And that fries my ass. You're too squeamish to even think about it. I certainly think about you being Jewish. Oh, come on, Nick. Are you gonna give me the liberal bullshit there's no difference between Jews and blacks and anyone else?"

"Yes. That's the liberal bullshit I'm going to give you."

"Well, don't. It tires me. Nicky, I *like* all your Jew-stuff. I like it that you're funny, and bookish, I like—"

"What if I started going on about your great natural rhythm and general physical superiority?"

"We *are* physically superior. You think we got a lock on boxing and basketball 'cause there ain't any white boys interested? Nicky, stereotypes don't spring out of thin air 'cause bigots have such great imaginations."

"We disagree."

"Goddamnit," she shouted, "why won't you shout at me if you're so angry? Did your parents teach you to be polite to colored folk? 'Cause the truth is, not only do you notice it, but that's all you notice! I grew up in a nice white town and went to nice white schools, I dated one black guy in my whole *life* and believe me his name wasn't Rufus or Jamal, I don't even know what I *am* sometimes, but all you see is *brown*. I've got to turn myself into I don't know what before you'll act like I'm *there*. And I don't care whose idea it was! I don't care if I liked it! You can't even *draw* me without turning me into an *ink* blot, some puddle of *tar!*"

"Let's save the art criticism for another day, shall we? Jesus, your kibitzing and your *kibitzing!* Maybe you wish I wasn't an artist, too. Maybe you'd rather sparkle all alone."

"You think I don't?"

Then we were speechless.

"I said it to hurt you, I said it to hurt you!" she cried. "Please, I just said it to hurt you! Where are you *going*? Don't walk away when we've just said things like this!"

"We'll continue when I can think more clearly."

"I don't want you to fucking think clearly," she said, beginning to cry. "I want you to think you know me well enough to lose your temper. Nick, will you goddamn *look* at me? At *me!* Nicky, this is *me!*"

:   :

Rayella hadn't had our advantages, and allowances had to be made. But she was still bad news, and we resolved to forget her.

The problem was, she was fun. And that was certainly more than you could say for either of us.

Over the next weeks, Charlotte and Nicky gave their days over to endless, earnest, slow-motion discussions about relationships and race that were like a game of chess played by mail in which both sides steadily lost. They filled my head with damp kapok, they made finding each word a killing effort. I longed powerfully just to lose my anxious face in Charlotte's lap, but Charlotte's lap was attached to Charlotte, whom I was letting down so badly.

But Rayella, now, Rayella didn't *care*. When I came home from work one night, she pinned me to the front door and blew me, never removing her silver sandals, yellow sweatpants, or azure tube top, a fictive woman with a real mouth, gorgeous and two-toned, and real fingertips that bruised my flanks. She then removed twenty dollars from my wallet and kept it. I took her to the Paradise Grill; she ornamented the butcher paper with big, exuberant cocks wearing mezuzahs and yarmulkes, which I quickly converted into palm trees, neckties, rockets. Deafening macaw-shrieks of laughter. Once home, we tore into each other. We'd sometimes rut with our hands literally closed around each other's throats, Charlotte chuckling and long-eyed, her coarse little crux jerking against and around me. Even our contraception was uncouth. I'd pull out and unloose a pearly stream across her belly, stupefying in its abundance. She'd dabble it over her tarry nipples as if playing with fingerpaints. It was the best sex either of us had ever had, and we only wished we were having it with each other. Afterward we'd kiss to avoid each other's eyes.

We tried, as I said, to ban Rayella, but without her we had nothing to talk about, and nothing to fuck about.

One Sunday morning, we were reading together on the sofa. We'd been getting along very nicely all morning. Charlotte had tucked her feet under my leg. It was nice. I was reluctant to move my leg, in case she'd think I was uncomfortable and take her feet away. After a while, she looked up from her copy of *High Performance* and said, "Nick? What'd you say was Julia's last name?" She passed me the magazine.

In the photo, Julia, clad in lace teddy and construction boots, brandished an axe over an old vacuum cleaner. Behind her, a row of Raggedy Ann and Raggedy Andy dolls sat in little chairs, arranged boy-girl, boy-girl. The caption simply indicated that Julia Hargreave was pictured performing *Ugly Girls Go to War* the previous year at InterAct, and that she'd returned there with a new piece. The photo was credited to a James Merriam. I had a bad feeling about this James Merriam. "Yep," I said. "That's her."

"You want to go?"

"You're serious."

"*Yes* I'm serious. Sorry. Why wouldn't I be serious?"

"You think I wanna get wound up in that *shit* again?"

Balefully: "Maybe you shoulda fucked her when you had the chance. Maybe you'd be a li'l calmer about it by now."

"As it happens, Charlotte, I don't feel calmer. As it happens, I feel the way I feel. Do *you* want to go?"

"Well. Just to get a look at her. Are you telling me you're not curious?"

"On a certain level, I'll admit—Fuck. This is a bad idea. You *know* this is a bad idea."

"I honestly don't think I'll mind it."

"But you always mind it. Whenever I so much as—"

"Okay *okay*. Well, I'd like to be given a chance to not mind it," she said. "Unless you just want us to agree I'm just screwed up and jealous forever?"

"All right."

"All right what?"

"All right, let's go see her."

"I said all right *what?*"

I said, "Well, all right, but I can't help thinking, you want to try and not mind this, but it's not you who'll pay if you fail to not mind it. It's me. You'll make me pay."

"That's a valid point," she said angrily. "We won't go."

"*Shit.* If only we could do one goddamn thing without discussing it and discussing it until it's raw and bleeding and deciding it twenty dozen different ways. Why don't *you* go, Charlotte, and I'll stay here? Then we don't have to worry about whatever my response is, and you can still see her."

"That's not a serious suggestion."

"Well, I was half joking, but it's worth some consideration."

"No, Nicky, like about two-thirds of the stuff we consider at length, it is not worth some consideration."

"Well, we're certainly in agreement about that much. Oh hell, Charlus. We don't even know what we're arguing about anymore. C'mere."

"You're right," she said, "but no huggies right now. Let's just say you owe me one."

:   :

InterAct: A Media Space was a reconverted firehouse a few blocks north of Grand Street. A stage stood where the trucks had once waited for alarms. Its offices were upstairs in the former firemen's quarters, which it shared with a tiny Ecuadorian wig factory. We bought our tickets – there was a pail on the ticket table marked *Air Conditioning Fund* – and then the plywood risers thumped hollowly as we climbed to a couple of seats just under a black ceiling criss-crossed with black pipes. The house was nearly full. There were a few well-dressed older folks, who might have been dutiful relatives. One silvery and august gent had a wrapped bouquet across his knees and a look of determined sportiness. The folding chairs squealed as we settled ourselves. On the PA I heard Etta James singing "I'd Rather Go Blind." Center stage, I saw a row of four large galvanized laundry tubs filled with water. Behind them, a metal shelf about six feet high held four TV monitors, one behind each tub. At the far right, a video camera stood on a tripod.

Charlotte examined the xeroxed program intently. It listed a mere three names. A gentleman responsible for Light/Sound Design got equal billing with James Merriam, whose credit read "Attendant." Julia's name appeared without elaboration in letters of modest size above the title: *The Water of Fond Remembrance*. A graduate of Miss Porter's and Bennington, Julia Hargreave had occupied herself for many years with forays into poetry, feminism, and various forms of spiritual legerdemain. She had been Associate Coordinator of an upstate soup kitchen, exhibited her photographs at CB's Gallery 313, and more recently studied movement and bodywork with the legendary... some name with a lot of consonants. Then the lights went down, and I could see nothing but the exit sign and some dashes of luminous tape on the stage, which marked the position of the tubs and equipment. We heard shuffling and rhythmic splashing sounds, and the first monitor came on, displaying the word *Child*.

The lights came up slowly. At first one could see little but the crown of Julia's head and her bright shoulders. The Attendant stood in the dimness at her side, operating the video camera. As the lights brightened, the word on the first monitor faded into a mottled whitish blur that filled the screen. Beneath it, Julia stood in the first tub, dressed in a white wedding gown, sopping wet from head to toe. Her face was obscured by a wet veil like a caul, but dark medallions of bosom and groin were in ghostly evidence. The cool concrete floor was sad in my nostrils. Julia's arms hung relaxed at her sides. She exuded a supernal aplomb. When the lights were up full, she lifted the wet veil from her face and smiled. "Damn," Charlotte whispered, "she's a beauty. Least you have good taste."

James Merriam was a short, muscular young man with a big grouchy face that probably took a lot of shaving, and a shaved head. He put me in mind of a circus acrobat I'd once seen. He'd been spotting his young daughter from the sawdust as she worked the high trapeze without a net, and his poised vigilance came to mind as I watched Merriam watch Julia from behind his camera.

"Whoops," Charlotte whispered. "I'll shush."

At last Julia spoke. "When I was seven," she said, "little Mason Beck tried to scare me with a rubber snake."

Here she produced a small rubber snake. I could have sworn her hands had been empty.

I'd heard this story before. She always told it well. But I didn't think it would do for an audience of a hundred, even with washtubs and TVs thrown in.

Julia regarded the rubber snake fixedly. There was a stifled, uncertain chortle from somewhere, then another, quickly choked off.

Finally, still motionless, she swept her eyes down and gave the audience a faintly troubled look, as though wondering whether she might possibly have heard something, and the laughter became general and prolonged.

"She ain't bad, either," Charlotte whispered.

"I knocked him down and took it away," Julia said, and got another laugh.

"And nearly every day for a while," she said, "little Matty would come up to me and say, Ju-lia, gimme my snake back. Ju-lia, gimme my snake. Now, I have to admit, I really didn't care much for the damn thing. I just didn't want him to have it. But what started to be cool was that I could do anything with that snake. I could make it male and I could make it female. I could make it ride through the air. I could make up little men and powerful queens and give them rides on the back of my flying snake. I gave Matty Beck a ride on the snake. He never knew. I gave Mom and Dad a ride on the snake. They never knew. I could make anyone fly on the snake, and they were better people for the experience."

As she spoke, she stretched out the snake to form a phallus, doubled it to make a vulva and poked through it a rhythmic finger. She rose on tiptoe to send it aloft and observed its progress with interest. She cited Cleopatra and slipped it down her bodice. The story ended when Julia and Matty were fifteen, having sex in a beached rubber raft. The image on the video monitor had slowly been coming into focus all this time, and now it could be seen: Julia's wet bodice, with the dark squiggle of the snake visible beneath the cloth. The Attendant took a felt-tip marker and traced its image on the television screen:

There was a brief pause. Julia's face conveyed the faintest gleam of impatience.

Merriam left his post, and without ado lifted Julia from the tub. She remained stiff as a doll. Once aloft, though, she gave us all a gracious little nod. He set her on her feet in the second tub. She'd dripped on the floor. Together they regarded the small puddle in silence.

Then he withdrew to his camera. The monitor above the second tub came on, displaying the word *Daughter*.

This, too, faded to a mottled blur.

For *Daughter* she told another story I knew well. When she was little, her father would pay her a silver dollar to walk up and down his back. "I mean, it wasn't really a silver dollar. We were rich, but for Christ's sakes, no one goes around with their pockets full of silver *dollars*. It was a half-dollar" – she produced a half-dollar coin, again apparently from nowhere – "with President Kennedy's shiny little face. He was so handsome." She palmed the coin, made it reappear, made it twinkle across her knuckles and vanish into her fist, her movements smooth and practiced. "Well, all right, it wasn't a Kennedy half-dollar either, because it was maybe 1960 and he wasn't even dead. But that's the way I'm gonna remember it," she said pettishly.

It's wonderful what a range of movement Julia found while standing with feet together, making only the most constrained and stylized of gestures. There was a sense she'd been stood in the tub as a punishment, even that the tub was filled with hardening cement and Julia was to be executed gangland-style. Still, she kept doing coin tricks, almost absently, as she spoke of the silent crunch of her father's vertebrae beneath her instep, of the smells of cologne, freshly shampooed carpet, tobacco, and fatigue, and all the while her face never lost its pleasantly composed self-centeredness. It was the solemnity that was so funny. Performance was a matter on which Charlotte had opinions, and she watched Julia with admiring eyes and an almost pained half-grin of concentration. At last Julia opened her hand to reveal the coin a final time, and the Attendant traced it on the television screen:

Again Merriam lay familiar hands beneath her arms and lifted her to the next tub. This time he tried shaking her a little, to dislodge the last drops from her toes.

The word on the third screen was *Slut*.

Julia said, "When I was nearly twenty, I got bitten by a snake. A real one."

My lips tingled. Charlotte shifted beside me.

"I'd been visiting my parents, in the company of one of the too many men of whom I have already made mention. And one day we were out walking in the woods. We were accompanied by a ten-year-old boy from town. This was some ten-year-old. He'd already asked if he could be my boyfriend, too."

Chuckles. Charlotte did not join in. Me neither.

"I told him I was undecided."

Laughter.

"I was."

More laughter.

"Anyway, he was supposed to be explaining to me about the flora and fauna, all the local flora and fauna, and he was making every last goddamn thing up as we went along. An artist. My usual luck," she said. "And eventually we came to this stinky little pond, with a marshy little island in the middle of it. Just him and me. We'd left my then-boyfriend snoring in the woods. And I asked the boy what the island was called. And he said, Julia's Island."

She went on. She mimed balancing on rocks. She sat with a splash in her tub to indicate falling. "Lay idly back in the thick grass," she said. "A lash of brightness amidst the stinky water," she said. Rising, she lifted the hem of her dress to display her right leg, then gracefully raised her foot – the unexpected movement drew another laugh, and she paused, foot suspended, with another wondering look – and set it on the edge of the tub. With a tube of lipstick she made two dots like the marks of fangs on her inner thigh and, as the boy fumbled out his knife and began to cut, a jagged stroke crossing a straight stroke. And on the screen of the monitor, James Merriam traced it:

She told how I'd pressed my mouth to her leg, how she'd pressed it closer, her fingers tangled in my heated hair, how I'd fumbled off my belt and given it to her, and the hardness of the sun-warmed buckle in her hands. "And I thought: *I am so much in this world. I am so much in this world now. I will be in this world forever.*"

In a low, clear voice, Charlotte said, "I'd like to leave now."

I hesitated.

"Please, Nick."

I saw as we left that *Priestess* was the final word on the final monitor. I tried to move quietly on the hollow risers, but more laughter arrived to cover the sound of our departure.

On the sidewalk, Charlotte blew out a breath. "What the hell was *that* about?"

"I have no idea," I said, blushing.

We walked a block or two.

She said, "All right. I'm upset."

"I noticed that, yes."

"And you were right. And I was wrong. Would you like to say about how you were right and I was wrong?"

"No."

"And you're angry at me."

"Very angry," I said.

"Don't blame you. And we're walking the wrong way."

We turned around and headed north.

I said, "How's your stomach."

"*Never mind my goddamn stomach.* Sorry. It hurts."

"Sorry. We'll go home and get your medicine."

"No." She swerved over and slipped her arm around my waist. "No, no, no, no, no. We'll go home and get blind fucking drunk, is what we'll get."

"All right."

"You're damn right it's all right." She rolled her head against my shoulder.

"That feels good."

"Good. We'll go home and get blind fucking drunk. Because we got no sense. Going to see her like that. No sense at all." I put my arm around her shoulders, and she laughed shakily. "*Well.* Ah sure hope that girl ain't quit her day job."

"Oh, knock it off, now. Please."

"Don' lose yo' sensa humor, chile."

"Come on, Charlotte."

"Ah thought you like Rayella," she said.

"Yes, but I don't want to discuss the *arts* with her," I snapped.

We skidded to a halt.

She whispered, "You don't need to insult me over that scatter-brained ofay bitch."

"Who said that? Charlotte or Rayella?" I said dully.

"We're in *agreement,*" she shouted, and kicked me savagely in the thigh. And I remembered the tattoo there, the one that wasn't supposed to mean anything.

:   :

It was three or four in the morning when I crawled on my elbows to her side of the bed. It seemed a very long way. "Let's…," I whispered. "Let's discuss the arts."

No sign from the dark knot in the sheets.

"Well, to start with," she said at last, "I ain't crazy about that thing on your leg."

"I hate it, too."

"Oh? I worry you love it. I worry you love it a lot."

"No."

"Don't you? Nick? Don't you?" Then she said, "What are you doing with the checkbook?"

I had about seven hundred dollars in the bank. I spent four hundred and fifty to get my tattoo erased. They used lasers.

EIGHT

Unrestingly Now · You, Swollen and Sly

I probably stuck with messenging longer than I should have. Problem was, I liked it. I'd bought a little steel-framed Bianchi, the sort of thing (fixed gear, no brakes) your average Joe couldn't ride a block without misadventure, and on it I became a nervy fellow who loved to stare down cabdrivers or lunge in front of downshifting trucks, pumping smoothly ahead with a throat that seemed lined with metal. I had a retentive memory and a detailed mental map of the city. I knew how to get on with dispatchers. I often pulled fifty-run days, and fifty runs is good money. Office workers struck me as quaint, in their closed rooms full of bric-a-brac. They were like old-time shopkeepers living above their shops. *My* life was all vectors, *a* to *b* in *x* minutes. Everything else was just something in the way. And out in traffic, when something got in my way, I had a sporting chance of getting around it.

Charlotte didn't make the Biennial, but it was a near thing, and Nan, impressed, finally gave her a one-woman show. The opening— another opening—was a success: little self-adhesive red dots appeared beside one piece after another. By the end of the evening, only five of eighteen paintings remained unsold. Charlotte never eased her grip on my back pocket the entire time, or ceased rubbing a doting cheek against my clavicle. Then she moved out. It took until midnight to get her boxes to her new place uptown, since we kept sending the movers outside to wait while we wept, and kissed, and swore we were both wonderful, and sorry, and doing the right thing, probably. After that, we went through a phase where we dated all the time, and then a phase where we went to bed occasionally and tried to see ourselves as friends, and finally a phase where she married a forty-two-year-old public relations consultant. He was short, handsome, talkative, button-nosed, and black. "I might maybe still be making mistakes," Charlotte said, "but I sure ain't making the same ones twice."

At the time of Charlotte's engagement, I was working at a big color lab called FotoPro. It was housed in the tunnels and chambers beneath the Chrysler Building, and though the pay was oddly good there, I suppose we were a subterranean lot. Louis the dispatcher, for instance. An unwholesome fellow nearing fifty, he was addicted to corn dogs with mayonnaise, which worsened his flatulence and ringed his lips with glistening white. At a messenger company, dispatchers are kings, but at FotoPro Louis counted for so little that they'd stationed him out in the hall with us. He had a desk, though, and we were lucky to find a seat on the single bench. (There was only room on it for three. Last one in had to sit on the stairs leading up to the street.) Louis always called me Funny Man. I don't know why. Perhaps he thought I thought something was funny.

Key was a spidery black seventeen-year-old possessed of preternatural energy and good cheer. He was convinced he had a promising future in crime. "First you need you an idea," he told me. "Good things happen to the man with the idea." His first arrest was at fifteen. You see, the government used to put up these pictures saying how teachers should Give Kids the Keys to the City. They showed these keys marked Natural Museum, Modern Museum… Now, there had to be at least a hundred oil paintings in each of those places, all of them worth a nice piece of change. And if you got you a locksmith to copy those keys on the poster, and let yourself in quiet when they closed… The first locksmith he approached had laughed at him, and Key had smashed his front window. He still thought it was a good idea, if only he hadn't got excited.

Army worked only on foot. So deeply wrecked were his mind and body that we gave him a place on the bench whenever he might come in. He didn't notice. At least sixty years old, tiny, pear-shaped, with wet, puffy white flesh and thick glasses, he'd drag one mashed foot forward, then the other, clutching at all times a ragged gray handkerchief which he'd worry with tugs of his gray teeth. "When I was in the service," he bleated, "we was all in the service, when I was in the *Ah-my*…"

Curtis's main gig was in the evening: salad man at a Queens diner. Most weekends he also did data entry at a catalog house. At twenty, Curtis had a wife, an infant daughter, payments to make on their Crown Heights bungalow, and plans for his own lunch counter. He'd been working two or three jobs since he'd quit high school. Returning from a run, he plumped down and napped until called. Even in sleep he looked furious, stout brown fists balled in his lap, upper lip bulging with purpose. He despised any middle-class white boy feckless enough to be working beside him. "You come here," he told me. "You amuse yourself."

"Just a fuckin' job, man." Oh, pitiful. Why did I try to talk street with him?

"You got college?" he demanded.

"Cornell," I admitted.

"Amusing yourself," he said, and never spoke to me again.

:   :

Louis droned, "*Funny Man*. Priority. Heller, Marketing, by noon. *Go*." I tucked the envelope into my bag and humped my bike up the stairs to the upper world.

I always felt like a bit of a mongrel when I had to make a run to Maud Heller et Cie. A high-toned cosmetics company, it staffed its offices with asthenic young persons sporting posh wardrobes and the faces of ill-natured angels. The receptionist for the marketing department was no exception. Her sleek fair skull was narrow as a collie's. She'd tipped it over a paperback, but at my approach, raised it and simply stared. I suppose she reserved her *Can I help you?*s for people in suits. "Rush package for" – I glanced at Louis's headlong scrawl – "J. Harkavi."

She didn't move. "Your people have made a mistake, I'm afraid. There's no Harkavi here."

"Are you sure?"

"I work here."

"Sorry. I was told it was urgent."

"Well, I don't doubt you, but I don't see how I can help you, either."

I knew how, but it would have ruined the knees of her forty-dollar Fogal pantyhose. "Perhaps if I could see a staff directory?"

"They're for staff use. Sorry."

I waited. She'd bent to her book again – Clive Barker's *Cabal* – propping her temple with one hand as though she'd forgotten all about me, and displaying a becoming sadness. For perhaps fifteen seconds I observed the faint green veins in her neck. "I was told it was important."

She looked up. "No doubt. I'm sure the best thing is to get back to your employers right away and straighten things out."

"I was told this had to arrive by noon at the latest. It's eleven forty-eight now."

"Yes," she said, and elevated a slim wrist so that I could see she owned a watch, thank you very much. Then she snapped her fingers. "Wait. Harkavi. Hargreave. Perhaps you've misspelled her name."

"I don't misspell names. We have someone on staff to do that." But she was depressing a stud on the phone and murmuring, "Julia?"

From down the hall I heard, "Fucking *what*, Sydney?"

When she stalked into the reception area, she resembled my Julia no more than *Harkavi* resembles *Hargreave*. Her face was seamlessly made up, with a red mouth like a badge. She wore a boxy taupe linen suit with a short skirt, high heels, and a cummerbund clumped with gold appliqué. Her hair was still lustrous and brown as beef blood, but she'd cropped it down to a poodle-poof atop her head. Her legs were hard in their taupe stockings, and a faint groove beneath the tip of her nose ran back between her nostrils. Her gaze shot straight from Sydney the receptionist to the package the messenger held, and she moved toward it with a hand extended. When I gave it to her, she muttered, "Thanks."

I said, "You're welcome."

She squealed and threw herself against my chest. "*Nicky!* What are you doing in this *getup?*"

"Earning a living. What are you doing in that getup?"

She released me and nodded, grinning. "I have a *job*," she said, and waved toward the receptionist. "Associate Marketing Coordinator for Skin Creams. It's wonderful. It just snaps my whole life together. I should have gotten a job *years* ago." Sydney examined Julia with frank hatred. "Sydney, this is Nick Wertheim. He's not really a messenger."

"Actually, he is," I said.

"Well, he's also a wonderful, um, artist."

Sydney smiled thinly. "A man for all seasons."

"Oh, Sydney, kiss my *ass*." Julia grabbed my arm. "I have no time, but come back and talk a moment. Don't worry, Sid," she called over her shoulder, "I'll make him wash his hands before I let him *touch* anything."

I don't know what I expected — a corner office with a Bokhara rug and a wall-sized aquarium full of Siamese fighting fish? — but Julia's cubicle was small and bleak, with a slough of papers on the desk. She slung the rush package onto the heap and propped her heels atop it. The triangular space between her thighs and her skirt seemed the mouth of a cannon. After a pause, she said, "Well. I guess we're both nervous."

"Not me. I'm having a fine time, standing here, looking up your skirt."

She swung her feet to the floor. "Ever the gentleman," she muttered.

"That's me."

"You really were such a gentleman, you know. That year."

"You know the Yiddish for 'gentleman'? *Schmuck*."

"I think that lessens both of us, Nicky."

"Oh, I dunno. That year I think we were both pretty less."

She was looking at her pressed-together knees. "I was very unhappy, and very manipulative. And I made you hate me."

"No."

"Didn't you?"

"I could never hate you, Julia," I said.

She snickered.

"I could never hate you, Ju-li-ah," she intoned.

"Oh, fuck you." But I'd begun to laugh, too.

"I feel so stupid."

"You look wonderful."

"Really? You like my clothes?"

"The clothes are entirely foul."

"Entirely. Well. Do you like my hair?"

"A grave error."

"Aha. The way I've decorated my office?"

"You haven't decorated your office."

"My tone of voice?"

"It is entirely possible that your tone of voice is worse than your clothes."

"And I look wonderful?"

"Very wonderful."

"Thank you. And fuck *you*. What stinking tone of voice am I supposed to have? I remember the last time I saw you with paralyzing clarity."

"We'd just mopped the kitchen. You kissed my cheek and wished me luck."

"You know exactly what last time I saw you I mean. And then you left me there! When I was ready to – Skip it. How *are* you? You disapproving little crap. I've missed you. Don't we always wind up saying this? First fuck you, then I've missed you? Well, *this* time I'm not letting you get away. Let's see. Tonight is not good, not good at all. Nor Tuesday – Could you come with me to a party on Friday? We wouldn't have to stay." She pulled out a beautiful leather Filofax and took down my address and phone. It was the same neatly jostling script I remembered from the check register at the soup kitchen. Suddenly hesitant, she said, "Is it really okay, this messenger stuff? I mean, slap me if this is wrong to say, but is there anything I can do?"

"It's all right. But yes, there is. You can tell that ravening bitch out there to kiss your ass again. If I do it, I'll lose my job."

"But I *do*, Nick. I tell her ninety times a day. She's this horrible little Smithie who thinks she ought to be simultaneously on the cover of *Vogue* and editorial director of Condé Nast and she'll never get anywhere because she's a horrible little tick whom people loathe and all her IQ goes into insults. Actually, it's *your* ass she ought to be kissing. If she got a good boff now and then, perhaps one could live with her. Would you do it, Nick? I'd be willing to put it on a cash basis. She's only twenty-*three-ee*," Julia said coaxingly. "Would a hundred be fair? Maybe she'd kick in a few bucks herself. You know, those biker shorts are very effective. I'm just talking like this, because, I'm just talking like this. Here's my address. Come by at, oh, nine? I will absolutely be ready at nine. Now skedaddle, before my staff starts thinking I'm furgling the messengers, like I'm always saying I will." She kissed my cheek and shooed me out the door.

As I walked by the reception desk, I heard Julia call, "Think about doing that piece of work for me, Nicky."

I smiled at Sydney and called, "I'll think about it."

Sydney extended a gleaming middle finger into the air.

Back at FotoPro, Louis eyed me around his corn dog. "You were there all fucking day." Mayonnaise had gathered at the corners of his mouth in two little clots, each almost perfectly spherical.

I said, "Louis, how would you like to make a fast hundred bucks?"

He said, "Everything's funny to the Funny Man. Sit down and shut up before someone stops loving you."

:   :

Now, a story, as I understand it, is a matter of What Does Our Hero Do Next? The difficulty in telling the story of a cement-assed depressive like me is that our hero does *nothing* next, and does it over and over. After Charlotte wrote and asked me not to call (*"It's not fair to Kent, or to me, or to you"*), I lapsed into a long inanition. I'd take aimless walks, skulking between the couples, ashamed of being seen alone, *again*. I'd drop into a chair to remove my boots, say, and find myself unable, one sock off and one sock on, to rise or stir for a half hour that seemed to last until dusk. I was subject to semi-involuntary naps that drained me as though I'd run a marathon, to a weariness amounting to terror at the thought of tiny obligations, and to small, half-conscious utterances when I was alone. *Can't. Please.* I rummaged through an alphabetized accordion file of skin magazines and consumed bales of dope, bushels of junk food, and if I was in the mood for a Scooter Pie and all they had at the bodega was Ding Dongs, a bud of hopelessness blossomed in my throat.

My family offered scant comfort during this period. Del, for instance: while her husband studied law, she stayed home in Mahwah minding their three children, and if you were not their three children, she couldn't quite see what you had to do with anything. Her youngest, I recall, was two. He demanded his bowl and flung it on the rug, demanded his bowl and flung it on the rug, and Del stooped to retrieve it, more times than seemed humanly possible, sometimes quietly pointing out that he'd get more oatmeal if he'd stop flinging it all over the room. He waited for her voice to stop, then accepted his bowl and flung it on the rug. Del seemed to regard this game of fetch as the only fit occupation for an adult. She regarded me primarily as good DNA going to waste.

Saul was by then nearing seventy, and looked it. Vertical creases divided his chin from his face. He resembled a ventriloquist's dummy. Though always meaning to move from our old house, he'd instead rented out one room after another to students. The closets were stuffed with research for his second book, a monumental history of strikebreaking in America from the first clashes with the Pinkertons to Reagan's mass firing of air traffic controllers. After a decade, he'd yet to complete a 120-page outline. A popular lecturer, Saul was still regarded at Cornell as a dismasted lecher whose tenure had been a mistake. "I can't even say I didn't live," he raged. "What I can say is, I gulped life without tasting."

Meanwhile, Suzanne was dating a vague-eyed thirty-one-year-old with inexplicable Prince Valiant bangs. He'd done the ashram bit in India, worked construction in Vancouver, sold peyote in Amsterdam and wind chimes in New Hope, then taken eight hundred dollars and lived a year in Tegucigalpa, trying to write a screenplay of *The Prophet*. He'd been around the world three times and had nothing in particular to say about it. Silently he rubbed my mother's shoulders, silently brushed her hair, silently crouched at her feet, a vestal attending a sibyl. Suzanne was then clerking at a spice store, the sort of place that stocked curative herbs and four different brands of wheatgrass juice, and as he gave her hair its nightly hundred strokes, clouds of spice filled the apartment. "Nicky, you look like something going bad in the back of the fridge. I'm afraid you don't deal well with celibacy. Anyway, if you're not ready for a partner, don't knock masturbation. You know, there was a time when Saul and I weren't having intercourse. We were still very close, physically, but it wasn't right for me just then to have another person inside me. And instead I masturbated constantly. And it was perfect."

"That's nice, Mom."

"Nick, you're twenty-eight. Do you think you could address me by my name, instead of my societal role?"

"How's it going, Suzanne. Thanks for dinner, Suzanne. What do you hear from the patriarchy, Suzanne. Like that?"

"Call me what you wish, Nicky. And do try to find a woman. You're not getting any pleasanter."

I'd been rooming with Adam for a while, and that wasn't going too well either. It had seemed natural to ask him to move in after Charlotte left; I'd been bitterly lonely and Adam, as always, had been broke. We'd hauled up four-by-fours and built a sleeping loft in the living room, and for a few days the apartment was filled with the ringing screech of the circular saw and the hot, fresh smell of cut lumber. I'm a child of the suburbs and I love hardware stores, love the yellow-green liquor at the heart of each carpenter's level, with its traveling bubble, the pegboards hung with widgets, each shaped by some mysterious purpose. We slapped white paint over our handi-work, then over the walls and into the gaping craters in them, frost-ing the BX cable and the rotting laths with cleanliness and high endeavor.

But I hadn't understood how much of my pleasure in Adam's company had always depended on my being able, at the end of an infamous night, to leave him and stretch out between clean sheets in the silence of my chaste, orderly apartment. Into this he now intro-duced all the random detritus of the Bunker, as well as an unending stream of quizzical women. Late at night I'd hear yips and moans and finally Adam's orgasm, a terrible sound, like a manhole cover being dragged over a manhole in which I happened to be cowering, nursing a headache. Adam had also grown overfond, I thought, of cocaine. Though he had the tact not to offer me any, he shared it with an alarming batch of new drug friends. The beads of stray piss he left on the rim of the toilet, the clicks and sucking noises he made drinking a glass of water, soon struck in my chest an unending chord of rage. Eventually we did not speak to each other without prior consideration.

A couple of nights after I ran into Julia, I was out at the Brite Spot with Adam and his principal girlfriend. We'd been out pasting up Detonators flyers since ten; it was now two in the morning. A galvanized steel bucket and a paste brush sat at my feet. We cradled beers in gummy hands. It was an ordinary night with Adam: he was trying to pimp me off on the bartender. "Maddy?" he called. "Come meet my friend Nick."

"Pleased to meet you, Nick. Since when do you have friends, Frankel?"

"Ah, everybody likes Nick. He's likable. Actually, Mad" – here Adam mimed having an idea – "you oughta know him."

"You think?"

"Absolutely. He's an artist."

"Oh, well, in that case."

"He is. I'll vouch for this man. You understand me? I'll *vouch* for him."

"He won't," I said sadly. "He's always saying he'll vouch for me."

"What're you two, an act?" she asked.

"You got no idea," Adam's girlfriend said. "You don't live with these drama queens."

Adam had met Catherine Gleason while she was waiting tables at an all-night Ukrainian diner. He'd come in from a thunderstorm and dried himself with a dozen napkins. Before taking his order, she'd plucked a shred of wet napkin from his hair. That was all he needed, was, in fact, a good deal more than he usually needed. Tall and almost thin, Cat had a neat white pouch under each eye, and viewed the proceedings from her vantage point atop a long and weary neck.

Maddy moved off. I did not detain her.

"*Somebody* ought to fuck him," Adam said. "He never *fucks*. It isn't *decent. I'll* fuck him if no one else is going to. You know, you *are* cute.

Oh, yeah. That big nose is very male, and all that prissy arrogance is kind of fetching. I mean, so serious, like a young Talmud student. Nice head of hair, too. It would be worth it just for the look on your face."

"Lay off, you fat little fruit," Cat said.

"He can take care of himself."

"No I can't."

Adam said, "Women –"

She said, "You don't know dick about women."

"I know about you."

"I'm not women. Half what you know about me's wrong, anyway."

"And the other half?"

"And the other half I haven't bothered to think about yet."

"So why do you let me go on if it's all such garbage?"

"It used to be entertaining."

"You do deserve better than us," I told her.

"Oh, Jesus," Adam said. "Nick, women do not want to be *conspired* with."

"Try me," Cat said.

"What Nick needs is enough pussy long enough to acclimatize him. He's a difficult case. He oughta be experimenting ceaselessly to find what'll work."

"Sure," I said. "I'll just fetch out my little black book and start with the A's."

"Please, not another hour of bright patter about how you're the least attractive guy in the world. Like, that's how you keep getting these great women to stumble things up with. 'Cause you're so repulsive. C'mon, this is New York. The streets are lined with pussy."

"Pussy," I observed, "pussy, pussy, pussy, pussy."

Hunched on his stool, Adam looked dense as an iron figurine. He cast his gaze down his cheeks then, as if fondly searching for some trinket on the dirty floor. When he lifted his gaze, it had no more human meaning than two polished spots on an iron mask. Very evenly he said, "You are starting to sicken me."

"All right."

"It's not all right."

"All right, it's not all right."

The weight of his cheeks was lethal.

He said, "I see you working up these little appraisals. Based on I don't fucking know what, because I don't know what you do in your life to get a basis. I see you sitting in your little shit. You think you can spread smartness over all your future actions like paint. Devise it all out first and act later. And that's *contemptible. Saints* don't get to do that. You're like someone by this river all his life, calculating the best spot to jump in, doing a whole fucking *essay* on rivers, and eventually you can be fucking *drowning* but you *still aren't even wet.*"

"I recognize—"

"*Don't goddamn recognize.*"

Cat poured herself more beer. "Drama queens," she said.

Adam made a plain effort to look at me afresh. "Listen." He fumbled in his jacket, then nodded. "Listen."

Cat stood.

"Now, Cat," Adam said. She walked out, head level on her long white neck.

"What was that?" I said.

He touched the pitcher, then applied beer-cold fingertips to his eyelids.

"My conscience," he said. "Come into the can."

He picked up the bucket and brush and ushered us into the single stall, where he locked the door and produced a white plastic vial. The screw-off cap had a miniature spoon on a hinge, built right in. Someone had a regular little industry, making these things. I said, "Do you get this from someone in the band?"

"I got this," he said, "from someone *real.*"

Unfolding the spoonlet, Adam dibbled up some powder and applied it to each nostril. He seemed about to sneeze or get a joke. I waited as if waiting to be kissed. When he handed the vial over, I recall being surprised at its lack of weight, and then I did as I'd seen him do. It cut into the tissues of my head like a wire. I shivered, tasting gasoline or sour wine, and said, "I saw Julia the other day."

"Huh. This is the first I hear of it."

"Your manner, tubby, does not invite confidences."

"All right. You saw Julia. And…"

I breathed. Each breath seemed to contain unusual amounts of oxygen. "She invited me to a party."

"And you plan to…"

"Go."

"Okay. How did she strike you?"

"Miserable. She's some sort of cosmetics executive now. She took me into her office, flung her legs around, and bellowed about the receptionist's love life."

"She sounds available."

"Yeah."

"That's your plan."

"Yeah."

"Fuck her and get the poison out of your system."

"Something like that."

"Okay. You know what? I like it."

I had a bitter taste in the back of my throat, and a sense of myself as an unpleasant fellow who could get what he wanted.

"I don't," I said. But that's the plan."

:   :

The doorman at Julia's building was a dignified, Irish-looking man of sixty or so. He bade me good evening warmly enough, but when I gave him Julia's name, he grew taller and older and aimed at me the deep, straight grooves bracketing his mouth. They met at his nose and looked like crossed halberds. "I'll tell her," he said.

He made no move toward the intercom. I nodded and walked past him.

No one answered when I rapped on her door upstairs, so I put my eye to the peephole. Of course, I couldn't see anything but a ball of light. Then of darkness. I said, "Hello?"

"Such a big brown eye," Julia said through the door. "Why did that calcified old shit let you up?"

"Aren't you ready?"

She opened the door a crack, leaving it on the chain. I saw a slice of unmade-up face, a bare shoulder, a bare knee. "You ought to know better by now than to show up on time, Nicky."

"I'm half an hour late."

"On purpose?"

"Yes."

"Clever. But an hour would have been cleverer." I smelled what I'd expected to: bourbon. "No biker shorts," she remarked, scanning me regretfully.

"That was my morning getup. This is my evening getup." I'd bought a new jacket in the goose-shit green then fashionable. With it I wore black jeans and spit-polished black Dr. Martens.

"Oh, getup getup. Blah. Listen, can you remember an address?" She gave it to me without waiting for a response. "Just a few blocks away. I'll be there soon as I can. Don't be resentful. Are you resentful? Liar. Kiss," she said and, opening the door as far as the chain would allow, raised her face.

There was no question of kissing her cheeks; she'd pressed them against the steel of her door and its jamb. I kissed her, and her tongue flashed into my mouth. Then she pulled away with a pop and said, "Nnnnnnh," her eyes half-closed.

"Half an hour," she added, and closed the door.

The party was in a corner duplex overlooking Central Park. You

entered onto the second-floor balcony and, to the pulse of synthe-
sized French dance music, gazed out and down over a gleaming
wooden floor traversed by celebrants. The place was cavernous and
white and nearly bare except for an immense fifties sofa in mauve
tweed and a gigantic unframed painting of a towering, faceless figure like a tornado of gray snot. This I recognized as a Jedd Garet, and
probably worth more than my father's house. You descended a steel
staircase that rang under your feet, and by the time you touched
down on the surface you understood yourself to have a role in some
vague but resplendent enterprise, global and new and worthless in a
stirring way. They'd set up a bar, and that is where I went. On the bar
sat a galvanized tub filled with ice and rubber-stoppered bottles of
Grolsch, which, as I remember, were then selling for about three
bucks apiece in the better groceries. I pulled one from the tub, and a
bartender offered me a napkin and a plastic cup, neither of which I
wanted, both of which I took. Then he removed the bottle from my
hand and poured some of it into my cup. He kept the bottle. I
thanked him. Nearby, a heavyset, pretty-faced man in paisley sus-
penders was saying, "So by now he's down about ninety grand,"
which in those days was a lot of money." I saw I'd be waiting for Julia
for quite some time.

For nearly two hours, I wandered alone and occupied myself
with drinking. The bartenders were very nice about giving me a new
glass and napkin with each beer, and taking the bottle away. I supposed the people in suits had come straight from the office, where
they were boss, and the ones in evening wear had come from the
opera or something. There were actually a few folks who might have
been from my neck of the woods. For instance, a young man with a
shiny, shaved saffron head and a powerfully curved nose. He wore a
double-breasted suit, immaculate red canvas deck shoes, and a fez. I
strolled toward him with some notion of conversation, and he met
me with, "And whose little Christmas tree ornament are you?"

"Sorry?"

He regarded me with concupiscent goodwill. "Or perhaps I should say Hanukkah bush. Oh, now, don't let's begin in a snit. I take whatever all back. Edgar Reyes." I told him my name, and we shook hands. "I simply meant that you've obviously been imported from the real world to sparkle the place up. And I *entirely* approve. I just wanted the name of your sponsor."

"Sponsor. You know, Edgar, I'm kind of tired."

"Just so," he agreed, "who do I think I am? But look around. Would anyone willingly talk to these people, even if one were these people oneself? No, Socrates, one would not, and so you'll see them all absolutely *fanning* out, a real scavenger hunt, to bring back bits of brightly-colored writers and artists and, well, *us*, to line their nests with. For instance, those bitty things in jeans who look like models? Are. Actually, I think the caterers supply them. You say which wine and how many models. But for you and me, someone actually had to go out and *snout* us up, as if we were truffles. You can't help loving the rich. They try so hard."

"If they're so dull, what are you here for?"

"Gossip," he said dreamily, "and gash." In his mouth, the word was plush and syrupy. "And you?"

"Well," I mumbled, "I'm not interested in gossip."

Edgar put his head back and laughed sumptuously. "Oh, *very* nice. I knew you were talkable-to. Look, I probably ought to tell you that I'm working, sort of. I edit one of those downtown style rags—since you didn't recognize my name, I won't humiliate myself by telling you which. Not, granted, much of a magazine, but we have fun, we have fun. Anyway, a surprising number of these people love reading their names in the boho press, and that's where *I* shine in. You see them sending their cars down to pick the paper up outside Veselka. They could get it at their own newsstands, of course, but above Fourteenth Street we charge a buck fifty."

"Aren't you rich?"

Amused: "Oh, no."

"How do you know *I'm* not rich?"

What a gorgeous laugh he had. "Oh... the way you stand. As though you had your SAT scores tattooed on your dick. No, no, it's entirely charming, and I'm sure it *works*."

"Intermittently."

"And you're going to tell me whose ornament you are? You're not bashful? Not ashamed? Shame's lethal," he said gravely.

"I am here with my friend Julia."

He smiled widely, open-mouthed. "Ahhhhh," he said, his voice syrupy again, "our li'l Miz Hargreave."

"Cram it, baldy," I snapped, and turned to go.

He laid a hand on my arm. "I most humbly apologize. I'm doing nothing to improve your situation."

"I don't have any goddamn situation."

"You've been stood up. Oh yes. You claim to be here with Julia? A plain untruth. Our Miz Hargreave does not make quiet entrances. Well, I am your ally for the evening, whether you believe it or not, and as it happens, no one is more competent to aid you in making alternative arrangements. Let's see. There are any number of plausible young things. We want one who values intensity over ebullience. We want her restful; I believe you've had enough excitement. Not mercenary. Able, perhaps, to carry a conversation some considerable distance without much help. What, you've spotted one already?"

"Yes."

"And drawn her to you with a glance. Here she comes. I am superfluous. Wertheim, you intrigue me increasingly. Hello, Sid. Don't you go underestimating this young man. That's what I've been doing. Bye now."

She said, "Bye, Ed. If you say so, I won't."

Sydney wore a sleeveless tobacco-hued sheath that resembled an immense and immensely chic dirty undershirt. Her velvet pumps had flat heels. Even so, her eyes were level with mine, and if she'd straightened fully from her lissome slouch, she'd have sent that constant gaze of mild and almost perfectly controlled incredulity right into the center of my forehead. She said, "I have a confession. I saw you an hour ago, wandering around alone. I was just going to let you rot. But that's not what I wanted to say. Somebody ought to apologize for the other afternoon, and as the one who probably least gives a damn, I suppose I'd better. I'm sorry, Nick. I'm sure I was quite unpleasant."

I took a fortifying swig. " 'Quite unpleasant.' Is that really what passes for an apology around here? You were a prize bitch," I said with relish.

"I do do it well, don't I? But I much prefer the way you said it to Julia. A *ravening* bitch."

"Well, if you were listening in, you deserved whatever you got."

"Of course I wasn't listening in. She came and told me."

"Oh."

"Yes. 'Oh.' And that she'd offered to pay you fifty dollars to sleep with me. Because what I needed to stop me being such a horrible little Smithie was a good 'fuck.' Or no, what was it? A good 'bang.'"

" 'Boff.' And it was a hundred."

"Really? You know, I feel much better now. You're an old – it's not my business, of course – friend? Well, I gather she's changed. And I warn you, you're not going to get it."

"It?" I said coolly.

"It. Friendship, or sex, or… whatever it is you want, that's what you're not going to get. She's grown genuinely nasty. Believe it or not, Julia and I were friends when she first came to the office. Before she decided she'd rather hate me. For what, I don't know. Being sober, or younger, or prettier."

"You're prettier, are you?"

Sydney nodded, not much interested in the question. "But it could have been anything. Snobbery."

"Can't say she's ever struck me as a snob."

"Of course she hasn't been one to *you*. Middle-class intellectuals are off her social scale."

"But you're not."

"Nope. The Platts were pretty established in this country for about a century and a half before anyone heard of the Turrells. And now we're pretty busted, so I get it from her both ways."

"That's tough."

"All right. But I'm not the one being snotty now. I'm just speaking plainly. I thought you people appreciated that."

"You mean *you Jews?*"

"You artists."

"Oh." I flushed.

She laughed delightedly, swaying back and forth and pointing. "*Gotcha!* Oh, I got you! And it was *easy!*"

"All right, you got me."

"Oh, stop. Stop pretending you don't like me."

I began to smile. "All right."

She said, "You're something of a bitch yourself. I was going to just let you trudge around. You were so unhappy, and I was glad. I don't know how you got so completely on my nerves the other day – well, yes, I do. Because I could see myself so clearly in your eyes as just this little horror."

"Two bitches."

"Fraught," she agreed.

A pause.

"Rrrrrrrrrravening!" she said happily, making a claw of one hand and sweeping it through the air.

We laughed. "Sydney, what are you doing here?"

"But this is a Heller party, really. The Conservancy Board *is* the Heller Board, once you scrape off all the old lichen who don't know *what* board they're sitting on anymore. Why else do you think Julia got invited? Because she's such a hostess's delight? You know, it's so funny talking to an old beau of hers, or old friend, or what*ever*. I had a real schoolgirl crush on her when she came here. I was thrilled she thought I was glamorous – she's probably made fun of my little stint of modeling, but she didn't think it was funny then – and anyway, back then I'd've died to meet someone who'd known her forever. And here you are, and you seem more clueless than I am. I hope not. I hope you can talk to her. Because she's growing darker and darker, and no one's doing anything to stop her. Certainly not me; I hate her now. As you've no doubt noticed."

From behind her back she brought one of those fabulous beers – she'd gotten the whole bottle, I noticed – and took a pull.

"Nice that it was a full hundred instead of fifty, at any rate," she said.

"I'll say. I could use the money," I muttered.

She laughed. "If you like, I'll tell her you earned it."

"You're too kind."

"Oh… it's not as kind as all that."

We smiled uncertainly.

Then Julia's voice rang out:

"Ah. This must be one of those miniature Japanese drinks you read about. The Japanese are doing great work in miniaturizing drinks. Any chance of making this American-sized?" A local hush. The bartender accepted a drink from a slim hand and poured a few more shots into it, face blank. "Much obliged," Julia said, and hove into view, her forehead damp, her plastic cup brimming with whiskey. In a miniscule black dress she clicked across the parquet floor like a thoroughbred approaching the starting gate. "Well, *hello*," she said. "Are you young things setting a date and time?"

"Bit soon for that, Julia, wouldn't you think?" Sydney said. "No telling when you'll be done with him."

"Sid –"

"Yes. I know what I can kiss, thanks. You've mentioned it before. And since you're waving it all over the room tonight, I'm not likely to have forgotten about it."

"This is all very tactically unsound, young Sid."

"Do you think you're sober enough to remember to have me fired?"

"Yes."

"Well, poor unfortunate me. Goodnight, Nick." She walked off.

A pause.

"That's a lovely getup," I said.

"Oh, *stop*," she cried. "I come to these things. And I just act so badly."

"And then you act forlorn about acting so badly. Don't get sloppy on me, Julia."

She looked up with wet eyes. Then, with lips pressed shut, she worked her jaw in a savoring manner, as though her mouth had been filled with something interesting, if not necessarily pleasant.

"You've turned sensible, you little shit," she said.

"No. I don't think I have."

"And how about our young Sid? Have you ever seen such skin. And her *legs*. She used to model, you know. She probably told you. She tells everybody. Tell me, what goes through a man's mind when he sees something like that?" she said, and looked hopeful.

"A hundred bucks," I said.

She was downcast.

"You wanted us to be buddies again," I suggested, "discussing the merits of the Jewess at the Co-op store."

"Don't you get tired of being smart about how awful I am?" she said bitterly.

A pause.

"You sort of wish she'd do something awkward," I admitted.

Julia sighed in gratitude. "But she doesn't! Not *ever*."

"No?"

"And it would make me feel so *good!*"

"I've been looking forward to seeing you," I said sadly.

"Yes. You bought a new jacket." She reached out and plucked a few tiny threads from my sleeve, where I'd snipped the label away. "I've been looking forward to this, too. Somehow it embarrasses me to admit how much. I knew you'd have your little lectures ready, but at least you'd bother to do that. Most people don't. Things haven't been so terribly bright, lately."

She tipped her head back and drained her drink. Julia's throat was an inevitable fluid curve, like water poured from a jar. She held the plastic cup suspended to catch the last few drops. Then she noticed me watching, and made a little show of shaking the last drop into her mouth. She raised the cup like a chalice and took a hieratic stance. "The priest and the prophet reel with strong drink," she droned, "they are confused with wine, they err in vision, they, um, stumble in giving judgment. For all tables are full of vomit and no place is without filthiness. Isaiah."

"Based," I said, "on a true story. What are you writing these days?"

"Nothing. I've given it up. Who have I been kidding with this gumbo of half-pretty thoughts? I'm a *business*person now." She let her mouth hang open on the *w* of *now* while she studied my reaction, absently brushing the cup back and forth against her pendant lower lip. "How are *you* working, if it comes to that?"

"Diligently."

"No divine spark, eh?"

"I don't know if I'm a particularly sparky person."

"Is that why you come sniffing around me? What a horrible question, I forbid you to have heard it. But aren't you getting any good work done at *all?* I'm serious, Nicky, I think of you as someone with occasional access to the larger things. You're not just some little nail-biter."

"Are you starting again?"

She leaned close and touched my forearm. "Did I *stop?*" she asked, and began to laugh. *"Run, run while you still can!"* she cried, and laughed helplessly, her face shiny. "And the horrible part is, you still want me. It's so sick."

"I dunno. You're looking pretty good."

"Really, how good could I look? Quick," she said merrily, "before it comes again, how *are* you? You seem kind of ragged."

"That's about right."

"You look like you're at the stage of judgment. A very low place. Like, you're shit, and everything's shit, but you, you're *intelligent* about it. I bet you keep a notebook on your crap job and all the crappy things, and someday it'll be revealed as beautiful? That's how I spent *years*. But Nicky? That day never comes. I think that job's bad for you. You should quit."

"And do exactly what?"

"Your *work*," she said sternly. "You can always find some crap job for money. Walk me over to the bar. I'm dry."

"Let's sit and talk a little more."

"Don't be a prissy-boo. Come on. Nick, this is annoying. Well, I'll be right back."

She set off. I thought about calling after her, but even I could see that, when trying to get an alcoholic into bed, one does not improve one's chances by pointing out how very much she's drinking.

And then I thought about having thought that. *"Julia,"* I called.

She walked back, elaborately patient. "Yes, Nick?"

"Don't drink any more tonight."

"No? Why not?"

"Just don't."

"Why not?"

"Because you're an alcoholic, Julia."

That had sounded stupider than strictly necessary.

"And you," Julia said, "are a swarthy little Pharisee who's going to go home the way he generally does. With nothing. Goodnight."

After she'd gone, I noticed people staring. I stared back at them one by one, and they looked away. There was a glass door in the corner, leading to a balcony. It looked very cool and empty out there.

It wasn't cool, of course; when the latch clicked behind me, warm darkness wrapped itself around my face. Across the way was the concrete dome of Hayden Planetarium, sharply illumined. Around it, the trees were an ashen black-green and, lit with harsh spotlights, seemed gripped by some glamorous crisis.

In a while Julia came through the glass door. She held out her hands to me, as if to have her knuckles rapped with a ruler. I brushed them away. She leaned beside me at the railing. Then she hugged my arm and pressed her face into it with a child's unconditional desire for comfort. "I love this power station so much."

"This planetarium."

"That's what I meant, that it looks so powerful. Don't you love the shape and how it's lit up and clean?"

"Yes."

"Oh, I'm doing this so badly. I was so nervous about seeing you, and I kept on having a little more, a little more, and then I was sloshed. And then I thought, okay, I'll be dissolute and fascinating. But I'm just doing this so badly."

"We're neither of us winning any prizes."

"Oh God, that last drink was such a mistake. I'm going to be more drunk in a little. I can feel it swirling up, all hot."

"Are you sick?"

"Am I feverish? I feel so feverish. Fevered. May have to go back in the bathroom."

"Come on, I'll take you."

"*No. Please* let's just stay out here and be like this a little more. Were you saving that up to say? Me being a drunk?"

"Nope. Didn't plan to say anything."

" 'Cause you didn't think I'd listen?"

"Because," I said bleakly, "I was hoping to get laid."

She nodded. "That's reasonable."

"Is it?"

"Oh, yes. But, Nicky, not tonight? It's so awful, sleeping with people when you're drunk. So messy and swushing-around. Don't you see how it would be so awful? But you *should* get laid, you really should. It's no fair, your coming here and being so patient and looking so nice and going home without getting anything. There are lots of girls here. There's Sydney. I think you should go home with Sydney."

I made some noise of exasperation.

"You should! I've been *thinking* about it! Look, Sid and I used to actually be sort of buddies, before she decided my soul needed a good swabbing down with Lysol or something, and I actually do still care about her. She'll do this lethal little pas de deux with one of these fat-faced young beauts. Then at the penultimate moment she'll bolt like a bunny and they'll both go home alone and *miserable*."

"So instead she should perform this lethal pas de deux with me."

"But her last boyfriend was just *like* you. She only likes Jews or Armenians or something."

"Or something."

"At the conclusion of the evening I shall offer up a blanket apology for every hideous thing I've said, and you may beat me with an extension cord. Until then, piss off." She returned her forehead to my shoulder. "Nicky, *please* just take Sid home. You're both young. And *sober*."

"I am not," I said crossly, "sober."

"We can try again some night when I'm not horrible."

"Are such nights common?"

"They occur. At intervals. Rat. Go on, now."

I was silent. Then I nodded.

"Okay," I said. "I think you're right. Enjoy the party. I'll call you." I bussed her cheek, then turned and set my hand on the knob of the glass door.

Julia seized my elbow and spun me around. "You *slut*," she snarled, and I began to laugh at her. "You scrawny, ugly, *ugly* little Wasphound. You whore, don't laugh," she said, giggling. "You would've done it, wouldn't you?" I put my arms around her, as I'd been aching to do all evening, and she slipped her hands under my jacket and embraced me tightly. "You would've done it, you would've done it," she sighed. I said, "Julia, for God's sake, let's get out of here."

She yawned into my chest. I laid my temple atop her cropped head. She pivoted my head with a deft twist of hers, so that we were face to face, and I smelled her breath, like sugared ozone. She noticed me smelling and sent a big puff into my nose. Then she began to exhale over my cheeks, my chin, my forehead, my neck, whipping her face deliriously back and forth, her parted lips a fraction from my skin, until I took hold of her skull and clamped my mouth across hers. I heard small noises from the back of her throat. Someone came to the glass door, then went away. She pulled her mouth free and said, "Oh God. Is that you against my belly? Oh, I have to *pee*." Chuckling, she dropped her forehead against my chest. "Actually, I have to do worse."

"Come on, I'll take you."

"*No*. I don't want it to be like some... You just wait here, and it'll be fine, and then we'll go. Can you trust me to come back here and it'll be fine?"

"No."

"You're right. But I don't want you to be right, I want you to trust me. I've said such terrible things, but I'll feel so much better when I come right back here, and can't you see how it would turn everything awful if you were just being a caretaker?"

"No."

She bit my lower lip. She had a cat's knack of knowing just how hard she could bite without breaking the skin. "I want you to take me home," she whispered, "and get me... out... of this... *getup*."

"Oh, for God's sake go to the bathroom."

She mooched off, her shoulder blades rubbing slyly together, like a cat's.

I leaned on the railing again and looked across at the planetarium. I was drunk myself, but not too drunk. The alcohol seemed to have thinned everything out and left it clear. In a while, I'd go in and hunt for Julia. "Nick, my dim young friend, you are going to *pay* for this," I said aloud. On the sidewalk below, tiny people went about their business. I gazed down benevolently. As I watched, Julia appeared among them and began marching toward the park.

By the time I skidded out the front door, the sidewalk was empty of Julia, and I ran toward the park, toward a small shadow sinking into other shadows, framed by stone gateposts. I cried, "Hold it!" The darkness of its head glinted white, as if it had turned its face toward me. Then it slipped inside. When I reached the gate, a figure was just fading out of another streetlight's glow, deeper into the park. "Julia?" I shouted. It seemed to enter the woods around the amphitheater. I thought I'd found the spot, but blundered through the brush and gained only a deserted path winding up through black trees toward the miniature castle above the lake. I trotted down around the looming wooden hull of the theater, then up along shallow, curving stone steps. The path divided and looped. She could have stepped off anywhere. I fought my way through the trees to the edge of the bluff. Below, I saw the shadow-thronged bleachers, a sloping bluff whose veins of mica twinkled in the moonlight and, within a little cove, a disturbance like cream troubling stale coffee.

By the time I got there, Julia was crawling out through the rushes and mud, hugging her purse to her belly. Her makeup was barbarously dark.

"Thought if I could cool off it would just *stop* everything. Just *stop* it," she explained as she lurched to her feet, "but then I fell in. I mean, I dove. But I lost my shoe. See?" She lifted her stockinged foot and sat abruptly, spraddle-legged, like a toddler. I hooked my hands under her arms and hoisted her to her feet.

She said, "Get your fucking hands off me. Wait, hold it, I'm gonna fall. There. That was easy."

"All right," I said. "Let's go."

"Go?"

"Let's get you home, Julia."

"Home? With you? Was that really what we decided?"

"Yes," I said. "I believe that was what we decided."

She thought about it. She seemed honestly puzzled. "That doesn't sound right. Is that really what we decided?"

"Yes."

She looked at me much as Christopher had once looked at the leftovers. Her cheekbones lifted and her lower teeth seemed to lengthen in distaste. "So that was what we decided. You *have* been waiting for your moment. But I'm afraid I'm not quite drunk enough after all. Why don't you trot back and try your luck with Sydney?"

Then she began plucking bits of wet leaf from my lapel.

Very quietly, I said, "Julia, did you drink anything more after you went inside?"

"Only a nice cool beer," she confided. "They give you these wonderful bottles."

I turned her toward the street and she began to limp along next to me on her single high-heeled pump, swinging from side to side like the baton of a metronome. I kept an arm around her waist. If she stumbled again and I tried to hug her upright, she'd probably slide out of her sopping dress like a cooked eel slipping from its skin. As we approached her building, she looked around curiously. Then her nostrils flared and she elbowed me away. She kicked off her shoe and, leaving it in the gutter, walked by the doorman under her own power. She stepped into the waiting elevator, gripped the rail on the back wall as if it were the barre in a ballet school, and gazed composedly at the paneling in front of her nose.

"Julia? I've forgotten your floor. What floor, Julia?"

"Whatever you like," she said courteously.

"Julia, what floor do you live on?"

"Oh… nineteen?"

I punched nineteen. As we rose, she slipped bonelessly to the carpet. I left her there. When we reached nineteen, I hoisted her up and slung her over my shoulder. "Don't recall your apartment number offhand, do you?" With her flank, hot and live as a bird's breast, against my ear, I fumbled her purse open and rummaged through weedy water for her keys. One was stamped 19K.

Inside, the neatness amazed me until I realized she must have a housekeeper. There were a lot of earth tones and nubbly fabrics, wall-to-wall dusk-blue carpet, an inoffensive antique breakfront that seemed to have been polished by committee. Like a high-class hotel room. A poster for *Ugly Girls Go to War* in a plastic stationery-store frame. I didn't want to ruin her furniture, so I set her down on the doormat. That looked uncomfortable. Good. I dropped her keys by her head and turned to go.

She began trying to crawl, like a rabbit half-squashed by a car.

Oh, all right. I slipped my hands beneath her thighs and shoulders and scooped her up again.

She vomited down the front of her dress.

My God, she'd strangle – but I didn't turn her over at once; I worried about staining her carpet, perhaps because it had the same poodle texture as her hair. I bundled her into the bathroom and set her before the toilet. She began to retch again, a deep, ratcheting sound. "Uh," she said, "uh Gah. Uh Gah. Oh Gaaah."

She brought up a few last strands as I stroked her neck and said, "It's all right, it's all right. *What's* all right? You witless cunt. Are you done?"

"P'weh. P'wuh. Pfuh."

I scooped a little clean water from the sink into her mouth and she spat. By this time Julia was puke-slick from chin to knees. I lowered her into the tub just as she was and ran it full of warm water. She whimpered: I was trying to drown her. Then smiled dreamily, as if being drowned were the best lascivious fun one could imagine, and her knees parted. I closed them and sudsed her up. I gripped the back of her neck and dunked her soapy head; she folded easily at the waist, tried to blow bubbles, and emerged giggling. A golden cloud enriched

the water. "Simpler," she managed. "Oh, absolutely," I agreed, drain-
ing the tub. "Much simpler this way. You don't need to do big business as well, do you? Presumably not, or I'm sure you would have. No
need to stand on ceremony with old Nick." She shivered in the empty
tub and I began to refill it. I pulled her dress away from her flat chest
and ladled water down there. I didn't look inside. Well, I did. My God,
what did it *matter* – I'd already seen everything Julia had, hadn't I?
Chewed on it, in fact. I lifted her out and dried her roughly, clothes
and all, while she grunted in fear and tried to fight me. Then I
dumped her on her bed: Julia, goodnight and goodbye. She shivered.
Let he· ne caught her breath and shivered again. Oh, for Christ's
sake. julia had no more sense of modesty than a newt; wouldn't she
rather I got her out of this sopping muck? Jesus, didn't I deserve a little thrill for all my grief and trouble and the cockteasing and the fetid
ruin of my new jacket? Yes. No. I turned and strode to the door.

Then I strode back and stripped her furiously naked, flinging her
soaking pantyhose against the wall. They stuck.

A stranger's body sprawled before me, pale, the shaved armpits
shockingly white, each bone or muscle separate and comely. Her
flanks rippled like a gazelle's haunches when I shifted her into the
center of the bed. The triangular garden had been trimmed into a
sort of lush exclamation mark whose dot was her anus. Her tiny
breasts had vanished; her long nipples sat on dainty ribs. The nipples
were hard and granular, and her entire sleek body was goosefleshed.
She squirmed a little with the chill and cuddled her elbows into her
sides.

I wasn't really the sort of man who would rape an unconscious
woman, was I?

It was an interesting question.

I lifted and turned a slim leg, touched her pale buttock with a
forefinger where it joined her inner thigh, held her long foot. The
heavy calluses had been smoothed with pumice. I set my palm on
her belly. She moved her hips vaguely and I withdrew it. I ran my

hands over her cropped head and she licked my wrist. Quite clearly she sighed, *"Chris."*

A malign leer eclipsed her features: the full, dreadful face I'd only glimpsed before, gathered savagely around a hard little muzzle. Like childhood dreams of chasing endlessly after someone you cared for – there was something you had to say, something important – and when you caught up, you saw a countenance distorted and bestial, crude jaws ready to rend, just as you'd always known they'd be. I wondered which face I'd kissed through her half-opened door.

But it was already sweetening into sleep. The X on her inner thigh, my neat stroke and her jagged one, gleamed. I touched it with the tip of my tongue. This had to stop. Firmly, I kissed the crest of her cunt: goodbye. I brought the covers to her chin and turned out the light. It was perfectly clear, then as now, that I'd been at a party with an old friend and ex-lover, and that when she'd passed out in the mud I'd done the only decent thing: taken her home, held her head while she was sick, gotten her sodden things off, and put her to bed. It was perfectly clear, then as now, that I'd been at a party with a strange and unfriendly woman, and that when she'd passed out I'd taken the opportunity to strip her naked and sniff over her body. I told myself, incorrectly, that someday this would all make sense. Scrubbed free of makeup, Julia's eyelids and lips were pale and swollen, and beneath the tip of her nose lurked that faint, avid, animal cleft.

In the kitchen, I tried to clean my jacket with paper towels, then left the keys on the counter. Downstairs, the doorman ignored me as I stepped out into the warm, jumbled night.

Spattered as I was, I couldn't get a cab to stop; I took the subway instead. When I fit my key into our lock at home and pushed, I was met with a hellish clattering. Inside, I saw someone had balanced the paste-brush and metal bucket against the door, so that they'd fall if the door was opened. Adam came roaring down from his loft half-awake, like a monstrous child on Christmas morning. *"Did you get lucky?"*

Bending, I picked up the bucket and brush. "The moment," I said, "wasn't right."

He sagged against the wall. "You just… what? You just *talked?* You were supposed to fuck her and get the poison out. You were supposed to get over her."

"I think I'm over her anyway."

"*You?* You have never gotten over anything in your *life*. I'm getting out. I am getting out of here. *You're* the poison. You are *poison*."

"I don't blame you."

"I said I'm moving *out*."

"I heard. Lower your voice."

"And all I wanted," he cried with outthrust arms, "was to get you a little pussy."

"You think you could give that word a rest?"

"YOU *FUCK!*" he screamed. "I AM NOT GOING TO CARRY YOU ON MY BACK ALL MY LIFE!"

:   :

Toward lunch on Monday – it was slow, and I'd spent the morning yearning up through the plastic swinging doors at the stairs leading to daylight – Louis barked, "*Funny Man*. Maximum, Heller, two coming back."

I froze. "Which floor?"

"What, if it's not your favorite floor, you won't go? I gotta Maximum."

"Send Key," I managed. "He's been here on his butt all morning."

Key bobbed to his feet. "I got it," he chirped. "I'm there."

"*Sit down*." Key sat down. "I'm sending *you*. Who in fuck do you think you're talking to?"

"I just meant that I didn't feel that great. Don't. Maybe I should just. Go home?"

"All right," Louis said reasonably. "You little piece of *shit. What did you do last time you were at Heller?*"

Curtis woke and examined me with mild, sad interest. Army bundled his handkerchief against his breast and moaned.

"You were there all fucking day," Louis said. "You steal something, Nicky? Hit on a receptionist? – ooh, that made you jump. Leave your tag on the wall? Piss in the elevator? You heard me right. You think I haven't fired little geeks like you for worse'n pissing in the elevator?"

"I," I said. "I didn't piss in the elevator."

"He speaks. Now, tell Poppa, what did you do to the fucking receptionist that you don't wanna go back?"

"Louis?"

"Yes, Funny Man?"

"You have mayonnaise on your mouth, Louis. You always have mayonnaise on your mouth. In the corners, two little dobbins. When it's fresh it's pretty much white, and then after an hour or so it's more sort of yellowish and, and, you eat these *corn* dogs. They give napkins away with those things, Louis. Free. Do you have any idea what it does to a person of even moderate sensibility, Louis, to take orders all day from some gritty little slob to whom it doesn't ever occur, apparently, who apparently can't be *bothered*, not to mention all the farting, Louis, I quit. I *quit*."

My bike ticked crazily as I wheeled it toward the stairs.

As I passed Curtis, he muttered, *"Amusing himself."*

Must Welcome Turmoil as a Central Friend

The idea was that *slam* would be a downtown 'zine, but with corporate backing and, more to the point, hundreds of pages of glossy national advertising. A great deal of thought had gone into the premiere issue. The art director set the headlines in a digital font designed to look as though it had been banged out on an old typewriter. Before delivering it to the printer, she xeroxed the expensive fashion photography, in order to attain the proper savor of cheapness. Though its parent conglomerate occupied a monolith on Sixth Avenue, *slam* was published out of a rehabbed tenement on Avenue B. It augmented its staff with local artists and rockers. Of course, the editor-in-chief was a company man: the forty-one-year-old wunderkind behind *Golf Entrepreneur* magazine. He was also, as it happened, the brother of a Sag Harbor orthodontist who owned three of my lithographs and wanted to do me a good turn.

Looking back, I'd say I was born to be an office manager. It is a position in which you are paid to be fussy and controlling. It did not bore me to take inventory, or to ponder the excellences of competing brands of light bulb. The wunderkind was delighted with his humming copiers and supply closets that were a dream of order, and

I was not displeased with my generous and regular paycheck. I also approved of my coworkers, with the possible exception of an Israeli copy editor named Dori Schreuder.

Dori was a portly young woman who seemed always to have slept in her clothes. You had just, she suggested, woken her for some damn fool reason. Deadlines left her unflustered; each day at five-thirty sharp, she'd rise with a grunt, leaving marker uncapped, denim skirt rucked up on one side, coffee mug half full, work half done, and away she'd amble, hips majestic. She had the face of a newborn animal whose eyes are only reluctantly open, and ill-kept short hair, more beige than blonde. But her limbs were round and potent, her chest dizzyingly heavy, and her sexual aplomb absolute. By this time, I'd learned to experience desire as hatred. I watched Dori as she sauntered off each night, my loins churning with hate.

Spite, in those days, was my meat and drink. Spite hauled me from bed each morning; spite sent me about my business; spite squeezed my eyes shut each night. Though I'd sworn to purge my life of chaos, though I'd sworn I'd never speak to Julia again, I still spent hours haranguing her in terrific solitary sessions which left me as queasily sated as if I'd gorged on cheap candy. I'd never told Julia off! This was now as maddening as never having fucked her. Narrowing my eyes, I rehearsed by the hour the things I'd say if I ever saw her again. Julia brazen, Julia contrite, Julia soused and clumsy, phoned me entreatingly in the small hours, found me hollow-eyed (her handiwork!) in a low dive, saw me strolling down the avenue with someone better. *Forgive!* she cried on some bile-swept darkling plain. Her little black dress in tatters. *I'm afraid you've used up your allotment of forgiveness,* Nick murmured through a pitiless smile. *But I love you!* she cried. Nicky, crisply: *Then God help the people you love.*

slam made a great to-do of its boho personnel, and each month ran a photo of a representative staffer in its contributors' notes. They featured their office manager in *issue three.* It was a very flattering portrait. I'd tied back my hair and looked fetchingly intense, and the bio reported that here was an innovative young printmaker from whom big things could be expected. I was at my desk late one evening, trying to draw from the intent, dark, close-set eyes a smidgen of courage and calm, when I became aware of a silent figure at my shoulder. I humiliated myself further by quickly turning the page, then flung down the magazine. "Oh, Narcissus," Dori said, chuckling. "Careful you don't fall in your pretty pond."

I snapped, "Would you care to go screw yourself?"

"Another of your funny American idioms. Oh, translate, please."

" 'Would you care to have coffee with me?' "

"Better a drink."

In the bar, I tried to find out how in hell Dori ever found work as an editor. The subject bored her. I still don't know. Her written English was bloodlessly correct, but she'd shuttled since childhood between Tel Aviv and Amsterdam, where she was born, and her spoken English… "Out on the street" was *Odd Anne they strayed*. She loved to say *you know*, which she pronounced *you knew*. "The buildings are so big here, and the dogs, you knew, so little. I see things on leashes that back home we would be killing them as vermin. The men never go in the sun, and so when they take off their clothes, you knew, they look like children. And the women, excuse me, so ugly. In Amsterdam they look at me and say, Who is that fat cow? But here everyone thinks I am *beau-ti-ful*, and oh, they must meet me."

"Not me. I thought, Who is that fat cow?"

"So," she said, smiling hungrily, "not always so nice."

"Hardly ever nice. Why'd your family move so much?"

"You see? This American niceness to foreigners. You are concerned for my fam-i-ly background."

"That's it. Could you answer the question?"

"It is too boring."

We continued squabbling lazily. Then, what I thought was an aimless walk led us to her Hell's Kitchen tenement. Brusquely, I asked to come up. She walked inside and let me lunge through the front door before it clicked shut. Upstairs, Dori had a lightless shotgun apartment of truly ambitious squalor. "My roommate is away. Else we could all have a nice talk about her family. But now we must be nice, you knew, all by ourselves."

An ambush of some sort? Fine. Let's get it over with. I hooked the back of her neck and dragged her toward me. That was the first time I saw her look surprised.

"Just the kiss. Not, please, the demonstration of how tough you are."

We kissed. It was a kiss of astonishing delicacy, and went on for quite a while, and my spite began to disintegrate into details: the bread-scent of her saliva, a white gleam in the hollow of her ear, the buckle on her brassiere as it stubbed my thumb through her T-shirt, like the massive lock that dramatizes a chest of fairy-tale treasure. My hand drifted out and landed on a breast. Dear God. I opened her shirt with worshipful fingers. She let her brassiere slither down her arms.

I offer no apology for what I thought then.

I thought: It's not every man who gets a second chance with Melissa Perlman.

:   :

I gave Dori a drawer in my dresser, where she kept a few changes of clothes, which I'd wash whenever I did my laundry. I was hard-pressed not to smirk each time I laundered one of her bras. They seemed to be the collaborative effort of a sailmaker and a blacksmith, and I folded each one cup into cup with awe. I fixed us dinner nearly every night. The bottom of my wok glowed blue as lightning. Dori read while I cooked, and seldom complimented the food or thanked me, and in fact she sustained her great body on finicking half-portions, but I could smell how good it was and knew she could, too, and her small face was blissful as she ate. I began a major new suite of etchings. She liked to watch me working, and liked to hear me talk about it. We did splendidly unimaginative things, like seeing movies. My patience with movies is slight, but Dori didn't see the point of exerting her critical faculties unless paid to do so, and found them all engrossing. While I squirmed and snorted, she sat upright, mouth slightly open, and eventually, never taking her eyes from the screen, brought a fist down on my restless thigh. A sincere blow. We soon developed a procedure agreeable to both of us: if I disliked the film, I'd leave and meet her outside the theater when it was done. Meanwhile, I took walks and savored the city. There's a certain hammered-lead glint that clings to midtown cornices in fall. The gravel factory, prison, and vast Pepsi-Cola sign along the ocean-stinking East River are grander to me than pyramids and more venerable – speaking more directly of the great human currents of greed and ingenuity – and sighting along the basin of the Washington Square fountain, with its spigots sealed by iron caps for winter, I knew I was privileged to be part of one of history's great cities in its days of brilliant decline, like Imperial Rome, like Victorian London, and since I knew this great city contained, on a worn velour seat in a darkened theater, a plump and clever woman who would spend that night with me, then my place in it was fully established, and my contentment complete. I did little chores for her: removed and planed her balky kitchen door, put in a new faucet. "Someone taught you to do that," she accused in wonder. Afterward we lazed on a grassy incline in Central Park. "So lucky to be able to do this," she said. "Your arm is nice where it is."

"What arm. That's a perfectly blameless arm. That arm is around your waist."

She snugged it still higher, so that her breasts were squashed together in the crook of my elbow. "Oh yes, blameless. Nicky?"

"Yes, Dutch Girl?"

"Say again how you like me."

"You're my flying circus. You're my all-girl orchestra."

"Someday I wish a park like this, all to my own."

"This *is* your park. I just bought it for you."

"Oho. You did not say you are rich."

"I'm not. I'm busted from buying this park. You better take good care of this park or it's the last park you get from me."

"It is the most wonderful park I am ever given."

"Thank you."

"You are so nice to me, I will give you half my park. What shall we do with our park? We don't let anyone in who isn't on our side," she said seriously.

"Good idea. Those people down there, are they on our side?"

"I can't tell," she said uneasily. "Go ask them."

"In a minute. I'll ask them in a minute."

I kissed her. Even her tongue was leisurely, fat, and firm. The grass chilled our legs. The vertical faces of the skyscrapers bordering the park retained a gold luster, separate from the gathering dimness in the trees around us. It was time to think about getting home. Dori removed her open raincoat and settled it over us like a blanket. She unsnapped her jeans beneath it and tucked my hand around the humid nest within. "This is good for thumbs." I'd mashed my thumb earlier with the crescent wrench. "You must keep on to do nice things for me. When we are home you must bring to me my favorite books and you must cook me a good dinner."

"I just fixed your sink and bought you a park. Get off your rump and cook it yourself."

"I will cook you dinner. What would you like?"

My fingers paused. "You cook?"

"I do all the cooking for my family since I am nine."

"You never told me that."

"It is too boring. Shall I cook you Chicken Kiev?"

I didn't answer.

"You will make me come in the middle of my park," she observed, "with people walking to and fro."

"And we don't even know if they're on our side," I reflected.

She looked tormented.

I said, "They're on our side. Of course they're on our side. You're going to come."

The lights along the paths blinked on. Shadows stretched across us.

"I will cook you Chicken Ki-*effff*. I will cook you DUMPLINGS!"

The raincoat rattled, then quieted.

"This is our park now," she hummed. "And in your hand, that is your park. All yours."

Oh, marvelous, marvelous, I hadn't really understood this whole sex thing before. Why had no one had the kindness to explain? Julia had been... (a hallucination! Julia who!?). And my trysts with Rayella had been like some wrenchingly gratifying work of pornography. But with Dori, everything was actual. The world was flesh: hers. White and poreless, it could be warm, private, and nourishing, or chill, heavy, dense, and sweet, like half-thawed frozen pound cake sneaked from the fridge at midnight. Those indestructible forearms and hips, that small, pacific brow – with a gear or bundle of lightning bolts in one hand, she could have been a municipal caryatid in sun-smoothed granite, representing Progress or Rural Electrification. And her tits were lustrous, heavy, bomblike, murderously large, bearing faint silver stretch marks like the surface of wind-rippled snow, and nipples like pale grayish-pink ponds, which wrinkled into nuggets at my touch. You felt you had to do something about them. Either I gathered everything together in a cramming, smothery embrace, crushing her face, bosom, and trapped hands into my chest and muffling her moans, or I heaved back and hammered myself into her so that they wobbled in great independent figure eights, which forced me to grab them, which stopped the wobbling, which forced me to let go so I could watch them again. It maddened me to have to choose while sucking, to leave one nipple unattended. By mashing her breasts together, I could get both into my mouth at once. But then you couldn't do as good a job.

"Nicky, my God, your mama, didn't she breast-feed you?"

"Yeah. But she *stopped*."

For all Dori's amused grouchiness and female bulk, her cries when I entered her were small and bewildered, like a small child unjustly punished. A better person than I would have found nothing arousing about this, probably. But I was rough, and loved to inflict pleasure, to bite and slap and wrench her from one posture to another. With alacrity she dropped to her round knees, buried her face in crossed arms as if counting to a hundred in a game of hide-and-seek, and presented her bum. The delicate white flesh showed the least mark. I could see that nothing but my thumbs and teeth had ever happened to her. On this pearly screen bracketed by my hands, I saw Amsterdam, a big village full of windmills and legal pot, all wholesome as Gouda cheese, smug and swaddled in North Sea oil money; I saw the hygienic Israeli desert, marching Sabras purged of second thoughts by a common foe, a sun like an autoclave baking everything clean. I'd come to view sex as a long-deferred retribution for life's teasing – take *that*, and *that* – and maybe, with Charlotte, I'd hesitated to wreak vengeance on a member of an oppressed minority. But here was a chubby, snooty Dutch girl who'd never known a whiff of trouble. Fine. *Let her have it.*

From time to time I'd retreat to the bathroom, not needing to urinate so much as to see my face in the mirror, to verify that my character and humanity had not been entirely schtupped away. Then I'd stumble back to bed, and up it would start again.

"Ah, if anyone knew how good I felt, they'd arrest me."

"They are not so interested to stop your good time. This you must learn."

Then she slept. As much as Dori loved sex, I believe she considered it the foreplay of sleep, and she often retired before me. When I lifted the blankets, a wall of heat and scent rolled out as if I'd opened the hatch of a female furnace. She lay on her stomach, guarding her head with both arms. Her legs were splayed and her breasts squeezed out to either side of her mightily tapering back in two fat white crescents. I wanted her to throw a leg over my cold and meager body, but she slept motionless and, resolved not to disturb her precious sleep, I took her warmth as if stealing.

I was a thwarted little item, I thought comfortably as I nuzzled the nearer white crescent. Raised in a sexual maelstrom administered by taboo females, I'd chosen as my heart's desire the queen of the inaccessible. Periodically she'd sweep through my life like Halley's Comet, and in fury at not having her I'd bitch up whatever contentment I'd improvised with someone else. Julia wasn't to blame, of course. Any more than Halley's Comet would be to blame if it obliterated the earth. Now, here was Dori. She was fond of me – she'd sleepily hugged my face into her starboard breast – and refused to take me seriously. What luck! In a year I'd be thirty. I saw myself as mature, hard, finished with romance. And if I'd truly learned how not to wreck good fortune... Here I rolled Dori, sleepily complaining, over on her back. With my head crammed into her bosom like a hand crammed down between the sofa cushions in search of lost dimes, I reflected on how much nicer it was to be smart than to be stupid. There was simply no comparison.

Later, bruised and wet, she whispered, "Remember you are always my *chayaton*."

Her little beast.

:   :

Adam was delighted to reconcile, and ecstatic to see me doing so well. He knew just what I should do about Dori.

"Adam, you don't even *believe* in marriage."

"I sort of do. In emergencies."

"Well, I'm not in love with her," I said experimentally.

"Oh, don't *say* that," he said. "Why would you want to not be in love with her? You are *blossoming*. There are roses in your kike cheeks."

"Don't go waving your glass at Maddy. You're not having another."

"Fine. I'm not having another. My concern here is that you not make the rest of your life a shrine to that rich psychopath. 'Cause I think you cherish this little niche. You're gonna go on, all brave, but this little corner of you's gonna remain tragically empty, and you kinda dig that. What I say is, *stuff* that little corner. And I know just what with. Why don't you love Dori? She's smart and easygoing and likes you and has breasts that are visible from outer space."

"I love who I love, Adam."

"Jesus, you're fabulous. I could eat you with a spoon when you're like this. You can still get married."

"Between us, that's what I want."

"You do? Fuck. That's wonderful news. So why are we arguing?"

"Conditioned reflex. *Ah.* Thank you."

"I was holding that. Can't I sit and hold an empty glass?"

"Sorry, Maddy, he was just gesturing. Would you take this? and I'll have another, and he'll have a Coke."

"Fuck you," Adam said to me.

"Thank you," I said to Maddy.

"Don't be true," Adam said, "to a heart that's cruel."

Most of Dori's actions were governed by an implacable and all-encompassing laziness. In the mornings, she groaned like an old woman when she had to stand, then cranked her head down for a sniff under each arm. Since her porcelain skin never seemed to sweat, only twice a week or so was the entire edifice subjected to an epic sudsing. Then, after pulling on T-shirt and skirt, she often kicked underwear and pantyhose along the floor to the foot of my laundry hamper. It was too much work to bend down and put them in. It was too much work to record her checks. The bank was always happy to tell you when you were out of money. It was pointless work to close the bathroom door. I recall her on the toilet, panties around ankles and book on knees, half a sandwich balanced on the sink. She read constantly, including an imposing array of Great Works, but favored the effortless: Harlequin Romances, princess-and-winged-dragon novels, cheap mysteries. These she finished in a sitting. With longer works, she found it most convenient to mark her place by smushing down the corner of the page. I gave her some bookmarks. "Thank you. When I read one of your books I will use them."

"As you wish, Dori. I was brought up to respect books."

"And I was brought up to respect people, that you shouldn't treat them like bad children over nothing," she said sunnily.

Even in English, her third language (first came Dutch, then Hebrew, and a grammarless but functional French came fourth), she read faster than anyone I've ever known, and our evenings advanced to the steady slap of turning pages. She finished *Anna Karenina* in two nights.

"You did not."

"So. I did not."

"Who said, 'You ought to be able to inoculate people against love'?"

"Vronsky. At the Princess Becky."

"Betsy. What did he and Anna do at the end of that evening?"

"Shake hands. After, he kisses his palm where she has touched."

"While thinking what?"

"That soon he screws her."

"What happens to Vronsky?"

"He goes off to war."

"What's the matter with him?"

"His teeth hurt."

"Jeepers."

"That I am your little schoolgirl now, you like it? I shouldn't get so many right answers maybe, and then, my Karenin, you could, you knew, *punish* me?"

We seemed to spend a good part of our time swapping genial insults. This sometimes worried me, and always puzzled me. I was happier than I'd ever been, and this apparently freed up my energies to pursue a perfected irritability. The world seemed to be saying, *Hey, we were only fooling with you. You okay? Got your girlfriend and everything? No hard feelings, all right?* But I wasn't inclined to let the world off that easy. I was furious no one had helped me be happy; I'd had to find Dori all by myself.

Still, my nagging did not upset her; she seemed to regard it as so many love bites. I didn't think she *could* get upset about anything until she came in one evening without her big handbag. "Mugged," she remarked. "Is there wine?"

"My God, are you all right?"

"If I am not all right I say so. Wine."

I gave her wine.

"Stupid boys, I think. I think they don't know to do anything better. In Amsterdam we have the same, but there they think they are *poli-ti-cal*. They shove me down. Nothing. I land where I am fat. Please sit, Nicky, or I shove you down, too."

"Sorry. I'm calling the cops."

"*No*. It is over. Forty dollars and my tampons and my credit card. Not so much."

"They've got this book of faces. You might recognize them."

"This is more than forty dollars of trouble. You may call to stop out my credit card if you must call."

"Well, I admire your serenity," I said with some resentment. "It's a rare quality."

"No shit. In this city, everyone is so *proud* to be upset all the time. So proud of their bad temper, so proud of their therapy, that everything is the end of the world. But with wit! And if nothing upsets you, you are a stupid bumpkin. I am also upset, but what I cannot stand is all the oh oh oh! when it is done with. This is spoiled and stupid. *Let me drink my wine.*" I'd put my arm around her.

Her face disappeared into the glass, like a child drinking juice.

"You are only being nice," she said. "Nicky, I apologize to you. I don't like, you knew, to be hit. Because I had a mother that she beat me. As in the camps she was beaten, in Belsen. To bleeding."

"Oh, Dori."

"Yes. This is why I am now unreasonable. She is a pianist, so they make her a typist. When she makes mistakes they break a finger, so then she is not a typist anymore. Nazi smartness. But she lives, and after she marries. My father she does not beat because he will break her jaw, so she beats me and beats her boyfriend." She sighed. "And so my father comes in, and cries and asks me, a little girl with a bloody nose, what he must do, that he has married a woman who beats his daughter. Well, he is drunk. They both drink. Then he dies — a hem-orr-hage from all his drinking — so the boyfriend makes her stop drinking and still she beats, only now her aim improves. Now I am twelve, thirteen, and when I come to menstruate, she puts on the floor an oilcloth, and this is where I sleep, and best of all she likes to beat me when I am getting dressed, because I dress, you see, like a *whore*. She beats my belly, she beats my bosom. And in comes the boyfriend screaming and because he is skinny she beats him in the chin. Oh, everyone is against her, and she must go. So to Tel Aviv when I am five, and back to Amsterdam when I am seven, and so like this. For years! Now, that she cannot forget Belsen, the great harm done her, this I can see. *But I can forget her.* And so I do. *Because I will die.* And first I must have something better than oh oh oh. To take a little hurt and cuddle it your whole life, this is your luxury. And I hate it. I hate it. And now, I am done to talk about it. Only once to you as a friend, so this is not a secret kept from you. I don't even think of it, you knew, but maybe the littlest bit. Oh, look at you. *You* will think of it, you will go oh oh oh for a year now. This is why I have sayed nothing. Stop it. My life is good a long time now. I have my good job that I can be so lazy at and a nice boyfriend to cook me dinner and tell me always what to do. Come here. Yes, like that. My God, the fuss you Jews make over life."

I lifted my head. "You Jews? And what are you?"

"I cannot, excuse me, consider myself truly Jewish in this way. I am too sensible."

Later she said, "Oh, Nicky, *you* are a Jew."

Who Plies Her Fangs of Difference Through Your Heart

I used to like doing hard-ground etchings on copper. It cost more than zinc, but permitted both delicacy and a fierce precision. I liked the entire process: scoring the metal with a hooked blade, cracking it along the edge of the kitchen table, beveling the edges with a flat file. I'd open a window before releasing the asphalt stench of ground and varnolene. When I'd applied the ground and let it dry to a silken black, I'd be ready to scribe the image through it in bright lines. Then I'd snug the plate in an old flannel shirt, take it to the printmaking studio where I rented time by the month, and immerse it in an acid called, as it happened, Dutch mordant.

When I was satisfied with the bite, I'd remove the ground with solvent. I'd warm the plate on a hot plate and work the ink in with a bunched black rag until my fingertips were cooked. Then I'd wipe it down with a clean rag and let the plate cool before finishing it with the edge of my palm dried with talc. Finally, when the copper gleamed sullenly around the inked lines, I'd arrange it beneath a damp sheet on the press bed, spread the felt blanket, and click the switch. An electric motor would drone to life, and paper and plate would be drawn under a rumbling roller that dealt out tons to the inch. I'd peel the sheet back like a bandage and find a bearded man, say, gilding a calf's horns, a long knife tucked in his belt, or some blank-eyed sailors unknotting a bag of winds. As I mentioned, I'd started an extended series of etchings. My long apprenticeship was over, and I wanted a big project with which to declare myself, to exorcise years of cement-assed depression, a big story full of big doings. Everything considered, I'd decided to illustrate the *Odyssey*.

"What a *juicy* choice," Saul said when I came to visit. "There's no one like Odysseus, you know. A two-fisted whiner, king of this perfect narcissist's world. Troy burns, Achaians and Phaiakians plotz by the shipload, but all anyone cares about on Heaven or Earth is how godlike his thighs are and is he gonna get to see his wife. Lurching bing-bang from one crazy woman, one *disaster* to another, and running every time to Big Mama Athene to save his bacon, all the while wailing about this chick he hasn't seen in years—you know, he's perfect for you. Jesus, I've watched you futz around. You haven't taken the measure of your gifts. You have to stake a claim, Nickel, you have to take a big bite," said the wrecked child's lips below the disordered gray mustache. "You can't wait 'til you're ready. Ready's too late."

At Saul's elbow was a row of old file cabinets filled with the ever-ramifying notes and manuscript of *Strikebreaking in America*. My father's big bite. He seemed to have lost any notion of completing it. Instead he spent a good deal of time putting it in order, as if for a Saul Wertheim Archives. He also kept a journal which threatened to become a memoir. His bustle grieved me; it had a posthumous quality. My father had been back in New York for a year. Weary of the disregard of his department chair and of a new generation of comely and confused twenty-six-year-olds, Saul had finally returned to the city of his youth to lecture at Queens College and attempt a rapprochement with Suzanne.

Since the madman with the Prince Valiant bangs, my mother had been alone. Suzanne had always had a beautiful woman's vagueness about men. She was like a city kid who believes vegetables grow on shelves at the grocery. Now the years had led her into a wilderness of respectful boys and bright-eyed old coots. Her friends' parties were peopled with lonely women like herself. The occasional intriguing man would be someone's son, and have an air of wanting to show her his report card. She solaced herself with paperback mysteries and chamomile tea. She joined a drawing club which met in a Spring Street basement, and manufactured zaftig post-impressionist nudes hemmed about by jigging polygons. When I went to visit Saul, I found her seated on his ottoman, hugging her knees beneath a long muslin dress, being pretty and good and pondering her options. "A big bite," Saul said, distractedly petting a small brocaded pillow, and Suzanne sighed with fellow feeling.

To be expert in beautiful work, to have good character, Homer sang. I'd planned a portfolio of forty-eight etchings, two for each Book of the poem, each plate facing the excerpt that inspired it, all elegantly bound – I'd gotten pretty good at that – in an edition of forty-eight. A graphic summation of a lifetime's thought, like Matisse's *Jazz* or Miró's *A toute épreuve.* With glee I anticipated years of labor: Odysseus blinding Polyphemos and rogering Circe; Odysseus pouring ditches full of honey, milk, wine, and barley and howling for his dead mom; Odysseus cold-cocking Iros, stringing the great bow of Eurytos, casting off his beggar's rags and regaining what was rightfully his: pretty much everything. The big *goyische* lunkhead was just the ticket, with his blissful egomania and his operatic tears; he hauled the line from the tip of my burin and wrapped it around himself with heroic speed. Meanwhile, I was luckier than Odysseus: at the end of my day's wanderings through debonair swathes of sugar lift, beetle-leg scratches of drypoint, and succinct ensigns of *chien collé,* I'd get to lie down beside my wise and faithful queen. Fatigue humming in my shoulders, I'd gather Dori's refulgent whiteness into fingers permanently edged in black, like a mechanic's. *"Upon a corded bedstead in the echoing portico,"* I'd cackle.

"Yes, Nicky."

"Deep-girdled women!"

"Yes, Nicky. Sleep now."

For about a year, I produced marvelous fat sheaves of work. But after Dori's mugging, everything began to go sour, first of all with Dori herself. I lost my knack of affectionate admonition. And if I quit, it reduced us to good manners. Dori seemed to bait me then, seemed relieved when I was again my bitchy little self. Tenderness enraged her; it was for victims. "Social worker!" she sneered. "I should not have sayed anything." Besides, in my case, tenderness was a lie. Sitting stolidly beneath her inverted bowl of beige hair, her tiny features dead in her white face, she maintained she knew the real me; it was spelled out in bruises and toothmarks across her bosom and bottom. All she asked was to continue undeceived. My reasoned responses sounded tinny, hateful. I was a mosquito tormenting a mare.

And back at work, I jabbed like a mosquito; my burin raised rashes. I'd lost the artist's necessary arrogance: the assumption that there is worth in the sinew-dictated hesitations and leaps of one's next line, as helplessly *you* as the sound of your sneeze or the postures you assume in sleep. I was back to the sorry state in which each new line had to justify itself. No, had to justify twenty-nine years of big talk and antlike industry. Blessed with a good start on a given plate, I'd grow timid and miserly, and dither about until I'd turned it to dreck. Then I'd resort to irony and dither further, as if ugliness had been my goal. I ruined hundreds of dollars' worth of copper, then retreated to paper and filled sketchbook after sketchbook with puzzled noodlings. At last I began to make new blank books, book after book, and leave them blank.

Fourteen months after it began, *Suitors' Tune* bogged down for good on a plate representing Ares and sweet-garlanded Aphrodite lying together in the brazen-floored house built for her by her husband Hephaistos, the crippled smith of the gods. Suspecting an affair between the two, Hephaistos had fashioned hidden snares to truss them together when next they shared his bed. When the trap was sprung, he cried:

Father Zeus and all you other blessed immortal
gods, come here, to see a ridiculous sight, no seemly
matter, how Aphrodite daughter of Zeus forever
holds me in so little favor, but she loves ruinous Ares,
because he is handsome and goes sound on his feet, while I am
misshapen from birth, and for this I hold no other responsible
but my own father and mother, and I wish they had never got me.

One day I came in after work to discover Dori examining one of my sketchbooks. "What is this?" she said, and showed me the page:

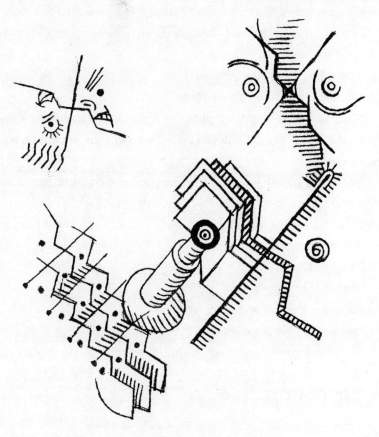

"I didn't know you were here," I said. My right thigh twitched. I had a squarish scar there, pale and puffy as a smallpox vaccination. I'd told Dori it had been a tattoo I'd gotten for an old girlfriend. Amused, she'd inquired no further. Now, thinking of her mother's tattoo – a functional row of blue numerals – I felt a familiar shame.

"I came in," Dori said. She had a key, of course; she was at my place more often than hers, and why call to tell me when she was coming, when I'd always been so glad to see her? "What is this?"

I decided to tell her.

At first, Dori was prepared to be amused again. "Ten is a young boy. Already your heart is so smit-ten?"

Well, of course I'd seen Julia again. I told her about the reservoir.

"But so then she wanted you. I thought your suffering was that she didn't want you. Tell me, it wasn't exciting, to be watched like that?"

That wasn't the *point*. I described our agonizing year of half-platonic friendship.

"But this is years later! You *waited?*"

Well, no. I explained about Terry.

"But then there are other girls. So if she has changed her mind when she comes back and doesn't want you, why do you not be with other girls?"

No, it was months after her return that she changed her mind. When she came back, she'd actually offered to relieve me of my virginity at my sister's wedding.

"So then you *did* screw!"

I'd said no.

"But so then it's *you* who don't want *her.*"

No, it was the way she'd offered.

"She has to offer the right way?"

Look, I acknowledged it was stupid. It was trivial. We should forget it.

"But to you it is important."

I tried to explain how twisted things got around Julia. I described the Conservancy party and its mucky aftermath.

"But she is drunk. So you leave her there in her mud and it serves her right."

Well, no, I hadn't, actually. After much soul-searching, I'd stripped her mucky clothes off and put her to bed.

"Oh ho. And were you excited?"

That wasn't the point! How did she think I *felt?*

"Excited."

The point was, *my feelings had been trifled with.* (I tried to think of a more damning phrase than *trifled with.*)

"But a hundred times by now you have a chance to screw her! After she offers herself so *terribly* wrongly at your sister's wedding, you can offer yourself! And do it correctly!"

But I was seeing Terry then.

"But you don't care about her. And anyway, soon Terry breaks up with you."

But then we were too sad.

"Oh, Jesus Christ."

Look, Julia was impossible. Dori had to take my word on this.

"Then it is simple: you never see her again!"

Right. That's what I'd already decided.

"Then what is the problem?"

The problem was that my fucking heart had been broken. The problem was that I loved her—I meant, I had loved her—and she didn't love me.

"But Nicky, my God, everyone has this pain. This is like saying, Oh, it hurt when I am teething as a baby. Nicky, listen, I will get drunk, and you can undress me and wash me and *me* you can screw. You see, Nicky? Times, you knew, are better now."

I swore.

"I think sometimes you don't like that I want to screw. Yes. Rather you would keep being clever and analyze. You like to be smart better than you like to be happy. Sometimes I must screw you to sleep so you will not smart all my happiness away. And oh, Dori, about your mo-ther. Oh, Dori, about the camps. Let me make more smart deductions from the shitty details. Give me many more details to be smart about."

She wrote English perfectly. Had she ever thought of putting a little effort into the way she spoke?

Dori assumed a look of concentration and farted.

"Very good," I said. "You did that without a trace of accent."

:   :

"I want a favor," I told Adam at the Brite Spot. "I need to use your apartment."

"Oh, no." He set down his glass with a clunk. "You stop jacking around, now. You just marry that girl and quit pushing your luck."

"I can feel it all piddling away, Adam. I'm just no good with Dori anymore. We're always *at* each other. And she won't talk about it. She won't talk about her mother, or about Belsen –"

"Nick, you *putz*."

"She thinks it's all morbid voyeurism. I won't let the past be past."

"Imagine that. And you wanted my place to meet exactly whom?"

"I have to talk to her. Face to face, or it's not real. She's poisoning everything."

"She's not doing dick, pal. She's not *around*. Forget her."

"That's the point! I've been trying to since I was ten, and I *can't*. I have to end it in so many words, Adam. I have to say, look, *here's* what's you've done with your tinkerbelling around. I have to do something with all this rage. It squirts out every time I move, in pissy little droplets. Adam, maybe Julia's fucked off forever, but I have to *tell* her to, so I'll believe it."

"You yourself said, every time that daft bitch reappears –"

"But that's it. For once, I'm not passively waiting for her to reappear. I'll meet her on *my* terms."

"Terms. Nick, I am begging you."

"And, I'll admit, I want to hurt her. I want to say things that will hurt her. She's hurt me so much! I don't care if she didn't mean to, I don't care if I sat up and begged for it! I'm *choking* on this backlog of things I haven't said. My life's so lopsided! Why should *she* always be the one to do the hurting? I know it's childish, I can hear myself. But maybe the only way for me to quit being a child is to *be* a child, to just *get her back*. Do you understand?"

"Of course I understand, Nick. I just don't give a shit."

"It's called 'closure'?"

"I am begging you."

"So. I guess I can't have the apartment."

"No," he said wearily. "You can have it. Just don't expect me – Yeah, you can have it."

The next morning, as I waited for her to leave so I could call Julia, Dori was unwontedly sluggish and affectionate, as if it were the old days. She licked my neck, she pinched my calves. Never had she seemed so fat. I reminded myself that I was not scheduling a rendezvous with another woman per se, that I was instead proposing to undergo an ordeal which would be not just chaste but unpleasant, so that I could free myself to love her, Dori, better, and none of this seemed any more convincing to me than it does to you. I got Dori's pants on by the simple expedient of shoving her down and wrestling them over her upraised legs. She chuckled amorously, twined arms and legs around me and forced me down against her softness. "You are good to me," she murmured, and I wanted to scream like a steam whistle. At last she was gone. Dialing Julia's number, I was subject to an internal sleet which left my forehead a mass of curdled fire. "This is Nick Wertheim," I said in the cadences of a man reading from a prepared text, which I was. "I'd like to see you."

Julia's voice sounded the way talcum powder smells. "Of course. You sound upset."

"I'd *like*," I grated, "to see you."

"I *said* yes, Nicky. Can one ask what all this—"

"Can one ask. Jesus, what lousy dialogue. You don't talk like that."

"I am talking like that. All right, I'm free tonight, and I'm free Wednesday—"

I threw my script on the floor. "I want to see you tomorrow night," I said at random.

"I guess I can—"

"Seven o'clock," I said. "Here's the address." Then I hung up.

Adam was somber the next evening as he let me in. "Okay. I'll be at Cat's. Here's the keys. You got the place all night."

"I will not," I said, "need it all night."

"Okay."

"Actually, I'd rather you came back. Say, around ten. I'd like there to be some definite, um. End."

"All right. How do you feel?"

"All right. Like an asshole."

"Well, that's reasonable."

We laughed. "I do think I need to do this, though."

"Well, you know best, sugar. I'll see you at ten."

I didn't expect her to be punctual and she wasn't. Seven o'clock came, then seven-thirty. At eight I called and got her answering machine. I hung up. I went and sat in the window awhile, and then called and hung up twice more. At eight twenty-five, her message was different, and concluded, "If this is Nick, I will be there just as soon as I can, and I hope you will be, too." It was well past nine when a cab stopped at the corner and Julia got out, and by then I had my forehead mashed against Adam's window grate like a bear in a zoo cage. She stepped briskly down the sidewalk and disappeared directly below me.

She'd gained weight. She'd worn a neat, royal blue dress, and looked pretty.

When I opened the door, she entered with a nod, holding a black clutch purse in both hands. She was plumper than I'd ever seen her.

Her hips were womanly, their movements decided. "I'm sorry I'm so late," she said without emphasis. "Well, from the sound of you over the phone, I didn't know whether to bring a diaphragm or a bullet-proof vest. I only own one of the above-mentioned, as it happens, and that's how I decided."

"Well, there'll be no need to put it in, I can tell you that much."

"It's in."

"I see. Jesus. Is that what you think I asked you here for?"

"I don't know. You wouldn't let me ask."

"All right," I said. "How to begin." *No self-deprecating irony, damnit.* "All right. Julia, we have known each other for a long, long time." Oh, this was wretched. "The last time I saw you…" Do finish a sentence, *please.* "The last time I saw you, certain things were said… were said, and *done*, as well…" Julia watched me with real concern. Her legs, in their gray stockings, were crossed at the ankles, her fingers laced in her lap. I gulped a breath. "Fuck. *You*," I said.

"All right. But I do think I have a right to ask."

"No, I mean Fuck You's why I asked you here."

"I see."

"Can we please," I said in a frenzy, "stop saying 'I see'?"

"The dialogue still doesn't please you? Well, it don't thrill me either."

"Are you drunk?" I snapped, adrift.

"Yes."

"I see," I said helplessly.

"I'm very frightened. You are being very frightening. I don't know what's worse, the thought of what you might say, or… I suppose there are some pretty terrible things you might, in all justice, say. Or something you'd do. Or just watching you have this, this *seizure*."

"You are over two hours late!" I shouted.

"And I said I was sorry!"

"You said you were sorry."

"I kept deciding to have another. You sounded simply distorted with hate."

"But you figured you'd put in your diaphragm, in case the mood turned romantic."

"It occurred to me that you might rape me."

There were intelligent new lines at her eyes. She had the mouth of a pretty woman saying reasonable things. I stared at it numbly. She said, "Nick, what do you want from me?"

"Common sense, common courtesy. Common *decency*."

"I assume I said or did something terrible the last time we met."

Quietly, I took a whiff. Mouthwash, strong. She said, "It's worse than you think. I start each day the moment I get up. Nicky? I have blackouts. Won't you talk to me?" Slowly, she said, "I wasn't ready. So you went without me. And then, some run-in with Sydney Platt."

"Whom you fired."

"I never had any authority to fire Sid. They fired *me*. I think she got my job. Anyway, after that… I have some idea we were walking under trees. I woke up." She closed her eyes. "Naked. Dirt on my clothes. Did I fall? And traces of vomit. Did I… " She swallowed. "Do you think you could help out a little. Nick, this is so difficult for me."

"All right. You got drunk. You jumped in Belvedere Lake. I took you home. You puked on yourself. I washed you and put you to bed. Then I left."

"There must have been more, for you to hate me this way."

"Your manners weren't too good, but I wouldn't think they would be, under the circumstances. I just saw that there was no further point in knowing you."

She closed her eyes, then opened them. Then she was almost businesslike. "I see. Will you at least tell me if you're happier these days?"

"It doesn't concern you. Nothing about either of us concerns the other anymore."

"Well, if you can't forgive me, Nick, I wish you'd forget me. No human being should have to support the weight of feeling you seem to have worked up over me. No matter what she's done. May I leave now?"

"Yes."

Her lashes were wet. "You know, I've thought of you, in the past year or so. And I would have this little daydream that you thought well of me. I would imagine that you visited me, and scolded me for all the stupid things, and gave me good advice. I had this reverie that you cared for me, and were sorry to see me in such trouble. I mean, are you? Do you think it just serves me right, or are you sorry to see it?"

"Yeah," I said.

"All right. I guess it was too much to ask. Well. Goodbye then. I do hope you're happy. And I hope someday you see that, even if I've done a bad job of it… Nicky, please believe in my friendship. My imperfect friendship. And my love."

Startled, I looked into her face. I found pity there. As if I'd made no progress at all, as if I were still that furtive freak cringing over her drunken body.

I said, "Then God help the people you love."

She didn't move, she didn't speak. I went to the door, opened it, and found Adam sitting on the stairs. "You were gonna be done by now," he apologized.

"She's all yours," I said, and left. This was how Saint George would have felt if he'd slain the maiden instead of the dragon. Because she was easier.

:   :

I trudged home in a stupor of loathing and self-loathing. The worst thing I could do, I reasoned, was to make too big a deal of this with Dori. But how did you make no big deal of seeing Julia? Mention it casually; just another of the day's events? Not mention it at all? But wouldn't keeping it secret be making something of it? The exchange had been inexorable, like a plate rolling under a press. I decided to take Dori's stoic example: I'd say nothing. At home, I found she'd let herself in. She didn't ask where I'd been. She slept that night with her cheek on my chest, leaving a small trusting puddle of saliva. The next evening, Adam asked me over. I imagined he wanted to tell me I'd been cruel. He could go fuck himself.

He let me in, unhappier than I'd ever seen him. "Well," I said. "You were right. It was a mistake. I feel more full of hate, more wound up in Julia than ever. And yes, I behaved badly, and yes, I hurt her. Though part of me's wild with regret for not hurting her worse. All right. There's no good way to end this but to end it. My anger is my anger. What concerns me now is Dori. You're not listening, are you?"

He said, "Julia just left."

"Did she now. You two are becoming regular little pals."

"Julia just *left*."

"Oh," I said. "You mean… Julia just left."

He nodded and wiped his stubby hands on his pants.

"Well." I looked at my watch. "About twenty-one hours. That's kind of a compliment to you, I'd say. Tell me, pal, how is she?"

"Hit me," he said.

"Hit you."

"You should've seen her after you walked out of here. I don't think I've ever… She was just leveled. Like *Dresden*. I'm not trying to excuse myself. She cried and cried. I took her to the Brite Spot, and that helped, and then she said, ah…"

" 'Can't we go somewhere where everyone isn't looking at me,' " I said reminiscently.

"Don't –" he began.

I regarded him.

"I know you, Nick. Goddamnit, you vengeful little shit, you don't get over things. I don't want you to do to me what you did to Julia. Paste me one. Go ahead. I'll let you."

The look on his face was interesting. I kept thinking how interesting he was to look at just then.

"No," I said. "You gobbling mutt. Live with it."

And I left. Things were getting very simple around here.

Late that night, as I slouched nude at my drawing table, doodling snares and ruined torsos, I realized Dori was watching me from the bed. She must have been feigning sleep for hours. She said, "If something goes on it's all right that it goes on. Only you must tell me."

"What are you talking about?" I said calmly.

"Your Julia! You have seen your Julia! You go out, and you do not tell me what, and after you are strange!" She rhymed it with *flange*. "And this is for *months* now you are strange! And I have not that I… If you have, that with other girls you are meeting…" She was losing her English. "I am so *miserable!* I don't sleep! It is the middle in the night and I don't sleep! I am *thin!* You must tell me! Please, you must only tell me, and then I am all right again."

"Dori, I am not seeing anyone."

"Not your Julia?"

"Last night," I sighed, "I met with Julia. For the first time in two years. I'm sorry. I should have told you. I didn't want you to worry. We did not sleep together, Dori. We didn't even shake hands."

"Then what?"

"I… had some things I wanted to tell her."

But Dori believed me. I could tell by her look of consternation. "And tonight? More things?"

"Tonight I saw Adam. We had a fight. *He'd* slept with Julia. He expected me to be upset. I was."

"But you do *not* sleep with Julia?"

Her consternation was growing, as if only a lunatic would not sleep with Julia. "Right! I do *not* sleep with Julia!"

"You do not sleep with anyone."

"*Right.*"

"Then this," she hissed, "all this is about nothing."

"Well, if by 'nothing' –"

"ABOUT *NOTHING!*" she roared. "And for nothing you drive me *crazy!*"

"What do I do to drive you crazy?"

"Everything. I don't knew. You put the eggs in the dimples."

"What?"

"You take from the carton and put the eggs into the little dimples, in the door, the frigerator door. One by one. I want to scream."

"Avert your eyes."

"It is not that, but everything. All the little things you do like *death*. You pose. When you are speaking to me, always you pose."

"How do I pose? Dori, I'd think, after everything you've been through –"

"I said you *pose*. You *peaaauuse*. You *PUUUWWWWWWSE*."

"Ah. I pause."

"*Yes!* Before speaking you must give a little *pawwwse*, because that I am so unreasonable and you must think what best to say to the poor crazy woman. *But I am not crazy before I meet you!*"

"Me neither. Look, I'm going for a walk." I reached for my pants.

"You stay *here*," she said, and effortlessly jerked me back.

Here my rage became, as it were, official. "Fine. I stay *hee*-ure. Why didn't you just say –"

"Why must I say? You have eyes! But to you I am a big cow nothing upsets!"

"Dori, you go out of your way to *present* yourself as a big cow nothing upsets."

"*I cannot make you happy! You will not let this!*" She waved the clock. "And now, three o'clock! And awake!"

"So fucking what? I don't believe a woman who's survived your troubles, whose *mother* has survived *her* troubles, is getting so worked up over a little sleep!"

"You think Belsen makes sleep less important? This is more of your stupidity. Belsen makes sleep *more* important! Yes. Sleep against Belsen! Sleep against craziness! Sleep against every bad thing in the world! *There is nothing more important than sleep!* Nothing more important than a good meal! Than a kiss! Than a drink when you are hot! Than one *hour* of happy boredom! What is not important is this *shit* that you sing about, this stupid love for a woman who treats you badly, *who is never there,* but that is all *good,* you knew, because your love must all be in the head, not for a woman who warms you at night and shakes you when you worry. *And you don't let go!*"

"Goddamnit, Dori, this is simple jealousy over a woman I will never see again and over feelings *I goddamn well cannot help!*"

"And don't *want* to help! You *love* these feelings! You think they are the best, the high-est *part* of you. But they are *shit!* One hundred years ago she kisses you and fifty years ago she teases you and today, today you spend all day hating her! You think I am jealous? *I want you to screw her and then it will be over!* I want you to screw her *every day,* just so when you don't go see her you are with *me,* instead of always somewhere else on a high shitty mountain in your beautiful soul making songs of how true your feelings and how badly she has treated you and your wonderful wonderful pain! With all the grief in the world one cannot escape, no, this is not enough, you will make more grief that no one needs, and this is *shit! No one wants this impossible love of yours! No one wants your shitty love!*"

I slugged her.

It was a roundhouse right to the jaw with all my weight behind it, a real beauty. I remember one white leg kicking awkwardly out, her great breasts jogging upward in unison, her face reduced to a child-like roundness, and the feeling of my dick swinging against my leg, and a warm connectedness traveling up my arm, a secret new conduit. I felt that I rose as she did, a skyrocket of exhilaration, until I was standing over her child's face, shrieking, *"That enough? That enough? You want more?"*

And then I sat down.

I wanted someone to kill me.

I couldn't look up. My tears dropped into my palm. Dori stood. "Get up, please," she said. "It is I who am struck, not you."

I cowered upright. It seemed unbearable to be naked. I could raise my eyes no higher than the beige tuft at her hips. "Look at me," she said.

"I can't," I whispered.

"Look at me."

I looked at her. "I am here," she said. "We are still both here. Now, no hysteria."

Her cheek glowed. It would soon be one dusky bruise from eye to mouth.

"I'm sorry," I whispered, tears running down my chin. "I'm so sorry. Dori, I'm so sorry. Hit me back. Please, just –" I stopped. I was quoting Adam.

"I don't hit as a favor, for you to feel better."

"Please… please forgive me. Dori, don't leave me."

"You, you, *you*. I forgive you," she said, "before my fanny hits the floor. Still, I must decide what to do, now everything is so clear. Please, without more talk. I would like to sleep."

"I'll sleep on the couch."

"It is warmer with you in the bed."

We drew the covers up, and she arranged herself against me just as she did every night. "I understand everything, you understand everything, and I *will* get angry, that I am hit but it is all you and your suffering. Oh, I still like you so much but I don't think I can live my life with a man so miserably weak. I wanted, I think I wanted, to live my life with you. I don't think so now. I will tell you in a few days." She settled in.

"Nicky," she said, "I can't sleep if you are whispering. Nicky? Are you praying?"

I shook my head.

I'd been whispering: *Not again.*

And Now You're Anyone's to Take Apart

But Dori decided the next day. She quit *slam* in the morning, and that evening emptied her drawerful of clothes into a plastic trash bag as I held it open before her. I was ready to cast myself at her feet, but no contrition of mine could possibly have been as perfect as her composure. We had, she conveyed, made our decision long ago. We were even happy about it. No further action on my part was required. She ambled back and forth, hips majestic, gathering up stray belongings, then headed for the door, taking with her a bulging trash bag and all the good things of the world: the unruffled amusement in her small eyes and the limping lilt of her voice and the nourishing white weight of her flesh, marked with a constellation of tiny adoring bruises and the one large valedictory bruise on her jaw. Outside, hugging her possessions, she inclined her head in farewell. Numbly I inclined mine. A few days later, I nerved myself to call and found she'd gotten an unlisted number.

When *slam* folded after *issue twenty*, my coworkers remarked on my equanimity: I still hadn't shaken the sense that no action on my part was required. I soon got an even better-paid job as studio manager at a computer animation firm. I opened a money market account and signed up for automatic deposits. When the quarterly statements arrived, I studied the mounting figures with curiosity. It seemed unnecessary to call Adam. It seemed unnecessary to make new friends. It seemed unnecessary to work, and so I didn't. Now and then I'd produce another sketchbook, experimenting with different materials and bindings. I stacked them neatly along the wall when I was done. I did not draw in them. I did not print. I turned thirty, then thirty-one, my fingernails pink and new-looking.

In the winter of 1992, in the middle of a near-zero week, our century-old boiler broke down just as I'd felt the first tickle of a sore throat. Overnight this turned to a high fever, and I called in sick for the first time in my life. I could scarcely hold anything in the gelid pit of my stomach. Whatever stayed down soon streamed from my bowels as a villainous gruel. By the third day of my illness, I tottered to the bathroom half-hourly. Wrapped in my parka, I'd drowse on the wintry bowl, watching my knees quiver, nursing a headache that tasted of brass.

I began losing weight. It gave me an odd sense of accomplishment. I felt purified, as if I'd been fasting, readying myself for visions in some secret inner chamber of my illness. And slyly I noted: after thirty-one years, I finally had an excuse to feel as bad as I generally did. But along with all this was the shame of unfitness. I didn't call a doctor, or try to find a warm place to stay. On the fourth day I woke in a cage of zinc pipes and waxy tubing. Three nonagenarian rabbis drooped over me, their legs preternaturally long.

"What's he in the hospital?"

"From sadness."

"Hoo hoo hoo."

We debated for a while, and presently I discovered I was not in the hospital, but alone in my own bed. It occurred to me that I was very ill, and that I ought to quit jackassing around and do something about it.

Not for the first time, I mourned the loss of Adam. He would have dropped everything and taken charge. His ministrations might have killed me, but at least he'd be there. Who else could I call? I had no real friends at work. I had not spoken to Charlotte, Essa, or Joey for years. Del was hours deep in the suburbs, and then there was her toxic self-satisfaction. I lay on the couch to ponder. When I tried to rise, my legs folded and I rapped my chin smartly on the floor.

I came to almost at once, thinking, *I've passed out! I've passed out!* This seemed very grave. I tried to scramble to my feet, went dim again, and dropped to all fours. I'd soiled myself slightly – I could feel the warm, acid spot against my tortured bum – and I could not get up. Tears of panic filled my eyes. *I could die here.* Passivity had bought me death.

The spell passed and I limped to the phone. Now I knew who I had to call. Thirty-one, and running to Mommy. All right, it beat dying. Head aswarm, I punched out the number from memory and heard a motherly *Hello?* She sounded peculiar, but I had my own troubles. "Listen, Mom, I'm sorry to bother you, but there's a problem."

"Um, Nicky?" Julia said. "Did you want… someone else?"

A pause.

"I better hang up," I said.

"Are you in trouble? May I ask? Nicky, you sound *dreadful*."

"The heat's out. Listen, I'd better hang up."

"You have no *heat*? In this *weather*? Are you in the same place?"

"You don't know where I live," I said desperately.

"It's in my Filofax. I'll be right there," she said, and hung up.

The woman to whom I opened the door might have been Julia's aunt. Iron rivulets traveled her hair. She wore clean, worn jeans, a gunmetal cashmere turtleneck sweater with matching gloves, and a long coat of quilted, plum-hued silk, which had no buttons or zipper. One kept it closed by hugging oneself. A shimmering camisole of youth had slipped from Julia's shoulders, revealing in all her mortal nudity a prettyish, plumpening woman entering middle age with grace and skill and a charge account at Bendel's. She walked past me as if counting the number of paces it took to reach the center of the room. "Nicky, you look like a sink full of dirty dishes," she said. Then, frightened: "Nicky, you *have* a sink full of dirty dishes. This place is... *messy*." She picked up a sketchbook from a nearby stack – I noticed there were a very great number of them – and flipped through it with gloved fingers. She seemed about to ask what I'd take for the lot. "Nicky... are *all* these books blank?"

Whipping off a glove, she set a palm to my forehead. "Well, you *are* living the life," she said in a temper. "Starving and consumptive in your freezing garret."

"I'm not consumptive."

"Yet. Come on."

"Come on where?"

"Nicky. You cannot stay here. It's *cold*."

"Taken up good works, have you? Among the deserving poor?" I was feeling very devil-may-care. I thought I might shit my pants any minute.

"Why don't you rest your voice?" she said, not fondly.

Outside, gusts of snow blundered at my face, and then we were in the waiting cab, with its wet-dog smell. As we struck each pothole, I gritted my teeth, clenched my insides, and prayed for various kinds of continence.

I doubt the doorman at Julia's building recognized me. He was solicitous, and walked us to the elevator, and asked if the gentleman would require assistance, and offered to send the kid to the pharmacy, and called her Miss Turrell. "He loves you now," I observed as we rose. "What did you do to him?"

"Talked. And gave him an especially good Christmas tip, but mostly I just apologized, and he forgave me. Not everyone's like you."

When we stepped into her warm apartment, I wanted to weep. It seemed the most wonderful thing one person could do for another was to bring him someplace warm. She marched me across the living room. "Where are we going?" She seated me in an armchair and marched off. "Where are *you* going?" I wondered if I could reach the toilet without falling. She reappeared with a bathroom scale in her arms, tucked it beneath my feet, and muscled me upright upon it.

"What do you usually weigh?"

"One thirty-five?"

"One-eighteen. I'm taking you to the hospital."

"I wish you wouldn't," I said dizzily.

"Why not?"

"…I don't know anyone there."

"I'll introduce you around. We'll all go see a movie before they treat you for malnutrition. For God's sake, Nick, you weigh ten pounds less than *I* do. How long have you been *starving* yourself?"

"But I'm not."

"Then what?"

"It's, um."

"*Um?*"

"The other."

"You have diarrhea."

"I wish you wouldn't say that." It conjured a violent squelching lurching in my bowels. "It's such an awful word. We used to call each other that on the playground. You got the diarrhea. You diarrhea-head. Just hearing the word seemed so dreadful. Listen, could you help me up a minute?" I said as I half-clambered, half-slid to the carpet and commenced a wild lopsided canter along an extravagant arc I hoped would send me through the bathroom door. Julia said, "*Wait*. Let me –" and I caromed off an end table, toppling an antique porcelain lamp patterned with rampant dragons. She scooped it one-handed from the air. Off flew the shade. Blinded by glare, I pivoted on one collapsing leg and ran straight into her. "*Oooof?*" she said, as I fell to my knees and, staring up into her delicate and newly oval face, lit from below by the streaming rays of the unshaded lamp she held like an unsheathed sword, shat myself.

A meditative pause.

"Nicky, are you all right?" She reached down to help me up.

I thrust out, getting a palmful of soft shoulder and another of soft breast – when had she grown *breasts?* – and shoved her off balance long enough to scuttle into the bathroom and slam the door. Wriggling up onto the toilet, I wrenched my pants down with a sob of effort, and let go. The familiar acidic rush, barreling through me like an express train. There was more, much more. My vision went briefly gray. Could one shit oneself to death? I regarded the ochre mess of my undies and hoped so.

"Nicky, really, are you all right in there?"

"No."

She opened the door. "Oh, poor Nicky. Give me those."

"Go away."

"Oh come on. What have you got I haven't seen?" She helped me remove my soiled things and took them over to the sink to rinse. "Well, I'd say we've broken the ice now, wouldn't you?" I've seen Julia look at a gallon of screwtop white wine with genuine squeamishness, but she worked soapy thumbs through my shit as if flicking lint off a silk scarf. "It's just dehydration. You're pooping too much, poor honey."

"Now what are you doing?"

"Running a bath. If you won't come with me to the hospital, at least I can get you cleaned up."

"It's been too cold in my place to wash," I said sheepishly.

"I didn't know you *could* get dirty. A little grime suits you. But I know how you hate it. There. Give a call when you're ready to get in. Oh, for God's sake, I promise not to look." She left.

I tidied myself as best I could, and flushed. The bath was filling up. I turned off the taps and raised a leg over the side. The exertion left me dizzy. Julia appeared, said *"Nick,"* and helped me in. "Well. It's improved with age, I'd say. Acquired a sort of roguish charm."

"I thought you weren't going to look."

"Did you believe me?"

"No."

"Then I didn't lie." She began working shampoo into my hair.

"Ah."

"Feels good?"

"Feels good."

"Good. Oh, what are you cackling about?"

"But when the water had come to a boil in the shining bronze, then / she sat me down in the bathtub," I told her, *"and washed me from the great cauldron / mixing hot and cold just as I wanted."*

"You're either raving or quoting. Raving, one hopes."

"I always liked the part about mixing hot and cold just as he wanted. It sounded so nice. That was Odysseus. Being bathed by Circe."

"Who turns men to swine, thanks very much. Lean forward. Oh dear, your shoulder blades. Does that at least mean the water's just as you wanted?"

"A bit cool, actually."

"I'm going to scald you. You can't possibly want it this hot."

"Ah. No. It's wonderful."

When I'd been bathed and wrapped in a big towel, I was so tranced with sweet, clean idleness I couldn't close my hands. "You'll sleep now, all right," she said, and handed me two tiny white tablets and a glass of water. "These'll stop you up. Lomotil. I have a supply from when I used to get the whiskey shits. But we should try and get something into you." She made me drink another glass of water, and stirred up soft-boiled eggs with shredded toast, and sprinkled it with pepper. "This used to be my hangover meal. The pepper keeps you from getting nauseous," she said proudly.

"You're very good to me."

"I'm enjoying this immensely."

"You sure are."

She laughed. "That may be true, but it's ungracious to say so. It's only a little bit vindictiveness and liking to see you off your high horse. It's good to have someone to do for. I've been absolutely scheming what I can make you for breakfast."

"I guess I'm staying over."

"Do you think I'm sending you back to that tundra?" She took the bowl from me, unfolded the sofa bed, and made it up with quilts and several feather pillows. "Why don't you get right in? And then you can sleep anytime you want."

"I think I'll sleep now. Please do whatever you were going to. I don't think anything could keep me awake."

"I'll just sit here awhile and read, then."

"So strange. You don't know how many times I've sworn never to see you again."

"I do know," she said with infinite sadness. "Goodnight, love."

:   :

Julia sat beside me on the sofa bed, legs crossed at the ankle, wearing a gray sweatsuit. She had a number of these. I was wearing one myself. I'd sweated through two others during the night. Each time, my muttering and yawping had brought her out to change the soaked sheets, and she'd smoothed rubbing alcohol over my body, to reduce the fever. This transformed me into plumes of cool smoke with no connection to any earthly trouble. Toward morning the fever had broken. By nine I'd put away a big bowl of eggs and toast, and presently a proper lunch of sandwiches. Now I was lying back in a clean warm sweatsuit (much too short), in a clean warm bed, my bowels sedate, feeling invincible and very aware of Julia's round cotton-clad flank several circumspect inches away from my ear. We'd been talking for hours; she was telling me now about her second husband. It appeared she'd been busy, too.

"Look, here's what my day was like by the time I met Ray. I got up at, oh, half past noon. I bathed – that took about an hour. Another hour deciding what to wear. Then do my face and, around three, I was ready for breakfast at one of two coffee shops I'd gotten used to. I'd peek in the window, and if there were a lot of people at the counter, so that I'd have to sit right next to someone, I'd go to the other. I had to sit at the counter, you see, because sitting alone at a booth made me feel too pathetic. But at the counter, I was just stopping by, it wasn't my *life*. There'd be a glass case full of desserts, with a mirror in back. In between the pies I could see this carefully dressed woman of middle years. Going a little soft under her jaw and in the upper arms. Carriage good. Eyes a bit dicey. Holding up quite well for, oh, fifty or so, but unfortunately I was thirty-nine. If both counters were crowded, I went back home and cried. If I sat down and they didn't have my favorite kind of pastry – I couldn't bear the ones that were all wet and dismal inside, or the ones that were all sugar and made you feel like a child. I wanted the nice ones, with just a little cinnamon and sort of flaky – anyway, I'd breakfast and then go home and cry. Otherwise, at four in the afternoon, I was ready for my morning walk. It had to be over before five, because by then people would start coming home from their jobs, and since I'd been fired, I didn't want to see them.

"Then I met Ray. I was on a bench by the boat basin in the park, hoping someone would bring out a toy sailboat, because the sails were so white and clean and always made me feel good. And this funny little man with a waxy little gray beard sat down next to me. I remember he had on a tight herringbone jacket and awful brown double-knit slacks and one of those canvas fisherman hats, very frayed and dirty, the brim turned down all around to the level of his eyes. He didn't strike me as one of those crazy people who think they look just great that way. He didn't strike me as crazy at all, though I knew he must be. He sat there, feet on the ground, palms on his thighs, very comfy. I asked him what he thought he was doing.

" 'Praying for you,' he said.

" 'Who the *fuck*,' I said, 'asked you to?'

" 'Almost done,' he said.

"He was not anywhere near done. And then he listened to me weep for quite a while, as if it were interesting.

"Well, it was a strange courtship. He gave me his card, and *scolded* me when I tried to give him mine. He didn't think that was proper for a young woman. We had dinner, and he quite calmly asked me if I'd mind paying, because he was broke. When he was young he'd been a Presbyterian minister, and then he'd started studying architecture, but his practice had never been a success, and he'd been supporting himself as a draftsman in other architects' offices. And quite recently he'd quit his job in order to address his own work more *fully*. But Ray actually stopped my drinking. He could see no reason for it, and, since he'd had to pay a bit of attention to his own health, he was well informed on the medical consequences. He thought I'd do better out of the city. And so, in due course, we went. And *there* all hell broke loose. Oh, dear. I became, all at once, quite the little expert on alcoholic withdrawal. Sometimes my skin would just *roar* all over with heat, and then I'd be all a sort of chill, oily sweat, all sliding. And the depressions, and the euphorias, all nauseous, and then at the least thing, I'd be *seized* by such *rage*, I thought my face must be striped red and blue like a baboon's. And I'd *hallucinate,* I'd see little flames. I'd see them licking at the edges of everything. I called them my Sly Flames. But the worst thing was my imagination, which I lost all control of. I'd take walks, and see a white flower, say, and decide that its roots stretched to the center of the earth. It was an agent, sent for my soul. If I smelled it I would be confused and lie down, and the lower things would get me. And so on. Not that I literally believed this, but *I could not stop imagining it*. And so I'd run and tell Ray. And he listened. Not patiently, but as if it didn't require any patience.

"Well, it wasn't a bad life, not all of it. At least I was writing quite a bit. And Ray would work in the dining room. It had good light and a big table just right for his drawings. His drawings were circular and just huge, and he drew them on pearly sheets of plastic, with a sort of plastic ink, so if he scraped away a line, you could actually pick it up between your fingers, like a hair. He'd been working for years on this theoretical circular city based on the Hindu mandala. He told me the natural expression of physical forces through space is inherently curving and bifurcating. He'd say, 'Try herding a group of marbles across the floor with your hand and you'll see what I mean.' Different layers of the design were on different overlays, and he needed my help to unroll them and get them lined up over each other, as if we were spreading sheets on a bed. You know, Nick, I've missed that judging little look on your face. But it wasn't *all* tosh. I mean, if you manage somehow to draw back the veil, and then try and talk about it, of course you're going to sound like a fool, because whatever's behind the veil can't be talked about."

"You think he drew back the veil?"

"Well," she said with a sour-pickle twist of the mouth, "he drew back *some* veil."

She shifted beside me, first lightly grunting as if in warning. "Does it bother you, me chattering away by the hour like this?"

"You know it doesn't."

"You're supposed to say I'm not chattering. Ask me anything about your African princess and about Adam and his drugs and your little cheerleader, sorry, gymnast, and Key and the corn dog man and your Israeli girl and *especially* about your Israeli girl's bazooms – I could certainly pick *them* out of a police lineup. You piglet," she said, and shoved me with a socked foot. "So don't you tell me about chattering. And I want to hear more, too. It's lovely to listen to you being the crazy one for a change. Oh, that's one of the things that drove me crazy about Ray, that we couldn't just sit and swap stories. Some nights I'd just lie in bed and listen to him moving around and pretend I was telling him all sorts of things, and then pretend he was telling me what he thought of all that."

"Listen to him? Where was he?"

"What do you mean?"

"Where was Ray while you were pretending to tell him stories and he was moving around?"

"His room," Julia said unwillingly, "was next to mine."

"Separate rooms, Julia?"

"What a nasty-minded little boy you are." She gazed off and away toward better things.

"Poor Julia. You, of all people, marrying someone who didn't want to fuck."

She looked at me severely. Then her eyes widened and she said, "Oh, Nicky. I can't believe it *either!* You see, I'd muss up the bed and make it all rumply, and he said I snored. He liked to lie there just so, like a wooden soldier. I kept wondering what was *wrong*. Nicky, I was prepared for any fruitcake rationale for our marriage, but it never occurred to me he was simply being practical. He wanted someone to fix his meals and tidy the house and pay for everything, and look nice so he could look at her, and he was just too sick and odd to be interested in anything else. I mean, at first he liked me to say and do things, little shows. But then it wasn't even that. I remembered that year in Ithaca and felt such *sympathy* for you. He wasn't even a real minister! He'd dropped out before they ordained him, and he got me to agree that didn't matter. Oh Nick, he was insane. From time to time I may be something of a nutter, but Ray was the genuine article. Never an instant's doubt. It made him so strong over me. Even at the end, while I was explaining that the landlord and the computer dealer and the grocer all had letters from my attorney stating I would no longer be responsible for his debts, and the rent was paid till June and after that he was on his own, and grateful as I was he'd gotten me sober, I wasn't about to repay him by finishing out my days as leading lady in his *folie à deux*, even then all I got from him was a peevish look at not making himself clear. To this day, I'm sure he thinks if I hadn't got all hysterical and female he'd've repaired the understanding. A phrase of his meaning won the fight."

"Poor Julia. How long *has* it been?"

She flushed. Unwonted privation had marked and softened her face. "That is a very improper question."

"Have you divorced him?"

She flushed deeper. "That wasn't necessary. We, ah, performed the wedding ceremony ourselves."

"Oh."

"Yes."

"Read the vows yourself?"

"And wrote them. Of course."

"Who pronounced you man and wife?"

"He did."

"Poor Julia. Who was the maid of honor?"

She smiled slightly. "I was."

"Well," I said with some asperity, "I hope, at least, that you had the *catering* done by professionals."

Here she began to laugh. She threw back her red face, and the shape of her throat regained its old clarity. Before she'd quite stopped laughing, she bent double and kissed me neatly on the mouth.

At once she stood, smoothing down the front of her sweatpants. "Chatter chatter. You should get some sleep."

Chin on mattress, I watched her pillowy gray rear retreat. It moved as if she expected at any moment to feel teeth sinking into it. A charming idea, I thought. Funnily enough, I actually was tired, and fell asleep soon after.

:   :

I woke near evening. My clothes had been laundered and folded. Julia was in her bedroom. Through her door, I heard faint music. I washed and dressed and was foraging in the kitchen when she entered in a worn blue bathrobe. "Well, look at you. Like a colt's first steps. I'm filled with motherly pride. Sit down and let me fix you something. That was another of Ray's notions, that I should, ah, take responsibility for my own nourishment. As a recovering alcoholic. It wasn't his worst idea."

"I'm fine. Take your bath."

"I think I will. I usually have a good soak before dinner. It's one of my pleasures. I pay close attention now to all pleasures that aren't drinking."

"I wouldn't mind fixing us dinner now, like the old days. I don't think I could be contagious, at this point."

"We'll see. Fix yourself a good snack, and I'll have my bath."

"Need your back scrubbed?"

"You are making a marked recovery," she said, and swept from the room.

I knew I was being clumsy, but I didn't think that mattered.

There were some nice vegetables in the crisper, and some eggs and farmer cheese, and I set about making a frittata, with a little mace and thyme, very perfumy. I folded up the sofa bed – I was still a bit weak – then set the kitchen table for two. There was a prettier table in the living room, but it was large and formal. I preferred to have us sitting knee to knee. I was cutting some bread when Julia came out in her robe. She observed the two places at the table. Her wet hair was done up in a towel. It seemed to me that she'd arranged her turban with some care. "That smells so good. I'm not cooking dinner?"

"You can cook another one later. I'll be hungry again."

"You are making a *very* marked recovery. Would you like me to run down and get you some beer? It's supposed to be strengthening."

"Water's fine. Sit."

"Shall I dress? You're dressed."

"Sit."

After we'd eaten, I seated myself on the sofa. "Come sit with me," I said, holding out an arm, and she sat beside me, and I draped my arm lightly around her. She gave my near knee a quick rub with one hand: *There.* Then she sat up and tucked her robe down between her legs, and relaxed again. Then she sat up once more, and poked at her turban. She couldn't get it quite even. She dropped her hands to collarbone level and considered, then pulled it off and shook out her hair. It flicked against my face. She said, "Sorry," and dutifully refitted herself to the space under my arm. She gave my knee the same *there* rub, to indicate that now we could get on with the business of sitting. Struck by an inspiration, she raised her brows – I couldn't see them, but her scalp stirred against my cheek – and said, "Would you like to watch some TV?"

"Fine."

"I don't have the remote."

"I'll get up and find it in a minute."

"Surprised you can get your arm around me."

"None of that."

"Quitting drinking's easy. Losing twenty pounds is hard."

"You're doing fine."

She sat up and turned to me a celebratory face. "You know, I *am* doing fine. I really am. I've been sober for one year and, let's see, almost fourteen weeks. And I'm doing things I enjoy that won't hurt me. And it's wonderful."

"What are you w–"

She clamped a hand over my mouth. *"Don't say it."*

I laughed into her palm.

"I do not care to speak right now about what I'm working on, not with you sitting there getting ready to make faces and remarks, you scrawny little *bully*," she said, removing her hand but keeping it poised. We laughed again, and she gave me a quick fond buss, an apology to my silenced lips. Slightly moist. Her hair swung around my face as she drew back: scent of shampoo and clean scalp. She tucked her head under my chin, and we sat that way, my fingers in her hair, her cheek on my chest. "What a long time we've known each other."

"What a terrible few years you've had." I traced a streak of silver in her hair.

"No, I've been going gray for almost ten years. I used to dye it."

"It didn't look dyed."

"It's not supposed to."

"You even…?"

"Oh, this?" She patted her lap. "Forgot how recently you'd seen that. No, there was never that much grey down there, and I'd just *pluck* 'em."

"Ouch."

"Yes, ouch. All that lovely beauty didn't come cheap."

"Don't talk about your beauty in the past tense."

She sat up.

"Nicky," she said, "I can't. I just can't. I'm flattered, and probably much more pleased than I ought to be, but I keep myself much more to myself these days. And I didn't bring you here to tease you, or take advantage of your weakened condition—"

"You're not," I said, taking hold of the lapels of her robe and drawing her gently forward. "I'm taking advantage of your weakened condition." Lightly, I kissed her immobile mouth.

"I am a middle-aged woman with white hair and a big fat behind and I refuse to accept that you still want me."

I kissed her again. This time her lips moved uncertainly against mine. I stood and drew her slowly up by the lapels, so that she could either stand or have her robe pulled from her body. She stood. I kissed her, and she took my cheeks in her hands and kissed me back. Her mouth was cooler and sweeter than mine, and her lips a bit thinner than when I'd kissed her last. I could feel the trembling of her jaw. I undid the sash of her robe and let it fall open, and set my hands on her soft bare hips. I did not look at her body. She held one hand before her groin and with the other tried to hide the swell of her belly. I slipped the robe from her shoulders and let it slide to the floor, and looked.

"You're looking at my breasts. I have breasts now."

"Yes."

"I grew them when I got so fat. I feel so naked."

"You are naked."

"That must be it. I wish you'd say how pretty my breasts are. I wish you'd say something."

They shone, her new breasts and her shoulders. Her softened belly and thighs gave back less of the light. Beneath her rounding abdomen, her brown muff seemed wide as the blade of a shovel, and I grazed it with my knuckles. Still humid from the bath. The hips had opened into unfamiliarly generous slow curves, and veins and tendons showed clearer on her big feet. Untouched, her nipples had contracted until they were dark as bittersweet chocolate. "They're like a girl's."

"Oughta be. They're new. The one blessing about getting so fat. The way I eat, and all the drinking. By rights, I should've been fat *aeons* ago. Oh."

I'd dropped to my knees and was rubbing my face in her cushiony stomach. Now I'd taken her hips and was trying to pivot her. She didn't want to pivot. "Turn *around*. What a beautiful behind."

"Oh. Oh your mouth there. *Ni*-cky! Don't look at my cellulite."

My face still planted between her buttocks, I burst out laughing. She leapt forward.

Holding her fanny: "Nicky, I saw *sparks* when you did that!"

"Come down here."

She knelt and we kissed again. She began to tremble. Her buttocks were rich in my hands. I smoothed one hand down her belly and tenderly took hold of her cunt. It unsealed its wetness along my middle finger. "I can taste my ass on your tongue," she said dreamily. "And you're so dressed. You *like* this, me naked and shaking and on my knees and you're all dressed."

"It's not bad."

"Are you going to fuck me, Nicky?"

"Yes."

"What a long time we've known each other."

"Nm."

"I didn't think we'd ever do this."

"M."

"Oh you're moving me down there. Oh God, oh god oh god oh god oh Nicky stop, oh *God* I'll come right now *stop*."

"I want you to."

"*No*. If I do I'll go away and I have to be here with you right now. I have to be here with you naked and knowing you're going to fuck me."

She undid my pants, and dipped her hands inside as if dipping water from a stream.

"I've loved you so long," she said.

:   :

One of her bedroom curtains had been closed crookedly, and revealed the early darkness outside. Julia lay on her back with her knees drawn up and her feet resting on my chest. I knelt with my thighs bracketing her soft haunches and my erect prick lying along the groove of her cunt, as I had eight and a half years before. But now her nipples were so hard it seemed they must hurt, and her hands were loose and open at her sides, palms up – the palms looked as soft, pretty, defenseless, and endlessly fuckable as her opened cunt.

When she closed her eyes, the fatigued lines around them deepened, and she looked older, and as though she had been sick with desire for years. At the same time, with her knees pressed back against her shoulders, her buttocks and the bottoms of her thighs were tautly chubby, the skin childishly white and soft. The shadowy skin around her anus gleamed dully. Her labia were a girlish pink. The plush rise of her pubic bone fell away into a shallow declivity along the furrow of her vulva, and into this the undercurve of my erection fit as precisely as a peach pit into a halved peach. She breathed shallowly and did not seem to know what to do with her hands. Finally one alighted between her own breasts and the other on the back of my penis, and she traced its length with a fingertip. When I shifted, she drew back her hand. I kissed the soles of her feet and extended her legs up along my body, and she tried to twine her ankles behind my neck as I leaned forward, bending her double, and kissed her mouth. Her hands were captured between our chests. I felt my entire weight resting on my prick, which glided subtly back and forth. It struck the soft ledge at the entrance of her cunt and stopped. A fractional adjustment, and I would slide smoothly inside. I knew she would not stop me. This was irresponsible; I would do no such thing, and so thinking, I made a fractional adjustment and slid smoothly in. She cried out, and I stopped.

Her cunt was perfect; it was like the other side of my own skin.

I did not move. In my face gathered an angelic peevishness. "We don't want you pregnant," I murmured at last. A lie. I wanted her pregnant with one child of mine after another; I wanted her tangled to me beyond hope of rescue.

"In the drawer?" she whispered.

With a bitter effort, I pulled out of her and jerked open the drawer of the night table. In it was a sealed box of condoms. The condoms by the solitary bed were the most gallant thing I'd ever seen. I rolled one on and knelt above her again.

I slipped into her as an oar slips under the water, as a tired man slips into sleep.

I kissed her nipples in turn, and teased them with my tongue and teeth. My glans was crammed against her cervix, my balls lay against the infolding of her buttocks. Her breasts, hands, and thighs were a jumble against my chest. I placed my tongue deep in her mouth and set my ring finger over her anus as if stoppering a flute. The cleft of her ass was stretched wide, was now a shallow depression open to the light, still faintly dewy. The dusky skin around her anus felt white: the secret, mushroomy feel of flesh that is usually folded together in darkness. I began to move inside her.

The sensation was of light, sensed rather than seen, passing through pebbled safety glass to touch the back of my head, more than twenty years before. I was in the city with my parents, visiting friends in an old building by Riverside Park. A spiral staircase behind the elevator led from the dark lobby, which was tiled like a public restroom, to the roof. I loved to stand at the bottom of the stairwell and look all the way up to skylight at the top, and then to climb up to the ninth floor, just under the skylight, and look down. *I was there, and now I'm here.*

I set my thumb on the silvery scar inside her thigh. I wanted her to remember.

Then I hooked my arms tightly around her, one behind her neck and the other curled around her rump. After a few thrusts, she screamed into my mouth. Restraint was unthinkable this first time; a few strokes later, I screamed into hers.

Almost at once I struggled upright and knelt between her legs, gawping down at her. I was too dazed to do otherwise. She lay there, stirring in a disorganized manner. She seemed to have forgotten how to close her legs. She stretched creamily and tried to wriggle closer. Her legs got in the way. With two fingertips I smoothed the twin creases where her vulva met her plumpening thighs. I spread my hand on her soft belly, imagined it swollen hard with our babies. I took hold of her feet and pressed them back as if they were in an obstetrician's stirrups.

"I like you sucking my breasts when you're inside," she remarked. "You hunch up like an earthworm, so you can get to them."

"You came," I said stupidly.

"No. But I'm so close. I feel like your prick is still inside me. Oh, I'm still so close."

I set my mouth against her streaming cunt. The taste was rich and sedgy, like honey cut with pondwater. "Don't!" she cried. "Oh…" I noticed with some surprise that I was still hard and, securing the condom with two fingers, wedged myself into her again. "You *can't!*" she insisted, and twined her legs around mine. The thrashing of her hips grew more and more erratic. "Please!" she said hoarsely. "I'll die! I'm so! I'll die!" I slipped an arm under her waist and, rolling, pulled her over on top of me. "Do what you need to," I suggested. She pressed my shoulders to the mattress and went to work, puffing and straining, her face swollen and red and the creases silvery with sweat.

"Can I –"

"No! Let me – *LET ME*."

She began to thump her loins down on mine as if trying to knock something loose, grunting and gasping, stopping and starting again. Finally she was overtaken by a feral, hissing orgasm. My prick was caressed by the beating wings of sticky angels.

I rolled back on top of her and, as she wept, began to fuck her again. Her legs flinched together, and then she began to ripple against me, crying as if heartbroken, her wails punctuated by a quaver each time my hips struck her rear. Her wet mouth was criminal. "Oh, you've done this to me. You've done this to me. Oh God, I'm making you happy." I grasped her by the ankles, turned her over, and began to fuck her from behind, so that her white buttocks rippled with each impact of my hips. I gripped her silvering hair like reins.

"Shoot," she sobbed, peering up at me over her shoulder. "I need to see you shoot."

I withdrew and, turning quickly, Julia stripped the condom from me. Then she lay back and, straddling her, I knee-walked up her body. Eyes closed, she searched upward with her open mouth like a baby bird. She weighed my scrotum on a flattened tongue. I thumbed myself into her mouth. As when I was seventeen, her face reformed around the circumference of my prick, became wedge-shaped and made for sucking. Her wet eyes gazed up at me, large and senseless. At the base of my belly I felt a spreading stain of irrevocable wine, and then her throat moved matter-of-factly as she swallowed.

This time I sat back deliberately, to enjoy the dizziness. The night was full of things done the first time because they were inevitable and the second time because they were, apparently, possible.

I cast myself down and lay beside her. "You're little," I murmured, "you're all little."

"A runt," she said, and sniffled.

"You're so little and so beautiful."

"*Fat* runt."

"You've *always* been so beautiful," I said irritably.

She tried to bind my wrists with my hair, she masked my face with it. I knotted it loosely to hers. "You were crying," I said.

She kissed me quickly, thrusting her sour tongue into my mouth. "Ha!"

"Ha."

Soon the night had grown larger than any night could be. It began to fall apart, divide into epochs: The First Entrance; Before He'd Come in Her Mouth; The First Trip to the Bathroom; The Side by Side Period. I thought about kneeling between her legs, easing myself inside for the first time. We were beginners then. I'd learned things about her body I had already had time to forget, and when I learned them again, I was surprised, nostalgic. I dozed off and she nudged me awake. "You were sleeping with your hands tucked up under your chin, like this. And your spine is so poignant. Do you suppose you've got more than the regular number of vertebrae? I wanted you to sleep forever, so I could watch."

"So you woke me."

"Exactly. Or I wouldn't be able to tell you how dear you looked."

I woke again to find myself snouting blindly into her from behind. Outside the window, the new snow glowed. She was a squid, darting away in billows of ink. I worked contentedly and with no great pleasure, because it was better to be inside than out. With full wakefulness came the knowledge that I would not come. Besides, I ought to be wearing a... condom, that's what they were called. I withdrew and examined my prick, which was numb and looked very odd to me. I lay on one elbow, thoughtfully stroking it, as she hunted vaguely around behind her with her bottom. Her body had been remaking itself in sleep: it was now a night-body, sleek and younger and faceless. She lifted her rear hard against my palm, as a cat will arch its back against a stroking hand. Then, rocking from side to side, she worked herself up on her knees until her rump was in the air and her face and breasts pressed into the bed. I found a condom and knelt behind her. I spat, not unkindly, on her anus.

"Yes. Put your long dark prick up there."

When I was all the way home, her rectum contracted around me like a wedding band. "That's the ticket," she groaned.

"Does it feel good."

"Yes."

"Doesn't it hurt."

"Yes. Yes. Oh, ow, *don't move.* Just let it sit in there and cook. Tell me how you're fucking me. Fucking my fat ass." She waggled her buttocks beseechingly. "Oh. Oh. I've given you everything now. I've given you everything. Didn't you want this."

"Yes."

"I can't get my *breath!*" I fell forward and pressed my forehead between her shoulder blades. Still coupled, we rolled over on our sides. I gentled her mons with fingers already chafed to tingling by her pubic hair. I was scarcely moving. She pulsed erratically inside. "You keep poking my lungs. Oh, I'm making you happy."

I turned into light and emptied out completely into her.

When we collected ourselves, we trudged single file to the bathroom. There she plumped down on the toilet and I sat on the edge of the tub. She sighed and disburdened herself. I got up, cursorily washed myself, and sat again. My knee came to rest against hers. It was warm. I had no opinion of it. Another musical plop, like a low note played on a marimba. The frittata. I clumsily kissed her mouth, went back to bed, and passed out.

:   :

I was aware of someone's cheek against my chest. A woman's cheek. Snowlight had begun to seep between the dark curtains. Blankets had slipped from girlish new breasts. She'd scooted down; it had not occurred to her to draw the blankets up. The cheek against my ribs was matter-of-fact. I might have been a pillow. Her arm was stretched down against my body. Her nipples were disks of shadow. I twisted gently at the nearer one until it was stiff, then watched it go lax. Then I did the other. I lifted away the blankets and watched Julia's body assembling itself in the dimness. She slept on her back, round legs gracelessly spread, mouth open, her face exhausted and serene. It was like that drawing where by shifting your focus you can change the goblet into two faces in profile: I could change Julia into a pretty, plumpening, middle-aged woman with one nipple erect and one not. Finally she stroked my neck and deeply kissed my foul-tasting mouth. "There you still are," she said peacefully.

"Hello."

"Hello. Fooling with my breasts. I dreamed there was something going on."

"Hello," I said.

She made herself even smaller and huddled into my chest, her lips against my breastbone, her feet crossed one over the other. She looked wonderfully pretty. She murmured, "Where're all the blankets."

I drew them up over her.

"*Thought* I had some blankets." She kissed my breastbone.

"I wanted to look at you."

"Take a girl's blankets," she said. She wriggled around to relish having blankets and to warm them up inside again. "You're very satisfactory to sleep with. Get my arms *all* the way around you."

"Now I can't see you anymore."

"See me later. All you like. Hush now."

"All right."

"It's no good. I'm awake. And I was looking forward to sleeping in 'til noon with you, until some disgraceful hour when you'd ordinarily be bustling about."

"I think you could sleep again."

"Maybe I could." She smiled up through her tangled hair at me. "I remember you as so sensitive and inventive. I never dreamed you'd be such a little whoremaster. Know what really hurts?" she confided.

"Your ass."

"You guessed," she said, disappointed. She slid out of bed and reached for her robe.

"Where are you going?"

"Can you eat something?"

"Yes. Leave off the robe."

She laughed and let it slip from her shoulders. "All right."

Her buttocks wobbled as they left the room. An efficient wobble.

I listened to her clacking in the kitchen. Eventually she returned with clear broth and toasted bread cut from a dark, dense loaf and spread with hummus. Straddling my lap, she fed me, holding the bowl between her breasts and resting the plate of toast on my ribs. "What if you gained a pound for every one I lost? How would that be?"

I said, "You know what a *shabbes goy* is? Rich Jews used to pay Gentiles to come to their houses on Saturday and turn on the lights, cook the meals. Everything a *frum* Jew can't do on the Sabbath."

"What's it like, growing up in a Jewish house?"

"Who knows? My folks were about as Jewish as June bugs. I know about *shabbes goyim* from Isaac Singer."

I'd dropped a few crumbs on my chest and she dabbed them up with her tongue. "Is that what I am? Your goyum?"

"Goy. It's what I'd like you to be."

"Easy, sport," she said, laughing. "That could easily be construed as an offer of marriage."

"It is," I said.

Laughing nervously, she said, "Well, let's not run away with ourselves."

I hadn't meant to say anything, but now I had that dizzy feeling, that feeling of divinely sanctioned foolishness I'd had as a kid hanging headdown from a tree: I could launch myself into space and know that I'd come up smiling. It seemed that all my foolishness had been blessed in retrospect; it had brought me to this moment. Julia watched me take the bowl and bread from her and set them aside. Then I opened my lips to speak, and she quickly covered them with a hand.

Reflexively, I kissed her hand. Then I was silent.

She carefully got off of my ribs and seated herself on the mattress. She drew her knees up and hugged them and looked at nothing in particular.

"I'm – I already have someone, Nicky," she said. "I'm still with Ray. It's a – different relationship now, but I am still with him."

"Well, then that's that," I said very rapidly. I said it as a sort of reflex. I hadn't quite heard what she'd said. I knew it must be very terrible, but… "Ray. You left Ray. You kicked him out."

"But we didn't sever things altogether, I'm afraid. Simply because we couldn't seem to share a house, or even… Well, I certainly won't say that the sexual matters are *trivial*, but… I'm sorry. I can see I should have been clearer. I can see that now. But I didn't want to spoil things."

"You didn't want… to spoil things?"

"I wanted to finally give you everything. And if I came right out and… Didn't you always want us to have this?" she pleaded.

"You said you'd loved me so long," I said.

"But I have! You have always been one of my very dearest, most *important* friends! Even when we hated each other, I always thought of you, and you were one of the people whose good opinion I've always most cared about, and about your happiness… And you're very attractive, I always thought we, hoped we might get around to…" She gestured at us. "But it was never… Nicky, it was never that way."

"Friends?" I said.

I got out of bed and began hunting around the floor for my pants.

"I've made a mistake," she said. "Oh, God forgive me, I've made a mistake. I think we should talk about this."

I found my pants and underpants and set about putting them on.

"It's just, you sounded in such trouble on the phone. And I thought, if I could just be good to you for a change. And you were liking me again. And, I was just, enjoying doing things for you… I mean, Ray is very independent, emotionally, he doesn't… Can't you please stop tying your shoes? Nicky, please. I couldn't bear you hating me again. I couldn't bear it. I've had to bear so much. *Please* listen. I thought this would be a good thing. I thought we could have this single good thing. I didn't understand. I didn't know. I knew we'd always been drawn to each other. And I'd always felt there was something between us, a sort of covenant—"

"FRIENDS?" I screamed.

Her eyes on me were large and senseless again.

I touched my face with my fingers. It did not seem possible that it was still attached to my head.

"Friends? Covenant? What are you talking about?" I asked. "Julia? For the last twenty years, what have you been talking about?"

She did not answer.

"Why did you bring me here? A single good thing? Julia, what does that mean? Did you think it would be a good treatment for dehydration? Did you think it would be interesting? Did you think it would make another piquant little moment for some *poem?* Another little lash of brightness? What *shit. I* was the one who got stung. All my life, all my *life* I have been poisoned with you." I'd begun to shout. Her face, first frightened and pale, grew expressionless. As I continued to shout, it grew whiter and more still. She seemed naked and old, with a scarred leg. "And it's not fucking *poetry* to me. It's not something I can re*write* if I don't like the way it *sounds.* It's my life, it was my life, and how did I spend it? Loving *you.* Waiting for *you.* For what? Who asked me to? Who in fuck's name told me that Julia May Turrell was a good idea? A rich brat with a witty wardrobe! A splay-legged poetaster! A sexual dilettante, a fucking emotional *tourist* who can't keep her mind on the same man or the same *genre* for three weeks running and every bit of love I've ever been offered I've slapped aside because it wasn't *yours.* I cut my dick off every morning to be a friend to *you,* I sat over an empty page and *pissed* myself over *you,* I listened by the hour to *you* pondering Chris and Christ and Daddy and your fucking *rabbit*, and now, and now, at the end of all the words, I get – more words! I get a sort of covenant! And thank you very much and good-bye! Oh, why didn't somebody blow my brains out twenty years ago if I didn't have enough of them to run for my life the minute I saw you? *Loved? Loved so long?*" I wailed. "There is no love in you, Julia."

Her face was growing dim, like a white stone sinking toward the bottom of a pond. She still hadn't moved when I slammed the door.

:   :

That moment started three days of incessant screaming, writes Tolstoy of the death of Ivan Ilyich, *screaming so terrible that even two rooms away one could not hear it without trembling… he realized that he was lost, that there was no return, that the end had come, the very end…*

Actually, there wasn't a peep out of me.

The sidewalk sparkled in the lamplight. It seemed to quiver when my heels struck it. Here and there I noted random crusts of snow. The light before dawn was crawling and granular and TV-blue, and the chill seemed very new and sensitive. The world was subsumed by a sort of Brownian motion, so that everything stirred subtly and continuously and there was no rest.

I experimented with jauntiness. *Well, at least…* [Good. More.] *Well, at least I got to… at least I finally got…* I tried to be Adam about it: *Fancy fucking!* No. I recalled Julia's caresses, her cries, it seemed impossible –

None of that.

"This is stupid," I suggested aloud. I'd stopped walking and was facilitating the continued beating of my heart by gripping the steel grating over a shop window.

I detached myself and began walking again.

This *was* stupid. What, after all, had changed in the last forty-eight hours? My fever had broken and I'd had a night of splendid sex with someone I'd always wanted. Closing a chapter of my life, basically.

Fun, too. There. That was the way. I was over the worst of it. Wasn't I, really, to be envied? After all, Julia's caresses, her cries –

Nicky, it was never that way.

At any rate, let's keep walking, shall we?

For God's sake, I was still sick, I was just weak and nauseous, it was not my soul but my gut, I probably just needed to vomit to feel better. Gosh, did I need to vomit. I went to the curb, bent down with hands on knees, and tried to vomit.

Eeeeurkkh. Kh. Khhh. Kh? Any moment now.

Please let me vomit.

Goggling face toward the gutter, bottom toward the stars, I saw that I would not even succeed at this.

The pain was quite remarkable and, straightening dizzily, I believe I said as much aloud. Then there was the prospect of feeling what I felt for an indefinite period. I tacked over to a phone booth and enacted a little tableau of there being no one to call. Then I cut that silly shit out, but did not release the receiver. I told myself to release the receiver. I managed it and was greatly encouraged, and then discouraged that I'd been reduced to being encouraged about being able to let go of a phone.

In this way I walked clear across town. York Avenue was empty. Beyond it, the grinding rumble of the cars moving on the FDR Drive, like that of the earth moving on its axis. The sidewalk led to a ramp, the ramp to a pedestrian overpass. When I'd crossed over the highway, I leaned on the railing at the other end, looking down into the cold East River and filling my chest with its ancient, oceanic smell. I was aware of moving cars behind and below me. I was aware of presenting another tableau: a young man with a lot on his mind. It all seemed very bad art. I went down the stairs and circled behind them. Here graffiti-slashed concrete made a snuggery, out of sight. It was foul with urine; someone had recently lived here. The railing was awkward to lean on. It curved inward, probably to keep people from climbing up on it. But I managed, and then balanced atop it, steadying myself with a light hand on the wall, and looked across the East River.

About one hundred yards of dark gray water separated me from Roosevelt Island. Three illuminated towers rose along the river, and behind them, three immense striped smokestacks from the power plant, topped by red lights that blinked in unison. The river was glassy, the water flattened by oil and filth. A tug was nosing a vast gravel barge downstream. A dark radar antenna revolved on the tug's mast. The barge seemed too large for the narrow channel. The wind was bitter. The night's darkness was weakening. I wondered if anyone could see me, if anyone thought I was going to kill myself. I wasn't, of course, but I thought it might clarify my wish to live if I stood there balanced above the freezing water. And if I fell in and was removed from consideration, that would be a sort of bonus, what they called serendipity. Dear God, what a pukeworthy way to think; anyone who could think like that would improve the world by leaving it. I'd climb down from this *mishegoss* at once. But that seemed cowardly. The tug was passing, it had passed. Wait for another? Would there never be an end to my dithering? *Now.* I startled myself with a long, flat swan dive, entering the water quickly and easily.

The cold snapped through my body like a vast spark. For an instant I didn't know where I was. Then cold and black pressure, and the departing propellers grinding in my ears. Now all I had to do was breathe in. Still, this was the East River. I didn't mind dying, but I didn't want to get this stuff in my mouth. My head broke the surface and I took a sheepish breath, then sank to try again, my water-filled clothes moving around me with a sort of soggy delay; they'd sprouted internal cords to saw my loins. Shouldn't suicide be less uncomfortable? This was heartening stupidity: after all, people didn't die while considering silly shit like this. Oh yes they did; that's just how they died, and I saw I didn't want to die after all. But when I broke the surface again, it was difficult to breathe; the muscles of my diaphragm were seizing with the cold; I was already sleepy; already the cold didn't seem so bad; already it seemed fussy to mind the thick water I swallowed, water so cold it tasted clean. I tried to recall the definition of *hypothermia*. I peered over the wavelets. Both banks were lined with sheer concrete sea walls. If you swam to the island, there were boulders you might be able to climb. This seemed like a lot of trouble, and maybe I'd better just sink. I was born a ditherer and I was going to die a ditherer.

I began swimming, moving each limb as if it were a separate piece of luggage I was heaving up a narrow staircase. I stopped and undid my coat, hurting my fingers on the zipper, and then swam out of it. The island was not far away now, perhaps the length of a swimming pool, but it didn't seem to be getting any closer. I saw I was barely wiggling my arms and legs. I'd only thought I was swimming with all my might. Then the barge's trailing wake swept me smoothly under, and I heard the propellers again, as if they were very near, and slammed against something hard which I was almost too numb to feel. It was more like the notion of falling down and hurting yourself, everyone thinking you were silly. When I could, I clambered up the boulders, chirping and squeaking, and over the low railing on the sea wall, and then I was sitting beneath a streetlamp, on firm ground, in air that briefly seemed warm, gagging up oily water. I was pleased, about as pleased as I'd been to let go of the phone.

I got up and began bumbling along, giving out little cries, my jaw rattling in my head, until I found another pay phone, then forced my hand into my sodden jeans and came up with a few coins. This time I dialed without hesitation.

"Adam?" I said.

"Nick? What? Are you okay? Nick?" He was asleep.

"I," I said, "Julia. Julia's..."

"Oh, sugar," he said, "will we ever have any brains?"

:　　:

There's an all-night diner on the main street of Roosevelt Island, and I waited there over hot coffee in which I could still taste the oil of the river, shuddering and blinking. Adam arrived in forty minutes. He bustled me at once into the men's room and stripped me. He'd brought an old coat, a towel, and a paper bag of dry clothes: jeans, two flannel shirts, wool socks, a heavy sweater. These were Cat's; his own would be too short. The underwear was his, and I had to hold it up with one hand while pulling on Cat's jeans with the other. He'd also brought a pint of bourbon, with which he spiked my coffee as the counterman frowned, and he tried to make me eat a slice of apple pie. Then he hauled me off to the tram, hugging me and whispering to me among the early commuters as the car rocked above the black water I'd swum, now far below and metalled with morning light. By then I'd given him the gist. "Let's get you home," he said, full of sorrow, and took me to a bar.

I've retained nothing of the next two days but isolated details of amplified clarity. I was standing at a pinball machine, feeling hale and warm, if a bit confused, and several people, Cat among them, were admiring my score. The bourbon was doing me a world of good. I was pissing extensively between two parked cars while two young women stood sentry with their backs turned. I know one of them wore an add-a-bead necklace. At another point: a bowl-shaped light fixture, fastened to the ceiling by a knurled brass knob, speckled inside with the bodies of flies. I watched very carefully to see if any of them moved. I recall leaning against a plate glass store window, thinking how foolish it was to have put the legs way down there on hinges, so that all you had to do was bend at the waist and you'd fall over. I recall Adam shaking a pint of bourbon, another one, and peering inside. "If you slosh it up good, you can get a head on it," he reported.

"No you can't."

"Well, it goes away, but look, there's little bubbles that travel up."

Finally I awoke, sober, in Adam's apartment, my cheek pasted to the couch with my own vomit. It was daylight again. I didn't know what day. I guessed I'd find out soon enough. I felt quite well, but very tired and thirsty, and I went right back to sleep.

TWELVE

And Now You're Anyone's to Find and Mend

My phone rang around nine-thirty the next evening. I considered letting it ring. I was feeling washed-out and ill and oddly velvety in the ears. When I picked it up, I heard a young woman's fluting, sweet-and-sour Brooklynese voice. "Forgot, huh?"

"I'm sorry, who is this?"

"Leah Birney. Don't even remember me, huh? Why'm I not surprised?"

"Oh my God. Did I, ah, meet you the other night? Did we agree to meet?"

"Stingy Lulu's at eight. I just got back home."

"Oh my God."

"Well, I got my reaction now, so I guess I can hang up."

"Please don't. My God, Leah, I'm sorry. I wasn't in very good shape."

"Tell me about it. Look, it's no big deal. I didn't have plans, and I figured you wouldn't show, but you were sort of interesting. I dunno. Next to your friend who never shuts up. You were just so sad and so horribly skinny. I figured, fine, date another junkie."

"You've dated more than one?"

"I thought I dated all of 'em. I figured you were the one I missed. I was so relieved you were just a drunk, 'cause they last longer."

"Actually, I'm not even a drunk."

"Yeah, I got all that too. Um, the girl, Julie or whatever, and the whole deal since you were ten and got your tattoo. Maybe the tattoo was later."

"Leah, I'm terribly sorry. Can I meet you somewhere right now?"

"No, this is actually what I expected. I just wanted you to know. I have my Lean Cuisine dinner here, I have my book. It's fine. If you're thinking I was probably some knockout, don't worry, I'm not some knockout."

"Let me buy you dinner, Leah. Then I'll leave. Please. I have to learn how not to fuck up everything I touch."

"Well, good luck, but isn't that your problem, not mine? I'm gonna hang up now."

"Don't hang up."

"Can't I hang up?"

"Don't hang up."

"I guess I'm not hanging up yet. Um, I have to ask, what do you weigh?"

"Wouldn't you like to see me sober?"

"You kept saying that last night. It was almost charming."

"Is it almost charming now?"

There was a long pause. "I must just be so stupid."

Leah wore a mauve dress, pretty awful, that I could yet see was of good quality and quite successful on its own terms. A small, acute, plain face, and a plumpening torso perched on gangling legs. Her thick dark hair was cut short in a manner that was clearly no trouble to care for, and really not all that much trouble to look at. Her long-nosed face was freshly made up, her eyes level, polite, and almost unhumiliated. She was a trouper. I said, "You look very nice."

"Die. I dunno what I'm doing here. Like some *social* worker."

"Did you have a friend the other night? With an add-a-bead necklace?"

"Oh, don't even try. All right. She did. You remember us now?"

"No."

"You're a piece of work. You made more sense when you were drunk."

"I really am sorry about that."

"Why? You were incredibly polite. You were really-am-sorrying all evening. You were telling me the story of your life, but you kept turning to my friend so she wouldn't feel left out, and all she wanted was to get *away* from you. It was so funny. You could barely stand up and you were trying to take care of the whole bar."

"Meanwhile here you are, agreeing to meet me because I'm so horribly sad and et cetera."

"Um, point taken."

"How about your life story?"

"Don't try and put this on an equal basis. You're the jerk, and I'm putting up with you. That's our basis."

"All right."

"I was a nerd in high school, and when I got tired of that, I became a hussy. It worked, too. Except I did it wrong, I slept with all the losers. I *liked* them better than the winners. And when I grew up I was Miss Nice, but I still had addict boyfriends."

"I'm sure it's more complex than that."

"Not tonight it ain't. *Ohhh...*" Leah's *oh* was like her *um*: the high note forced from a water glass when you stroke a wetted finger around the rim. She let her head drop forward. She had a pretty nape, and perhaps she knew this. "You're nice, is one problem. Did you really jump in the river?"

"Yes. What do you do, anyway?"

I felt her sigh of defeat against my forearms. "Actually, I'm a social worker."

We ate in near silence. Afterward, we sat gentling coffee mugs with fingertips and palms. Fairly flirtatious stuff, these little displays of tenderness with the mugs. I congratulated myself on having effected, in my condition, what seemed to be an actual date. At the door of her apartment, I pecked her cheek. Thanks and goodbye. I steadied her, or perhaps myself, with a hand on each of her shoulders. This reminded me, as if across a span of years, how good it was to touch someone, and I put my arms around her.

All I meant by so doing, if I meant anything at all, was to file an application to appeal for permission to lie down with her someday when I was further from death and had not so recently been such a schmuck, but this was probably not the impression I gave. I felt a stirring of decision in the soft muscles of her back. Then she turned her mouth determinedly to mine. Here she became competent. Unhurriedly she brought me upstairs, divested us of clothes, sighed over my bruises, produced and deployed diaphragm and condom, made me comfortable within her, locked her ankles behind my waist, and said, "Don't wait." Several minutes later, she repeated: "Don't wait for me." I hadn't been waiting. It would have seemed presumptuous.

Soon enough I grew tired and, politely as I could manage, withdrew. I lay beside her, stroking her face and flanks. It was the body of a plain woman in her thirties, distinguished only by the length and narrowness of her limbs. Her belly and breasts looked well used. She accepted my caresses without necessarily accepting anything else about the situation. "You saved my life," I said.

"Yeah. And what happens when you're not brokenhearted anymore? I'm sick of saving guys' lives."

Still, in the morning she was gay, and made a little game of wrapping my shirt around her like a robe. My shirt would have made quite a serviceable robe for Julia – I fought off memory – but Leah was tall and the effect was cheerily indecent. "I hate that I got so emotional last night. You must think I'm a real whiner. But it's just I don't get to go with that many guys I like, and I've decided you're right, and just to enjoy this for however long it lasts. Don't stare up my skirt like that. Shirt."

"It's my shirt, and I'll stare up it all I want."

"That is so incredibly rude. I am talking seriously to you and you're looking between my legs. Well, look then," she said, happy for the first time, and clambered on top of me. The shirt fell open around us like a tent. In the filtered light within, the body above me seemed simplified, as if daubed on a cave wall or lavatory door: two bobbling chalky circles with dark centers, a dark triangle and, at the zenith above my nose, a dark dot. The whole business then descended plump on my face, blotting itself from view.

"Not that I object," she said after a while, "but what are you doing?"

I'd been rubbing my ear against her stomach. "It kind of prickles."

Soon I had a roaring earache and a fever of 104°. I wound up in the hospital after all.

:   :

After breakfast they removed the IV drip from my arm and Leah entered, shrugging. "Um, I do this for a living, anyway, visiting people here. On the other hand, it's not like I don't already have a caseload. Anyhow, we get a blood test out of the deal, which I was gonna make you take anyway, and they're gonna let you go now. But you know what I was thinking, a little before? If he dies, I'm stuck being his girlfriend forever."

"I am not going to die," I said resignedly.

Leah Birney's mother was a Bay Ridge housewife of uncertain temper and health, and her father was a successful importer of fruit-shaped refrigerator magnets. She'd helped raise two younger brothers, who had both married young and grown staid and prosperous. They adored her and hated her strenuous, ragtag life; they still hoped that a sexually improvident old maid of thirty-four might yet luck into, say, a tolerant widower bent on a second marriage, and in this way taste a little of their own happiness. Republicans both, they gave stolidly to any lefty cause she recommended. Her apartment was full of their gifts: black appliances studded with blinking digital readouts and a massive beige sofa with a strip of gold-hued mirror along the base, which Leah thought was very snazzy. I came to know this sofa well.

We seldom spoke during the week, but each Friday night Leah and I would meet at her office or mine. Her clothes, as when I'd first seen her, would be good and careful and just perceptibly wrong. She accessorized with bead wristlets her clients made for her during crafts hour. When she caught sight of me, she'd start forward with a game little smile. Her legs were unmanageably long; she seemed always to be learning to ride a bicycle. By this time I knew something about unrequited love, and it was odd and terrible to see how Leah looked at me: as if she'd been caught peeking. I knew what she saw, too: an ugly boy, all bones, flying politely into the river. I had about me the glamour of calamity. Worse, I knew she understood her situation. The best thing I could do for her would be to leave. But this I would not do. I was in extremis, and I liked her. Maybe Julia had always felt the same way about me.

We'd stroll silently through Tompkins Square Park, sit silently through gaudy art films, drink silently in fusty bars, grind silently against each other's bodies and wake, Saturday morning, on opposite sides of the bed. After brunch Leah would avert her eyes and say, "Um, I'm gonna go now." Julia might yet sweep through my life again like Halley's Comet, obliterating all romances in her path, but there didn't seem to be much she could do to this one.

One Friday afternoon, Leah called me. "Um, hi. I should've called earlier. I need a favor. You can say no. What if it wasn't just us tonight, because there's this friend Cassie, who keeps saying I'm avoiding her, which I am. She's sort of baleful. We used to all be in this group thing for fucked-up teens, and some of us got better, but she's been in this bad rut where she never leaves her apartment and her mother pays her rent, which is at least cheaper than the hospital, where she's also been. You can say no. I didn't ask how your day was."

Leah's friend Cassie was slim and fair, but her forehead was deeply seamed, and there was something doglike in the jut of her head. The walls of her apartment were covered in maps, some expensively framed and some thumbtacked one over the other, even on the ceiling. Her lampshades were also patterned like maps. She seemed to like them. When she saw me, her face closed like a fist. "Wasn't it gonna be just the two of us?" she said to Leah.

"I thought I'd bring Nick along," Leah said imploringly.

"What do you, need protection? 'M I that scary? She always has a boyfriend. Some of 'em sound pretty shaggy, but they're there. So, what's this one about?"

She was one of those shameless people who use their misery as a flail. I said, "Leah, let's go."

Firmly: "Nick's an *artist*."

"Then you can draw my picture." Cassie put hands on hips and struck a pose. "Right profile, left profile? Whatever you want. I got nothing but time."

"All right. I'll need some paper."

"Really?" they said.

I figured it beat talking to her.

In fact, Cassie had a choice of drawing pads. She'd taken, of course, a stab at art. I posed her with hands cupped in lap like one of Ingres's young gentlewomen, and gave her head a demure quarter turn. She held herself studiously still. I remembered all the things my subjects tended to like: a hard pencil and a thin, careful line – they think this looks "realistic" – and shadows clouded with a thumb. I set down smooth hair and large eyes. I was generous with her eyelashes; they cost me nothing. I was reticent about the grooves in her forehead. The drawing was a flat fraud, a lampoon of everything I'd struggled for over the past twenty years, and I found myself working with unusual fluency. Finished, I turned it to face her. She looked from the drawing to the two of us, as if afraid we were engaged in some terrible hoax. "That isn't me," she said, hoping to be contradicted.

Then a smile crept across her face, and she became insipid and pretty, became, in fact, much like my drawing. She tucked it away, and we got our coats. She was painstakingly pleasant throughout dinner, then kissed us each on the cheek and said she wanted to go home and look at her portrait some more.

After that, Leah and I had our usual Friday night and Saturday morning.

An hour after she'd left, I got a call. "Hi. It's me. Is it all right I'm calling? You were so good last night. I had to say that. You made her so pretty. It's 'cause you're kind."

"C'mon, Leah. It's because I didn't give a shit."

"Yeah, well, you've developed a very kind way of not giving a shit."

"Sounds madly attractive."

"You'd be surprised what us girls have to learn to be happy about. Oh, I'm not saying what I want. You came with me! I asked you to come see my terrible friend because I was scared, and you came with me!"

"It was no problem."

"But I never ask people for that! I do that for everyone in the world and I never ask for it back, and you came with me! And now, 'No problem.' Is this something else you just very nicely just don't give a shit about? Should we break up?"

"I don't want that."

"This is so stinko. *I* should leave. Why are you this Gumby, this *lump?* What *happened* to you?"

"Same thing that's happening to you."

"Oh, nice. And I hate that we're apart on Saturday night. Why don't you ever say, 'No, I want you to stay'?"

"Fuck that," I snapped. "I'm through saying, 'Oh baby, don't leave.' If you don't want to go, don't say you better go now."

"Well, I hate that we're apart on a Saturday night."

So after that, we weren't.

:   :

Del and I have a lot of snapshots of Suzanne; she always loved to be photographed. One of my favorites was taken years before my birth. She's at Jones Beach with Saul, wearing what must have been one of the first bikinis ever manufactured. She's twenty-five or so, a tall cutie with the curves of a chorus girl and the eyes of a coyote. She looks marvelously happy, and scarcely aware of the blocky little adulterer who's wound an ambitious arm about her waist. A full head of curls sits barbarously on Saul's scalp. His wide-set eyes hold less expression than the twin whorls of hair on his chest. He seems an interloper, pawing Suzanne's hip on sufferance. But forty-odd years later, Saul was still my mother's man.

There was no talk of remarriage, or even of moving in together, but on Friday nights they'd wait hand in hand outside the Thalia to see Paulette Goddard or Jean-Luc Godard. Or Saul would put on a dreadful corduroy hat, which seemed designed to identify him as a neighborhood character, and, though I'm sure he meant to saunter, strut like a windup toy down upper Broadway, nodding with seigneurial benevolence to impassive Koreans guarding astroturf-lined bins of produce outside twenty-four-hour bodegas, and Suzanne would drift along at his side, scattering over the general bafflement the benison of her apologetic smile. Into Saul's favorite coffee shop they'd go, where he gobbled sweets and she read her book. "We know each other," Suzanne said. "That's the chief thing, at our age."

"Not only at your age," I assured her.

They asked Leah and me over for dinner once, and the four of us spent the evening in Suzanne's small kitchen, eating one dish as we cooked the next, refilling wineglasses, saying *when* and *excuse me.* My mother fixed a separate pannikin of potatoes for my father and burned them hard, the way he liked them. Saul flirted firmly but civilly with Leah, and Suzanne spoke to her as a fellow veteran of the exigencies of progressive politics and makeshift sex. My parents had attained a seemly academic shabbiness, attractively spiced with hints of past dissipation. It was a pleasant evening, and we told each other we'd have to do it again. But soon after, Saul called me up and said, "You got time to come by?"

At the tone of his voice I was already reaching for my coat and keys.

The creases in Saul's face gleamed as if carved into a block of lead. "Sit," he said. "That was quick. Did you take a cab? You can't afford that. There's not a fucking thing in the house, you wanna go grab a bite? Sit. These ninnies can't seem to agree on much, except that it's cancer all right, the pancreas, and inoperable, and will probably move fast. Chemo either may or may not slow or reverse it; the fucks have been talking to their lawyers or something. She's at Sloan-Kettering. The tests take it out of her worse than the fucking tumor. I think she'd like to see you, do you have the time? I don't like her there. The room has no light. I've been talking to people, we may move her. You want a beer? Excuse my tone," said Saul, who had never apologized for his manners in his life. "I'm a little on edge. We thought she was just not in the mood for anything. For me. Maybe if we'd gone in earlier. Stupid," he said, tears sliding down his face, "stupid, stupid, stupid, stupid. Look, you wanna get some Mexican? I'm starving."

The room Saul had so disliked was a perfectly ordinary double room with a good-sized window. Of course, there was that pervasive chill staleness of disinfected decay. Suzanne smiled and held out her arms to me. She looked marvelous. A few years back she'd begun tinting her hair a becoming dark-honey hue. Her softening flesh had clarified her cheekbones and clavicle. The ridged veins in her forearms and hands seemed athletic. She wore owl-feather earrings and seemed dressed for an assignation. She was three months away from death, and soon would have a neck like twisted twine and knuckles that seemed filled with milk, but just then she was, as Leah would have said, a knockout, in a skimpy gown dotted with tiny faded blue fleurs-de-lis, and it was obscene and terrifying for her to be in bed in the middle of the day, surrounded by the dying, the old, and the tacky. She did not want to discuss her condition or the tests. They were all very unsatisfactory. What she wanted to discuss was my upcoming marriage.

She said, "I'm sorry I was so tough on Julia. She's spoiled – of course, it's difficult for the rich to be anything else – but there's a lot of good in that girl's heart, and I think she'll make you a good wife."

"Okay," I said.

"You don't agree? It's all right to have second thoughts, Nicky. I certainly did."

"We'll discuss it later."

"Wait. Julia's not rich. I mean, Leah's... Wait. I'm getting confused."

"It's okay, Mom. Actually, I don't see Julia anymore. I'm afraid we didn't part on good terms."

"I'm sorry."

"It's nothing, Mom. You're medicated and you're tired."

"I'm tired," she agreed.

She trained on me the unaltered clarity of her toothpaste-colored eyes.

"Nicky?" she said. "Are we parting on good terms?"

I began to cry. "I love you, Suzanne," I said.

She said, "You little diplomat. Call me Mom."

:   :

After the funeral, Leah took charge. Her own beliefs were hazy, and both her parents among the quick, but she knew damn well what you did if you lost one. She invited the mourners back to my apartment, where we found a feast she'd ordered from Zabar's. My nose itched with pulverized sugar and the suave, oily scent of butter cookies.

Saul's face was like a charcoal drawing almost completely erased.

"Thank you," he told everyone. "You're very kind." "But she wanted to be *cremated*," Del moaned. And her ashes scattered in the Silver Crest woods. We knew that. Somehow, we'd forgotten. With nail scissors Leah snipped the placket of my shirt, then tore it with a brusque jerk. She did the same to Saul's, then to her own blouse. Then she swept the sofa cushions onto the floor before the sofa and seated me beside Saul, and herself beside me, and that's where we spent the eight days of shiva as a thin stubble gathered on my cheeks. I don't know the Gemara's position on sex during the days of mourning, but I know Leah's, and we made love almost every night. Her hard ankles seemed to corral me back into the world of the living. In the mornings, I felt something I'd never felt with a woman before. It was a source of no wonder at all that she was there beside me.

Even after I shaved and put the sofa cushions back on the sofa, my time with Leah retained a quality of desperate consolation, and we probably grew careless about birth control. Two months later, she suggested she might be going to have a baby.

"Might be?"

"Well, I *am* pregnant."

"Oh, good," I said, and my eyes filled with tears.

" 'Good'?" she said, hugging me in alarm.

I'd learned arithmetic from textbooks which you turned upside down to find the solutions to a page of problems. I felt I'd been turned upside down and shown the answer. My life should be taken out of my hands. "Now we can get married," I explained.

" 'Now'? I'll get an abortion."

"*No!*"

Bewildered, she began to cry, too. "My insurance *covers* it. I wasn't going to tell you, just do it. With your mom and everything. I didn't want to do this to you."

"That's... kind."

"Be *serious!*" she cried. "You're acting crazy! I'll get an abortion. Jesus, if *I* don't know where to get a good one, who does?"

"Marry me."

"No! I wouldn't want you ever to think I'd done this on purpose."

"Don't you see? It's all settled now. I love you."

"You *don't*."

"Well, I want to marry you."

"Oh God," she wept miserably, "I hope it's a girl."

The nice thing about deciding to get married, if you're a man, is that it's the last decision you'll be called on to make for some time. Leah spent most of the next few weeks strategizing with her mother and an armada of aunts. It appeared that by asking her to marry me, I'd succeeded in getting rid of her. But soon the appointed day arrived. The Birneys were real Jews; they had that drop of caterers' blood, and knew how to make an occasion unexpungeable. I peeked through the double doors of the ballroom at a seeming warehouse full of round tables decked with floral centerpieces and sateen table-cloths. The rented wedding canopy looked radioactive. A ceramic dove at each place bore a calligraphed place card in a gaping wound in its back. The cocktail napkins were printed with the date, the name of the hotel, the address of the hotel, my name, and the name of one Leah Birney-Wertheim.

Adam approached me, aghast. "Big trouble, pal. I've lost the ring."

"No you haven't," I said wearily.

"Oh, all right." He picked at his tux. He seemed distressed that it fit him so well. Some efforts had been made with Adam's hair, but thirty-two years of worshipping at the Church of the Momentary Impulse had left his face blotchy and wet-looking. "This is serious. We're in enemy territory."

"Actually, it's my wedding."

"Might have to fight our way to the exits," he said, squinting about. "Using bridesmaids as human shields. I got mine all picked out."

"Give me the ring, Adam. I'll get one of the waiters to be best man."

He kissed my cheek and said, "Promise you'll never change."

Soon Leah appeared on her father's arm. Someone had dressed her up as if she were getting married. We exchanged vows and I smashed the wineglass and kissed her, or so I'm told, and then she took my arm and walked me back down the aisle like a veteran cop escorting the bereaved away from the scene of a fatal accident.

And they struck up the band. The Detonators had lobbied hard for this gig – the Birneys' big idea was a ten-piece swing ensemble – and they meant to seize the day. They played "Hava Negila," they played "Autumn Leaves," they played "Alley Cat" and "Satin Doll." They played "Sunrise, Sunset" twice, Adam swaying soulfully back and forth, brow creased in dyspeptic exaltation. By the end of the evening, he'd collected a pocketful of business cards and an invitation to play a graduation party.

I danced with Cat. "That girl really wants to make you happy," she said, concerned.

"I am happy, Cat."

"Well. I hope you will be."

I danced with Del's eldest. "Oop, I'm not keeping kicking you on purpose, Uncle Nick. Well, *that* one was," she said, giggling.

"You're not supposed to kick the groom at his wedding, Alice."

"I'm breaking you in!"

I danced with Del. She was drunk, her face aflame with bliss. "You'd think you could've moved your butt a little," she murmured, smiling. "You'd think you could've given her this pleasure while she was alive."

"Shut up now, Del."

She kept smiling. It was, I saw, a smile of dislike.

I danced with my wife. Her hand on my shoulder was wifely.

Then Leah's brothers brought forth two chairs and half-forcibly seated us knee to knee in the middle of the dance floor. The elder wrestled off his tie, presented one end to Leah, and had me grip the other. The younger motioned the celebrants forward. And then everyone boosted our chairs from the ground and danced Leah and me in circles as we teetered in the air, joined by a black bow tie. Large men, her brothers were murderously happy. They could not contain their joy that I, a Jew! educated! money market account! had come along to make an honest woman of their crazy slut spinster sister. I figured it might've tempered their enthusiasm if they'd known Leah was preggers, but no, they'd assumed as much. "Who else makes a wedding in such a hurry?" one told me. "It's okay. It's good. You had a chance not to do right, but you acted like a man." Certainly the first time such an accusation had been leveled against me.

By eleven the older guests had left the dance floor, and the Detonators were playing a straight Detonators set. They even finished with the Mysterians medley, and since no one else knew what to do, Cat and I finally waded in and started unplugging the equipment. Leah joined in almost at once, her long dress snarling against the mike stands. She was laughing, her face dark and brilliant, and no one could have guessed this was anything but the happiest night of her life. The word, I thought, was *valorous*.

Everyone wanted to see her drink champagne, and of course she wasn't drinking. She'd take a shy nip and then I'd snatch the glass from her and drain it, to general laughter. People never tired of this stunt. By the time Leah and I got upstairs, I was moving with especial grandeur, and the hallways were particularly quiet. There seemed an important distinction between walking on hardwood, where your heels clacked, and walking silently on carpet. We chuckled and held hands. We'd brought the whole thing off splendidly. Our room, when we found it, had that commercial, clean, gray smell. I tossed my monkey suit in a corner and sat on the bed. Leah worked deliberately at her buttons. It was an expensive dress and she wanted to keep it nice. Perhaps she was thinking: *It might be a girl, and she might grow up to be my size.* Nude, my bride was lustrous, her shadowed skin somewhere between butter and silver. The Birneys had hired a professional makeup artist to do the women of the wedding party, and Leah's face was a sleek, long-nosed mask. I was too exhausted to brush my teeth. I swung my legs into bed and arranged the pillow, and drew my right knee up, as I always do before sleep.

Then it occurred to me that I might have left something undone. I rolled over on my back and tried to look expectant, as if I'd been getting comfortable in order to wait. Then I sat up. I tried to look… Then I figured I'd say… I believe it was the guilt in my face, more than anything else, which doomed us. She saw how relieved I'd been to stop pretending. I saw she hadn't been pretending at all. She sank down beside me, eyes stunned. "I know," I said. "I know. Let's please not talk. Let's just go to bed."

"We are in bed."

"I meant – make love."

"Love?" Leah said. "*Love?*" she shouted. "We made a mistake," she sobbed, "we made a mistake. Oh God, we made a mistake."

:   :

In memory, the months that followed were all silence and flat sunlight falling through the windshield of Leah's father's Lexus as we drove, almost calmly, through the suburbs. We were looking for a neighborhood we could agree on for twenty years or so, someplace near a good school. Someplace where we could afford separate establishments after we'd split up. We'd made a success of our wedding. Now it was time to start planning for our divorce.

There was the question of timing. Our guests, who had brought such heartfelt gifts – an electric yogurt maker adorned with sienna wheat sheaves, a five-hundred-dollar gift certificate at Maurice Villency – must not feel mocked. Leah's parents must not be made to seem like fools. On the other hand, we couldn't wait too long; our child mustn't get used to parents who lived together. Eventually we agreed to separate two years hence, when he (we'd had a sonogram) would be eighteen months old. Maybe one or both of us could remarry; maybe he'd reach man's estate believing himself entitled to a happy second marriage.

"You're dreaming," Leah told me. "Divorce fucks kids up."

"So I've heard. Are you willing to stay with me until he's grown?"

She was slumped against the window, watching the lawns glide by. She pivoted her head against the glass: *No.* "If he grew up, little by little getting hip to what kinda couple we are… Besides, I frankly don't think I could take it. I feel like you opened up each part of me and spit in it. No, *I* did. Did your parents love each other a lot? Mine too, it was a big romance. My mom was just a queen, with all the guys bowing down, and I always thought it was so disgusting of me to even want what only queens were supposed to get, but maybe it'd be okay to have guys as long as they were cruddy. As my men go, you're not that bad."

"Thanks."

"Fuck you, pal. The life preserver doesn't owe the drowning man any manners. I mean that you're actually nice, and funny, even if you are damaged goods and a pouter. And I love you. I thought it would be okay that I got someone I loved, because you don't love me at all, so I'm paying for what I get, in pain. And now I just wonder how I could have despised myself so much. The look on your face. You settling for me, this fate you're manfully accepting. That she's this fascinating goddess, and I'm this dowdy thing. You don't like my *clothes!*" she said, and began to laugh. "Now *that's* what I can't get over. I like my clothes so much. You don't even like my sofa!"

"It's funny, the things that bother you, but I hate that fucking couch."

"You know what *I* can't stand? Your sense of humor."

"I thought I was funny."

"But it's all so mean. No, it's the drama, like, *See, even in my misery, I can still zing out the old one-liners.*"

"Well, you have a bit of that quality too. *This, this too I can bear.* I suppose I mind it particularly because I'm the *this too.* I did want us to stay together, but that was before I became the worst thing that ever happened to you."

"Oh honey. Do you just feel really horrible?"

"It feels *chronic*, more than anything else. As though I could feel exactly like this for the rest of my life."

"I *know*. Why didn't we just fix all this when it would've been easy?" she said. "Now everything's gonna be so difficult."

Eventually we found a house a ten-minute walk from where I'd grown up. A sizable affair, but crumbling and therefore cheap. The blue-and-white plastic mailbox for the *Bergen County Record* looked just like those I remembered from my youth. It was odd to see one waiting at the foot of my own driveway. We dragged the Canada Dry box from the rental truck with all the others. It was worn velvety, its sides flexible as thick felt, the corners armored with packing tape. Hankering for a reconciliation, Del had given us bread and salt to inaugurate the new house, and a bear-shaped plastic squeeze bottle of honey, for sweetness.

When Leah was due, we returned to the city hospital where she worked, and where she knew the reputations of everyone on the OB/GYN staff. It was an eleven-hour labor. I am told this is not particularly long. She clenched my hand, thrust it away, sought it again, frantically. Beneath the sheet my big gangling wife seemed misshapen, inhuman, a prehistoric bird on a laboratory table, tormented by cruel scientists, venting horrid shrieks, and I understood that she was dying, that she would die of my folly as I watched, and I wanted to murder the matter-of-fact nurses for pretending this was an ordinary childbirth, and when Leah exchanged hospital gossip with them between bouts of agony, I hated her, too. Afterward, I knelt by her bed. Her face was shiny red and gray. The sheet had collapsed over her depleted body, and she nursed a tiny, sticky item with a head like a dark turnip.

Still, what orchid skin. What *lungs*. Each time he lost Leah's nipple, he'd holler, then stop, wondering who'd made that ungodly noise. We'd already agreed on a name; a beloved great-uncle of hers. I touched Nathan's tiny busy back, then Leah's cheek. She pressed my hand between cheek and shoulder as if it were a phone receiver. "It's so strange, all creeping and raining down inside," she reported. "Um, warmly. But it makes me so tired." Carefully she switched him to the other breast. He assumed this change was for the worse, and began to shout, but when the new nipple was plunked into his mouth, his scalp wrinkled with contentment. Soon he slept.

"Can I hold him?"

"He's your son."

He woke when I picked him up, and in my arms made panicked little scanning motions with his head: I smelled different from Leah, I felt different. It was all a terrible mistake. He gesticulated as I pulled the blanket up around his tiny shoulders. I could feel the clamp on his pipik. He was not, he decided, going to fall, not right away, anyhow. His arms and legs relaxed, and then his back. I would do to lean his head against for a minute. I was okay. He worked his jaw and prepared to go back to sleep, as if he belonged in my arms, which, on reflection, I supposed he did.

Tenderly my wife reminded me: "This doesn't change anything."

The nurses wondered what in hell we were talking about.

:　　:

I remember lying side by side with Leah on the couch with the mirrored base, watching the immense TV her brothers had bought us, our big house shadowed and half-empty, our bodies curved around Nathan like the gunwales of a boat. He'd lie between us, a drunken mariner resting a loose red fist on each of our bellies. I remember us all in the ancient orange Volvo we'd acquired for three hundred and fifty dollars, rolling along Route 17 on some nocturnal expedition. I remember us as one of a billion little clans huddled in a billion grottoes, watching illuminated logos wheel above us through the corporate night.

Life was errands. You had to buy toddler-proof latches for all the cabinets and covers for all the light sockets. You had to buy a fine sturdy stroller Leah could not lift unaided, and then a flimsier one that she could. You had to buy tiny clothes more expensive than your own, and a car seat that cost a quarter of the price of your orange Volvo. And there were many moments of panic in the basement or bathroom, when you saw it was time to call the super, then remembered: there wasn't any super. I found out how many phone calls it takes to replace a water heater. I figured out how to replace a motor mount in our washing machine with epoxy and an old rubber glove folded small. Meanwhile, Leah wanted me to teach her to cook. Her culinary philosophy, I discovered, was based on curry. She had a childlike faith in its power to make things interesting. Still, I like curry. So, at an early age, did Nathan. At night, I'd bend to kiss his cheek and be met by a blast of it on his breath.

Nate soon became a long-faced boy with dark lashes and a brow prone to furrowing. His grip was powerful; he was going to be a bruiser like his uncles. He stood early, but hated to walk without something to hang on to, a table or wall for preference, your hand if you insisted. Often loutish with strangers, he was happy and open with his family. When Saul came to visit, he'd change Nate's diaper with a surprisingly deft roll and flick, then pause with a measuring palm across his grandson's swaddled rear, and Nate would peer slyly around at him, then scramble away in hopes of being chased. He was a particular pet of Del's youngest daughter. She'd call him her special boy and her fat boy. Nate was thin, but he'd stick out his stomach at her request, and sometimes when she'd made no request, to their great mutual satisfaction. He liked to have two or three books open at once, and would shove at a bird from one and a lion from the other, trying to bully them into conversation. His first word was *lamp*. This sprang forth when Leah turned on the first light of the evening. He accompanied it with a sort of semicircular *voilá* gesture. In short, it's all very fine and large to plan to divorce as soon as your child turns eighteen months old, but quite another thing to pick a day and leave.

I recall the weekend we finally decided to act. Adam and Cat had come to visit that Friday evening. Adam was still clerking at Sam Ash, supplementing his income with increasingly lucrative guitar lessons, and now and then playing a Detonators "reunion" gig at CB's or Brownies. The two of them now had a tiny fourteen-month-old daughter named Deirdre. She impressed Nathan no end. He lifted to me the asking-permission face before he approached her, then pushed her carefully around the lawn on a skateboard. She rode on her belly, dragging her hands and feet to hinder him, all with an air of scientific inquiry. In the morning I made my apple pancakes, Nate's favorite food, the proper preparation of which took so long that Leah scrambled some eggs to tide us over. In the afternoon Adam helped me pour a new cement stoop for the back door, into which the kids set their palms. Cat and Leah hiked up their pants legs, sunned their legs, and regarded us with an air of bemused joint proprietorship. They could have been lanky, weary sisters, one dark and one fair. Then we all sat around in lawn chairs – Cat and Adam had brought their own so we'd have enough for everyone – and got tolerably snockered on beer and debated whether I'd built the form level and was the cement supposed to be that color.

Nate had taken a real shine to Adam on this visit. He kept wanting to jump from Adam's belly to the carpet. He wanted Adam to come on our after-dinner constitutional. Nate would zigzag across the sidewalk, indicating this and that with a finger and an expectant look, hoping that whatever it was – post-hole digger, bale of peat moss, sprinkler nozzle – would be fun, and that he could have some of it. Though as he tired, he seemed increasingly to want reassurance that whatever it was was not actually his fault. At bedtime, he wanted Adam to come brush teeth with him. Nate was proud of his toothbrushing skills. He'd hold his brush under the running tap, fascinated, then methodically eat the toothpaste off it, paddling his fingers in the water all the while.

Later, Adam and I sat on the front steps with a pint. It was cool and pleasant out. A nimbus of incipient weather ringed each streetlamp. My hands were raw from the cement, and it felt nice to hold the smooth bottle. Our families were asleep. "It's good to see you, pal," Adam said.

I nodded.

"It's been some couple of years," he said.

"It has."

"I gotta admit, this fatherhood thing scared the shit out of me."

"Yep."

"Then I thought, if a candy-ass like Wertheim can hack it…"

"You calm down," I noted, "when you get too tired to do anything else."

He hesitated, then said, "You two're still planning…?" He set his hands together, one still gripping the pint, then spread them apart, fluttering his available fingers as if miming the dissolution of a dandelion puffball.

I said, "That was the agreement."

He took a somber nip and passed the bottle.

"Why?" I asked.

"Well, you know, what with the kid and everything. I've been thinking, why not, you know, fuck it. Get married. Settle down. Quit all the chasing. And I look at you and Leah, and, you know, you two look okay. But you're just waiting for the right moment. Aren't you?"

By the time Adam's station wagon wallowed backward down our driveway late Sunday afternoon – Cat waved, and Deirdre looked purposefully ahead – we were all tired and overstimulated. Leah pronounced herself dead and retired to the tub. Nathan was playing with my wooden cooking spoon. He held the bowl of the spoon in both hands, handle pointing forward like a dowsing rod, and walked around the house touching things with the end of it. You could touch things even when quite far away. Some days he wanted the spoon with him for hours, and tried to eat his meals and read his books without letting go of it. At a certain point, however, he began to throw. I'd warned him about this a minute ago. Now he let the spoon drop, giving it a little shove as he released it that really no reasonable person could consider throwing. He looked over to see how I was taking this.

"What did I say? Pick it up, now."

He stepped on it experimentally.

I took it from him. "No-*oo!*" he said reassuringly, and reached out both hands to indicate that nothing of any consequence had occurred and that I was free to give him back the spoon. We'd start fresh.

"Sorry, bud. I told you twice."

His face curdled and he began to cry. I'd been waiting for this since Adam and Cat left. It was nice not to be waiting. I was in a sort of localized bad mood, encompassed about by an unemphatic calm. Nathan stamped in a circle and ran squalling into the bathroom, and by the side of the tub did a little dance of grievance.

Leah did not open her eyes. The water's surface was a hair-thin silver necklace dividing her into pale and paler. "Yes, *chochem*, I know. Life's tough. You do whatever your father told you, and don't come running to me." Seeing himself outgunned, Nathan ran out again, wailing now with a note of formalized protest. "Isn't he getting kinda old to be in here?"

"I'll close the door," I said, only a little pointedly.

We heard the springs on Nathan's rocking horse as he rode furiously away. I closed the door. "Did you have a good time?" I said.

She nodded. "Is it just me, or was Cat vamping you?"

"She's been with Adam a long time. She thinks that's how people act."

"There was a lot of letting down straps. There was a lot of walking around holding her top up with one hand." She sighed. "I think she wants an affair. These bored housewives are murder."

"I don't like this new running to the other parent thing."

"Well, you better shoot him."

"It would be loud."

"Yeah. Are you gonna do her?"

"Sure. While I'm running errands, there anyone else you want me to do? Should I stop by the market and do the deli girl?"

"Yeah. Let's get some pastrami out of the deal. If it's lean, I'll know you were thorough. Oh, I'm just witchy 'cause I had a good time, and now I have to go in tomorrow and deal with everybody's problems. I wanna tell 'em, 'Do what I did when *I* was fucked up. Go to social work school. It's your turn.' And I'm crampy. It's cramp time."

I set my palm on her submerged belly. Her dark muff stirred driftingly. I ducked my face under and kissed her stomach. We heard the springs stop.

Amused: "Nice gesture, but you just got water up your nose for nothing. No one wants their belly kissed when it's awful in there like this." Nathan began hammering on the door.

I laughed and opened it. "What do *you* want?" I asked him.

"*Spooooooo*," he crowed, grabbing my pants legs and swinging from side to side.

Eventually I got Nathan settled. He read dozily on the couch, pressing an arch-shaped green block to the center of each page. Leah emerged in a light summer dress, scratching her legs with long fingers and looking about with a dissatisfied air. All was tidy again except for a few of Nate's toys, which couldn't be said to count, or else the place would never be describable as tidy. The beer bottles were rinsed and in the recycling bin, the cast-iron griddle wiped to a dull gleam. The crumbs had been sponged from the kitchen table. It was pale oak and we'd been very pleased to find it at a flea market. It had only needed a few split places fixed with C-clamps and Elmer's glue. In the kitchen window hung a new triple-decker wire basket filled with Bermuda onions, garlic, apples, and the heel of the pumpernickel we'd eaten all weekend. I'd meant to buy one of these gizmos for a long time. It was proving very handy. The house was getting into some kind of shape. It boasted a new roof and double-glazed windows. We'd gone further into debt for them, but any time we sold, we'd get our money back and more. All this was in order, all this Leah surveyed moodily. "I'm ready to jump out of my skin," she remarked.

She'd developed an almost boastful way of complaining: *This is my life. About all these things I am entitled to complain.* Now, though, I heard in her tone something additional. "Let's go to your island," she said.

"My island."

"Out in the gravel pit. We've never been."

It was kind of a courtesy to me, her not bothering to pretend we weren't about to have a talk.

Leah put Nathan's hat on, so he knew we were going out. His eyes widened at the illimitable prospect of a world where Adam and Deirdre visited and you stuck your hand in cement and had apple pancakes and then you put on a hat and just generally did special things without a letup. Then he remembered how tired he was and got teary, and campaigned to bring the book along, and the block, and maybe the couch. We compromised by giving him the spoon.

We crossed the road, which he seldom got to do, and approached the woods on the other side. Here were rocks and shrubs and a trifling stream and a section of cyclone fence woven with diagonal white and green metal strips. Nate looked at all this and decided he wanted it. When we let him go on the far side of the road, he galloped off waving the spoon. *"Nathan,"* Leah said.

He stopped dead. Her voice had not been loud, but it was the telling-you-for-the-last-time voice. This was unfair. His mouth curdled again. "You're okay," she said gently. "I just mean don't run away from us."

"Let's try something, bo," I said. "I'll bet you can walk down to the lake all by yourself without your hand held, and not get too far away from us. Now *that* would be good." He considered. It sounded all right. He wasn't convinced we weren't putting one over on him. Still, he began walking, his small back purposeful.

I'd remembered the path to the gravel pit as a long one, passing through many distinct regions of the woods, but we were on the shore quite soon. Nate perked up at all the water. "Got! Got!" he screamed, and jigged on the banks making wild, inclusive gestures. In twenty-five years, some of the stones leading to the island had rolled out of line and were useless for balancing, but a lot of muck had washed up around the remaining ones, so that there was very nearly a land bridge. I jogged over it with Nathan on my shoulders, and Leah hiked up her dress and waded along beside us. We set him down on the grass.

He looked fretfully around and said, "I don' *wa-han*' it."

Nate was very tired now, and incalculably far from his regular places to nap. We pointed out that he could nap right there on the grass, in the middle of a lake. You had to admit that was special. Presently the spoon dropped from his fingers. The sun was setting; his eyelids were translucent in the orange glare. I took off my shirt and spread it over him, then lay back in the grass beside Leah. She hugged her knees and brushed lake-scum from her shins. "What was all that kiss on the belly in there?" she said.

"Just aid and succor."

"I like 'succor.'"

"It sounds good," I agreed.

"What was it about?"

"I felt like it. Lay off."

She settled down astride my hips, and leaned over me, palms on my chest. Gravity made her cheeks petulant.

"Nate's two," she said.

Hopefully: "I had a good time this weekend."

"I had a good time, too. You were so good with the kids."

On the strength of that, I put my arms around her. We looked over at Nathan, who lay beneath my shirt, motionless but for the minute rising and falling of his stomach. I pulled her down against me.

"I should've said I liked having my belly kissed," she said. Her dress enveloped me, as my shirt had enveloped Nathan; the orange sun was filtered through calico. Slipping my hands under the hem and over her dewy buttocks, I noticed she was naked beneath. We checked Nathan again. I undid my pants and eased down the waistband of my shorts. With a practiced hand Leah welcomed me inside her and then sank down, releasing against my temple a heated sigh. The gravel pit gleamed, a gray halo around us, Leah's mild internal grip the fulcrum of it all. In a minute we'd disengage. It was nice under her dress. I touched with my fingertips the V of hair at her cropped nape, so like the trail of a duck across a pond. I would miss Leah's lengthiness and her unwavering sad regard. I would miss the oak table we'd fixed so that it was fine. Nathan slept on, shoes trustingly akimbo, as if his world could never change. It occurred to me, out of the corner of my mind's eye, that if Leah were to get pregnant again, she would not have the heart to make me leave. This was an unworthy way to think, and I decided not to think about it. But all the same, I began to move with increased purpose. When Leah gasped and tried to rise, I locked my arms around her back.

Afterward I drowsed between her knees, avoiding her eyes. "We didn't use anything," I began.

"Yeah," she said.

But she was trying not to smile. "My period's two weeks *away*. Can't you even count? You're so easy. You never knew what hit you."

I sat up. "Fuck," I whispered from the bottom of my heart, "*you. You* never knew what hit you. Don't you tell me I'm easy. I've knocked you up."

"You tried."

"I'll try again, goddamnit."

"You never knew what hit you," she crooned. "You never… knew… what… hit you."

THIRTEEN

You Will Not Understand, But Will Endure

People say they've reached "understanding" when they've had a chance to forget everything about a situation that puzzled them in the first place.

Over the years, my memories of Julia have grown simple. They've resolved themselves into tiny scenes, still and portentous, as if meant to be stamped on coins.

In all that time, I've seen her only once.

The kids and I were down in the shop. A torpid late afternoon in August; the standing fan roared in the corner. We'd recently splurged on one of the new hand-held air conditioners. Suzanne, five years old and a born voluptuary, was rapt as the stream swept her face. Nate, who was eight, declined: "It just makes it hotter when you stop." I squirted him anyway. It's best not to encourage martyrs. Then I turned the machine on myself, sighing as the coldness flowed over my throat. At this faintly embarrassing juncture, I heard the jingle of the bells above the entrance to the store.

Her hair was quite gray now, and very long, pulled down her back in a sort of clamp fashioned of silver and turquoise. A single silver and turquoise earring weighted her left lobe. Bangles chattered on her wrist. She wore a white garment like a djellabah, which shrouded her from collarbone to toes. The years had clarified her brown eyes to a dark gold. She still had a young woman's carriage, and the shape of her face was lucent and even more beautiful, but her eyes, I now saw, were pouched, and her mouth seamed with a few almost invisible radial wrinkles.

"This is so unfair," she said. "You look just the same."

I saw Nathan gazing at her bangles and earring and complex white dress and deciding that she was wonderful, and also that something terrible was going to happen, some resplendent catastrophe from which he wasn't sure he wanted to be spared. Suzanne granted Julia a single appraising glance: one of these rich dames who never cough up a dime. Julia surveyed them both, seeming to wonder to whom she should present her credentials.

I said, "Suzy. Nate. This is Julia…"

"Turrell-Prine."

"Ah."

"How do you do?" she said.

"Yeah," Suzanne said.

Julia gestured toward the name blazoned on our front window in gold-leafed letters I was used to reading backward: *Wertheim & Birney*, BOOKBINDERS AND STATIONERS. "And is 'Birney'…?"

I said, "Yes. Why don't I ask her to come down?"

"Oh, I don't know about that. My. Look at all this." We'd set up my workshop in an open area behind the counter, so that I could work and cover the register at the same time. People lingered to watch me; it was good for business. I'd been restoring someone's treasured old copy of *Middlemarch*. A corner of the half-title page had been torn away; I'd rebuilt it almost invisibly with layer on layer of rice tissue. I'd rebound the book in dark mauve morocco, giving it a well-rounded spine with full shoulders and a French groove, which I prefer. This one had discreetly raised cords in deference to the period, and fresh-sewn head- and footbands in taupe and teal. I'd just been getting ready to gild the foredge. Sheets of gold leaf and a little dish of dank-smelling glair sat waiting. George Eliot might not have approved of this frou-frou, but the client had asked for it, and I enjoyed doing it.

We liked to say that we sold both paper and everything that could be used to make a mark on it. Beneath the glass-topped counters lay rows of angled pen nibs; Sumi-e ink-sticks; brushes of sable, bristle, sponge, and bamboo; vine charcoal; plastic pens filled with faux silver ink. We even sold hexagonal no. 2 Venus pencils that clattered xylophonically when they rolled across a desk. But the shop's reputation rested on our handmade blank books. We got orders from stores in seven states for everything from desktop-covering accountants' ledgers finely ruled in mint and rust, to palm-sized *carnets de poche* with a leather loop in which to snug a pencil. We bound the books in linen, muslin, vellum, leather, rubber, wood, and galvanized steel, and used hot-press bristol smooth as a shaving mirror, near-translucent antique laids that were tissue-thin at the watermark, deckle-edged papers from Rajahmundry made with algae, wool, wheat, and hot-colored silk threads. "Can I see the ones in there?" Julia said, and I unlocked the glass case at the rear of the store where we kept samples of our specialty work. She paged through a tiny vellum diary blind-tooled with stars and ellipses, an album bound in azure sheepskin with an outlay of rusted metal screen cut from our old back door, and a simple writing book in pewter-toned calf tooled in silver with a few lines suggesting water. Its endpapers were patterned with a stamp I'd carved from a bit of maple. A field of crimson stars beneath her forefinger. I said, "Once you've got the stamp, you can use it as often as you like. I always thought that was a nice design."

"Well," she said.

"Yeah."

"It's beautiful. I'd like to buy it."

"You can't," I said. I tore off a sheet of brown paper and wrapped the book. My movements were deft and reflexive and I believe I was

making a point before her of being someone who waited on people in a shop. Suzanne looked on disapprovingly. Business was not so good we could go around giving away the stock. Nathan held open a shopping bag, which no one else was allowed to do while he was in the store. He seemed an acolyte. Julia took the bag meekly.

"Well. Thank you for my book," she said.

"My pleasure," I said.

I almost added, *Come again soon.*

She stood holding her bag before her, grasping the handles with both hands, heels together and feet pertly out-turned.

If she was going to show up like this, she could at least have something to say.

I said, "Why don't I ask Leah to watch the store? And we'll take a walk, and, ah. Catch up. Nate, Suzy, you two keep Julia company."

"You have only one earring," Suzanne told her.

"Yes, do you like it?"

"And a metal thing in your hair."

"It's nice," Nathan whispered.

"Well," I said, "I'll be right down in a minute."

I went upstairs. Leah was working on the ordering. The kitchen table was obscured by catalogs and old invoices and the printout from our last inventory, all arranged in a system of interlocking heaps comprehensible only to Leah. I could tell she thought I'd just run up to pay a little visit. Then her gladness faded into puzzlement. "Guess who's downstairs?" I said.

She pondered, then finally sighed.

"Did you at least ask where she saw the ad?"

"Leah, I'll send her away."

"Oh, quit sending people away all over the place." She rubbed her nose. "It was a nice day, too. So. What's my part in this little opera? Sorry – I'm not allowed to tease you?"

"I don't think so, no."

"Well, calm down. You look like you been cheating on me with a platoon of lingerie models. She must be a hundred years old. Oh hon, what do you want?"

"I want to talk to her. You could come say hello, if you liked. But I want to take a walk with her for ten minutes, and see why she's come and... I can't sit there, in the middle of... Ho boy."

"Breathe," she advised from habit.

From downstairs we heard the jingle and slap of the screen door, and someone walking briskly down the front steps.

"You're losing your girlfriend," Leah told me. "I'll be right down."

I went downstairs and into the front yard. The engine of Julia's little gray car was just turning over. If she drove off before I got there, the matter would be out of my hands. But she hesitated when she saw me, and I reached into her window and closed my hand over hers, and took the keys from the ignition. "I don't know what I imagined I was doing," she said. "I cannot imagine what I thought I would accomplish here. Hello, Nick."

"Hello, Julia."

"May I have my keys? If I promise to be good?"

"All right."

"Thank you."

"You're welcome."

"I suppose I'm ready for that walk now, if you still want to take it – or perhaps not. Do you remember, when we met at your sister's wedding, and you talked about not trusting your legs to hold you?"

"So. Let's just sit here for a while?"

"Yes," she said. "Let's."

I walked around to the passenger side. The shopping bag rested on the seat. It was odd how natural Julia looked with a shopping bag. She moved it to the floor, and I got in and closed the pearl-gray door. We watched through the shopwindow as Leah came downstairs and slipped behind the counter. She did not look our way.

"It took me a while to find you," Julia said. "You're not really right off the exit."

"So we've noticed."

"But people do find their way here?"

"Enough of them."

"That's good."

"I guess we might be in trouble if we depended on the walk-in trade. But we also do some mail-order."

"Ah."

"It's a lot of trouble. It's been a while since we've put a mailing together. And mostly there's a lot of stores that handle our books. That's where our margin is."

"They're such beautiful books. Actually, I already own some. You put this little label in back? I was so proud of you when I saw. Assuming it *was* you."

She had not let go of the wheel.

The kids were behind the counter, out of sight. I knew about where they must be from the way Leah stood.

"I've thought of you, quite a lot, in the past ten years," she said. "Does that surprise you."

"Quite a lot? I guess it does."

"And you've thought of me."

"Yes."

"And you're sorry you thought of me so much. Well, I don't blame you." She considered. "You were supposed to be the one who didn't fall in love with me, Nick. None of the ones who did would talk to me, after a while. So I didn't want to notice how you felt. I thought I could somehow keep you, that way. And it was so stupid, and led to such badness. Not that you weren't cruel to me, too. Sometimes."

"I know."

"I suppose I had all these… pictures of how it would be to see you," she said. "I thought you might revile me. I thought, I supposed I hoped, you might be happy, for some reason, to see me. But you're just sort of watching to see what I'll do next."

I smiled. "You have to admit, it's an interesting question."

"Tell me, at any rate, that you're not as calm as you look?"

"No. I'm not calm."

"You were so wild when you left that night, and still so sick. I didn't know what you'd do. I thought you might harm yourself."

"Well. Here I still am."

"I felt I'd done you such harm. Not just that night, but always. I wondered if maybe I shouldn't leave you alone, wherever you were. If, possibly, I'd taken my proper place in your life as this madwoman you should have had sense enough to avoid. But I couldn't bear to think you were alone, or in trouble. I wanted you to be happy. And now I've come, after all these years, and seen for myself, and you seem to be doing so well. And" – she smiled crookedly – "I don't seem to like that, either."

"How are you, Julia?"

"I'm all right."

"You've married again?"

"Yes."

"Congratulations."

"Thank you. I don't suppose you're being sarcastic?"

"No."

"Well, thank you."

"What's he like?"

"Me. Not like me, really, but the sort of uncle person that was always around when I was growing up, and let me practice being a little femme fatale. Someone like that. And now I'm apparently old enough to marry."

"That's handy."

"Ben knew what he was getting with me, and oddly enough that's what he wanted."

"Oh," I said, "I guess I can imagine wanting that."

She smiled at me genuinely then, that quick, complicit, slightly shamefaced smile. Then she looked off through the windshield again. "He's sixty-eight."

"I see."

"And his health is not good. That's what no one will quite believe, to look at him. He's one of these very ruddy little men, all bounce, but… He was very straightforward, and wanted me to know what I might be in for. Heart."

"I'm sorry."

"And sometime in the next few years, I think he'll have to leave me behind. And when that time comes, I will need my friends. I will need them very much."

She hesitated.

I shook my head.

After a moment, she said, "All right. That's fair."

"I'm sorry."

"No, don't apologize. It's fair. Well. I wanted to know, and now I know. I do have one further question."

"All right."

"Are you… Nick? Are you sorry you knew me?"

I shook my head again. I found I didn't have to think about it.

Her eyes grew wet. "Well. I guess that's as much as I'd really hoped. Thank you. In fact, I was thinking, if, when I saw you… Well. I want to give *you* something." She took an envelope from her purse and held it out to me. It was heavy cream-colored stationery. I weighed it in my hands, admiring the quality of the engraving.

"Why don't I read it later," I said.

Gratefully: "Yes, perhaps that's best."

I tucked it into my breast pocket.

"Well," she said, "I'd say your wife's been a good sport long enough now, wouldn't you? My address is on the notepaper. Perhaps you'll write me sometime? Well, in any case. Thank you for my book. Goodbye, Nick."

"Take care of yourself, Julia. Goodbye."

When the car had vanished around a curve of trees, I walked back and stood in the door of the shop. Leah was making a to-do of being busy at the register. I came around the counter and leaned on my elbows beside her. She was counting the day's receipts. "Closing up?" I said.

"I thought we could. It's slow." She did not remark on the envelope in my breast pocket, but tamped a stack of bills even with an awkward palm. I laid my temple against her softly bustling shoulder. She said, "They take it out of you, these old girlfriends. There oughta be a law."

"Leah, I swear to you. You won't be hearing and hearing about this."

"You're allowed to tell your story."

"You and the kids are my story."

"No," she said. "She's your story. We're your life."

She closed the ledger and kissed the crown of my head, then stepped around me and went upstairs.

I remained with my elbows on the counter as the shadows began to thicken and stir across it. Then I turned on the light, put the envelope away with the ledger and the receipts, and went out to sit on the front steps. A small evening breeze was shuttling across the front yard. Through the screen door I heard Suzanne stumping officiously about upstairs. The scent of curry began to warm the cooling air. I breathed it in.

Eventually I heard Leah telling Nathan to go fetch me, and heard my son's oblique, stealthy progress down the stairs. The screen door opened and shut. Then he leaned his slight weight into me as if by accident, as he did when something had been unsettling him. I reached back and closed my hand around his ankle, and he set his forearms on my shoulders as if I were the railing of a balcony, and looked at whatever I was looking at. The curve of trees into which she'd driven was deepening, and dusk gathered above it like steam above an iron pot. The bone of his ankle in my palm was warm and narrow as luck.

FOURTEEN

Snakebite

A lash of brightness catches you off guard
in childhood. It completes you. You change size
in dreams of smelly water, catch your eyes
impersonating something bright and hard
as sun and moon wear hot grooves in the sky
and you lurch toward conclusion. Here your strange,
illumined limbs betray you. You must change
unrestingly now. You, swollen and sly,
must welcome turmoil as a central friend
who plies her fangs of difference through your heart.
And now you're anyone's to take apart.
And now you're anyone's to find and mend.
You will not understand, but will endure,
snakebit, and never dreaming of a cure.